En

Don't be whiskey *have a good, stiff drink. Do anything, but get away from her.*

Jed muffled a sound of anguish and tore his eyes from the vision in front of him. He made himself creep away from the bush. Straightening to his full height, he walked back to camp.

As Megan waded out of the water, she heard a rustling sound in the bush alongside the bank. Abruptly alert and feeling exposed, she grabbed the towel to cover herself and peered up at the brush.

''Is someone there?''

It was nothing, she assured herself, as she hurried back.

Jed watched her return to camp. Before he could look away, she turned her head and met his gaze questioningly. Heat raced over his skin as he averted his eyes.

Dear Reader:

Harlequin offers you historical romances with a difference—novels with all the passion and excitement of a 500 page historical in 300 pages. Your letters indicate that many of you are pleased with this shorter length. Another difference is that the main focus of our stories is on people—a hero and heroine you really care about.

We have some terrific books scheduled this month and in the coming months: Cassie Edwards fans should look for *A Gentle Passion*; the second book in Heather Graham Pozzessere's trilogy, *Rides a Hero*, tells Shannon's story; *Samara* by Patricia Potter is the sequel to her award-winning *Swampfire*; Nora Roberts's *Lawless* is an unforgettable Western. You won't want to miss these and any of the other exciting selections coming from Harlequin Historicals.

Please keep your letters coming. You can write to us at the address below.

Karen Solem
Editorial Director
Harlequin Historicals
P.O. Box 7372
Grand Central Station
New York, New York 10017

Wild Horizons

Jeanne Stephens

Harlequin Books

TORONTO • NEW YORK • LONDON
AMSTERDAM • PARIS • SYDNEY • HAMBURG
STOCKHOLM • ATHENS • TOKYO • MILAN

Harlequin Historical first edition March 1989

ISBN 0-373-28618-X

JEANNE STEPHENS

discovered early in life the pleasures to be found between the covers of a good book. Today, her many contemporary romances, mysteries and children's books have won her wide acclaim. In addition to being the four-time recipient of the Tepee Award, presented annually by the Oklahoma Writers Federation to a promising Oklahoma novelist, she has also been named Oklahoma Writer of the Year by the University of Oklahoma. *Wild Horizons* was written with the love of the American West, given to her by her own Cherokee Indian heritage.

Prologue

1845

It was Vinnie Foster who finally told Megan why the other girls shunned her. Vinnie didn't want to, but Megan kept after her until the harried girl blurted out, "It's because your mother works at the Gilded Lily."

Megan was hurt. And yet, she told herself, she should have sensed the envy in her classmates' sidelong looks and nasty giggles. "They're jealous because their mothers aren't beautiful and exciting like mine. Every last one of them wishes Kate were her mother!"

"Oh, Megan...let's not talk about this."

"Admit it, Vinnie! They're jealous."

Vinnie was exasperated with Megan for backing her into a corner and she said more than she had ever meant to. "They're not jealous, Megan—far from it."

Megan's eyes narrowed angrily. "And what is that supposed to mean?"

"All right, if I must say it. Nobody wants a mother who does what your mother does, no matter how beautiful she is."

"My mother is a singer! There's nothing wrong with that."

Vinnie stared at her. Evidently Megan actually believed what she was saying. Somehow she had succeeded in blind-

ing herself to the truth about her mother. But she had to
accept it sooner or later. "She isn't a singer, Megan. She—
she entertains men in her bedroom."

Megan slapped her. "Liar!"

She had believed Vinnie was her friend, her only friend.
But a friend would not say such an evil thing about Kate.
Megan wasn't sure exactly what "entertaining men" in-
volved, but she knew instinctively that it was a grievous sin.

Mrs. Valentine, the pastor's wife, came into the room.
She looked from Vinnie's red face to Megan's white one.
"Young ladies, you'll be late for dinner."

Vinnie burst into tears.

Mrs. Valentine frowned and patted Vinnie's blond head.
"What's wrong, Vinnie?"

"Nothing," Vinnie whispered, and ran from the room.

"I'm not feeling well," Megan said quickly. "May I
please be excused, ma'am?"

Mrs. Valentine pursed her lips thoughtfully. She was a
plump, motherly woman who operated a private school for
girls in her home. Four of her students boarded with her and
her husband, a Baptist minister. "What's been going on in
here, Megan?"

"Nothing, ma'am." Megan wouldn't meet her eyes.

"Very well." Mrs. Valentine tapped her foot. She was a
naturally curious woman and it irritated her to be kept in the
dark about goings-on among her students. "If you won't
answer my question, you'll go to bed without dinner."

As if she could eat! Megan thought. "Yes, ma'am." Head
down, she walked from the room. Instead of going to the
dormitory at the back of the house, where the girls who
boarded with the Valentines slept, she slipped out a side
door and ran all the way to the Gilded Lily. Her mother had
told her never to come there, but she had to see Kate. If she
could just talk to her, Megan told herself, Kate would as-
sure her that Vinnie's accusation was a vicious lie. It
couldn't possibly be true, but she needed to hear Kate say it.

Her mother was a singer. Kate had told her that many times. She boarded Megan with the Valentines because she worked at night and couldn't leave Megan alone.

Megan knew which room was her mother's bedroom. One night about six months previously she had run away from the Valentine house, intending to find her mother and beg her, once again, to let Megan leave the Valentines and live with her. It wasn't that the Valentines treated her unkindly. The pastor was a quiet, bookish man who always seemed a bit distracted at home. His wife, on the other hand, was warm and talkative—but she wasn't Megan's mother.

As Megan had approached the Gilded Lily on that night six months ago, she had seen her mother in an upstairs window, and then Kate had disappeared and the light went out. She must not be working tonight, Megan thought as she hesitated. Then she retraced her steps, not wanting to disturb her mother after she'd gone to bed.

Now, for the first time in her life, Megan entered the Gilded Lily. She used the back door. The ground floor was a gambling hall and saloon. It was not yet six o'clock and only a few men sat at tables scattered about the room. None of them noticed the girl who hugged the shadows as she crept up the back stairs.

The upstairs hall was deserted. The odor of stale tobacco mixed with the scent of perfume in the dim, airless hall. Megan was trying to decide which door was her mother's, when she heard Kate laugh. Following the sound, Megan went to a door and turned the knob quietly. She opened it a crack and looked in.

Her mother lay on the bed with a fat man whom Megan had never seen before. Kate wore a sheer negligee and the man had his hand on her breast. In a state of shock, Megan stared at the man's bare, beefy flank for an instant, not understanding what she saw.

Then her heart began to crack, and a roaring started in her ears. She made a small sound like a wounded animal, but no one heard her. What are you doing, Mama? she thought. Oh, dear God. She could not move. In the bedroom Kate rolled atop the man, her long, dark hair shielding their faces like a satin screen. Instinctively, Megan stepped back into the dark shadows of the hallway. Her thoughts were barely coherent. The man was naked, his pale flesh covering disgusting blobs and rolls of fat. Who was he? Why was Kate behaving like a—a . . . She entertains men in her bedroom. They were . . .

"No," Megan whispered, staggering back against the wall. She felt hot and the smell of cheap perfume was suddenly overpowering. The walls were pressing in on her.

Fighting her nausea, Megan fled to the stairs and stumbled down them and outside. No one had seen her, and when she reached the dormitory at the Valentine house, she realized she had not been missed. Everyone was at dinner, oblivious to the fact that Megan's world had just crashed and lay around her in rubble.

She grabbed the basin from beneath her bed. The soul sickness wracked her body until she was weak and sore. Shaking, she huddled on her bed, turned her face to the wall and wept for the death of her childhood.

Chapter One

April 1850

Megan stood on the threshold, her face as white as her starched collar. Her loose gray dress, with its high neck and long sleeves, concealed the ripe curves of her young body, but it could not hide her lovely face. Her cornflower-blue eyes were framed by an unruly mass of ebony hair that was, as usual, coming loose from its pins.

Saddle tramps passing through town had been seen to stare after her as though spellbound, then turn away, assuming from her modest attire and downcast eyes that she was the protected daughter of strict parents and clearly unapproachable.

Everybody in Independence, of course, knew that her mother was a whore.

Megan stared, as though frozen, at the gaunt-faced man who perched on the bed, dressed in long johns and cowboy boots, his bony knees grazing his chin.

"She—she's gone, Abner."

"Who...?"

"Kate. She's dead."

"Ah, no, Meggie."

She stood rigid and dry-eyed, but the white-knuckled hands clasped at her waist trembled. Abner started to rise, his underwear forgotten until he glanced down at himself.

"Gawdawmighty! I'm nearly buck naked!" He dived for the dusty britches hanging on the bedpost under a battered flat-crowned hat. He jammed the hat on his head and kicked off his boots. His back to her, he tugged the britches up his long legs, then shoved his feet back in his boots.

Megan seemed to find nothing odd in his embarrassed haste. She hadn't even noticed his state of undress, he realized with relief. Her eyes were turned inward. Was she still seeing Kate?

He went to her, drew her quickly into the room and closed the door. Mrs. Herman, the owner of the boarding house, would throw a fit if she saw Megan in his room. She'd put the worst possible interpretation on the situation because it was Megan. Like most people in town, Lizzy Herman was waiting for Kate Riley's daughter to "go bad." Once Abner had tried to tell Lizzy there wasn't a sweeter girl in all of Missouri than Megan Riley, but the old biddy had merely sniffed and said, "Wait and see. Blood will tell."

Abner led Megan to the only chair in the room. "Sit down, sugar," he urged when she remained standing. Finally noticing the chair she sank into it and wrapped her arms tightly around herself, as though she feared she might fly apart at any minute.

She looked like somebody who'd had the breath knocked out of her. As Abner watched, worried, she took a long gulp of air and let it out with a slow, hissing sound.

"Why isn't Sadie with you?" Sadie Robison was the woman hired by Kate to live with Megan in a little house with a picket fence on the edge of town. Sadie had been with Megan for two years, ever since the Valentines had moved away.

"She was out—gone to the general store—when Waddell sent a stable boy to fetch me," Megan said. "He said Kate was dying." She shivered. "I didn't even know she was sick." She gazed into space, thinking she knew very little about her mother. Ever since she'd learned, five years ago, that Kate was a prostitute, she had wanted nothing to do with her. "Dr. Bastion said she'd had congested lungs for a week, but she seemed better this morning. Her fever had gone down some . . . but after noon, it shot up. . . .''

"Did you get there before—"

She gave a quick nod. Her blue eyes filled with tears and she dashed them away almost angrily with the back of her hand. "I wanted to send the boy away, Abner," she said in a trembly voice. "I haven't been in that place for five years. I never wanted to go near it again. But when he said she was dying, I couldn't get the words out." She dropped her arms and plucked at the coarse material of her dress. "I don't think she expected me to come, but I could tell it pleased her."

"'Course it did, Meggie." Abner squatted awkwardly in front of her and took one smooth hand in both of his gnarled, calloused ones. "You were her child. She loved you."

He had told her that many times through the years. When she was younger, Megan had argued that if Kate loved her, she wouldn't have turned her over to the Valentines to raise. But that was before she'd understood the meaning of the other children's taunts—"Harlot's daughter!" "Your ma's Royce Waddell's whore!"

Megan was a young woman of nineteen now, three years older than Kate was when she birthed her. Old enough, Abner thought, to understand that most people couldn't live their lives cloistered in neat white houses surrounded by picket fences and flower gardens. It wasn't Megan's fault. Between them, he and Kate had done everything they could to protect her from harsh realities.

"I hated her, Abner." She expelled the words in a rush, like tainted food. "But I guess a part of me loved her, too. I didn't think so until I saw her like that . . ."

"I know." He squeezed her hand. "Why don't you let me take you home now. Sadie's probably wondering where you've got to. Besides, you hadn't oughta be here. Folks'll talk."

"They'll talk, anyway," she said with a bitterness that tore at his heart. "I'm Kate Riley's bastard."

"Meggie—"

She stiffened. "Why didn't she send me away from Independence years ago! Why did she keep me here where everybody knew!"

"I guess she wanted to see you now and then, even if it was only from a distance." He stood. "Come on. I'll take you home."

Megan rose and, with a little cry, threw her arms around him, hugging his bony frame with all her might. "The preacher will conduct a graveside service tomorrow," she said, her words muffled by his chest. "I went to him right away, before I came here. He doesn't want to have the service in the church. He says the congregation would object."

"Kate would've wanted it outside, anyway, sugar." Once a long time ago Kate had told him she only felt clean out of doors.

"I don't suppose they'll want her buried in the church graveyard, either. If only the Valentines were still here.... Well, I'm supposed to let Pastor Donovan know where, but I—I don't know—"

"I still own that forty acres west of town. We'll bury Kate out there." He'd bought it eight years ago, thinking of the time when he could no longer follow the cattle herds, imagining the two-room house he'd build, tight enough to keep out the winter wind, with a porch for long summer evenings. But lately he'd been thinking this part of the country was getting too crowded, and he was getting too old to be a cowboy. For some time now he'd battled an itch to sell his land and settle in the West. It would mean leaving Megan behind, probably never seeing her again, so he'd put it off.

"Thank you, Abner. Will you come by in the morning and go to the funeral with Sadie and me?"

"You know I will, Meggie." He patted her shoulder and wondered what would become of her now. She might be nineteen, but she'd lived a sheltered life with the Valentines until she was seventeen, and since then in that isolated little house at the edge of town with only a middle-aged spinster for a companion and a broken-down cowboy who visited briefly when he passed through. Thank God this trip had coincided with Kate's death. In spite of her resentment toward her mother, these next few days weren't going to be easy for Megan.

It was a chilly, windswept morning, but the sun broke through the clouds just before the two carriages arrived at the land. Abner had hired two men to come out at dawn and dig the grave on a gentle hillside beneath a cottonwood tree. Abner, Megan, Sadie and Pastor Donovan alighted from the first carriage and walked toward the hill. The grave diggers waited about a hundred yards from the grave, leaning on their shovels, watching.

They look like vultures, Megan thought, the way they're hovering there, waiting for us to take care of our business and leave. Then they could swoop down and cover the coffin and its contents, as though Kate Riley had been a blot on the face of the earth to be quickly hidden and forgotten.

Royce Waddell stood beside the second carriage, smoking a cigar and gazing after the others, who didn't acknowledge his presence. His eyes were closed to slits against the smoke and wind. After a minute, he ground the cigar beneath his boot heel and followed them. He stood apart from the mourners, his black, narrow-brimmed hat in his hands, his eyes fixed on the grave, where the casket already rested. Megan wished he hadn't come.

The Baptist minister had stiffened with disapproval when he saw Waddell step down from the second carriage. Waddell owned the gambling house with its second-floor rooms where Kate and the other fancy women lived—scarlet women, Pastor Donovan called them from his pulpit.

As Megan darted a glance from beneath her lowered lashes at Royce Waddell, she remembered that the preacher had a name for him, too—spawn of the devil. The gambler was a barrel-chested man of medium height, with black hair and a thick mustache twisted on each side to points that curled upward in the middle of his lean cheeks. He wore his customary black suit with white shirt and string tie. The gray eyes that lifted to meet Megan's in the instant before she could look away held no expression. Blank eyes, Megan reflected. Blank and as cold as Missouri in January. Carefully avoiding further eye contact with Waddell, she pulled her coat collar up against the wind.

Her thoughts were not so easily diverted. What is he doing here? she asked herself resentfully. He cared nothing for Kate, only the money she brought him. Why had he come where he wasn't wanted? Perhaps he had done it out of arrogance or spite.

Megan felt Abner squeeze her shoulder gently, and she pulled her mind away from the gambler and tried to concentrate on the minister's reading of a scripture from Ecclesiastes. Pastor Donovan's voice, which boomed with righteous indignation in church, sounded frail without walls to contain it. Megan had continued to attend the church the Valentines had established, out of respect for the people who had raised her, but she'd never liked this preacher, who had taken over the Reverend Valentine's pulpit.

The wind whipped away the preacher's words as soon as they were spoken, and Megan had to strain to catch even a few of them. "A time to be born and a time to die . . . God shall judge the righteous and the wicked . . ." It sounded anything but comforting, and she gave up trying to hear.

Sadie muffled a sob with her lace-edged handkerchief and dabbed at her eyes. Megan's tears for her mother had been shed the day before, tears of bitterness, pity and love. Dry-eyed, she stared at the polished, black toes of her high-laced boots until the final prayer was said.

The grave diggers waited only until the small group of mourners had started back down the hill before they began to fill the grave. The hollow sound of dirt hitting the casket made Megan's throat tighten. She clutched Abner's arm and detected a faint trembling. Surprised, she looked up at him, wondering how he had felt about Kate. She didn't know if Abner visited the rooms above the gambling house when he was in Independence. She didn't want to know. But she had often wondered about his visits to her through the years, going back as far as she could remember. He had known her mother before Megan was born. Had he loved her?

Royce Waddell was waiting at the bottom of the hill. "Miss Riley, I'd like to have a word with you, please."

Megan felt Abner stiffen. "She's got nothing to say to you, Waddell."

It wouldn't take much for Abner to start throwing the fists that were already balled at his sides, Megan realized. And Royce Waddell was the sort of man who would strike back, even in these circumstances. Wouldn't that be a fine way to end her mother's funeral service! "It's all right, Abner," Megan said hastily. "Wait for me at the carriage. I'll be right there."

Abner continued to glower at Waddell. "You sure, Meggie?"

"Yes."

Pastor Donovan was already in the carriage, fidgeting impatiently. Abner took Sadie's arm and led her away. Slapping her hand on top of her hat to keep it from blowing off, Megan looked up at the gambler. She despised the man. She wouldn't have trusted him, even if he'd had no connection with Kate. The ice-gray eyes that peered down at her were no longer blank, she noticed; now they were sly and calculating. It was hard not to look away.

"What do you want, Mr. Waddell?"

"Kate paid your rent until the end of the month."

"I know that. What has it to do with you?"

A mocking smile curled the lips beneath the black mustache. "I won't be able to keep up the rent payments, Miss Riley. I don't make contributions to charity. I am a businessman."

"I know what kind of *business*man you are," Megan said, flaring. "And I'm not a charity case! I wouldn't take your money if you begged me!" The gall of the man!

Waddell went on, unfazed, "As you know, Kate also paid Miss Robison's wages." Noting the quick dismay in Megan's eyes, he added, "I see you hadn't thought of that, either."

"I've just buried my mother. I've hardly had time to think of anything else." Surely Sadie could find employment with a family in Independence or back in St. Louis, where she came from. Megan had no money except for the gold coins Kate had pressed furtively into her hand moments before she died. "I saved this for you, Meggie," Kate had whispered. "A nest egg to see you through till you decide what to do." The legacy might take care of rent and food for a few months, but only if she let Sadie go. "I learned nursing from Mrs. Valentine," Megan said, remembering the frequent trips to church members' houses to care for the sick and dying. "Perhaps Dr. Bastion will give me work as his assistant."

"You'll slave twelve hours a day for a pittance. Surely a pretty young woman like you can do better than that."

His tone gave Megan a creepy sensation down her spine. She stared at him uncomprehendingly. After a moment, she said, "My friends are waiting."

Waddell stepped in front of her, his back to the carriages. "I'm willing to hire you, Miss Riley." He spoke too quietly for his voice to carry to the others. "A good-looker like you can make decent wages, and the job comes with a room and three hot meals a day."

Swift comprehension nearly knocked Megan down. For an instant she was too shocked to speak. Finally she sputtered, "You—" Hot fury gushed through her. "You lowdown slimy scum! You are beneath contempt! I'd kill myself, Royce Waddell, before I demeaned myself by working for the likes of you!"

Something mean flickered in the gray eyes. "That's easy to say when your belly's full and you've got a warm bed to sleep in," he drawled with maddening calm. "When you get hungry enough, you might take a different attitude. If you decide to come and see me later, I won't hold those rash words against you. Scruples are for those who can afford them, Miss Riley. Think about it."

"The preacher is right," Megan shot back. "You *are* the spawn of the devil. Don't you ever come near me again!" She spun on her heel and walked away from him, her back stiff with outrage.

Waddell tipped his hat and laughed, the sound a harsh sacrilege carried on the brooding moan of the wind. He ambled to his carriage, climbed up and reached for the reins.

Abner lifted Megan to her seat. "What's wrong, Meggie? What did that bas—" He darted a glance at the preacher and amended, "That skunk say to you?"

"Nothing I'd care to repeat." Her cheeks still burned from Waddell's insult. "Let's get back to town." She gripped her coat lapels beneath her chin. "It's getting colder."

Waddell had turned his carriage around and, whipping his horses, headed toward Independence at a smart pace.

Abner glared darkly after the retreating carriage. "I'm surprised he showed his face here today." He exchanged a speculative look with Sadie.

"You shouldn't be." The preacher sniffed piously. "That sort knows nothing of propriety."

Megan knew Pastor Donovan was thinking that they had just buried another of Waddell's sort, and she had an irrational impulse to defend her mother. Strange, when she'd condemned Kate herself while she was alive.

Again Megan wished that the Reverend Valentine could have been there to conduct the service. Though he'd been a quiet, retiring man at home, his sermons had been delivered in a rich baritone that rang with the love and mercy of God. The Reverend Donovan seemed to serve a different God, one who was stiff-necked and vengeful. Megan bit her tongue to keep from lashing out at the minister, knowing there was no defense she could make for Kate.

Sadie made a clucking sound and patted Megan's gloved hand. "There, now. He's not worth upsetting yourself. Whatever he said, don't let it rile you."

It wasn't easy to follow Sadie's advice. It infuriated Megan that Waddell apparently had thought she'd consider his proposal. He'd come to the funeral specifically to make it, the disgusting swine! Still, he'd forced her to face the fact that her sheltered, secure existence was gone with Kate.

"I knew I shouldn't have left you alone with him," Abner said.

"No, it's as well you did," Megan replied with rigid composure. "He reminded me of some things I should already have considered. I have some hard thinking to do now."

Wishing he had words to comfort and reassure her, Abner tugged on the reins wordlessly and turned the horses toward town.

"Sadie, you have to think about yourself and your future," Megan insisted as she replenished their teacups. They were still at the kitchen table, after a lunch of goat's cheese and thick slabs of homemade bread layered with butter and wild plum jelly. "I can take care of myself. I'm a grown woman. Most girls are married by the time they're my age."

So would Megan be, Sadie thought, if she hadn't had to live under the twin curses of illegitimacy and her mother's profession. The few decent young men who might have courted her had been dissuaded by their families or the jeers of their peers.

It had been selfish of Kate Riley to keep Megan in Independence. Sadie remembered her own feeling of having been duped when she'd learned the woman who had hired her as companion to her seventeen-year-old daughter was a prostitute. But by that time, she'd been at the job for a week and had already grown fond of Megan. She had always imagined that Megan could be the daughter she might've had if she'd married. So she'd stayed, knowing the time was not far off when she'd have to leave her charge and seek other employment. Now that time had arrived.

"What will you do, Megan?" Sadie questioned.

Megan lifted her cup in both hands and drank slowly before replying. "I don't know yet. I've thought about applying to Dr. Bastion for a nursing job, but I don't want to stay in Independence.''

"You can come back to St. Louis with me. I still have nieces there. I'll find employment and—''

Megan shook her head emphatically. ''No, Sadie. It's dear of you to offer, but I have no intention of burdening you. You mustn't worry about me. I'm young and able-bodied. I'll manage.'' Her brave words covered an inner anxiety that neared panic in the middle of the night when she couldn't sleep. How she would manage, she had no earthly idea. ''I mean to give you a month's wages as compensation. You can stay with one of your nieces until you find work. When will you leave?''

Sadie frowned in consternation. ''Pay me? Just how do you intend to do that, girl? If Royce Waddell said there would be no more money, you'd better believe it.''

"Oh, I believe it. I wouldn't take a penny from that vile man, anyway. But—'' Megan leaned forward. ''Before she died, Kate gave me her savings. She slipped the money into my hand when no one was looking.''

"I imagine she feared one of those creatures who hang around that place would take it away from you if they knew.''

"Probably, but the point is I can afford to pay you a month's wages, and have enough left over to keep me for a while.

"I don't want to take your money.''

"I insist. Now that's the end of it.''

Sadie let the subject drop. ''I'd best write my nieces I'm coming then. On second thought, I can get there as fast as a letter. I'll go to Crow's General Store and see when the St. Louis stage is expected.''

Megan rose from her chair. ''Let me do that for you.'' A walk would help relieve her restlessness. ''On the way back, I'll stop at the boarding house and ask Mrs. Herman to send Abner around to bring your trunk in from the shed.''

Still in the black dress she'd worn to the funeral, Megan donned her coat and hat and set out at a brisk pace for Edgar Crow's general store.

Independence was only a cluster of buildings jutting from a sea of prairie grass, but it was a major supply center for westward-bound emigrants. Megan passed log cabins and houses of whitewashed clapboard, finally reaching the business establishments. The town's main street, was well rutted by horse hooves and wagon wheels. It was crowded with oxen, mules and horses and men—trappers, Indians, Spanish traders and gamblers, but the largest group were the emigrants with their eyes and hearts set on the vast land far to the west. Whips cracked, wagons creaked, shouts and raucous laughter split the air. Above the din was the ringing of blacksmiths' hammers.

On either side of the muddy street, warped planks of timber were nailed together as storefront sidewalks. Rows of plain frame buildings housed the town's businesses. Hand-painted signs identified the flour mill, the livery stable, wagon shops, saddleries and harness makers, saloons, several hotels, hostelries and general stores.

The Gilded Lily, with its swinging doors, stood near the center of town. Tucked in among the other buildings were hastily constructed blacksmith sheds.

Megan picked her way through the sloppy ruts to avoid passing in front of the gambling house. The Crows and the young man they employed were all busy with customers when Megan entered the general store. Within the past few weeks, the throngs on the streets of Independence had swollen to bursting as emigrants shopped for supplies for their journey. The town merchants were doing a booming business.

Content to browse through several new bolts of bright fabric and enjoy the aroma of fresh ground coffee and spices, Megan was in no hurry to conduct her business. She led a lonely life and she treasured the rare occasions when she could mingle with other people who knew nothing of her history.

As Megan fingered a piece of pink-and-white checked gingham, a voice at her shoulder exclaimed, "Isn't it pretty?"

Megan looked into hazel eyes that appeared too large for the thin, pale face. The young, blond woman was taller than she and thin as a rail. Like the other customers in the store, she was a stranger. Which accounts for her friendly overture, Megan thought. "Yes, it is. I was imagining it made up with a full skirt and puffy sleeves."

"Trimmed with white lace," the young woman said wistfully as she stroked the cotton fabric. Her hands were red and chapped. "Are you going to purchase enough for a dress?"

"No." Megan's response was automatic. She was so accustomed to choosing fabrics and styles that called no attention to herself that she didn't even have to think about it. Kate Riley's daughter would be branded fast and loose if she wore frocks that showed off her figure, as other young women did with impunity. "Are you?"

The young woman gazed longingly at the gingham, even as she shook her head. "It wouldn't be appropriate for crossing the continent in a prairie schooner." Her glance was drawn to the counter at the back of the store. She shrugged and lifted her chin. "I must be practical, Thayer says. Oh, I'm being rude. I haven't introduced myself. I'm Carolyn Goddard. Thayer is my husband."

"Hello." Megan returned Carolyn Goddard's friendly smile. "I'm Megan Riley. Are you going to Oregon or California?"

"Oregon. We're camped outside town. My husband is buying supplies for the journey right now. How about you?"

"I live here. I've never been more than a few miles from Independence in my life," Megan told her. "When are you leaving?"

"Within the week. Our wagon master, Mr. Dossman, wants to be on the trail as soon as we can."

"How wonderful. You must be eager to leave."

"Ye—es," Carolyn Goddard said. "As long as we're going, the sooner the better. To tell you the truth, I wanted to stay in Illinois. I have a four-year-old son, Johnny, and I wanted him to grow up with his grandparents and cousins. But nothing else would do Thayer." She glanced toward the counter where a stocky man in a homespun jacket and dark felt hat was paying Mrs. Crow for his purchases. He looked to be ten or twelve years older than his wife. "He says Illinois is filling up with a Godless rabble. We were fortunate to join a train of good families, many of them from our home state."

The man at the counter turned away with his arms full of parcels. He scanned the store until he located his wife. His heavy-lidded eyes widened as they looked from Carolyn to Megan and back again. Evidently he didn't approve of his wife striking up conversations with strangers. He strode to the fabric counter.

"Megan, this is my husband. We were admiring the pink check, Thayer."

Thayer Goddard nodded stiffly in Megan's direction. "Come, Carolyn. We'd best get back to camp. Rose Schiller has her hands full with her own brood. We shouldn't leave Johnny with her any longer than we have to." His eyes were very dark, almost black, and the glance he flicked over Megan was mean spirited and suspicious. He didn't look at Megan again, and he didn't smile. What an unfriendly man, Megan thought, not the sort she would have imagined paired with Carolyn.

Carolyn gave Megan an apologetic look, then followed her husband from the store. As Megan watched them go, the germ of an idea stirred at the back of her mind. She turned and moved slowly to the counter. The proprietor, Edgar Crow, handed a package to a tall man who was dressed in dark clothing, even to the hat pulled down over his eyes.

"Here you are, Dossman. Will that do you?"

"Yep."

"Well, now, Megan, how can I help you?" Crow asked.

Dossman reached for the parcel, turning to glance at Megan as he did so. His eyes were obscured beneath the shadow of his hat, his finely shaped mouth crooked into a faint smile. He touched the brim of his hat, edging it up an inch. "Afternoon, ma'am." His voice was deep and resonant.

Megan tipped her head, trying to see his eyes. They were brown, fringed by gold-tipped lashes, and they were staring boldly into hers. "Good afternoon, sir." Something had happened to her voice. It sounded reedy and too high. Heat suffused her cheeks. Dossman's grin made lines crinkle about his eyes and deepen in his bronzed cheeks. As he stood surveying her, it hit Megan like a fist in the stomach just how handsome he was. She didn't know what else to do but stare back into his compelling, watchful eyes.

"You're the wagon master," she blurted, and again felt heat rush into her cheeks, as hard as she tried to prevent it. "I—I was talking to a member of your party a minute ago— Carolyn Goddard." Megan never talked to strange men, yet she couldn't seem to keep her tongue still. "Is this your first trip to Oregon?"

His expression became closed and guarded. "No," he said shortly. He gave her a brief nod. "Good day to you, ma'am."

She put her hand to her throat unconsciously and it was a moment before she realized she was staring after him. She turned quickly back to the counter. "Did I say something wrong?"

"Dossman's wife died out in Oregon a couple of years ago," Crow said. "When you asked if this was his first trip, I guess you reminded him of what happened when he was there before.... Sorry you had to wait, Megan. We've been meeting ourselves coming and going around here for the past three weeks."

Megan sent a glance over twenty or so browsing customers. She didn't recognize a single one of them. "Are all these people headed west?"

"Yep, they've got the fever. Once it gets hold of you, you can't rest till you've run clean out of ground and are dipping your toes in the Pacific Ocean." He pursed his lips morosely. "They've all read this." Crow pushed a flyer across the countertop so that she read it:

LAND! LAND! LAND!
FREE LAND! RICH LAND!
In the Oregon Country
Plenty of homesteads for all!
Start a new, prosperous life in Beautiful Oregon!

Crow shook his head. "They've no idea of the hardships they face on a two thousand mile trek by wagon. I've heard some horrifying tales from the wagon masters, but them—" he gestured with his thumb "—they don't want to hear any of that. They think they're going to Paradise. As for me, I'll stay right here in Independence and sell 'em their supplies and go home at night to a snug house and a clean bed."

"I'd love to go west. It would be quite an adventure."

He chuckled. "Well, you're young." His gaze was kind, and she knew he was thinking about Kate's death, but he didn't mention it. He probably didn't know how to offer condolences in a case like hers. "Now," he said briskly, "what can I do for you?"

"Oh!" Talking to Carolyn Goddard had made Megan forget her mission. "I'd like to know when the next stage leaves for St. Louis."

Crow eyed her curiously. "You going there?"

"No. Sadie Robison is."

He pulled a much fingered piece of paper from beneath the counter. "St. Louis, eh? Let me see. Yes, here it is. Next stage is expected through here Friday morning sometime." He put the paper back on the low shelf. "What about you, Megan? You wouldn't be getting married, now, would you?"

She didn't mind Edgar Crow's inquisitiveness. He was one of the few people in Independence who treated her with kindness. "No, I'm making plans of another sort. Nothing definite yet. Thank you for the information, Mr. Crow, and good day to you."

Back on the busy street, Megan heard with heightened awareness the hammering and banging from a dozen blacksmith sheds, most of which had sprung up within the past month. The same thing had happened every spring for the past several years. Repairing wagons and shoeing horses, mules and oxen for the westward journey provided plenty of work for every blacksmith within miles.

The noise that had earlier been but an intrusive din now struck Megan as exhilarating. She made her way between a buxom middle-aged woman on horseback who was attempting to shield her sunburned face with a faded parasol, and three men dressed in country homespun, earnestly discussing the endless acres of rich, virgin farmland awaiting them out West.

She turned north into the wind and headed for Lizzy Herman's boarding house. She was so absorbed in her thoughts that she hardly noticed the sting of the gusts on her cheeks.

Chapter Two

Megan's dainty parlor always made Abner feel clumsy and not very clean. White, ruffled tieback curtains framed the gleaming windows. Every step he took left a boot print in the soft pile of the flowered rug. He wished he'd thought of that when he bought the rug for Megan in San Antonio. Doilies crocheted by Sadie Robison's never idle fingers covered every flat surface.

Cradled among the starched ruffles of the doilies were glass vases and gewgaws, all looking too fragile to be touched. Not that Abner had any inclination to touch them, but he feared he might do so inadvertently. Most of his fifty-two years had been spent in wide-open spaces with rough men and stinking, bawling longhorns. Only for Megan's sake would he tolerate this frilled and flounced room, where there was barely enough space for a man to get a good breath of air.

He managed by planting himself in the sturdiest chair in the room and staying there until he was ready to leave. As usual, Megan served him coffee and a sweet. Today it was a man-size slab of walnut cake. He didn't get sweets on the trail, and that and Megan's company made his visits tolerable.

"Thank you for bringing in Sadie's trunk, Abner," Megan said as she refilled his cup. She carried the pot back to the kitchen, then sat on the plump-cushioned sofa and watched him wolf down the cake. She had spent a restless hour since returning to the house, awaiting Abner's arrival. She had asked Sadie to stay in her bedroom with the door closed while she talked to Abner about a personal matter.

Now that he was here, she was finding it difficult to broach the subject she wanted to discuss. Though she had practiced over and over what she would say to him while she waited, she was fidgety from the audacity of it. If he said no, she had no other plan for her future. "Sadie will be leaving for St. Louis Friday."

He looked up with a frown. "So soon?"

"There's nothing to keep her here now," Megan said with a shrug intended to loosen her taut shoulder muscles. It didn't help much. "She has to support herself, and I can't pay her. She has nieces in St. Louis she can stay with until she finds work."

His mouth tightened. "That's fine and dandy for her, but it seems like she's spared no thought for you."

"That's not fair," Megan said quickly, hoping Sadie couldn't hear what they were saying. "I insisted that she leave right away. She wanted me to go with her, but I refused."

"Why? That sounds like a good idea to me. Here I've been worrying about what you'll do, and you've turned down your only chance to get out of Independence! I thought that's what you wanted."

"It is, but not as a burden to Sadie." Megan rose and wandered to the front window. She fingered the starched curtain apprehensively.

"What do you mean to do, Meggie?"

She dropped her hand and turned back to him. "Royce Waddell offered me a job."

Abner rose half out of his seat, dislodging the china plate from his knee. Catching it just before it crashed to the floor, he fell back in his chair. "He *what*?"

This wasn't how she had planned to start at all, Megan thought with dismay. Was she trying to manipulate Abner into going along with her plan by implying she might be reduced to following in her mother's footsteps? She was more desperate than she'd realized. But she couldn't manipulate Abner, who had always been kindness itself to her.

He set his empty plate and cup carefully on the floor beside his chair. "So that's why he wanted to talk to you in private. I'll kill him!"

"No," she rushed on. "I don't think he'll bother me again. I told him to stay away from me."

Abner's Adam's apple bobbed up and slid back into place. "I'll tell him again, damn his hide! So he gets it straight in his filthy mind."

"Please don't do that. I have enough to worry about without tales of you and Waddell fighting over me being spread all over town."

The black look stayed on Abner's face as he watched her pace nervously from the front window to the one looking out on the side yard where yellow daffodils bloomed.

Megan felt her courage deserting her and knew she must say what she had to say before it left her altogether. Somehow she had to get the conversation back on track. "Abner," she ventured finally, "do you remember what you told me last spring?"

He looked blank. "I must've said a lot of things last spring. Which one you referring to?"

"You said it was getting too crowded in Missouri. You said you were thinking about giving up the cattle drives, selling your farm here and going west."

He gazed at her, disconcerted by the abrupt change of topic. She was uncharacteristically restless today, though that was probably due to Kate's death and Sadie's leaving. It had finally hit her that she was on her own for the first time in her life.

He forced his mind to focus on her question. If not for Megan, he'd have gone west already. "I don't remember saying that," he lied. "If I did, I was just talking to hear my head rattle."

Her face fell. "Oh. I thought—well, you sounded serious at the time."

"Maybe I was, a little," he conceded, "but I've decided not to go. I want to keep an eye on you."

She pounced on the opening he'd provided, going to kneel beside his chair. "But you can do both."

He gazed at her without comprehension. "Both? What are you getting at, Meggie?"

"We could go to Oregon together. Now let me finish before you say no." She looked up at him, her blue eyes pleading. "I've thought about it all afternoon, Abner. It's the perfect solution, don't you see? I've heard men on the street talking about how rich the land is out there. And it's free! Imagine, you could have your choice of acreage. What do you think?"

Abner stared at her.

"Abner?"

He asked quietly, "What would you be doing while I was working my acres of free, rich land?"

"I don't know," she said impatiently. "I'll find something. I can learn to farm. I could even take in sewing. I'm very good with the needle. Settlers have been swarming to the Oregon Territory for five years. There should be ample opportunity for somebody who's willing to work hard. Best of all, Abner, there won't be another soul in more than two thousand miles who knows anything about me."

Her face was alight with excitement. But this idea of hers was an impractical dream. There were so many things she hadn't considered. "Listen to me, Meggie girl. To set out on a journey like that you'd need a good wagon, horses and oxen and six months' worth of supplies. That all takes cash, a lot more than I've got."

"I have money," she cried triumphantly as she jumped up and ran to the small mahogany table against the wall. She pulled open a drawer and lifted out a handkerchief knotted around a ball of coins. She untied the kerchief and placed it in Abner's hand. "Kate gave it to me. She said it was my nest egg."

Abner stared down at a handful of gold coins. There had to be several hundred dollars in the hoard. Kate must've been saving for years to provide this legacy for her daughter. He was holding Kate Riley's heart in his hands. For one dreadful moment, Abner's vision blurred and he thought he might actually get teary.

His continued hesitancy worried Megan. "Isn't it enough?"

His vision cleared and he looked at her. Gently he touched her shining black hair. "It might be," he said, "but there are a few things you haven't thought about. In the first place, it's too late to sign up with a wagon train this year."

"No, it isn't. There's a party headed for Oregon camped outside town right now. The wagon master's name is Dossman. I spoke to him in the general store today. They're leaving in a few days. You can talk Dossman into taking us. I know you can, Abner."

"Meggie, slow down a minute. Those trains are made up of families. Do you really think they'd take in an old cowboy traveling with a pretty young woman? My Lord, girl, you talk about starting over—"

"I've already thought how we can do it," she broke in. "We'll say I'm your daughter. We can say my mother died recently—that much, at least, is the truth."

Abner shook his head, but she ignored him and went on talking. He dropped the handkerchief full of coins at his feet and held his head in his rough hands. He listened to her and tried to think how to make her see the impossibility of what she was asking without breaking her heart.

"You could go out to their camp tomorrow and talk to Dossman, then come back to town and start getting our rig together. I can help you. It'll work, Abner. After all, you *could* be my father."

His head shot up, but he saw she hadn't meant it the way it sounded.

She gazed at him guilelessly. "You're the right age," she said, and he dropped his chin to his hands again. No, of course, she hadn't meant that he could actually be her father. How could she know he'd often wished it were true? There was even a remote possibility he was. About nine months prior to Megan's birth he'd paid Kate a visit before leaving on a cattle drive. But many men had visited Kate, some of them with regularity. Any one of them might be Megan's father. Some were far more likely candidates than he. But he was the only one who had established a relationship with Megan. Probably he was the only one who would be proud to be her father. This plan of hers was crazy, of course, but by God, if there were more time...

"Oh, Abner, I haven't said it right. Maybe it sounds stupid and impossible, but I have thought it through. It's asking a lot of you, I know, but you did talk about going last year, and I thought maybe you were still interested." She paused. "Aren't you going to say anything?"

What could he say? That he didn't want to go? Ah, he wanted to, all right. Should he say that she was talking like a silly child? That would be callous, and it would hurt her. She might be determined enough to go out to that camp on her own and talk to the wagon master. She'd be wasting her breath, of course. No wagon master would take along a single woman alone.

Finally he straightened. "Let me think, Meggie." He couldn't bear the eager pleading in her eyes any longer. He rose, stepped over the coins at his feet and went to the door. "I don't think we could be ready in three or four days, but let me check around." He had to get out of the close, cramped parlor. He couldn't bring himself to say no just like that. He had to at least pretend to consider it. He'd come back tomorrow with a couple of belts of whiskey in him to dull the pain of her disappointment.

He closed the door quietly behind him, but to Megan the click of the latch sounded ominously final.

Jed Dossman crawled out of his bedroll as the first pink tinge of dawn rimmed the eastern horizon. A white mist hung over the broad waters of the Missouri River, near which his party was camped. The covered wagons were arranged in a circle, as they would be on the trail. Within the circle, the party's livestock were penned and tents sheltered sleeping men, women and children. Other families had opted to sleep in their wagons.

Jed smelled coffee and heard the clatter of pots from the Schiller wagon. Rose was preparing to cook breakfast for her husband, Reuben, and their six children.

Jed dressed quickly in the early morning cold, his muscles drawn tight to keep from shivering. Then he tied his bedroll and stowed it with his gear. His horse nickered as he came around the wagon, and he placed his hand on the stallion's quivering flank.

"You'll get your oats, boy, after I've had my coffee."

He did his own cooking, but had fallen into the habit of sharing each day's first cup of coffee with Rose Schiller before anybody else was up.

"Morning, Jedediah," Rose greeted him as he approached her cook fire. She lifted the tin coffeepot from a bed of embers, filled two tin mugs and set the pot back. "These mornings are still right cool. Makes you appreciate a good, hot cup of coffee." She was a big, rawboned woman who handled her brood with a firm hand and enviable patience.

"It sure does, Rosie," Jed answered. Squatting on a log, he blew on his coffee, savoring the heat of the fire. Rose mixed flour, baking powder, lard and milk in a bowl for biscuits. She worked on a couple of boards laid across two barrels containing grocery staples.

"You made up your mind yet when we're leaving?"

"Monday," Jed replied, "as soon after first light as we can manage. I had hoped to be gone a week ago. Hadn't counted on the repairs taking so long."

Rose nodded and began to hum softly. She often hummed as she went about her work, he'd noticed. Jed found Rose a comfortable person to be around. She reminded him of a younger version of the grandmother who had raised him and had died four years ago in Indiana. Other than his grandmother, Rose was the only person who always called him by his full name. Jedediah. She said it was a fine, pa-

triarchal name and prophesied it meant he'd one day have
a big family. He didn't tell her she was full of bull.

As the sky lightened in the east, he nursed his coffee and
gazed out over the wagons, tents and livestock of the camp.
There were twenty-five wagons and ox teams. Some of the
party had arrived in farm wagons unfit for the journey.
They had tarried near Independence for two weeks while Jed
oversaw the strengthening and caulking of the wagons and
made sure each family had at least a six months' supply of
groceries and other provisions, including grease buckets,
water barrels and plenty of heavy rope, as well as spare
wagon tongues, spokes, axles and wheels.

The overenthusiastic guidebooks and flyers circulating in
Missouri, Illinois, Iowa and Indiana promised a leisurely
journey of a mere four months. But the guidebooks were
wrong. Jed knew they would be lucky to reach Oregon by
October, and they could be delayed by any number of ca-
lamities until November or December.

Jed was no stranger to trouble.

He thought about Penelope, eighteen when he'd married
her and barely twenty when she died. Back in Indiana, he'd
been drawn to her fragile, blond prettiness. Something
about that girl Megan in the general store yesterday had reminded him of Penelope as she'd been when he first knew
her. It wasn't her looks. Penelope had been a green-eyed
blonde. The girl in the general store had stove black hair and
the bluest eyes he'd ever seen. No, it was something in her
manner, a freshness, a sweetness, with an underlying
strength.

Back then, before they'd started for Oregon, he hadn't
known that his new bride was a spoiled child, reluctant to
struggle against the unaccustomed hardships. Eventually
he'd realized that what he'd thought was an untried strength
was really a bullheaded insistence on always having her own
way.

Penelope had never dreamed of the rigors involved in
going west when she'd agreed to it. Jed had known that, but
he had stupidly counted on the journey stripping away Pe-

nelope's childish ways. They hadn't gone two hundred miles before he knew he'd made a terrible mistake. After the lark of the trip had worn off, she had cried incessantly. But worse was to come.

Single-handedly, he'd built a one-room house and worked the land he'd claimed, while Penelope sat for hours, pining for the comforts of Indiana and begging him daily to take her home. He should have admitted defeat and done as she wanted.

He could close his eyes and remember her green eyes following him after he rescued her from that trapper, tracking his every move in mute accusation, piling guilt upon guilt until he thought he would buckle from the weight of it. Sometimes he almost thought she'd died just to punish him.

He stood, muttering a curse. Rose stopped humming and watched him drain his mug. "Help yourself to more coffee."

"No, thanks, Rosie. Better get to work."

The camp was stirring when he reached his wagon. He was feeding the stallion, when a man spoke close behind him. "I'm looking for Dossman, the wagon master."

Jed left the bucket of oats wedged between two tree stumps where the stallion could reach it and looked up at the gaunt man astride a bay mare. The stranger sat the mare with an ease that came from long hours in the saddle and his face had been weathered to a lean, lined hardness by exposure to the elements.

"I'm Dossman."

The stranger shifted and leather creaked as he dismounted. He tied the mare's reins to the nearest tree. "Claunch is the name. Abner Claunch." He cast a long look over the camp. "Understand you're headed for Oregon."

"That's right."

Claunch met his look briefly, then studied the munching stallion. "Fine horse you got there." He paused and cleared his throat.

"He's not for sale."

"I don't want to buy him. I was wondering if you'd consider taking another family with your party."

Jed assessed the man before he spoke. Claunch seemed nervous. He wondered if he was running from the law. He wouldn't be the first man to escape a noose by going west. "You've left it a bit late, Claunch. We're pulling out Monday."

"If I can be ready by then...?"

Jed walked over to the stallion, who was nosing the empty bucket, and loosed him from the stake. "Suppose you tell me why I ought to take you on at the last minute like this," he said as he led the stallion toward the river.

Claunch followed him doggedly. "Wouldn't think one wagon more or less would matter to you."

"Maybe. Maybe not."

"If you're worried I can't carry my weight, you needn't be. I'm used to hardships, and I'm good with livestock. I been a trail driver most of my life."

That fit with his ease in the saddle, Jed reflected, but it didn't explain the nervousness. "You just woke up this morning with Oregon fever. Is that it?"

"No, that ain't it. We was set to go with another party. They left about two weeks ago. My wife took sick after we set out. By the time we got to Independence she was bad. She died last week."

Jed shot a look at Claunch over his shoulder. Claunch met his gaze steadily. If he was lying, he was damned good at it. "Sorry to hear it."

Claunch shuffled his feet, making his spurs jangle. He looked at the scuffed toes of his boots. "After she died, my daughter and me decided to go on like we'd planned."

"What'd your wife die of?"

"She took a fever she couldn't shake. It wore her down till she couldn't fight it no more."

"How old's your daughter?"

"Nineteen. She's a healthy, hardworking girl, Dossman. We can carry our share of the load."

"Your rig ready to go?"

Claunch hesitated. "It will be, by Monday."

The stallion finished drinking and Jed led him back to the wagon. Claunch made him feel vaguely uneasy, yet his story sounded all right.

"It's no picnic," Jed warned. "Before we get there—if we get there—you'll wish you'd never started."

"I know what I'm doing. I ain't no greenhorn."

Jed shrugged indifferently. "Tell you what, Claunch. You and your daughter show up here at dawn Monday with a rig and provisions that pass my inspection, and we'll talk again."

"We'll be here. Much obliged, Dossman."

Jed watched him mount and ride away. Shaking off his uneasiness, he told himself that if Claunch was lying, he'd probably never see him again. If, as he claimed, his wife's illness had prevented his departure with an earlier party, he'd have some kind of outfit already and it was possible he could be ready to leave by Monday. If not and he was starting from scratch, there was no way on earth he could get an adequate rig together by then. To begin with, wagons were nearly impossible to come by in Independence, and when one did change hands the price was dear.

As Abner rode away from Dossman's camp, he was astonished at the easy way the lies had slipped from his tongue. All he'd had to do was remind himself he was doing it for Megan. He felt other emotions, too—apprehension over what lay ahead and a dawning anticipation as he imagined Megan's excitement when he told her Dossman had as much as agreed to take them.

He had lain awake most of the night, thinking. At first he'd tried to decide how best to tell Megan he couldn't take her to Oregon. But as the night wore on and his thoughts went down side roads of speculation, the undertaking began to seem more and more possible. He knew Megan didn't know what awaited those who went west, but she had always had it in her mind to leave Independence if she ever managed to save a little traveling money. She had spirit and determination, and she'd need every ounce she had to see her through to Oregon.

Still doubting they could equip themselves in time to leave with Dossman's party, he had gone by the livery stable before dawn to ask about wagons and a team. By a fortunate twist of fate, only moments before an Iowa family had left their rig with the stable owner to sell. The trip to Independence had been so fraught with bad luck that they'd decided to go back to Iowa by speedier means, horseback. The stable owner had promised to hold the rig for Abner until noon. The asking price was high, but it was the only wagon for sale in Independence.

Finding that rig, more than anything else, had made him decide to ride out and talk to Dossman. The wagon needed some repairs, but he could have it in top shape by Monday. Now Dossman had given him a chance to join his party. It was exciting to be making plans to homestead out West. Abner had almost convinced himself that finding the rig and Dossman's reaction were signs of supernatural origin.

It appeared that either God or Satan was behind this venture. He would find out which soon enough.

Chapter Three

Saturday afternoon, satisfied that final repairs and stocking of provisions were on schedule, Jed rode into town for a couple of hours of relaxation. It was likely to be the last idle time he'd have for months. Entering the Gilded Lily, he sauntered to the bar and ordered a whiskey. Leaning an elbow on the bar, he pushed his black felt slouch hat back on his head and turned to scan the gambling hall. Several tables were occupied by cardplayers, with a couple of painted women in red, low-necked dresses wandering from table to table, replenishing whiskey glasses and laughing at suggestive remarks.

The bartender, "Curly," a bald man with a round belly, poured liquor into a shot glass and set it in front of Jed. "Better wet your whistle good, Dossman. You ain't gonna get fine whiskey like this between here and Oregon."

"That's a fact, Curly," Jed agreed. He downed the shot and felt its heat settle pleasantly in his stomach. He slid the glass toward the bartender. "Hit me again."

"When you leaving?"

"Monday morning, bright and early."

A man slid his white-shirted arms onto the bar next to Jed. "I'll have a taste of that, Curly."

Jed turned his head and met the cold, gray eyes of the owner of the Gilded Lily. He turned back to the bar and wrapped his fingers around his glass.

"Howdy, Dossman."

"Waddell." Jed didn't like Royce Waddell. He'd seen dark bruises on the arms and face of one of the prostitutes and had questioned her about it. She'd shrugged and said Waddell could get nasty if he thought you were faking illness to keep from working or holding back extra money left by an appreciative customer.

"Heard you say you're leaving Monday."

"Yep." Jed lifted his glass and sipped.

"I was in Crow's store yesterday. He told me Abner Claunch is getting ready to go with your train."

"What's it to you, Waddell?" Jed asked with a prickle of irritation.

"Ain't a damn thing to me," said Waddell with seeming amiability. "It seems awful sudden, is all. Last I heard Claunch was fixing to head back to Texas and sign on for another cattle drive."

Wishing Waddell would go talk to someone else, Jed turned around and planted both elbows on the bar behind him. "No law says Claunch can't change his mind," he muttered. Jed's gaze wandered over the room in search of a card game that showed signs of breaking up. He'd enjoy playing a few hands of poker if the stakes weren't too high.

"Crow told me Megan Riley was in his store, buying a hoard of provisions. She had a list as long as your arm. She said Claunch had made it out."

Jed glanced at Waddell. "It's no concern of mine who Claunch gets to buy his provisions for him."

Waddell sipped his whiskey and studied Jed. "Maybe it should be. You must be interested in the character of the people you welcome into your party."

Waddell talking about character? What a laugh. "What do you have against Claunch?"

"Tell me something, Dossman. What did Claunch tell you? How did he explain his sudden decision to go out west?"

Jed frowned. He didn't like the feeling he was getting. It reminded him of his uneasiness during his conversation with Abner Claunch. "It sure wasn't sudden, from what Claunch said. He was set to go with an earlier party, but when they reached Independence his wife was too sick to continue. After she died, Claunch and his daughter decided to sign on with another party."

Waddell gave a startled hoot of laughter. "Daughter! Claunch has got no daughter far as I know. He sure hasn't got no wife, nor ever has."

Jed's eyes narrowed. "Why would he tell me a story like that when he didn't have to? I can always use somebody who knows his way around livestock. Makes no difference to me if he's a bachelor or not. Besides, how does he plan to explain it when he shows up without a daughter?"

"He won't show up alone." Waddell reached for the whiskey bottle the bartender had left on the bar and replenished his drink. He nodded toward Jed's glass and Jed shook his head, noting a glitter of shrewdness in Waddell's gray eyes. What in damnation was the man trying to say?

A robust, red-haired woman in a ruffled black dress that exposed half of her plump breasts sidled up to to the bar. She smiled at Jed. "Hi, cowboy. Wanna buy a girl a drink?"

"You're interrupting a private conversation, Dolly," Waddell grunted, without looking at her. To Jed he said, "I figured Claunch had something fishy up his sleeve when Crow told me about Megan Riley buying the provisions. She must be going west with him. Only thing I can't figure is where Claunch got that much money. He's been in Independence nearly a month now, and he's dropped a bundle here at the Gilded Lily. He can't have earned much more than that on his last trail drive." He draped an arm familiarly around Dolly's waist. The prostitute, who had been listening intently, leaned against him.

Dolly looked up at her boss. "Can I say something?"

Waddell scowled at her. "I told you, not now."

"But I know where Abner Claunch could be getting money. It's probably Megan's."

Waddell spared her another dark scowl. "Megan doesn't have that much money."

"Kate gave her money before she died," Dolly said. "I was there. Kate slipped it out from under her pillow and gave it to Megan when I was seeing the doctor out. She acted like she didn't want anybody else to know about it, but I turned around before Megan put it in her pocket. It looked like a lot of money to me. Kate must've been putting it away for a long time."

Jed sensed the sudden tension in Waddell. "You got a good look?" he asked Dolly.

"Good enough. It was a handful of gold coins."

"Who *is* Megan Riley?" Jed demanded.

"She's—" Dolly began.

Waddell gripped her arm and pushed her away from him, more roughly than was necessary, Jed thought. "One of your customers just came in, Dolly," Waddell snapped. "Go take care of him." He watched her hurry away before he answered Jed's question. "Megan's a pretty little tart, Dossman. Doesn't surprise me in the least that she finagled Claunch into taking her west. Megan's mother worked for me upstairs. She died a few days ago, so there's a grain of truth in Claunch's story. Now that Kate's gone, Megan won't have the added income her mother gave her."

Waddell paused to study Jed's reaction. Jed remained grimly silent, and Waddell went on, "Megan set herself up in a private house with an old maid companion to make herself look respectable. Kate didn't know anything about her daughter's activities. She thought Megan was as pure as the driven snow, that she'd make a respectable marriage. That's why she sent Megan whatever she could scrape together every month. But the apple doesn't fall very far from the tree, does it?"

Waddell twirled his shot glass between his fingers. "Megan has regular customers, like Abner Claunch, but it'll strap her to keep her little love nest going without Kate's help. Too much competition from the Gilded Lily and the other houses in town. Out West, she won't have much competition—for a while. She stands to make a bundle."

"Are you saying Abner Claunch plans to take a whore to Oregon with my party?" Jed demanded.

"Appears that way to me." Waddell took a swallow of his drink. "She may have the morals of an alley cat, but she's a raven-haired beauty. Megan could cause a peck of trouble before you get to Oregon."

Jed muttered an angry curse. Waddell didn't know the half of it. Once it became known what Claunch's "daughter" really was, there would be a few upstanding family men in the wagon train who couldn't resist paying her a visit.

Something else was nagging at Jed, too. Megan was not a common name, and the girl Edgar Crow had introduced to him in the general store was named Megan. She'd seemed intensely interested in the fact that he was taking a party to Oregon, too. Could she be Megan Riley? A growing certainty in his gut told him she was. And he'd thought she was sweet and innocent! He'd even compared her to Penelope.

Hell, he was no better judge of women than he'd been when he asked Penelope to marry him. But Megan Riley was a beauty, all right. There would be men in his party who couldn't resist her. Those who managed to, and every last woman in the bunch, would make more trouble than Jed could handle.

Damn Abner Claunch for trying to take that woman along, masquerading as his daughter! Damn himself for letting Claunch put one over on him! He'd *known* there was something wrong with Claunch. As much as he disliked Waddell, he owed him gratitude for telling him about Megan Riley. "Thanks for the information, Waddell," Jed said. He left the bar abruptly and asked to join two other men who were starting a poker game at a corner table.

For another few minutes, Waddell watched Jed with calculation, a new scheme already taking shape in his mind.

Jed spent the next hour winning almost fifty dollars at poker. Earlier he'd entertained the notion of finishing his afternoon of leisure in one of the rooms upstairs. But when he pocketed his winnings and left the card table, he found all of the available women spectacularly unappealing.

Jed's disinterest was due in part to his preoccupation with what Waddell had told him. His anger at Claunch still simmering, he left the Gilded Lily and went to Crow's General Store, hoping to run into Claunch and give him a piece of his mind. But Claunch wasn't in the store, or at any of the livery stables when Jed looked in.

By the time Jed had checked them all, his anger had faded. He headed back to camp, deciding to let Claunch go ahead with his hasty preparations until Monday morning. He'd wait till Claunch showed up with his pretty little chippy at the camp to tell him they would not be allowed to accompany Jed's party. He'd enjoy watching Claunch squirm as he told him why. It would be interesting to see Megan Riley's reaction, too, when she realized she'd spent her mother's savings for nothing.

Megan squeezed the last of her belongings into her trunk and, sitting atop the flat wood lid, barely managed to fasten the metal clasp. With a weary sigh, she surveyed the bedroom. She was leaving behind most of the furniture and taking only necessary bedding and clothing. Still, the room had a deserted look, as Sadie's had after her departure the previous morning.

Sliding off the trunk, Megan walked into the parlor to make sure she'd packed everything Abner would allow her to take. Most of the wagon space would be needed for foodstuffs, spare wagon parts and other necessary supplies. There would be little room for furniture, though Megan clung to the hope that Abner would let her take her beautiful blue-and-rose floral carpet, which was rolled up against the wall.

She had left an extra house key with Edgar Crow, who had agreed to send his sons over to haul the remaining furniture to the general store. He'd promised to sell what he could and send her the money when she let him know where she'd settled.

Abner would come by later in the day to inspect what she was taking and make sure it would fit into the wagon. Suddenly remembering her nursing supplies, which she'd accumulated while helping Mrs. Valentine, Megan ran back to the bedroom and hauled a faded brown carpetbag from under the bed. She set the bag on the trunk, then wandered back to the parlor.

She flopped down in the carved oak rocker, which she would have to leave behind, put her head back and closed her eyes. She was tired from all the activity of the past few days and too excited to get much sleep. Two more nights in this house, she told herself—just one more full day, and I will leave Independence behind forever.

Abner had warned her that the journey they were undertaking would be fraught with perils and hardships. But she wouldn't let herself think about that now. After all, thousands of people had made it safely to California and Oregon; she and Abner would make it, too.

Jed Dossman had struck Abner as a capable wagon master, and Dossman had traveled to Oregon before. That counted for a great deal, Abner said. The one time Megan had seen Jed Dossman, she'd sensed his strength and intelligence. He certainly was handsome, too. She pushed that thought aside, telling herself that Jed Dossman's looks had nothing to do with what kind of wagon master he was. Furthermore, she had no business thinking about him as often as she had in the past few days. She was merely restless, she told herself.

She rose from the rocker and went to the window, knowing that with all Abner had to do, he wasn't likely to come until later. She pushed back the curtain, anyway, and gazed out hopefully. No one was in sight, and she dropped the curtain and went to the pantry, looking for a snack. The shelves were bare, except for half a loaf of bread, part of a smoked ham and some dried fruit. Along with the jug of milk cooling in the well house, the food was just enough to last until Monday morning. She reached for a piece of dried apple and munched it as she returned to the rocker, determined to relax until Abner came. If only she could fall asleep, the time would pass quickly.

She finally dozed off, but was awakened a few minutes later by a knock at the door. Instantly alert, she jumped up and ran to answer. "Abner, I didn't expect you so early," she exclaimed as she swung open the door.

It wasn't Abner; it was Royce Waddell. He removed his hat and planted one black-booted foot across the threshold. "Abner'll be busy at the livery stable for a good while," Waddell said. "As I passed I saw him pulling a wagon in to work on."

Megan gripped the edge of the door. "What do you want?"

"Much as I hate to be the bearer of bad news, Megan, there's something I need to talk to you about."

"Nothing you have to say could be of the slightest interest to me, Waddell." She tried to shut the door, but his foot kept her from closing it completely. "*Please* remove your foot," she said acidly.

He laughed harshly and leered at her as he pushed hard against the door and stepped into the parlor. "I think you'll be interested when you hear me out."

"Get out of my house!" Megan ordered, trembling with anger and the beginning of fear.

He sent a glance over the parlor, taking in the rolled-up carpet and the trunk and carpetbag visible in the open doorway of the next room. "Your house? This place belonged to Sam Delaney last I heard."

Megan took a step back. "As long as the rent is paid, it's mine! If you don't leave this minute, Waddell, I'll start screaming."

His eyes narrowed. "I doubt anybody would hear you. You're pretty far from your nearest neighbor."

In a growing panic, Megan darted for the bedroom and slammed the door. She was wrestling with the trunk, trying to shove it in front of the door, when Waddell pushed the door back. He stood in the doorway, watching her calmly. "Don't be afraid of me, Megan. I didn't come here for anything except what is rightfully mine."

Straightening, Megan poked at a black curl that had escaped the braid coiled at the back of her neck. She moved behind the trunk, putting it between her and Waddell, all the time watching him warily. "There's nothing in this house that belongs to you," she said scornfully, "or ever will." In spite of her effort to control her voice, it shook noticeably.

He lounged insolently in the doorway, a hand braced on either side of the door facing. "Kate stole several hundred dollars in gold from me," he told her, "and I've taken her room apart looking for it. Today I learned she gave the money to you before she died. I want it back, Megan."

"You're a liar!" Megan cried. "Kate saved that money from what she earned. She told me so herself."

His stance remained casual, but his gray eyes were coldly determined. "She couldn't have saved that much from her wages, not in twenty years. She took the money from the safe in my office."

Megan could not help watching his eyes. His gaze flickered across her face as he spoke, and then . . . moved to her breasts.

"I don't believe you!"

He shrugged. "Believe me or not, I mean to have my money."

She tried bravado. "Well, you can't. I don't have the money. It's gone, spent."

"I know where it is," he answered matter-of-factly. "In that rig Abner Claunch is working on at the livery stable. He'll just have to find a buyer. That won't be hard. You might even make a profit. I don't think the two of you are going to need that rig, anyway. You'd be crazy to try traveling two thousand miles alone."

"We're going with a wagon train," Megan blurted, and immediately wished she could call back the words. The less Waddell knew about their plans, the better. He didn't seem disconcerted by her news, however. He merely reached for her. She tried to dodge him but his hands gripped her upper arms. Somehow he had moved around the trunk, and now brought his face down close to hers. She could smell sweat and whiskey and cigar smoke, and she shuddered.

"I don't think you're going anywhere, Megan." There was a menacing softness in his tone. "But whatever you do, I want that money back before you do it. If I don't get it, I'll go to the sheriff."

"Let me go!" she cried. "You filthy swine!" His hands tightened, and she thought he would break her arms.

He shook her hard. "Damn you, what makes you think you're too good for me! You're nothing, a stupid whore's by-blow. I know you're not the innocent you pretend."

"All right!" she said desperately. "I'll get the money!"

Suddenly the front door crashed open, and both Megan and Waddell jumped as though they'd been shot. "Take your hands off her, Waddell," ordered Abner. "You got a cocked Colt .36 aimed at your backbone."

Waddell froze. "You have till Monday at noon, Megan," he warned. "I get the money, or I go to the sheriff." He released her and turned slowly, keeping his hands away from his sides and in plain sight.

"Get out of here," Abner growled, his eyes ablaze with fury. "And don't come back." He stepped away from the door, jerking his head toward it.

As Waddell walked past Abner he said with icy calm, "The next time I see you, Claunch, I'm going to kill you."

"Not if I see you first."

The two men stared at each other with hatred for a long moment, then Waddell walked out and Abner kicked the door closed with his foot.

Still trembling with fright and anger, Megan watched him holster his gun. He looked up. "Are you all right, Meggie?"

She nodded and walked to him on rubbery legs. He put his arms around her and patted her back. Megan pressed her cheek against his chest. "He wants the money," she said. "He claimed Kate stole it from his safe."

"He's lying."

"I know." She didn't believe Kate stole the money. Kate had been too afraid of Waddell. "But I told him I'd get the money. I didn't know what else to do." The sheriff was Royce Waddell's cousin; he got a free drink at the Gilded Lily whenever he wanted. Who was he likely to believe, Waddell or Megan?

"Everything's going to be fine, Meggie. I'll be able to finish the repairs to the wagon this evening. Then I'll bring it over here and we'll pack everything tomorrow. We'll leave before dawn Monday morning."

She closed her eyes and hugged Abner's skinny middle. Abner was right. Waddell had no way of knowing Abner had arranged for them to go with Jed Dossman's party. "He told me to bring the money to him by noon Monday. We'll be gone long before then." No need to tell Abner that Waddell had threatened to have her thrown in jail if she didn't return the money. By the time Waddell discovered they were gone, it would be too late for him to do anything about it.

"That's right," Abner said, but he was thinking that he should have known Kate couldn't have saved so much money from what Waddell paid her. She must have been holding back her tips for a long spell. Abner wondered how Waddell had figured it out. Well, it was too late for Waddell to do anything about it now. Abner suspected Waddell realized it was too late and his demand for the money was a way to force Megan into working for him to pay off the debt.

To make sure Waddell didn't bother Megan again, Abner decided to sleep in the wagon the next two nights. He'd wait till after dark to bring it to the house, and he'd pull it around in back so it couldn't be seen from the street. "Things are falling into place real good."

Megan took a deep breath and stepped back. She looked at him, her blue eyes bright with resolve. "We'll make a good life for ourselves in Oregon, won't we?"

"You bet we will, Meggie."

"Oh, Abner, I can't wait to leave this place!"

Chapter Four

Abner walked slowly through the dim house as he made a final inspection. When he was satisfied they weren't leaving anything they would need on the trail, he made his way back to the parlor. "Looks like that's all of it, Meggie. Can you think of anything we missed?"

Megan lifted a blue wool shawl from the back of the rocker and pulled it around her shoulders. Her heavy gray dress wasn't quite enough protection from the predawn chill, though later in the day it might be too warm. By then they'd be on the trail, bound for Oregon. She smiled at the thought, but then her glance fell on her beautiful carpet, rolled up against the wall. "My carpet." She sighed wistfully. "Are you sure there isn't room for it?"

Abner looked at the regretful pout on her lovely face and reversed his decision of the day before. "We can squeeze it in, I reckon. So long as you understand we could be forced to throw it out before we reach Oregon. We may have to toss a lot of things overboard before then, Meggie. But by then maybe it won't matter so much. Just surviving may be all you'll be thinking about."

Megan lifted her eyes to his. Every time Abner said something like that, she had a sinking sensation in the pit of her stomach. Last night she'd slept very little; she'd been too tense with excitement over today's departure.

As she'd lain awake, waiting anxiously for the dawn, stories she'd heard and given little thought to in the past had invaded her mind. Stories of Indian attacks on wagon trains, abductions, scalpings, tortures; stories of killing plagues that swept through trains, leaving the few survivors so weak and beaten they didn't have the fortitude to go on; stories of livestock drowning in flooded rivers and plunging off mountain cliffs; stories of shortcuts that led travelers so far from their route they became hopelessly lost; stories of insanity and starvation and even cannibalism. Perhaps she'd be lucky if all she had to deal with on the journey was leaving her carpet behind on the trail.

"I understand," she said.

Abner hoisted the carpet roll to his shoulder and clomped out of the house. Although she was leaving behind most of her furniture, she sound of Abner's boots on the bare floor echoed as though in an empty house. It occurred to Megan that the house *was* empty in an important way—for her it was empty of the human drama that made a house a home: marriages, births, family gatherings, even deaths.

She looked around her one last time. If she had known more happiness here, she might have felt sad at leaving. But all she felt was a vast relief at finally being able to close and lock the door behind her for the last time. Kate had made that possible. As Megan stepped on the porch and turned to fit the key in the lock, she murmured, "Goodbye, Mama." Whatever lay ahead couldn't be much worse than what she'd known the first nineteen years of her life, she reflected.

Abner had yoked and hitched the four-ox team and pulled the wagon around to the front of the house. He stepped down from the high seat as Megan crossed the porch. Tied to the back of the wagon were two mules, two mares and five head of longhorn cattle—three cows and two yearling bulls. "If we get there with only a single cow and a bull, we'll have the foundation of a herd," Abner had told her.

"It looks like a circus wagon," Megan said, laughing.

Abner swept off his flat-crowned hat and bowed low in front of her. "It's no circus, I promise you. Are you ready to go west, daughter?"

Megan giggled. "Yes, Papa, all ready."

His eyes twinkled. "No second thoughts?"

"Not a one."

He moved to help her up to the high wagon seat. "No, don't do that, Abner—I mean, Papa," Megan said. "You won't be around to give me a boost every time I want to get in the wagon while we're on the trail. I might as well start climbing in by myself." Grabbing hold of the rope that laced the heavy canvas top to the wagon's sides, Megan planted one booted foot on a wheel spoke and hoisted herself up. "Not very ladylike," she admitted as she settled her long skirts around her, "but I made it. I'll be going up and down like a monkey in no time."

Abner chuckled and climbed up to sit beside her. "You're about to get an education in how to get in a wagon and a lot of other things, that's for sure." He reached for the reins and cracked the whip. The oxen moved slowly forward.

Megan gripped the edge of the seat. "Bouncing on this hard board day after day is going to get uncomfortable," she observed. "Maybe I can find something to pad it with."

Abner grinned and flipped the reins, and the oxen plodded a little faster. "Somethin' I been meaning to tell you, Meggie girl. We ain't gonna be sitting up here all that much."

She gave him a startled look. "We'll ride the mares?"

"We'll be on mares, all right. Shank's mares."

"We're going to *walk* to Oregon!"

"Much of the way," Abner said, his eyes glinting with amusement at her stunned expression. "Gotta keep the load as light as possible, for one thing. Why'd you think I made you buy two extra pair of boots? 'Course, when you get absolutely tuckered out, you can catch a ride on one of the mares or on that lazy board I built yesterday."

The previous afternoon, she'd noticed him working on a stout oak plank that pulled out from the left side of the wagon, next to the tool chest, but she'd been too busy packing grocery staples in barrels to wonder long about its use. Besides, she thought Abner might be getting tired of her questions, though he'd answered them all patiently enough.

"The wagon bed sags in the middle, Meggie, so the load will shift toward the center." "The axle hubs are made out of sour gum, Meggie, because sour gum's right near impossible to split." When she'd referred to the outer circle of a wagon wheel as the rim, Abner had informed her that it was called the fello, not the rim.

Abner was right, Megan reflected, she still had much to learn. Her ignorance didn't daunt her; she would learn whatever she needed to know; she fully intended to do her share of the work on the journey. "I can walk as far as the next person," she said.

Abner threw an arm around her shoulders and gave her a quick hug. "You'll do fine, Meggie." A wide grin split his weathered face. He was looking forward to the trip as much as she, Megan realized.

The town was silent, the business establishments shuttered, as they passed down the main street. The plodding oxen beat a slow drumming on the drying dirt street. Megan was glad there were no curious idlers on the street at this early hour to stare after them. "I'm not sorry I won't see this town again," Megan murmured.

"I haven't shed a tear over leaving it, either," Abner said. "Couldn't stay around here, anyway, with Waddell looking to shoot me in the back."

"We'll never have to see Waddell's hateful face again," Megan said. "That's another good thing about leaving." As they passed the last wooden structure in town, she looked over at Abner. "Did you find a buyer for your land?"

"Been waitin' for you to ask that. I signed the deed on that forty acres yesterday. Had to take less than I would have if I'd been staying around for a while, but it gives us some cash for emergencies. I spent every penny of Kate's money on the rig and supplies."

"Do you think she'd say we put the money to good use?"

"Yep, I think she would," Abner answered with a sad smile. "She'd be glad you're leaving Independence, though she couldn't bring herself to encourage you to go while she was alive."

"I guess it wasn't the right time before," Megan reflected. "Pastor Valentine used to say everything happens in God's own good time. This must be God's time."

"Must be," Abner agreed, though he was remembering his feeling the day he rode out to Dossman's camp that it could be the Devil as easily as God who was behind this enterprise. No need to worry Megan with his old cowpoke's musings. Spending so much time on the open range gave a man some strange and fanciful notions. It helped pass the time.

"Abner," Megan said suddenly, "I just had a terrible thought. What if Jed Dossman won't take us with his party?"

"No reason why he should refuse. Don't borrow trouble, Meggie."

Megan nodded and lifted her face to the soft gray sky.

Nothing could keep them from getting to Oregon. It was meant to be.

Dossman's camp was alive with activity as Abner and Megan's wagon came in sight of it. Men hitched teams of oxen or mules to wagons. Women threw dirt on the ashes of their breakfast fires or herded excited children close to the wagons where they could keep a eye on them.

Abner pulled back on the reins. "Whoa, there!" He handed the reins to Megan. "Jerk back on 'em and holler 'whoa' if they take a notion to wander off. I'll find Dossman so he can inspect our rig."

Gripping the reins, Megan nodded. She noticed that the hide of the two oxen closest to the wagon quivered and they shuffled their feet restlessly. The smell of other livestock and the noise and activity were making them nervous. For the first time, Megan appreciated the blinders that prevented the oxen seeing anywhere but straight ahead. Abner had stopped far enough from the perimeter of the camp and facing away so that the oxen were looking out at open country.

She fixed her gaze on the line between land and sky where pink had given way to pearly white as the bright ball of the sun moved higher, nearer to peeking above the horizon. She'd had experience with the mare that Abner had bought her two years ago, but she'd never driven a team of oxen. She decided she wouldn't think about it; Abner would be right back.

Fortunately the animals gave her no trouble, but she was glad, when she stretched sideways and craned her neck to peer in back of her, to see Abner and Jed Dossman walking toward the wagon.

Something was wrong. Abner was grim and tight-lipped; he looked worried. Dossman walked around the wagon, his gaze flicking to Megan on the wagon seat. He stopped, hitched his thumbs over the tops of his hip pockets and stared up at her. His strong, solid shoulders were outlined by a dark cotton shirt. A fringed buckskin vest hung loosely on his frame and his long, lean legs were encased in light gray pants of a coarsely textured material. He was hatless. His dark brown hair appeared damp and freshly combed.

The wagon master looked strong, solid—someone to depend on, until you saw that the planes and angles of his handsome face were set in a hard, unrelenting expression. His dark eyes seemed to bore right through her. Was this some kind of test, to see if she was tough enough to go west? She sat straight on the wagon seat, tightening her lips and hoping her shiver of apprehension went undetected. Megan forced her eyes to remain steady as she met his stare.

"Good morning, Mr. Dossman." Securing the reins, she twisted sideways on the seat. Dossman made no move to help her down, but Abner hurried to the wagon in time for her to grasp his shoulder as, with as much dignity as possible, she jumped lightly to the ground. Straightening her dress, she turned to Dossman and said, "I'm sure you'll find our wagon acceptable."

Dossman shifted his weight. "The wagon's fine." His gaze scanned the covered wagon perfunctorily, then returned to Megan. "I won't be inspecting it, though. The wagon is no longer the issue, Miss *Riley*."

Megan darted a puzzled look at Abner, who gazed back at her unhappily. How did Dossman know her last name? Thinking hard, she assured herself that Edgar Crow hadn't used her last name when he'd introduced Jed Dossman to her. Abruptly she remembered her meeting with Carolyn Goddard. Had Carolyn mentioned her to Dossman? Frantically she searched for an explanation that would satisfy the grim-mouthed man before her. She swallowed. "Mr. Claunch is my stepfather—" she began.

"Don't bother, Meggie," Abner interrupted. "It's no use."

When Jed saw her stunned look his expression changed slowly to a mocking grin that made Megan avert her flushed face. "Even if I didn't know the truth about you two," Jed drawled, "your face would give you away, Miss Riley. I'm surprised you're not a more practiced liar. But maybe you've rarely had to resort to lying to get men to do what you want."

Fear crawled through her. Dossman sounded as though he had no intention of including them in his party. "Abner? What's he talking about?"

Jed couldn't help noticing the way shiny black tendrils escaped her chignon and curled around her face, and he couldn't help wondering how that mass of raven hair would look, loosed and flowing down her back, how it would feel to bury his hands in it. Hell, he told himself, it wouldn't be a unique experience—dozens of men already knew how she felt, hair and all.

"You aren't related to Claunch," Jed said, his eyes raking over her contemptuously. "Not by blood, and not by marriage. That's why you won't be traveling with my train. Claunch may be fool enough to be taken in by your scheme, but I'm not. I've known plenty of women like you, Megan Riley. You're—"

"That's enough, Dossman," Abner growled. "You've made your point."

Jed's eyes narrowed dangerously, but after a moment he merely shrugged. "No reason for you two to hang around

here, Claunch. You'll only be in the way.'' He glanced at
Megan one more time with a faint, but somehow chilling,
quirk of his lips. Then he turned his back on them and
strode away.

"Abner!'' Megan clutched his arm frantically. They could
not go back to Independence. Waddell would kill Abner the
first chance he had, and Megan would be facing criminal
charges before the day was over. "Go after him! You have
to make him take us.''

"He's not going to change his mind,'' Abner said grimly.
He would never tell Megan everything that Jed Dossman
had said before they'd reached the wagon. Dossman hadn't
come right out with it in so many words, but his meaning
had been clear. For some crazy reason, he'd got it into his
head that Megan was a woman of unsavory virtue and she'd
cause trouble among the men in his party. Abner had
cursed, argued and tried to tell him he was wrong, but
Dossman wouldn't listen. Megan would be mortified if she
knew the real reason for Dossman's refusal to take them.

Megan stared at Jed Dossman's retreating back and suddenly she broke away from Abner and ran after Dossman.
"Mr. Dossman, wait, please!''

Behind her, she heard Abner calling for her to come back,
but she couldn't. They had nowhere to go if Dossman refused to take them. Somehow she had to make him change
his mind.

Dossman finally heard her above the noise of the camp
and turned around to stare at her coldly. He was actually
enjoying her predicament, she realized. The man was a
monster. She opened her mouth to tell him so, but choked
back the words.

Instead she composed herself with great effort and closed
the short distance between them at a more sedate pace. She
was painfully aware that her desperate plea had carried
through the camp and people were stopping their work to
stare at her. She saw Carolyn Goddard and a small boy not
far from where she and Dossman stood. At least twenty
people were listening curiously, but she couldn't worry

about how she must look, hollering and running after Dossman like a harridan.

She lifted her chin and said in a restrained voice, "You have to take us. I spent every dollar I had to my name on that wagon and our provisions."

"That's your problem," Jed said. "It's not as if you have no trade by which to earn more money, is it, Miss Riley?"

Megan gaped at him. She had no idea what he meant by that—though she knew this man disliked her intensely, and for no reason. But there was no time to try to understand Jed Dossman; she was pleading for her life and Abner's. "Why won't you take us?"

"I don't think you want me to go into all of my reasons," Jed said, glancing at their small, but growing, audience. Damn, what a nuisance she was turning out to be. "It's reason enough that I've made it a policy not to take single women in this wagon train."

Megan felt Abner's presence at her side even before he touched her arm, but she didn't look at him. Her thoughts were scurrying wildly about in search of a way to change Jed Dossman's mind. She was sure further pleas, even tears would not move him. She was a single woman and—

The solution came to her in a flash. "We've had time for nothing else except making preparations for the journey. We thought there'd be time to get married Saturday or Sunday, but it—it was impossible."

"Meggie!" Abner muttered in a cracked voice. "What in tarnation are you saying?"

She would have to deal with Abner later, for now, all her powers of concentration were on Jed Dossman. "Please, Mr. Dossman, if you'll only wait until we can return to town and find a preacher. We should be back in less than an hour."

Instead of answering her, Jed was contemplating the man beside her. Megan finally glanced at Abner. His face was a study in shock. Seeing Abner's reaction, anybody with a brain in his head would have known that marriage had never been mentioned between them. Nevertheless Megan had to salvage the situation because there was nothing else for her to do. "I know you wanted to keep our engagement a secret, Abner," she said, begging him with her eyes to go along with her. "But I had to tell him. Mr. Dossman seems to have the wrong impression entirely about us."

Jed's mouth twisted sardonically. The little tart had given Claunch the shock of his life. Clearly Claunch had no objection to traveling with a fallen woman, but he'd never meant to marry her. If Jed hadn't been so angry, he would have had a good laugh at the older man's expression. As it was, he had to fight back an explosion of fury. For some reason, this new scheme of Megan Riley's to marry Abner Claunch riled him even more than her original scheme of posing as Claunch's daughter. He didn't pause to ask himself why.

"You just don't quit, do you, lady?" Jed snorted. "But I don't have time to dally while you wrangle this old cowpoke into making you an honest woman. We're ready to pull out of here."

Megan stared at him in confusion. She felt as baffled as she was hurt by his attitude. She shifted her gaze to the crowd, searching for a friendly face, some sign of support. She saw Carolyn Goddard smiling at her and said impulsively, "Carolyn, make him listen."

Carolyn came forward, still holding her son's hand. "Jed, have you forgotten? There's no need for them to go back to town. We have a preacher with the train. Pastor Glenhill can marry them."

A murmur of agreement rippled through the little knot of spectators. Jed threw Carolyn Goddard a dark look, his hands clenched instinctively at his sides. Carolyn was evidently taken with the idea of a wedding and wouldn't be diverted by his displeasure. "A wedding will bring good luck to the train," she said, looking around her for approval.

A big, broad-chested man spoke up. "Let 'em get married, Jed. We can tarry another ten minutes, and it'll be fine to set out on a festive note. It could be a good while before we have another reason for celebration."

Several other onlookers voiced their agreement. A tall, bearded young man called, "Put that poor old cowboy out of his misery, Jed. If he don't hitch up with that pretty little lady while he has a chance, she's liable to come to her senses and back out on him."

Laughter ran through the spectators, and Megan cringed, as much for Abner's embarrassment as for her own. At that moment she wanted nothing so much as to run away from the crowd of nosy, amused strangers.

"We ought to be thinking about getting to Oregon, Carolyn, instead of delaying for frivolity," Jed said tautly. "You may look on a wedding as good luck, but I doubt Claunch sees it that way."

"Oh, pooh, of course he does," Carolyn disagreed. "He's just embarrassed, poor man. Daniel Schiller—" She pointed at a gangly red-haired teenager in the group. "Go find Preacher Glenhill and tell him he's got a wedding to perform."

Not daring to look at Jed Dossman's angry face, Megan tugged on Abner's arm, pulling him back out of earshot of the others. "Abner, I'm sorry, but it's the only thing I could think of."

"Meggie, this is crazy," Abner wailed. "An old man like me wedding a fine, young girl like you? Why, I'd feel like some kind of pervert. And you'd come to your right senses in a while and wish it had all been a nightmare. No, Meggie, it's ain't right. We'll just have to find another wagon train to take us."

"You know it's too late for that!" Megan said urgently. "Getting married is the only way we can leave for Oregon right now, and we have to go today. Once we get there, I won't hold you to vows made against your will. I swear to you I won't do that."

Abner shook his head doggedly. "You don't know what you're saying, sugar. A wedding is a wedding, whether you want to believe it or not. Sweetheart, you got your whole life ahead of you. Someday you're gonna meet a fine young man and—"

"I can't go back!" Megan choked back a sob. "Oh, Abner, I didn't want to tell you this, but Waddell threatened to go to the sheriff if I didn't bring him the money by noon today. You know they're kin, and you know nobody is going to believe anything I say in my own defense. I probably couldn't even find a lawyer in Independence to take my case."

Distractedly she looked back over her shoulder and saw the teenage boy who'd been sent by Carolyn Goddard to find the preacher. Daniel Schiller hurried toward Jed Dossman. Another man accompanied him, a pale young fellow with white-blond hair slicked down with water. He was trying to button up a black suit jacket while carrying a large Bible in one hand. In that single glance, Megan saw also that Jed Dossman was watching her and Abner, his expression intent and furious.

"They've found the preacher," Megan said breathlessly, turning back to Abner. "If you can think of any other way out of this mess, I'd like to hear it."

Somebody in the camp rang a big cowbell, and a man's voice shouted, "We're having a wedding, folks, before we get started. Everybody gather over there where Jed's standing. Step lively now. We gotta get this couple hitched so we can head for beautiful, green Oregon!"

Realizing the situation was beyond his control, Jed walked over to Abner and Megan. "Mention a wedding to a woman, Claunch," Jed said, "and she's off and running."

Abner looked at Jed and back to Megan in an agony of indecision.

"Carolyn Goddard means well," Jed said. "She just doesn't know what's going on here." His dark eyes, filled with disdain, fixed on Megan, as though he thought she was some kind of criminal.

"Abner?" Megan said.

Abner shoved his hands into his britches pockets. "I wish I had time to think, Meggie. Maybe I could come up with another way."

"I don't believe Mr. Dossman will give us any more time." Megan faced Jed squarely, struggling to hide her dismay over his obvious disapproval of her.

Jed thought she played the part of the sweet innocent to perfection. If he didn't know what she really was, he'd feel sorry for her. He'd probably do something stupid like rescue her from a marriage to this cowboy who was old enough to be her father, maybe even her grandfather. As it was, he thought Abner Claunch was the one in need of rescue.

"She's using you, Claunch," Jed said harshly. "Think about what you're getting yourself into."

Megan's eyes widened in amazement. Seething with outrage, she clamped her lips tight against the urge to aim a scathing retort at the stubborn wagon master.

"This is no business of yours, Dossman," Abner replied sharply.

But Jed went on relentlessly, "All you have to do, Claunch, is get back in that wagon and drive it out of here. If you feel sorry for her, give her money. Or leave the wagon with her to sell and get on your horse and head for Texas. Nobody's holding a gun to your head. There's no reason for you to go through with this."

He made it sound as if she'd planned to marry Abner all along! As if she were desperate to get married! If not for Jed Dossman's arbitrary decision to bar them from the train— if not for his bullheaded stubbornness—she and Abner wouldn't be backed into this corner, forced to consider a marriage that neither of them would ever have thought of otherwise. Megan ached to slap Jed Dossman's face and tell him exactly how despicable she thought he was, but she didn't dare. He could still refuse to take them.

Jed read the fury in her flashing blue eyes and a lopsided grin slowly formed across his face, enraging her further, as he'd intended. "Make up your mind, Claunch," he warned, glancing at the crowd that had gathered, Carolyn Goddard and the young preacher, David Glenhill, in front of the pack. "The wedding party's waiting with bated breath."

Abner swore loudly, then turned Megan away from Dossman and spoke softly, close to her ear. "Meggie, it looks like we might have to go through with this. I can't take you back to Independence and you sure can't follow me around on cattle drives."

Megan had never before thought of going to Texas with Abner. "What's a cattle drive like?"

Abner heard the little flicker of hope in her question and answered her bluntly. "You don't take many baths and a bunch of cowpokes can get to smelling worse than the cattle. You hear more swearing than anything else, and the men can get real starved for a woman. No, sugar. There's no way you'd be allowed to go. But don't you worry none. We'll untangle this mess later."

Megan sagged against him. She hadn't seriously thought she could become a cowhand. They would go to Oregon, after all, though not as they'd planned or would have chosen to. She knew she would not feel like a married woman even after the ceremony, but she couldn't think about that now. It had come down to marry Abner or go to jail.

Abner took her arm and led her forward. "Tell the preacher we're ready, Dossman."

Jed gazed at the tall, gaunt man, shook his head and made a sound of disgust. "You're a bigger damn fool than I thought, Claunch, but it's your funeral. Pastor, come over here. Let's get this farce over with."

Megan had taken all the abuse from Jed Dossman she could tolerate. She whirled on him, her fists clenched, her face red with outrage. "Nobody asked for your opinion!"

"You got it, anyway, lady."

Abner grabbed her hand and pulled her away.

"What is wrong with that man?" Megan sputtered.

"Pay him no mind, Meggie," Abner soothed.

"He's the most arrogant, hateful—horrible beast I've ever met! He looks at me as if I'm dirt, and he doesn't even know me!"

"I reckon he's a woman hater," Abner said. "Just ignore him. It's none of his business what we do, is it?"

"None at all."

"Sir? Miss?"

Megan was so intent on her dislike of Jed Dossman that she didn't notice the preacher until he spoke. He was standing next to her, looking young and self-conscious and shy. Why, this must be his first wedding, she thought, and managed a weak smile. "It's very kind of you to marry us without any advance notice, Pastor. I'm Megan Riley and this is—er, my intended, Abner Claunch."

"How do you do, sir." Glenhill offered his hand and Abner's rough paw enveloped it. "Miss, if I may say so, you're just about the prettiest bride I ever set eyes on, even without a proper wedding gown."

Megan blushed. "We—I didn't have time to make a gown. Everything has happened so quickly."

"I ain't exactly duded up like a proper groom, either," Abner grumbled.

"It's what's in our hearts that counts," Megan said. "Isn't that right, Pastor?"

"Yes, ma'am." Glenhill's pale blue eyes were fixed on Megan as if he found what he saw almost too good to be believed. After a moment he cleared his throat, remembering his role. "Let's walk over there and stand beneath that tree, shall we? We'll pretend it's an arbor in a flower garden."

Abner looked at Megan and lifted his eyebrows. She suppressed a nervous laugh. "That sounds lovely, Pastor."

Hearing her, Jed rolled his eyes in contempt. "Make it snappy, Preacher," he barked. "We're pulling out in five minutes, whether they're hitched or not." With that he walked away to saddle his horse.

Megan glared after him until the minister touched her arm lightly. "You may stand right there, Miss Riley. And Mr. Claunch, stand here beside your beautiful bride."

Glenhill had positioned them to face the crowd. As Megan scanned the assemblage, Carolyn Goddard caught her eye and smiled. At that moment Carolyn's husband, Thayer, strode to Carolyn's side. He said something, and her smile faded. Carolyn shook her head and Thayer Goddard spoke again. Once more Carolyn shook her head. Thayer Goddard grabbed his young son's hand and, dragging the child after him, stalked through the crowd, away from his wife.

Megan realized Thayer didn't want Carolyn to witness the wedding, and was bewildered. Two strange men had taken an intense dislike to her and she couldn't understand it.

"Dearly beloved," the preacher began, "we are gathered here to witness . . ."

Megan wrenched her thoughts back to what the minister was saying, but hard as she tried, she couldn't make the moment seem real. The solemn words and the sacred vows seemed to come to her through a mist, as though she were hearing them in a dream. And the minister seemed to speak so quickly she couldn't catch all the words. She felt as though she'd lost her grip on the reins of her life and she was astride a runaway horse, incapable of getting off or of stopping. Too much was happening too fast, and all she could do was try to hang on until she could think things through clearly.

As if from a great distance, Megan heard the young minister say, "I now pronounce you man and wife. What God has joined together let not man put asunder. Mr. Claunch, you may kiss your bride."

Megan jumped when Abner bent and hastily brushed his lips over her cheek. His face was red with embarrassment. Cheers rose from the onlookers, and several women came forward to offer their congratulations.

Carolyn Goddard squeezed Megan's hand. "I'm so glad you're going with us, Megan," she said. "This is my friend Rose Schiller."

The woman with Carolyn was one of the biggest women Megan had ever seen. She stood almost six feet tall, and her hands were as large as a man's. Her sandy hair was bound in a single braid that was wound tightly at the back of her head. Her freckled face was merry and kind.

"You're the mother of that red-haired boy who went for the preacher," Megan said. "Daniel, I think his name is."

"Yes, I'm Daniel's mother," Rose said.

"And Aaron's and Ben's and Jude's and Mary's and Laura's," Carolyn added.

Megan smiled. "You're a brave woman, going to Oregon with six children, Mrs. Schiller."

"Pshaw, call me 'Rose,' Megan. Oh, mercy, Jed's yelling at us to head out. We'll be seeing a lot of each other, Megan. I hope we'll be friends."

"So do I," Megan said sincerely.

"Come on, Meggie," Abner called. "We have to get our wagon in line."

She ran after him and climbed in the wagon just as it started moving.

Far down the line ahead of them, she heard Jed Dossman's deep voice shout, "Stretch 'em out!"

Whatever else he might have said was lost in a volley of popping whips, oaths and calls of encouragement to the animals.

The hoofbeats of the horses and mules and the softer drumming of the oxen's tread created a steady rhythm on the hard ground accompanied by the creaking of leather harnesses and the squeaking of wagon wheels.

Abner walked alongside the oxen, driving them with his whip. Soon Megan could no longer see him because he was lost in the dust churned up by the hooves of the livestock. Megan soon realized the dust was another reason for staying out of the wagon while it was moving. Tossing her shawl behind her into the wagon bed, she climbed down and walked some distance away where the choking cloud wasn't so thick.

She looked up at the clear blue sky and her heart soared. The long journey was under way. I'm going to Oregon, she told herself, and that's all that matters.

Chapter Five

Before long, most of the other women in the train were walking, too. Children darted here and there, eliciting frequent warnings from adults to stay clear of the wagons and livestock. Megan could be thankful, at least, that she had no small children to keep an eye on every waking minute.

Two young girls caught up with her. "You're Mrs. Claunch, aren't you?" asked the older one, a tall, strawberry blonde.

Megan smiled, glad for the company. "I guess I am. I'll have to get used to thinking of myself that way, won't I?"

The younger girl, whose oval face, emerald eyes and thick auburn hair were precursors of a breathtaking adult beauty, skipped along beside Megan. "I'm Laura Schiller," she said, "and she's my sister, Mary."

"You're Rose's daughters. I should have known. Carolyn Goddard told me your names earlier."

"We never saw a wedding before today, Mrs. Claunch," Laura informed her. "I thought it would look more—well, special and important."

"Laura!" Mary scolded. "That's not a nice thing to say to Mrs. Claunch."

Megan laughed. "To tell you the truth, Laura, I always thought my wedding would be much different, too, with lots of flowers and a white gown. Sometimes, though, things don't turn out the way you've dreamed. This morning's ceremony was over so quickly I still can't believe I'm married."

"You'll get used to it in a little while, Mrs. Claunch," Laura said reassuringly.

"Mercy, will you stop calling me that? It makes me sound like a middle-aged matron. How old are you girls?"

"Fifteen," Mary said.

"I'm thirteen," Laura added.

"I'm not much older than you, Mary, even if I am a married woman. I'd like it much better if you two would call me 'Megan.'"

"All right," Laura agreed with pleasure. "But you better tell Mama you asked us to, or we'll get a lecture about being disrespectful."

"I'll do that the next time I talk to Rose. Which wagon is yours?"

"It's two back," Mary said.

Megan looked and saw, through a film of red dust, a square-built, balding man with a whip in his hand, walking beside the two lead mules of the six-mule team pulling the Schiller wagon. Behind him walked Daniel Schiller, his bright red hair shining through the dust like a beacon. "Laura, is that your father with Daniel?"

"Uh-huh."

"And how old is Daniel?"

"He's the eldest, sixteen. Aaron's ten, Ben's eight and Jude's six, only Mama calls him the hindmost 'cause she says he's the last one she means to have. When she says that, Papa swats her bottom and says the best-laid plans sometimes go astray."

Mary gasped. "Laura! Do you have to blab everything you know?"

Laura shrugged. "Nobody ever told me it was a secret."

"Common sense should have told you."

Megan was struggling not to laugh. "I won't tell anyone, Mary."

"How many babies do you want to have, Megan?" Laura asked.

"Excuse me," Mary intervened, "but I'm going to walk with someone else." She gave Megan an apologetic look. "There are times when I wish I didn't have a sister."

Mary dropped back several wagon lengths and began talking to another teenage girl. Laura said matter-of-factly, "I embarrass her sometimes. I don't do it on purpose, though."

"I'm sure you don't."

"You don't have to tell me how many babies you want if you don't feel like it."

"I really haven't thought about it," Megan said, and wished Laura would change the subject. She didn't even want to think about her hasty marriage, much less having babies. "Did you bring your schoolbooks with you?"

"Yes, that was the first thing Mama put in the wagon, and slates and tablets and pencils. I was kind of hoping she'd forget about them, but Mama doesn't forget things like that. We took a holiday today, but as soon as we're on the trail tomorrow we have to do our schoolwork in the wagon before we can do anything else. Except Daniel. He already finished the tenth grade and Papa said he was old enough to quit book learning and do a man's work. Oh, look, here comes Jed." Laura waved at Jed Dossman as he rode past astride a bay stallion.

Jed grinned and yelled, "Hello, Mistress Schiller. When are you going to bake me that chocolate cake you promised?"

"As soon as Mama will let me!"

Jed's gaze slid to Megan, and his smile faded. He tipped his hat to her and rode away. Somehow the gesture seemed more insolent than polite.

"Oh, isn't he handsome?" Laura exclaimed. "He's nice, too, and funny. I wish I were older so I could marry him!" She giggled. "Oops. Good thing Mary didn't hear that. She'd get beet red. I'll tell you something if you promise to keep it a secret."

"Promise," Megan said solemnly.

"Mary really likes Jed. I think she'd like to marry him, too, only she'd die before she'd admit it."

Megan had to bite her tongue to keep from saying that if Laura and her sister knew the Jed Dossman Megan had seen, they'd alter their opinion of him. She knew she had to keep her thoughts about the wagon master to herself. She was going to spend months in close proximity to the people traveling with the train, and the only sensible thing to do was try to get along with all of them—even Jed Dossman. "One of these days Mary will fall in love with a young man her own age and she'll forget all about Jed Dossman."

"I hope so," Laura said candidly. "Then maybe he'll wait for me to grow up."

Megan laughed and flipped one of the girl's auburn pigtails. "Oh, Laura, I like you."

Laura beamed. "Thank you, Megan. I like you, too."

The wagon train traveled northwest along the Missouri toward the Platte River in Nebraska Territory. There they would follow the Platte and its tributaries west, all the way to the Rockies. The greening land stretching all around them was flat, with few trees and even fewer hillocks.

They stopped for a "nooning" hour at midday to rest the animals. Those people who were hungry ate a cold lunch of breakfast leftovers. Others napped. Jed assigned several men and older boys to stand sentry while the others rested.

The day passed much too quickly for Megan. By the time Jed gave the command later in the afternoon to "corral" the wagons, she had had ample time for the full meaning of that morning's wedding ceremony to sink in. She was a married woman with a husband who would surely expect to share her bed that night. Although she had never had a serious suitor, Megan had come to understand the intimate details of marriage. Since that day five years ago when she'd witnessed what her mother did for a living, she had learned by observing animals and from Sadie Robison, who had a surprisingly intricate knowledge of the subject for a spinster.

Sadie's father had been a doctor, and she'd learned about the sex act from his medical books.

It was one thing to have a theoretical understanding of sex, however, and quite another to think about putting it into practice. Megan found herself avoiding Abner all day, except for taking him three sausage-and-biscuit sandwiches at noon while he stood sentry. She was grateful to him for treating her as he always had, like a daughter. If he was contemplating their first night as man and wife, he gave no indication of it. But that didn't keep the hours from passing with what seemed to Megan, incredible speed.

At Jed's command, the wagon train swung out in an arc, forming a big oval with two openings, which would be closed by ropes after the livestock had been watered and fed. A woodcutting party went out, returning later with enough wood for two cook fires. The women set about preparing the evening meal, the main meal of the day.

Rose Schiller insisted that Megan and Abner share their supper of sowbelly, beans, shortcake and coffee. The Schiller children drank milk from the family's milk cow; it was Aaron's chore to milk the cow each morning and evening.

"I tried to get Jed to join us," Rose said as they were eating, "but he's tuckered out and wants to bed down as soon as he can. I guess sleep looked more appealing to him than company."

"He rode or walked up and down this train all day," Reuben Schiller said, "making sure nobody was falling behind and helping those who were having trouble. No man can keep that up day after day. Jed asked Mason Glenhill, the preacher's brother, and me to be his captains starting tomorrow. That should take some of the load off him." Reuben was a ruddy, robust man who stood several inches shorter than his wife.

"I'll take over our wagon when you're helping Jed, Papa," Daniel volunteered.

In spite of what Rose and Reuben said, Megan couldn't help thinking that Jed might have joined the Schillers for the evening meal if she and Abner hadn't been included.

Abner spoke little during the meal, and though Megan made several efforts to participate in the conversation, her heart wasn't in it. After the children and the men had left, Megan began clearing the Schillers' makeshift table, two planks propped on cartons that were light enough for Rose to lift down from the wagon unaided.

"You leave that be, Megan," Rose chided. "I'll get Mary and Laura to help me with the cleaning up. You need to get yourself all freshened up for your wedding night."

Megan felt her face color and was thankful there was no longer enough light to reveal her embarrassment. "I *would* like to get out of these dusty clothes and wash off the dirt," Megan said, wanting only to get away from good-hearted Rose Schiller and her reminders of what the night would bring.

"You go along then," Rose said. "I'll see you at breakfast."

Megan hurried to her wagon, her head down so she wouldn't have to chat with anyone she passed. Abner was still sitting with Reuben Schiller and several other men near one of the dying cook fires, savoring the last coffee. Earlier he had brought her a bucket of water from the creek where the livestock had been watered, but she'd only had time to wash her face and hands before supper.

It was dark under the arching canvas cover, and Megan didn't think anyone passing at the end of the wagon could see inside. But as an added precaution, she bent between two barrels and stripped off her clothing. She dipped water from the bucket into a shallow pan and scrubbed herself with a clean cloth and lye soap. She wished she could wash her hair, but had to settle for letting it down and brushing it vigorously. There would be more dust tomorrow, and she couldn't wash it every night. It was thick and long and took hours to dry unless she dried it in the sun. She doubted that the opportunity for stealing off by herself for a leisurely bath and head washing in the middle of the day would arise very often.

The evening was cooling and she was shivering by the time she finished. She dried herself hastily and slipped a long, cotton gown over her head, drawing the clean-smelling fabric around her. She gave her hair a few last strokes and plaited it loosely. Then she shoved the boxes and cartons from the center of the wagon against the sides, unwound her bedroll and spread it in the narrow space.

She crawled under a quilt and stretched out on her back, pulling the cover up to her chin. She stared at the barely discernible hole where the canvas was gathered tightly at the end of the wagon. Somewhere in the distance a coyote howled forlornly. Megan burrowed beneath her quilt. She was still shaking but now it was not from the cold but from nervousness. God help me, she thought, what if I can't go through with it? She had to do her duty as Abner's wife—somehow. Megan Riley, she lectured silently, get a grip on yourself. The wedding was *your* idea. Abner didn't want to get married. You talked him into it.

After all, she told herself sternly, you are a grown woman. You knew what getting married meant. But, dear heaven, she hadn't allowed herself to think about that at the time, and she'd managed to keep such thoughts at bay most of the day. It was only as sundown had approached that she could no longer help thinking about it.

Her shaking seemed to be easing as her body warmth filled the cocoon formed by the quilt. She mustn't be quaking like a leaf when Abner came into the wagon. She willed her muscles to relax. She must look on the bright side of the marriage, she thought. She had known Abner all her life, and she knew he would never do anything to hurt her. She had great respect and affection for him. For most of her life he had been her friend and there were times when she had pretended he was her father. Those feelings were something to build on. Surely in time she could learn to love him as a husband.

Megan didn't know how long she lay there, reassuring herself. Eventually, her exhaustion from the walking she'd done that day overcame her anxiety and she drifted into sleep. Sometime later she jerked awake. She was still alone in the wagon. How long had she slept? Where was Abner?

Then she heard footsteps approaching, and her heart began to race. The footsteps stopped at the end of the wagon and she heard Abner rummaging through their goods, trying to be quiet. Every sound he made was amplified by her nervous state.

She wondered if she should say something, but her throat closed and she couldn't get a word out. Finally she heard him moving away from the end of the wagon. She sat up, peering into the darkness, but she couldn't see a thing. Abner grunted and let out a long sigh. It sounded as though he were under the wagon. Megan rose up on her knees and felt blindly for the other bedroll. It was gone. Abner had bedded down on the ground beneath the wagon.

Slowly Megan lay back down. Relief washed through her in an enormous, releasing wave. She felt as though she'd been given a reprieve from a death sentence. She felt guilty at her reaction, but the feeling lasted only as long as it took her to drop into a deep sleep.

The next morning dawned clear and bright. When Megan awoke, Abner's bedroll was already back in the wagon. She dressed hurriedly in a plain, blue cotton dress that buttoned high at the neck. When she left the wagon, she saw Abner leading their livestock to the water. A wispy breath of fog drifted low over the creek, slowly dispersing into a thin, transparent mist.

Hurriedly Megan gathered an armload of supplies and joined the other women around a big campfire. A party had gone out early to cut wood. She started coffee brewing in her pot and waited for her turn at an iron skillet. While slabs of bacon sizzled in the pan, she mixed griddle cakes of corn meal, baking powder and water and fried them in the bacon fat. By the time Abner had staked the livestock where there was fresh grass for grazing, she had their breakfast ready. There was sorghum molasses to go with the griddle cakes; with bacon and hot coffee, the breakfast was tasty and filling.

As they ate, she avoided Abner's eyes and heard herself chattering inanely. She felt Abner watching her, but when she managed to look at him, he smiled pleasantly and glanced away.

Wiping his plate with the last piece of griddle cake, he said, "I'll go get the team. Can you pack our things back in the wagon, Meggie?"

"Well, of course I can. I'm not helpless, Abner."

He grinned, seeming at ease with her for the first time that morning. "Nope. You look fit as a fiddle this morning after walking all that way. Are your feet sore?"

"A little," she admitted. "I'm wearing two pairs of stockings this morning."

He drained his tin coffee cup. "Jed'll be wanting to leave in a few minutes. We'd best get hopping." He plunked his cup down on the old quilt Megan had spread on the ground, rose and went after the livestock.

She should have talked to him about sleeping under the wagon, Megan thought, but she didn't know how to bring it up. It was easier to put it off and try not to think about the marriage at all. Maybe things would work themselves out in time without their having to talk about it.

She scoured the skillet and their dishes with sand and rinsed them with some of the water left in the bucket. Enough water remained to provide their drinking water for the day. Wedging the bucket between two boxes in a corner of the wagon bed, she set a pie tin on top of it and weighted it down with a rock. After stowing the quilt, dishes and cooking utensils in their proper places, she decided to walk to the Schillers' wagon and say hello to Rose.

Megan looked out over the prairie, admiring the cloudless blue of the sky and the way the dewdrops sparkled like tiny jewels on the grass. A white, stilt-legged water fowl flew above the creek and dipped down to stand, motionless and watching, at the edge of the water. Beyond, the prairie looked endless.

She didn't see the rock in her path until she stumbled over it and plunged forward. As she fell her arms flailed desperately in search of something to grab hold of to steady herself, and then she was caught in a strong grip and crushed against a hard chest. Her cheek scraped against a rough buckskin vest she would have known anywhere. Jed Dossman!

Jed had reacted instinctively, and now he stood, stunned and as motionless as a statue, with Megan Claunch in his arms. A black curl nestled against his neck. He could feel her breasts crushed against him. Her heart beat frantically against his chest like that of a frightened rabbit and her breathing was rapid.

The heat from her small body made beads of sweat pop out on his forehead. He tried not to notice the feel of her hair, silky beneath his chin, or the clean scent of her. He tried mightily to forget what he'd been thinking about just before she fell into his arms. He had seen her walking toward him and had noticed the thrust of her full breasts against the cotton material of her dress, the soft curve of her hips in the full skirt; and his hands had itched to span her narrow waist. He had been angry with himself for thinking of her in that way. It had reminded him too pointedly of the restless night he'd spent napping briefly and waking to discover disturbing thoughts in his head, thoughts of Megan and Abner Claunch lying together in their wagon.

Megan's arm was pinned beneath one of Jed's and something—a metal button, she thought—was digging into her earlobe. His warm breath fanned her forehead and his heartbeat was slow and regular beneath her ear.

"Please," she gasped. "You can let go of me now. I—I'm so clumsy... I'm sorry."

"Are you?" His tone was totally unlike any he had used with her before, soft and lazy and amused.

"You're crushing the breath out of me," Megan gasped, wriggling against him.

Jed was hotly aware of the erotic sensation her weak struggling was beginning to evoke. How easy it would be to bring his mouth down on her full, rosy lips. It would be like savoring wild honey—he could almost taste her. The woman in his arms was soft and feminine and so desirable it made him feel like groaning.

Suddenly he remembered who and what she was, and the insistent stirring of his body abruptly switched off. He grabbed her roughly by the arms and set her away from him.

Megan took a stumbling step back. "I—I appreciate you catching me like that." Her voice shook. She felt dizzy, her heart was pounding and she was weak and uncertain. She waited for him to say something, but he didn't. Nor did he move. Perhaps this was a good time to take the first step toward breaking down the barrier between them. They could not travel for months in the same train with things as they were.

She took a deep breath. "Thank you, Jed."

Jed fought an unaccountable need to reach out and brush a straggling ebony tendril of hair out of her eyes. He stiffened in response to the tenderness that rose in him. "I'd do the same for any saddle tramp," he muttered tensely, "*Mrs.* Claunch." His voice sounded hoarse.

Megan had not expected kindness from him, but his callous rudeness hurt her. She was tired of trying to figure him out, tired of letting him humiliate her. She had a right to expect the same respect he would give any other woman on the train.

"Stop saying 'Mrs. Claunch' in that tone of voice. You say it like you mean something vile. My name is Megan."

"Damn it all—"

"And don't swear at me!" Without any warning, hot tears filled her eyes.

Seeing the tears, Jed felt a prickle of alarm. Women's tears made him feel helpless, at a loss as to what to say or do. "Thunderation," he said gruffly. "Don't cry. People will think I hurt you."

Furiously Megan blinked back her tears. "My goodness gracious, we wouldn't want anyone to think a thing like that, would we?"

Her voice held equal measures of sarcasm and stubbornness. Jed wasn't sure he liked it. "I have work to do," he said, and touched the brim of the hat. "Good morning— 'Megan.'"

Her head held high, Megan continued on to the Schiller wagon. The two younger boys were still eating breakfast, sitting on the grass beside the wagon. Young Johnny Goddard was sitting between them, eating a biscuit. Rose was in the wagon, repacking food and bedding. Carolyn Goddard stood at the end of the wagon, talking to Rose.

"Hello, you two," Megan called.

Carolyn looked around and smiled. "It's Megan, Rose. My, you've fed your husband and repacked your wagon already? Nobody would guess you were a new bride."

"It has to be easier to cook for two than it is to feed a husband *and* children," Megan said. She went to stand beside Carolyn at the end of the wagon. "Rose, where on earth are you going to put all that bedding?"

Rose laughed. "Watch and learn, Megan. You'll be amazed how much you can stuff in a wagon if you know how to pack it." She pulled blankets and quilts over to the opening, where Megan and Carolyn stood, sat down and began winding them into tight bedrolls. "We were all too tired last night to set up the tent, but we will tonight. The boys slept on the ground, but it was still too crowded in the wagon. I hope you brought a tent, Megan. A wagon's too hot in the heat of summer."

"We brought a small one," Megan said, uncomfortable with the subject of sleeping arrangements. "Where are Mary and Laura?"

"I sent them down to the river to wash our breakfast dishes. If they didn't run into Jedediah, they ought to be back any minute."

"I passed Jed on the way here," Megan said, determined to keep her voice casual and her face composed. "He seemed to be headed away from the stream. I must say, he's not a very friendly man.''

Carolyn looked at her oddly. "He acted like he had something in his craw yesterday when you and he were talking. What did he say to you just now?''

"As little as possible,'' Megan said. "That's my point. I actually think he hates Abner and me, though I can't fathom why.''

"Oh, I don't think that's true,'' Rose said calmly. "I saw him talking to Abner several times yesterday.''

"Then I guess it's only me he hates.''

"Really?'' asked Rose. "That doesn't sound like Jedediah. Why should he dislike you?''

Megan threw up her hands. "I don't know.''

Rose tied a bedroll with a long piece of twine. "I expect he's just feeling a little blue. Lord knows, he's got enough reason to be out of sorts now and then. He lost his wife a couple of years back.''

"Oh." Thinking of Jed as somebody's husband was strangely disconcerting to Megan. "I remember now. The owner of the general store in Independence mentioned it. How did she die?''

Rose shook her head. "Jedediah never talks about her, not to me, anyway, and I haven't asked any questions.''

Carolyn glanced over her shoulder to make sure the children were out of earshot before she confided, "I heard he killed a man in Oregon.'' Megan and Rose stared at Carolyn, wondering if they had heard her correctly. "But I don't really think it could be true, do you?'' Carolyn went on. "I mean, if he killed a man, he surely wouldn't be going back, would he?''

"I've grown real fond of Jedediah, and I don't like gossiping about him,'' Rose said reprovingly.

"On the other hand,'' Carolyn mused, still following her own line of thought, "they say there's not much law in the western territories. I imagine there's more than one murderer walking around out there without fear of being arrested.''

Rose gave Carolyn an impatient look. "You can be sure that if Jedediah killed somebody, he had a good reason."

Megan was about to say there weren't many good reasons for murder, but before she could, an adamant male voice boomed from just behind her, "Carolyn! Bring Johnny and come to the wagon. We're going to have a Bible reading and prayer before we leave."

Carolyn whirled around. "Oh, Thayer—you scared the wits out of me." She turned back to the other two women, "Rose, Megan, I'll talk to you later." Then, under her husband's black and watchful scowl, she hurried to her son. "Come along, Johnny. We're going back to the wagon with Papa."

Assured that Carolyn and Johnny were coming, Thayer turned his stern gaze on Megan. The previous day she had caught Thayer Goddard staring at her twice in the same way as he was now. It made her want to rub her nose in case there was dirt on it. She shifted uncomfortably. "How are you this morning, Thayer?" she ventured.

"I'll be better when my wife and son are back at our wagon where they belong," Thayer answered curtly.

Megan wondered if he'd berate Carolyn when they were alone. What had Carolyn done that he could possibly disapprove of? Didn't he want her chatting with the other women in the train, or was it she in particular that he resented? Megan knew only that she didn't trust Thayer Goddard, and had an impulse to defend her new friend Carolyn.

"We were only chatting for a few minutes, until we start moving again," she said.

Thayer gazed at her broodingly, as if she'd spoken in a foreign language, and walked off. Megan and Rose remained silent until the Goddards were out of earshot.

"That man gives me goose bumps," Megan said, absently rubbing her forearms.

"Thayer has no sense of humor and that's a fact," Rose agreed. "He's awfully stern with Carolyn and Johnny sometimes, yet he seems to be a religious man."

"Religious fanatics can be dangerous," Megan said. "They want to remake the world and everybody in it to suit themselves."

"Mmm," Rose murmured. "Thayer does get a strange gleam in his eye at times." She sighed. "Poor Carolyn, but then she did choose to marry him."

"Maybe he's changed since then," Megan suggested.

Rose pushed the last bedroll into place at the side of the wagon. "Well, we'll be her friends. There's really nothing else we can do for her." She grabbed a damp cloth, climbed out of the wagon and began scrubbing jelly and milk off Ben's and Jude's faces. "You scallywags ate enough for four."

Mary and Laura returned from the river with clean dishes. "We're leaving!" Laura cried. "Papa said I could ride his horse this morning."

"After your lessons," Rose said firmly, "and if I catch you tearing around with your dress tail up to your ears, young lady, I'll swat your behind."

"Hello, Megan," Laura said cheerfully, as though her mother hadn't spoken.

Megan grinned. "Good morning, Laura. Mary, while she's riding—and as soon as you finish your lessons—will you walk with me? We'll take Ben and Jude and give your mother a rest."

Mary agreed, with Rose's enthusiastic blessing. Megan walked back to her wagon as Abner climbed up on the wagon seat to urge the oxen forward to their place in line.

She saw Jed on his stallion, galloping down the forming line of wagons toward her, and her pulse fluttered at the base of her throat. He looked so strong and confident, leaning forward in the saddle.

Why did she feel such a compulsion to stare at him, at his strong legs and the way the muscles of his arms moved against his shirt sleeves? An inexplicable warmth suffused her cheeks and she quickly turned her head, averting her gaze as the already familiar sounds of a wagon train on the move rose around her.

Chapter Six

Megan noticed the first grave alongside the trail five days after they left Independence. The mound of dirt was freshly dug. It couldn't have been more than a few hours old. Carved on the crude, tilting cross atop the grave was the inscription Nathan Brophy, b. 1821 Indiana, d. 1850 of cholera.

Megan was walking beside her wagon, carrying the whip. Abner had gone ahead of the train with Reuben Schiller to choose a campsite for the night. She hurried past, wondering if Nathan Brophy had left a wife and children who were now traveling to Oregon or California without him. It made her sad to think of him, setting out on the trail full of plans for the future, as he must have been, then falling sick and dying only a few days out. He would never see the land he'd meant to make his home, or his children grow up. Would never realize his dreams.

She pushed the thoughts of Nathan Brophy out of her mind and replaced them with the more pleasant ones of the friendly traveler they'd passed that morning, a Dutchman named Vermeer, with a wheelbarrow full with provisions. He had walked with their train for a while, talking to several people. He was going to California, he said. They had left him behind when he stopped to mend his wheel. Megan smiled at the memory of the stout Dutchman and his wheelbarrow. She didn't see how he would ever make it as far as California, but she admired his pluck.

Already they had met a few wagons going in the opposite direction, carrying the disillusioned who had grown fearful or homesick and turned back. No matter what lay ahead, Megan couldn't imagine wanting to turn back. There was nothing behind for her; her future lay ahead.

She came out of her reverie to see that the oxen had slowed to munch on the tempting grass. She had to flick the animals with the whip to get them going again. Rose Schiller, who was walking several wagons ahead, dropped back to talk to Megan.

"I think we should have a party Sunday to celebrate the end of our first week on the trail," Rose said.

"That's a wonderful idea," Megan agreed, pushing her thick hair off her damp forehead. "I heard one of the women talking about baking a cake over the campfire. Have you ever tried it?"

"No, but I will tomorrow night. Laura has been badgering me to help her make a chocolate cake for Jedediah. We'll serve it at the party—if it's fit to eat."

Whenever Jed's name was mentioned, Megan remembered how he'd caught her in his arms and she felt an odd queasiness in her stomach. The past three nights she'd gone to sleep thinking about him, while Abner continued to make his bed under the wagon. Their tent remained unused, rolled up in a tight cylinder.

Megan felt guilty about Abner, and promised herself at least five times a day that she would talk to him very soon about consummating their marriage. She knew that she owed it to him. The problem was, it wasn't Abner who filled her thoughts. It was Jed. She was ashamed of herself for that, and had prayed for God to rid her of her obsession with a man who was not her husband. Sometimes she thought that Jed must have cast a spell on her.

"I have a few jars of applesauce," Megan said. "I'll make an applesauce cake for the celebration." She was determined to see to it that Abner enjoyed the party. Perhaps by then she would have found the courage to talk to him about their relationship.

"I'll talk to some of the other women," Rose said. "Then all I'll have to do is convince Jedediah to make camp early Sunday so we ladies can pretty ourselves up for the party."

Megan's excitement faltered. "I don't have a dress fit to wear to a party."

"Make one," Rose said.

"Out of what?"

Rose pondered the question. "That blue dress of yours . . . all it needs is a lower neckline and a little lace to fancy it up a bit."

"What a good idea!" Megan's anticipation of the party had returned. She had several lengths of lace in her sewing basket and it would be the first real party she'd ever attended. She could already picture her blue dress as it would look after she'd remade it. "I'm so glad you thought of it, Rose."

"Honey, with two growing girls, I'm constantly making dresses over. I think I'll drop back and talk to Carolyn about the party." She turned around. "Oh-oh, the preacher's headed this way. Coming to see you, I'll bet."

Megan chuckled. "What makes you think so?"

"He's sweet on you, Megan. Don't pretend you don't know it."

Rose left her without waiting for a reply, but no reply was needed. The young preacher, David Glenhill, was making a habit of seeking Megan out to talk with her or lend her a book. Twice he'd ridden his horse alongside the wagon when she was sitting in the seat. He'd told her about his father, who was a minister in Ohio, and of his conviction that God had called him to carry the Gospel to the western territories.

Megan rather enjoyed David's company, and by now she knew he was a true romantic. He had idealistic notions about carrying God's word to the heathen Indians who, David said, were God's ignorant children and descendants of a lost tribe of Israel. David Glenhill wanted to introduce the Indians to their true heritage. He naively believed they would eagerly embrace it. Megan had seen drunken Osage

Indians on the streets of Independence. Contact with the white man had harmed rather than helped them. She doubted that the "heathen" David Glenhill planned to convert would fare much better.

"Good afternoon, Megan," David called as he ran to catch up with her. She had asked him to call her by her Christian name the first time he had sought her out, before she had realized his infatuation.

"Hello, David. What do you have there?"

He offered her a slim, much thumbed book. "It's my favorite volume of poetry. I thought you'd enjoy reading it."

Megan took the book. "I'm sure I will, David. Thank you."

He looked at her with adoration. The preacher's crush on her was harmless, of course, but Megan wished he would choose another object for his devotion. Perhaps she could find someone, play matchmaker. She would have to think about it.

She told him of Rose's plans for a party Sunday evening, and he immediately asked her to save a dance for him. Several of the men in the train had fiddles, which they brought out almost every evening. No one had as yet danced to the lively tunes, but a party would probably include dancing.

Megan and Vinnie Foster had surreptitiously practiced steps when they'd lived with the Valentines, who'd disapproved of dancing. Sunday evening would be her first chance to dance with a male partner. Unbidden came an image of herself and Jed, swaying and whirling over the grass in time to fiddle music. Swiftly she replaced Jed's image with Abner's, and then David Glenhill's.

"Of course I'll save a dance for you, David," she promised.

That evening, Megan and Abner shared their supper with the Schillers. To Megan's surprise, Jed joined them. The past few days he'd seemed to be avoiding her, though perhaps he'd only been busy.

After the meal the adults lingered over the last of Rose's coffee. Rose caught Megan's eye as she said, "Jedediah, I propose that we have a party Sunday night to celebrate the end of our first week on the trail."

Jed cast a questioning glance from Rose to Megan. "So that's what you women have been planning all afternoon. I knew something was up."

"My wife loves a party," Reuben commented. "She was the unofficial organizer of all the socials back home."

"Never went to many parties myself," Abner said.

"Nor did I," said Megan, and wondered at the odd look Jed sent her.

"So, Jedediah," Rose said, "you don't object?"

Jed shrugged. "Why should I?"

"Well..." Rose said carefully, "the women would like to make camp early Sunday so we can get ready." Seeing what looked like a refusal in Jed's expression, she added hastily. "We're going to take a stab at baking cakes over the camp-fire tomorrow night. I told Laura we'd make that chocolate cake she's been promising you."

Jed laughed. "Rosie, that sounds like a bribe to me."

With Jed's attention on other things, Megan felt her tenseness ease, and she joined the others in laughter as Rose poured Jed another cup of coffee. "We can't have a party without refreshments, can we? Will you give the order to make camp early?"

Jed threw up his hands. "Yes, I'll give you an hour, but that's it."

"Thank you, Jedediah," Rose said sweetly. "An hour is all we need, isn't that right, Megan?"

"An hour will be quite sufficient," Megan said, lowering her eyes. Jed was leaning lazily against a tree trunk, his long fingers curled around his cup as he watched her musingly. Seized by a restless need to move, Megan rose, picking up her and Abner's tin plates for washing. Still feeling Jed's gaze on her, she said guiltily, "You finish your coffee, Abner. I'll put our things in the wagon."

Later, lying alone in her bedroll beneath the canvas, Megan wondered if Jed would ask her to dance, and what she would say if he did. She fell asleep without coming to a decision.

She awoke early the next morning to the sound of Abner leaving his bed beneath the wagon. He was going to take care of the livestock. A few moments later she heard a male voice nearby.

"I want to talk to you, Dossman." It sounded like Thayer Goddard's voice, and the tone was aggressive.

"I'm on the way to water my horse," Jed said with a touch of impatience. "Make it snappy, Goddard."

"My wife says a party's being planned for tomorrow night."

"That's right."

"I disapprove of revelry on the Sabbath. I know it's hard to keep our standards up in our situation, but we have to try. Otherwise we're no better than savages."

Jed uttered a low oath. "You can disapprove all you want, but I don't expect you'll find much support for your position. Don't raise a stink over this, Goddard. Let these people enjoy themselves while they can."

"I don't care if everybody on this train chooses to defile the Sabbath," Thayer said furiously. "My family will not take part."

"That's up to you," Jed responded shortly. "If you'll excuse me now, I'll take care of my horse."

The men moved away and Megan lay staring at the pearly patch of early dawn sky visible in the canvas opening. Poor Carolyn wouldn't be allowed to join the party. How on earth did she bear being married to that man?

"Let these people enjoy themselves while they can."

Jed had sounded as though trouble were inevitable.

Megan remembered the grave of the cholera victim and shivered as she dressed for the day. They had been fortunate so far, with only a few head colds and stomach complaints among the members of the party. And they had lost only one animal. A cow had panicked and drowned when they'd crossed a broad branch of the Platte River that Abner said was called the "Big Blue." She wouldn't court disaster by thinking of the terrible things that might happen.

Abner was waiting for Megan at the foot of the wagon as she handed him their tin plates and cups and stepped down into the twilight. He wore the better of his two homespun shirts and his extra pair of britches and he'd slicked his hair back neatly with a wet comb.

"My, don't you look handsome," Megan said, taking his arm.

"You look mighty pretty yourself, Meggie."

Nervously she smoothed the skirt of her made-over blue dress. She had spent two hours that afternoon, working on it in the jolting, airless wagon, perspiration dripping off her nose. Having glimpsed a dim image of herself in her small, cracked mirror, she was satisfied with the results. The dress's neckline was now scooped low in front and trimmed with a row of white lace. More lace edged the three-quarter-length sleeves.

Then she had managed to wash her hair, using a pan of water in the wagon, and sit in a pool of sunlight behind the wagon seat, brushing it, until it dried. Now it was pulled back from her face with combs, the ends falling loose down her back, for she knew it wouldn't stay up when she danced. "Do you really think I look all right," she asked anxiously.

"Sugar, you look like the first flower of spring." From the level patch of grassland where the women had spread the refreshments on planks supported by barrels, they heard fiddles being tuned up. "I have to warn you, Meggie, I ain't much of a hand at dancing."

"Neither am I," she confessed as they approached the refreshment tables, "but we'll get the hang of it. Doesn't that music make your feet itch?"

"Nope, but the smell of them cakes makes my mouth water."

"Half of them fell," Megan informed him, "mine included. They're gooey in the middle."

"Just the way I like 'em," Abner said. Two campfires provided flickering light and Abner surveyed the cakes hungrily. Rose and Lacey Glenhill, the preacher's sister-in-law, were serving pieces of cake and pouring coffee.

"How many pieces can I have?" Abner asked, rubbing his palms together.

"One at a time," Lacey told him with a laugh. "What are you having first?"

Abner debated between chocolate and spice as Megan turned to watch three couples who were the first to start dancing. Without thinking, she searched for Jed, but she didn't see him.

"That dress turned out fine, Megan," Rose said, ladling a big slab of chocolate cake on Abner's plate. "You want a piece?"

"Not now," Megan said as she continued to watch the dancers. "I don't suppose Thayer will relent and allow Carolyn to join us."

"I doubt it," Rose said. "She told me she would try to get to sleep early. So she can't hear the music, I reckon."

"Thayer Goddard has a mean streak," Megan reflected.

"He'd call it being righteous," Lacey snorted.

David Glenhill appeared at Megan's elbow. "Abner, may I claim your wife for a dance?"

"You sure can," Abner said around a mouthful of chocolate cake. "I been telling her she'll end up with sore toes if she dances with me."

"I'll chance it," Megan teased. "You finish that cake, Abner. I mean to have the second dance with you."

She allowed David Glenhill to lead her to the flat area where several couples were now two-stepping to a fast, lively tune. Remembering Thayer Goddard, she asked, "Have you no reservations about dancing on the Sabbath?"

"No," David said without hesitation. "In the first place, this isn't the biblical Sabbath. The Sabbath was given to the Hebrews as a day of rest after six days of labor. The seventh day is Saturday. Not that I have any quarrel with those who call Sunday the Christian Sabbath. But the Sabbath was made for man, not man for the Sabbath. I interpret that to mean we should enjoy whatever day we choose to call the Sabbath above all others.''

''Thayer Goddard doesn't agree with you.''

''Thayer is guilt ridden.''

Surprised by his assessment, Megan asked, ''How do you know? Has he talked to you?''

''No, but I've noticed that when a man won't allow himself any fun, it's because he doesn't think he deserves it. He's punishing himself, you might say.''

''Sometimes, David, you surprise me with the things you say. You're an unusual minister of the Gospel. You know, you've never told me what denomination you're a member of.''

''I was raised a Methodist and schooled by the Presbyterians. But I've yet to find a denomination whose doctrine I agree with on all points. I just want to serve God in my own way.'' He bowed before her comically. ''Right now, God surely must want us to join in the fun, and this preacher wants to dance with the prettiest lady at the party.'' He took her gingerly in his arms.

''I haven't had much practice,'' she warned him.

''Nothing to it. Merely relax and follow me.''

It was easy, Megan discovered. Soon she was following David's lead with confidence, laughing, her black hair bouncing and flying out behind her. She noticed Abner watching them, and as soon as the music stopped she excused herself and dragged him into the midst of the dancers.

''Aw, Meggie,'' he protested, ''I got two left feet.''

Laughing, Megan planted his hand at her waist and rested her hand on his shoulder. ''So does Reuben Schiller, but he doesn't let it stop him.'' She had noticed Reuben and Rose dancing a jig together only moments before.

The music started and Abner began a hesitant shuffle. ''Like this,'' Megan said, taking the lead. He was good-natured about it and allowed her to keep him dancing through three tunes. Then David Glenhill cut in on them.

Megan couldn't help noticing that Abner seemed happy to return to the refreshment table.

Curling black tendrils framed Megan's glowing face; her long hair tumbled down her back in an ebony cloud as she lifted her face to smile at David and he swung her in a wide circle in time with the music. In the shifting, flickering firelight Megan's cheeks were rosy with exertion, and her blue eyes danced with pleasure. Her breasts strained against the cotton fabric of her dress and the airy white lace nestled against her darkly shadowed cleavage. She looked more desirable than she had ever looked in her life, and she was totally unaware of it.

Jed was dancing with Rose Schiller. Until a few moments ago, he had been lounging against the tail of a wagon out of reach of the firelight, cloaked in darkness. He had watched Megan dance with the preacher and then with her gangly, awkward husband.

She was the most beautiful thing he had ever seen, and he would have been less than human not to experience some reaction. Several reactions, in fact, a few of which he couldn't name. However, the stirring of sexual arousal was easily identified, and he thanked fate that his discomfort was hidden by the night. He had averted his gaze from Megan, but again and again it was drawn back to her, the way metal filings fly to a magnet.

She looked for all the world like an innocent girl on the threshold of womanhood, ripe for the plucking. Unbidden, the thought slipped into his mind that what he wanted was to get her alone, lead her into the darkness, cover her parted lips with his, feel her arms encircle his neck. He actually calculated how he might bring the fantasy to pass. Jed swore as he realized he was seriously considering a plan for seduction. He remembered that she had lain with more partners than he, and that she was now a married woman.

It was at that moment that Rose found him and coaxed him to dance, saying he was the only man present taller than she. He was having trouble concentrating on Rose's conversation, because he was watching Megan. She was laughing at something David Glenhill had said. She tilted her head coquettishly and lowered her lashes, and Jed felt a sharp stab of jealousy. Damn, he was acting like an idiot tonight. Megan Claunch was a practiced flirt who obviously didn't hesitate to use her guiles on preachers, the same as other men.

My God, being married to Megan must be hell for Abner Claunch. The previous night, Jed, patrolling the camp on guard duty, had realized that Abner was sleeping under his wagon. Had Megan kicked him out of her bed? Was that marriage in trouble already?

He saw Abner Claunch now, leaving the refreshment table, headed toward his wagon. Maybe Claunch couldn't stand watching his wife have so much fun with David Glenhill. Abner Claunch was an old fool for falling under Megan's spell, but Jed felt sorry for him nevertheless.

"Jedediah, you haven't heard a word I've said," Rose complained.

"What? Oh, I'm sorry, Rosie. What was it?"

"I said, I thought dancing would cheer you up. But you're still scowling like a bad-tempered brat."

Jed forced a smile. "Sorry, Rosie. I was lost in my thoughts."

"Uh-huh. I'd give a pretty penny to know what those thoughts are, but I know you aren't about to tell me. Oops..." Rose bumped into somebody and turned to apologize. "Excuse my clumsiness. Oh, its you, Preacher." David and Megan had stopped dancing. "Here, Reverend, let's change partners. Maybe Megan can cheer Jedediah up. I'm certainly not having any luck at it."

Before Jed could protest, Rose was swinging away with David Glenhill, leaving him facing Megan. The two stood there, surrounded by laughing, dancing couples.

Megan saw his jaw clench. "You don't have to dance with me," she said softly.

Jed found that her lowered gaze and suddenly demure manner angered him. "If you don't want to dance just say so," he snapped.

Startled, she looked up at him. "I didn't say I don't want to dance. I thought you—"

He cut her off, "Oh, hell, we'll be trampled if we don't move." His arm went around her waist, his big hand fitting itself to the small of her back as though it had been made for the purpose.

He moved with ease and confidence, Megan mused as they danced. Like some wild but naturally graceful beast. Her heart was beating rapidly, and she didn't know if it was from the intensity of his gaze or the way his body was touching hers at so many points. His hand at her waist was warm and oddly familiar. His other hand clasped hers, his fingers wrapped around hers. His chest brushed lightly against her breasts. She tried to hold herself away from him, hardly daring to breathe. His shirt was open at the throat, and she could see curling dark hairs on his exposed chest. She felt mesmerized as she stared at his throat. Her mouth had gone dry.

She was amazed at the steadiness of her own voice as she said, "I'm glad Rose thought of having a party. Everyone seems to be having a good time."

He bent his head to hear what she was saying. "Almost everyone," he said gruffly.

Megan knew he was referring to himself and wondered if he was trying to rile her. If so, she couldn't understand why. But, then, Jed was a mystery to her. She was determined to hold her temper. "Oh, well...of course, there are the Goddards...."

He made a little sound in his throat that could have meant anything.

When he said nothing more, she observed, "Thayer is an odd sort of man, don't you think?"

"He's a bully," Jed muttered. "I don't know why Carolyn married him."

Silently Megan agreed with him. She wished she'd thought of a more pleasant topic of conversation, but her store of topics seemed to be exhausted. She tried to relax, without much success. Nor was she any more successful in holding herself away from him. Had David held her this close? If he had, she hadn't been aware of every faint touch, every breath, every heartbeat. Jed's touch seared the small of her back, her hands, her thighs, her breasts, everywhere her body made contact with his.

Except for the morning Jed had caught her in his arms, she had never been this close to a man before. Somehow she had not been affected by dancing with David and Abner as she was with Jed. The strangeness of her bodily sensations was both frightening and tantalizing.

Nervously she cleared her throat. "You dance very well for a-a—"

He gazed down at her. "A what?"

She did seem to be stammering like a schoolgirl. "I only meant you don't seem the kind of man who spends much time in dance halls." She felt flustered and too warm. When he bent his head down to speak to her, his face was very close, so close that his lashes could almost brush her forehead. She lowered her eyes, breaking the hot intensity of his gaze.

"What kind of man do I seem to you?"

Like no one she'd ever known. "Oh...an outdoors man, I suppose. Are you a rancher—when you aren't leading wagon trains to Oregon?"

"Once I thought I wanted to be." He shrugged. "Now I don't know what I am."

She sensed that he was thinking of his wife, who had died. Perhaps his wife's death had ruined ranching for him.

"Is that what your father was—a farmer?"

Jed laughed. "Thunderation, no. He was a gambler who always lost, and a drunkard to boot. He died when I was twelve. I can't remember missing him at all."

"Oh," Megan said softly. "I think I understand. You must have wanted to be entirely different from your father, a man who does good, honest work, like ranching. It must be wonderful to work the land, away from towns and people, with no one to judge you harshly because of who your family was. You can be what you are—in your heart, I mean—and do what you want.''

Jed gazed at her curiously, moved by the wistful longing in her voice. ''Sometimes what you are isn't enough,'' he replied.

She couldn't guess what he was thinking, but she sighed, a soft, gentle expulsion of breath. The sound made Jed tip his head back to see her better. She looked up at him and smiled. ''If you can't be what you want to be where you are, then you have to go somewhere else and start fresh.''

''Somewhere like Oregon?'' he asked wryly.

She laughed, and her eyes danced. ''I would think a person can become anything he wants to in Oregon.''

He wondered what she wanted to be, if not a whore. Perhaps she really meant to become a respectable housewife now, cooking and cleaning and raising children.

As he looked at her, her laughter faded and her dark lashes lowered, shielding her expressive eyes. He might have told her she was going to a savage, if beautiful, wilderness, not a garden party. He might have said there would be no other woman there as lovely as she, and that if she had waited, she could have done far better for herself than Abner Claunch. He might have said he felt sick with denying himself the taste of her mouth. But he said nothing.

After a moment, he fixed his gaze on the darkness beyond the reach of the fires. He made a valiant effort not to be so exquisitely aware of how small and fragile her waist felt to his big hand, how close to his fingers was the softness of her hip, or how tantalizing was the light brush of her breasts against his chest. Wisps of her hair tickled his jaw like silk threads, and the scent of her invaded his nostrils. It would be so easy to let his hand flow downward until it cupped her hip, so easy to pull her closer until his hardness pressed into her belly.... He felt a reckless tingling in his loins, and a seductive heaviness that was very nearly impossible to fight.

Jed was beginning to sweat inside his clothes. She was another man's wife. He made a gruff sound low in his throat.

Megan peered up at him, frowning. "Did you say something."

"No, I think the fiddlers are taking a break."

As the dancers began to disperse, she took a quick step back, out of his arms, confused by her own reluctance to do so. She was surprised by the touch of sadness she saw in his eyes the moment before he banished it. He was a complicated man. And yet she had begun to feel almost comfortable with him before the music had ended. Perhaps she had mistaken him before; perhaps he didn't dislike her. Why should he? Perhaps they might even become friends.

"I know Rose thrust me on you, but I've enjoyed dancing with you," she said.

He looked at her thoughtfully, her fresh beauty overwhelming him once more. They now stood alone near the campfires. Everyone else had gathered around the refreshment tables, leaving them to look at one another, without speaking.

Laura Schiller broke the spell as she ran up to them, grabbing Jed's hand excitedly. "Hi, Megan. Jed, come and taste the cake I made for you before it's all gone. And later will you dance with me?"

Jed shook off his lassitude to grin at Laura and laid a hand lightly on her auburn hair. "Where are your social graces, Mistress Schiller? Don't you know it's the gentleman who is supposed to ask the lady to dance, not the other way around?"

Laura tossed her head. "If I waited, like Mama says I should, you might never ask me. I'd be stuck with fat Tucker Olmstead all evening. His hands are sweaty. Ugh!"

Jed threw back his head and laughed. After a moment he looked at Megan again. "Thank you for the dance, Megan."

"You're welcome."

He seemed reluctant to go, or perhaps she imagined that because it was how she felt. "Don't stay up too late," he said finally. "We leave at dawn."

"I'll be ready," she said with a sad little smile, and walked away from them.

Chapter Seven

Jed knew the moment Megan left the party, though he couldn't have said how. He simply felt that she was gone. After that, he disentangled himself from good-hearted Rose Schiller, who was urging more cake on him, and Laura, who wanted him to dance with her again, and walked into the darkness toward his wagon. He passed the Claunch wagon en route and heard Megan stirring inside, preparing for bed. He quickened his step, his errant imagination filling his mind with pictures of Megan in a state of undress, despite his best efforts to suppress them.

The snores he heard came from beneath the wagon. Abner Claunch was still sleeping on the ground alone, poor sod. Jed undressed in the dark and crawled into his bedroll, but he couldn't get to sleep. His mind remained busy with thoughts that should not have been in his head. Why was Claunch still sleeping under the wagon? Evidently Megan was still punishing her husband for whatever he'd done to anger her. Yet Jed had watched Abner and Megan together tonight, and they had seemed on good terms. A man would have to be crazy to be married to a woman like that and sleep alone. Jed remained certain the Claunches' present sleeping arrangement was Megan's idea.

He wondered how Claunch could live with the knowledge that his wife had lain with so many other men before him. Jed would want to kill every one of them if Megan were his wife.

Appalled at the direction his thoughts were taking, Jed rolled out of bed, dressed again and walked through the camp, satisfying himself that the men assigned to sentry duty were awake and at their posts. He was even more restless than usual tonight, and uncommonly alert. And he didn't think it was all due to his disturbing thoughts about Megan.

He felt a vague uneasiness that had nothing to do with Megan or the party. Perhaps it was because they hadn't seen an Indian yet. The plains appeared to harbor nothing but wild animals, but that was an illusion. Jed knew that Indians inhabited the country through which they passed, and he kept expecting them to make their presence known.

Once he'd assured himself that the sentries were at their posts, there was no good reason to continue wandering about the camp. He returned to his wagon and undressed for the second time. It was a long while before he fell asleep.

Megan awoke the next morning, shivering in her bedroll and coiled as tightly as a spring. Her skin felt clammy. She realized with distaste that her bedding was damp. Rain drummed on the canvas wagon cover and she could hear it dripping on her metal trunk. The cattle were bawling, and she heard the shouts of the men as they tried to get the train moving.

Groggily she sat up and reached for her heavy gray dress. She must have overslept. Fortunately she kept her and Abner's clothes in the metal trunk and they were dry. She dressed as quickly as she could, her movements hampered by her shaking.

Abner's bedroll had been flung into a corner of the wagon bed, and she wondered how long he'd been up. The bedding was wet, so she spread it and her own over their goods.

A few minutes later Abner came to the end of the wagon and thrust his head inside. "Meggie, Jed's gonna try to get a few miles down the road."

"In this?" Megan grumbled.

"We gotta keep going as long as we can. I'm in charge of the teamsters, and it'll be a chore to keep the livestock together and going in the right direction. I already hitched our team. I hate to ask you to get soaked, but somebody has to drive the oxen."

"I can do it," she said. "Here." She handed him a cold biscuit and some dried peaches. "I guess that's breakfast." She would have given anything for a cup of hot coffee, but there was no dry fuel for a fire, even if Jed would give them time to build one.

Abner stuffed the biscuit and fruit into a pocket of his wool poncho. "I've had worse breakfasts, Meggie girl. I have to get back to the livestock. You gonna be okay?"

"Don't worry about me."

He ducked out of sight and Megan found their shabbiest blanket, which felt damp like everything else. She draped it over her head and wound it around herself. Clutching it together in front, she stepped from beneath the dripping canvas and the rain poured down on her head in a torrent. She climbed into the wet wagon seat and reached for the reins and the whip.

Through the cold, slanting rain, she saw men and women struggling to bring their wagons into some semblance of a line. Most of the mule and ox teams were balking as the soggy prairie sucked at their hooves with every step. Megan huddled in her blanket, which was soon wet through, and whipped the oxen forward through the quagmire of mud.

They traveled about four miles and camped near a swollen stream, which they would have to cross as soon as the water was calm enough. Following Rose Schiller's example, Megan had cooked extra food each night for the next day's noon meal. She and Abner ate cold beans and cornbread in midafternoon, after the wagons were corralled and the livestock safely penned.

Although Megan had tried to protect their bedding, it continued to feel damp to the touch. Megan had changed from her wet dress into another from the trunk, but it, too, already clung to her skin. She wondered if she would ever be warm and dry again.

After they had eaten, Abner went to help feed and water the penned livestock. It was still raining. Megan tugged on her oldest pair of boots, draped her coat over her head and ran to the Schiller wagon. Rose and the five younger children were inside, eating a cold meal.

"Come in, Megan," Rose called when Megan stuck her head through the opening in the canvas, "if you can squeeze in."

Megan climbed over the end of the wagon and perched on an empty carton. Mary and Laura were huddled together with the two youngest boys beneath a quilt.

"What a dreadful day," Megan said.

"I hate it!" Laura exclaimed. "If only the weather could always be as nice as it was last week."

"It could be worse," said Aaron, a towheaded ten-year-old. "Jed said we'll probably run into snow before we get there."

Mary shivered. "Brrr. Don't even mention it."

"How are we going to sleep tonight, when everything we own is damp?" Megan asked.

"I just hope the rain stops before bedtime," Rose said, "but if not, the tents should turn most of the water. Did you manage to keep some of your clothes dry?"

"Yes," Megan said, "but they feel damp as soon as you put them on."

"My family's going to put on every piece of dry clothing we own tonight," Rose said. "That'll help some."

"Mama," said Mary, "I think Ben's got a fever."

"Oh, Lord," Rose said, getting up to feel the little boy's forehead. Ben, who had been about to fall asleep against Mary's shoulder, grumbled drowsily. "Ben and Jude have had the sniffles all day," Rose said to Megan over her shoulder. She brushed Ben's red hair away from his face with the back of her hand. "You feel bad, Benny?"

Ben nodded miserably, and Rose murmured in sympathy. "It's a mustard plaster for you, my boy."

"I learned something about nursing from Mrs. Valentine, the minister's wife in Independence," Megan said. "She swore by weak green tea with lemon juice for children's fever."

"There's not a lemon within miles," Rose said, "and we've no dry wood to heat the tea."

"I've seen Mrs. Valentine give it cold," Megan said. "Perhaps the tea without lemon juice would be beneficial." She rose and pulled her coat over her head again. "I'll soak tea leaves in cold water and add some dried lemon peel. Maybe I can make something resembling tea without hot water."

"Sure couldn't hurt to try it," Rose said. "Thanks, Megan."

"I think the rain's letting up," Megan said hopefully as she left the wagon.

As she skirted the end of the Schiller's wagon, Megan almost ran into Jed. She barely caught herself before she bumped against him. "I'm sorry, Jed," she said breathlessly. "I seem to be making a habit of falling over you."

His clothes were mud splattered, and rain dripped off the brim of his hat. He looked worn out. Megan had an impulse to smooth the tired lines on either side of his mouth with her fingertips, and she closed her hands into fists to prevent giving in to such madness.

Jed had seen her coming. He would have stepped aside if she hadn't spotted him. He had spent a hellish night, his head full of forbidden thoughts. All he could think about was her softness, the feel of her in his arms. All he could see was her eyes, dancing with merriment or filled with wistfulness. His memories, his need of her, invaded his blood. Even his flesh ached for her.

He knew that touching her was dangerous for him, and he had promised himself it would not happen again. He could not let himself get that close, and somehow he had to put last night out of his mind.

Gazing at her now, her slender, feminine body swaddled in a black coat, her wet but smiling face framed by the coat lapels, he thought she looked very small and fragile. He also thought her eyes had kindled briefly at the sight of him, but he could no longer trust his instincts. He was having trouble distinguishing between what was and what he wished could be.

"No harm done," he said, and before he knew what he was doing he had reached out and tucked the coat tighter beneath her chin. Disconcerted, he jerked his hand away and stuffed it in his coat pocket. "You shouldn't be out in this."

"It's not much wetter than in the wagon," Megan said. "Ben Schiller has a fever. I'm going to make cold green tea for him. Hot tea would be better, of course, but not possible."

"We've been lucky to have no fatal sickness in the train yet. Do you think Ben's illness is serious?"

"He and Jude have the sniffles. I think it's just a cold. Children can run a fever much more readily than adults."

His mouth quirked in an expression of irony. "How would you know about that?"

"I used to help the Baptist preacher's wife nurse the sick members of the congregation."

Jed's eyes widened. "A *preacher's* wife?"

"Yes. Why do you sound so surprised?"

Jed felt confused. No preacher's wife would make a companion of a whore. It must have happened before Megan went into her mother's profession. "I can't imagine you in the role," he said finally.

Frowning, she tugged the coat closer. "Why not?"

She was cold, and he wanted to open his coat and hug her to him and warm her with his body. There's more than one person in this train suffering from a fever, Dossman, he told himself. What he felt was the obsession of a crazy man. He could not have this woman; he was mad even to want her. He had to leave her alone.

He set his jaw; his hands clenched so tightly they hurt. He looked away from her. "You'd better get in out of the rain, and I have work to do." He strode away without another word.

Megan stared after him with a tight feeling in the area of her heart. Why was he always so prickly with her? He could laugh and tease with Rose or Laura, but with her he always seemed to be on his guard. He could not relax with her, and that made her sad.

Last night she had almost convinced herself they could become friends. But just now Jed had acted as though he had never danced with her or stood on the grassy prairie and gazed at her with gentleness and a strange yearning in his eyes. Disheartened, she walked on through the mud to her wagon.

The rain stopped about an hour later. Later still, Abner pitched the tent and he and Megan ate what was left of the cornbread, dipped in molasses. Then they rolled into their damp bedding to sleep without ever touching. Abner was so exhausted from handling the livestock all day that he was soon snoring loudly. Megan slept in fits and starts, waking frequently to the uncomfortable awareness of the damp and cold.

The next morning Megan left the tent feeling bone tired and achingly sore in every joint, but her heart lifted to see the sun peeping over the horizon. Already, wet clothes and bedding were spread over rocks and wagons for drying. Megan and Abner breakfasted on dried fruit and jerked beef, then went their separate ways, Abner to take care of their livestock, Megan to spread their wet belongings in the sunlight.

After she was done Megan checked on Ben Schiller. The little boy was still feverish and fretful, but he seemed to feel better than he had the day before.

"I got your tea down him," Rose confided. "Maybe it helped. Benny has always been our puny one. Whatever sickness is going around, it takes him faster and harder than the other children."

Ben Schiller was not the only member of the wagon train who was ill that morning. Several children were suffering with head colds. Hollis Glenhill, the bachelor uncle of Mason and David, had suffered all night with an ague, alternating between violent chills and a high fever. Lacey Glenhill came to Megan—Rose had told her of Megan's nursing experience—and asked what could be done for Hollis.

Megan dragged from her trunk the old carpetbag containing packets of dried leaves, bark and herbs, potions, salves and the careful notes she had made. She searched until she found the small packet of dried leaves labeled "boneset," the name Mrs. Valentine had given it. The plant undoubtedly had another, scientific name, but Megan didn't know it. If only she had a few pieces of dry wood for a fire, she could brew the strong tea from the boneset leaves, which she had seen benefit people suffering from high, intermittent fevers.

She rummaged through the goods in the wagon until she spied a crate made of wooden staves. The crate contained bags of flour, sugar and other staples, most of which were now damp. Megan emptied the crate, setting the bags on the wagon seat in the sun to air and dry. Later she would have to salvage what she could from them and distribute them among the other storage containers.

As she had hoped, the bottom of the wood crate was dry. She dragged the crate outside and broke it apart with the hatchet. When Rose saw the feeble fire Megan had managed to kindle, she contributed the bottom from one of her own crates. "If we can get a good blaze going here," Rose said, "we can feed it damp pieces of wood slowly. Maybe we can keep it going long enough to cook a meal."

"I'll help you," Megan promised, "as soon as I brew Hollis Glenhill's tea. Lacey says he's very ill."

"Yes, she told me," Rose said. "The preacher is taking care of Hollis's wagon and livestock for him."

"How's Ben?"

"He's had no fever since early this morning, but he's weak. I left Mary with him."

Megan got a bucket and headed for the swollen stream. The roiling, muddy water rushed past, barely contained within its steep banks. She filled the bucket, and as she started back to her wagon, she saw Jed stride his bay stallion, farther down the bank. He sat motionless, watching her, and she knew instinctively that he had been watching her for some time.

When she lifted her head and acknowledged him with a wave, he touched the brim of his hat abruptly, spurred his horse and rode away. She could have sworn he had been riding toward her before, but now he galloped off in the opposite direction.

When she reached the small fire that Rose was carefully tending, Carolyn Goddard had joined the older woman. Megan shook her thoughts of Jed away. "Good morning, Carolyn," she said warmly. "Haven't seen you in a day or two."

"Johnny's been sickly," Carolyn said, "but he's fit today. Laura's keeping an eye on him for me."

As Megan concentrated on brewing the tea, she noticed Thayer Goddard standing beside his wagon, staring at her. When she glanced up, he turned his head and stalked around behind the wagon, out of sight. What a strange man, she thought as she strained the water through a clean cloth before boiling it. Carolyn seemed tense and nervous lately, and Megan was sure her husband was the cause.

Megan brewed the tea, hoping its strength would mask the muddy taste that remained in the water. A few minutes later, she poured the tea into a clay pot and carried it to Hollis Glenhill's wagon. Lacey was inside, bending over the sick man. When Megan spoke her name, she rose hastily and came to take the pot from her hands.

Hollis thrashed about and muttered incoherently. "He's out of his head," Lacey said worriedly.

"It's the fever," Megan said. Hollis's skin felt hot and dry to the touch. "We have to get this bedding dry somehow."

"As soon as one of our quilts has dried, I'll get him to lie on it while I dry his bed clothes," Lacey said.

"Give him two tablespoons of the tea every half hour until bedtime," Megan told her. "I'll come and sit with him this afternoon to give you a rest."

"Oh, Megan, thank you. Do you think he'll be all right?"

"I don't know. All we can do is give him the tea and pray."

Going back to her wagon, Megan looked around her at the bustling activity in the camp. This prairie land was flat as a floor, and spinning around, Megan realized there wasn't a single tree in sight. There was no firewood, damp or otherwise. Their carefully tended fire seemed doomed to die quickly.

By the time Megan reached the fire, Rose and Carolyn had succeeded in gathering more pieces of crates from other wagons, but there wasn't enough wood to keep the fire going for long. Immediately they gathered as many iron skillets as they could set over the fire and fried griddle cakes and strips of smoked sow belly, using flour and meat from several families' stores. Before the fire died, there was enough food for the entire party's afternoon meal and extra for the next day.

"Next time it rains," Rose said as she flipped a griddle cake, "there'll be no hot supper. We're burning up all the wood crates folks can spare right now."

"How long do you suppose it'll be before we see trees again?" Carolyn asked.

"Could be a spell."

"We might be eating raw grain before we get to Oregon," Megan said, worried.

"We might, but we're getting into buffalo country, where we can gather chips."

"Chips?"

Rose laughed. "Dried buffalo dung, Megan. Makes good fire wood."

Megan stared at Rose, until she realized the woman was serious. "Oh," she said, and wrinkled her nose as Rose laughed again and Carolyn joined her.

That afternoon, after relieving Lacey at Hollis Glenhill's sickbed for a couple of hours, Megan saw that the stream had fallen somewhat, though she heard two of the men saying Jed had decided to wait until morning to cross. Megan's dress clung to her, and she felt sticky and dirty. There was time for a bath before sundown and suppertime, if she could find a secluded place along the bank.

Buoyed by the idea, she ran to her wagon and got a bar of soap, a towel, a clean dress and undergarments. To the west, the water ran in a straight line between bare banks as far as Megan could see. She walked east for some distance, following a bend in the stream.

Ahead she saw a line of scrubby brush on the bank, and when she reached the spot she discovered a rocky outcrop where the bank slanted gently down to the stream. She picked her way carefully to the water's edge where she would be hidden from view.

The current was still too swift to risk going in very far. She undressed hurriedly and waded in until the water reached midcalf. The water was cold, and looked muddy, but as she splashed it over her body with her hands, she felt much cleaner. Though she stood in bright sunlight, goose bumps rose on her flesh. Steeling herself against the chill, she vigorously rubbed the bar of soap over her body everywhere she could reach, working up a lather.

Jed had been following the stream, looking for the best place for a crossing, when he heard sounds of splashing. Instantly he had dropped low enough to be hidden from view. He didn't know who was down there. It could be a wild beast or an unfriendly Indian—he'd noticed a band of Pawnee in the distance that morning. If there appeared to be any danger, he'd go back to his wagon for a gun.

He crept closer to the bush in front of him and parted the prickly branches. He sucked in his breath. Megan stood at the edge of the water, naked as the day she was born. As he watched, she lifted her face to the sun and moved a bar of soap in circles over her breasts and flat stomach. Her black hair hung loose down her back. She circled the soap back over her breasts and lathered her throat.

Entranced, Jed stared at her. The sounds of the camp faded away. He heard nothing but the sound of his own heart beating thunderously in his ears. He thought, what are you doing? How could you crouch in hiding and watch her bathe? What if someone sees you? Dear God, she was beautiful—so beautiful it made his throat ache.

She bent down, throwing her long raven hair forward, and began washing it. The slender lines of her legs and waist, the gentle curve of her hips, the movement of her breasts as she scrubbed her hair, kept Jed there, his mouth dry, his blood heating and his body throbbing with desire.

Somebody might be looking for him right now, but he didn't care. He couldn't have moved if his life had depended on it. All he could do was look at her, knowing he would never get enough, and fight the fiery need to go down there and claim her for his own.

You're not going one step closer. You're not going to do that to Abner or to her or to yourself. She's not yours. She never will be.

He swallowed hard. His throat felt hot and parched and his skin burned. Every bone, muscle and sinew wanted her. Without being conscious of his own actions, he shifted his weight, moving a little closer to her.

Don't be a fool. Get back to camp. Get that bottle of whiskey out of the trunk and have a good, stiff drink. Do anything, but get away from her.

Jed muffled a sound of anguish and tore his eyes from the vision in front of him. He made himself creep away from the bush. Straightening to his full height, he walked back to camp.

As Megan waded out of the water, she heard a rustling sound in the brush alongside the bank. Abruptly alert and feeling exposed, she grabbed the towel to cover herself and peered up at the brush.

"Is someone there?"

There was no answer. Fearfully she scanned the line of bushes, but saw no movement and heard nothing more. It must have been a small animal, she told herself as she dried quickly and threw on her clothes.

When she was dressed, she sat on a rock and dried her hair as best she could with the towel, then brushed it back and tied it with a ribbon at her nape. When she got back to camp, she would sit at the end of the wagon and let the sunlight finish drying it. She still hadn't shaken the vague feeling that someone had been there, watching her. Right now she felt an urgent need to get back to camp, where she would be surrounded by other people.

It was nothing, she assured herself as she hurried back, only some small animal hiding in a bush. Yet her vague uneasiness didn't go away.

Holding a bucket of oats for his horse, Jed watched her return to camp. Before he could look away, she turned her head and met his gaze questioningly. Heat raced over his skin as he averted his eyes.

Something in Jed's look the instant before he glanced away made Megan's face flame. Had Jed seen her bathing? The question was too disturbing to entertain for long. No one had been watching her. She was imagining things. Nonetheless she'd be wise to find another woman to accompany her when she bathed after this.

Chapter Eight

May-June, 1850

Independence was six weeks behind them, and the rigors of the trail had taken their toll. Three weeks ago several families had lost much needed supplies when fording the Elkhorn River. All the river crossings slowed them down and at the Elkhorn there had been three hundred wagons waiting to cross ahead of them.

In the first six weeks on the trail, more than a dozen head of the train's livestock had strayed or died of disease or drowning. One of Abner's longhorn cows had disappeared during the night and was never seen again. Jed had set extra guards to watch the livestock during the night because of the bands of Pawnee and Sioux in the area.

Several families had lost their livestock feed to rivers, and when there was no grass for several days, they fed the animals flour and meal meant for human consumption.

Throughout the train, women were being forced to discard their precious belongings to lighten the load, Megan among them. Her eyes swimming with tears of regret, she had left her beloved floral carpet beside the trail three days ago after two of their oxen fell ill. Abner had replaced the two with their mules and the oxen seemed to be on the mend.

They'd had so much rain that some of the bedding was ruined, and everything smelled of mildew. When they weren't traveling through hub-deep mud they often had dust to deal with—dust everywhere, in their clothes and in their food. Occasionally the wind was so high they didn't dare make a fire.

The nights were cool, and some were actually cold. The number of physical complaints among the party had grown, and Megan's nursing skills and medical supplies brought people to her wagon almost every day, requesting her help. Chills, fever and stomach upsets were the most common complaints. Members of two families had come down with cholera and the remaining relatives had voluntarily separated from the train and started back to Independence, though no one expected the cholera victims to live long enough to see civilization again. As yet, no one else in the party had contracted the dread disease.

The last day of May was very warm, and they traveled twenty-five miles along the Platte River road over the bare plains. Upon starting that morning, they could see about fifty wagons ahead of their train and two herds of cattle. It took most of the men to keep their livestock separated from that of other trains. Finally Jed led them off the road entirely, and before the day was over, they had left the other wagons behind. By the time they stopped to make camp, they were within a hundred miles of Fort Laramie.

Once the livestock were tended to, Jed stopped near the Schiller wagon, where the Schillers and Abner Claunch were eating their evening meal.

"Want a plate, Jedediah?" Rose asked.

"No, thanks, Rosie." He glanced at Abner. "You're going to need your food for your family before we get where we're going."

"Megan brought me some supplies this morning. I finally talked her into letting Abner eat with us as long as she's caring for the sick day and night, like she has been lately. Why don't you throw your food in with ours, Jedediah, and eat with us all the time."

"I appreciate the offer, Rosie," Jed said distractedly. "I'll think about it." He had seen Megan returning to her wagon late last evening after nursing Hollis Glenhill all day, and early this morning he'd seen her retrace her step. Hollis's fever kept recurring, each time leaving him weaker than before. The man had lost so much weight he looked like a skeleton. "Abner, is Megan still with Hollis?"

"She's been with him all day," Abner answered, nodding. "He's worse than he's ever been from what she told me last night."

Over the past few weeks Jed had watched Megan's unflagging care of the sick. He had seen her go to her wagon some nights so exhausted she could barely put one foot in front of the other. He had fought a growing admiration for her compassion and strength, knowing that the more he saw in her to admire, the harder it would be to stay away from her. So far he had kept himself in check, but when he thought about the months that lay ahead of them on the trail, a feeling of panic rose in him. He left the others and made his way to his own wagon to eat.

An hour later, after washing and changing into clean clothes, he went to Hollis Glenhill's wagon. Pale light from a single candle flickered on the sick man's bed. Megan sat on a low trunk beside the patient, dozing, her cheek resting against a wooden wagon bow.

Jed climbed into the wagon and looked down at her for a long moment, waiting for his pulse to slow down to normal. He had been avoiding her, catching glimpses of her only from a distance, but he hadn't forgotten how beautiful she was. He had never seen her asleep and defenseless before. The delicate ivory color of her skin in the candlelight, the dark crescents of her lashes resting on her cheeks, the gentle rise and fall of her breasts beneath the cotton fabric of her dress made him weak.

The heat inside the wagon caused her dress to cling damply to her bosom. Her black hair was falling from its pins; a good portion of it tumbled over one shoulder. Her slightly parted lips were pink and moist looking. Jed had not expected to find her like this. Just looking at her started the gnawing hunger deep inside him, which he thought he had learned to tame these past few weeks.

He touched her hair. "Megan," he said softly.

She sat up with a start. "Oh, Jed . . . you frightened me." She stood and raked her fingers through her disheveled hair.

Watching her, his fingers itched to bury themselves in the rich, silken thickness of it. He stuffed his hands into his trouser pockets and smiled at her. His throat felt tight, and he had to clear it. "I'm sorry." His gaze shifted briefly to the sick man's flushed face. A faint rattling sound issued from the patient with every breath. "Just thought I'd check on Hollis. How's he doing?"

"Not well," she murmured.

His eyes returned to her. "You don't look all that good yourself. You're going to make yourself sick long before we reach Oregon if you don't get more rest."

The way he was looking at her brought an infusion of color to Megan's cheeks. Her heartbeat quickened and a sudden weakness swept over her. "I'll be all right, Jed."

It was impossible to stop looking at her. Jed forced himself to remember that a seriously ill, probably dying man lay between them. Still, it was an effort to keep his voice from revealing his emotions. "Where is Lacey? She should have relieved you hours ago."

"She's not very well today herself," Megan said. "I don't think it's anything serious, just an upset stomach. She hasn't mentioned it to me, but I suspect she's with child."

Megan's cheeks burned with renewed color. She shouldn't be discussing such an intimate female condition with Jed. His hair was neatly combed, his face smooth and tanned. He wore a fresh shirt and trousers. He looked so clean and strong, and much too handsome for any woman's safety. His eyes, shadowed in the dimness of the wagon, seemed to burn into her, and she dropped her gaze.

"Then I'll stay with Hollis tonight."

She looked up and shook her head. "No, I've just started him on a new medicine. I need to keep an eye on his reaction to it."

The smudges beneath her eyes and the hollowness of her cheeks suddenly angered him. She would kill herself taking care of other people. "Damn it, Megan," he said with a sigh of impatience, "what *can* I do to help you then?"

Megan smiled at Jed's impatience. Inactivity did not sit well with him. How healthy and vital he looked, with his large hands moving restlessly in and out of his pockets. He was frustrated, and she longed to reach out and clasp his hands tightly in hers. She understood the nervous agitation he was feeling; she had felt it herself the past few weeks, particularly when she caught sight of him.

"I would like a bucket of fresh water, if it's not too much trouble. Bathing Hollis's face and chest with cool water drives the fever down temporarily."

"No trouble at all," he said, looking into the darkness beyond the candlelight. "Where's the bucket?"

She took a step into the darkness, picked up the half-full bucket of tepid water and handed it to him. He reached for it, his fingers closing warmly over hers. For an instant they stood on either side of the sickbed, staring at each other as though frozen. His eyes were dark and hungry.

To Jed, her eyes looked wide and almost black in the dimness. They seemed to swallow him. When she pulled her hand away, he felt an overwhelming sadness that he was no longer touching her. "I'll be right back," he said hoarsely as he turned and left the wagon.

Megan stirred and shivered inexplicably in the warm, airless night. Bending down, she laid her palm on Hollis's brow. Perhaps it was wishful thinking, but he didn't seem quite as restless as he had been all day. He was sleeping deeply. Straightening, she stretched her neck and back to ease her sore muscles.

She needed some fresh air. She stepped out of the wagon and leaned against the end of the wagon bed to wait for Jed to bring the water from the river. It was noticeably cooler outside the wagon, and Megan lifted her falling hair with both hands to cool her neck. A chorus of cicadas sang around her. After a moment she tried to bind her hair in a loose bun at the back of her head, but found it a hopeless task. She had lost too many pins during the long day. Giving up, she removed the few pins remaining and shook back her hair.

She heard Jed coming before she saw him moving toward her through the night. He lifted the bucket and set it in the wagon. "Thank you, Jed."

He turned, all at once very close to her. Something taut and expectant quivered between them. Megan's breath caught in her throat. For an eternal moment they stood transfixed. Then Jed's hand went to her face, startling him as much as Megan. He hadn't known he was going to touch her, but she didn't move. Their eyes searched each other's shadowed features, probing and hungry.

They moved closer, as if in a trance. Not knowing how it had happened, Megan was suddenly in his arms, and his mouth sought hers blindly in the darkness and found it. His kiss was hungry and warm, and deep inside Megan something opened, like a flower reaching for the sun.

His hands gripped her waist tightly, his fingers clenching and unclenching convulsively. Then they were moving up her back, burrowing beneath her hair, pressing her against him.

Dizzily she became aware that her hands rested on his shoulders, and wrapped them tightly around his neck. Instinctively her lips parted to take in more of him. She was a stranger to a man's kisses, but Jed's seemed so right that without thinking about it she was kissing him back.

Jed made a sound at the back of his throat and took the kiss deeper. Megan's head swam. Jed, oh, Jed, I have waited for you all my life...my love, my love....The words raced through her brain, the dizzying revelation of them exploding her thoughts, and she moaned, every part of her crying out with the need and pain and desperation of loving him. Oh, Jed...Jed.

Jed was on fire wanting her, his blood roaring and his mind reeling. He had wanted her for so long, wanted to hold her softness and lose himself in the heady taste of her mouth, wanted to lie with her, to touch her everywhere, to possess her and make her his...his... She was another man's wife. The truth hit him then with a staggering impact. To possess her would be to take what was not his.

From some deep reservoir of honor he found the strength to overcome the onslaught of his emotions and tear his mouth from hers. He stared down at her, his chest heaving, his breath coming hard and with a savage sound. In his eyes was a dawning shock as he fought himself to keep from kissing her again. Already he missed the sweet taste of her mouth.

Megan looked up at him, her eyes wide and her whole body trembling. Her mouth was swollen from his greedy kiss yet ached for more. Now that he was no longer kissing her, sanity trickled slowly back, and with its return came shame. She was married to Abner. Oh, God, she had no right to want Jed with this desperate, searing need—no right....

Abruptly he released her, jerking his hands away as though from a flame. Megan felt bereft and longed to throw herself back into his arms, but knew that she could not. She could only stand frozen, stunned and in pain. She couldn't even speak. He looked back at her for an instant, and the anguish in his face was like the twisting of a knife in Megan's heart. Then he turned and walked away from her, into the night.

Hollis Glenhill died just before dawn the next morning. As Megan kept vigil by his bed during the night, Hollis had awakened several times and talked to her quite coherently. But she was not reassured by the patient's seeming improvement. She had seen too many people rally briefly before they died. It was as though they had accepted death as inevitable and somehow found strength and comfort in the acceptance.

Hollis talked to Megan about his childhood on an Illinois farm, and about the sweetheart who died before they could be married. Mason and David came to see him about eleven, and he awoke and talked to them for some time. The nephews were cheered by Hollis's recovery, and Megan said nothing to upset them. She didn't know the future, after all, and perhaps she was mistaken.

Hollis's temperature shot up again soon after their visit, and he died shortly after that as Megan bathed his fevered face with a cool, wet cloth. She sat with him until she heard the first stirrings of the camp, then went to inform Lacey, Mason and David that Hollis was gone.

The train's departure was delayed while a grave was dug and David read a familiar scripture over it: "'I am the resurrection and the life . . . he that believeth in me, though he were dead, yet shall he live: and whoever liveth and believeth in me, shall never die. . . .'"

Megan couldn't help contrasting the reading with the harsher one chosen by the Reverend Donovan for her mother's burial service. She closed her eyes for a moment and let the healing words flow over her. For an instant it seemed that David read the words for Kate.

Throughout the brief service Megan and Jed carefully avoided meeting each other's eyes. In the merciless early morning light, what had happened between them the night before seemed to Megan even more shameful and inexcusable. Somehow she had to excise the feelings she had for Jed from her heart. They were wrong.

She clung to Abner's arm as if her life depended upon it while David led them in singing "Nearer My God To Thee."

A great sadness rose in Megan. Afterward she squeezed each of the Glenhills' hands in turn, but could not utter a word. Her throat was thick with emotion, and she knew if she tried to speak, the dam would break.

Clutching Abner's arm again, she walked back to their wagon. "Meggie, are you all right?" Abner asked, studying her pale face.

They had reached the wagon and Megan only nodded as she climbed into the bed and sat down on her trunk. Abner stood over her, frowning, clearly concerned about her but not knowing what to do. To Megan's embarrassment, tears began trickling down her cheeks. She couldn't stop them, so she buried her face in her hands.

Abner knelt beside her and patted her shoulder. "Meggie, I know Hollis's death is hard on you, him being the first and all. But you did everything you could for him. Nobody could have done more."

"I know that," she mumbled through her fingers. "I'm sad about Hollis, but that's not why I'm crying... I'm...oh, I feel so stupid, bawling like a baby."

Abner put his arm around her shoulders a bit awkwardly. "Sugar, you've worn yourself out nursing the sick, that's what's wrong with you. You'll be all right once you get some rest. Look, I'll get one of the Schiller boys to keep our team on the road today. You don't worry about anything but yourself."

"No...no," Megan protested miserably. "It's not caring for the sick. At least that makes me feel useful."

"Why, what are you sayin', sugar? You've worked like a mule ever since we left Independence. You been as useful as anybody else in this train—more so, with your nursing added to everything else you do."

Megan lifted her tear-stained face from her hands. Abner was so kind to her, so gentle, and she didn't deserve it. Last night she had ... She choked back a sob and threw her arms around him, burying her face in his shoulder. "I practically forced you to marry me, Abner, and I—I've not been a decent wife to you. I'm—I'm so sorry."

"Now, now, Meggie girl." His voice sounded strained, and he didn't move as she pressed her face against his rough homespun shirt. He cleared his throat and added, "That wedding wasn't what either one of us wanted if we'd had any other choice. We'll get things worked out when we reach Oregon. There's plenty of time, so you quit fretting yourself about it."

Megan lifted her face and released him. She had embarrassed the poor man. What was wrong with her this morning? Perhaps Abner was right and she was overtired. "Don't pay any attention to me, Abner," she said, forcing a weak smile. "And you don't need to get one of the Schiller boys to help you. I'm still capable of keeping the team under control. I can't get any rest, anyway, while we're on the move."

"Well, if you're sure . . ."

She took a deep breath and rose. "I'm sure. Now go and get the team. I'll be fine."

Abner nodded and left the wagon. Megan sat, feeling drained by her crying, until he returned and hitched the animals. Then she got the whip and walked along beside them. The mules would be traveling with the herd today; all four oxen were once again hitched to the wagon.

They were lucky to have lost only one cow, Megan mused as she flicked the nearest ox lightly with the whip to remind him to keep moving. She really had much to be thankful for, she told herself. Not the least of which, she admitted, was the fact that Abner seemed determined not to consummate their marriage. Her sense of duty would prevent her turning Abner away if he came to her bed, but she was glad it wasn't going to happen, at least for a while.

After last night it had been hard to stand so close to Jed at Hollis Glenhill's grave and not shrivel with embarrassment. Jed had been miserable, too; his embarrassment had been obvious in the studious way he ignored her. Megan sighed, wishing there were another woman she could talk to about Jed and the confusion she felt over her feelings. She knew Rose Schiller would be a sympathetic listener and wouldn't repeat anything Megan told her in confidence.

Yet Megan couldn't bring herself to speak to the older woman. As far as Rose and everybody else on the train knew, Megan and Abner had a normal marriage. Megan felt she owed it to Abner not to disabuse them of that belief. She would not make him the object of other people's pity.

Later that day, when Jed rode past on his stallion, Megan found she could call a casual greeting, just as though he were any other man in the party. That made her feel a little better about herself. She would get over her feelings for him, she told herself stoutly. There was, after all, nothing else for her to do.

On June 11 they reached Independence Rock, a landmark for westward travelers where emigrants carved or painted their names following the tradition started by mountainmen and trappers before them. The rock, known as "the great register of the desert," rose one hundred thirty-five feet, close to the road and about a hundred feet north of the Sweetwater River. It reminded Megan of a giant bowl turned upside down.

Megan carved her name and Abner's on the rock with the edge of a spoon, along with the date—June 11, 1850.

"I don't know why I'm doing this," she told Mary Schiller, who was inscribing the names of her family. "Nobody I knew in Missouri will know who Megan Claunch is. They knew me as Megan Riley."

"We have to uphold the tradition," Mary said.

"That's how I feel, too," Megan said. "Oh, look, somebody has written the directions for a shortcut here." Megan leaned closer to read the faint, scrawled words.

"I'm glad Jed knows the best route," Mary said. "Papa says people have died taking a shortcut they heard about on the road."

"Mmm, I can understand how people could be tempted to do almost anything to cut a few miles off the journey." Megan looked around at the barren landscape. For the past few days they had been traveling through sand and dust. The days were hot and the nights cool, as the road climbed to higher altitudes. They were in Sioux territory, and though they had seen no Indians for some time, there was a constant wariness among the party.

"It's hard to believe we aren't even halfway there yet, isn't it?" Mary sounded discouraged.

"We should reach South Pass in about two weeks," Megan said. South Pass would mark the end of the first leg of their journey. The second half, Abner had told her, was much harder and would take longer than the first half, but Megan chose not to dwell on that.

Before they camped for the night, they crossed the bridge over the high, swift Sweetwater River. They had been on the road for almost two months.

By the time all of the party, their goods and livestock were on the north bank of the river, it was late in the afternoon and seemed even later because the sun had been behind a western hill for some time. Megan felt enormously relieved to be on solid ground again, for a strong wind had come up as they were crossing.

The wind seemed to be increasing every second. Megan had crossed the bridge on foot with the other women and children. Now she squinted against the stinging dust, trying to spot Abner and their wagon. The dust was so thick she could barely see two wagon lengths in front of her. She could just make out Jed and Abner, with several other men, struggling to keep the frightened livestock together and moving forward.

Alarmed, Megan ran toward the wagons. She located hers and climbed into the seat. Abner was now nowhere within her limited range of vision. She had to grip the edge of the seat to stay there. The wagon rattled and creaked and swayed frighteningly in the wind. The terrified oxen stamped and bawled, trying to free themselves from their restraints.

Megan grabbed the whip and attempted to gain control of the team. She sensed the oxen's panic as they lurched forward, wanting to get away from the stinging dust and the howl of the wind. It didn't occur to her to jump off the wagon and abandon their belongings. She clung to the seat, screaming commands that were snatched from her mouth by the wind.

Still clinging to the wagon seat with one hand, Megan stood up and threw her arm back, preparing to bring the whip down on the oxen. The wind grabbed the whip from her hand and sent it flying into the dust.

The oxen picked up speed and within seconds were running out of control in the midst of dust so thick Megan could see nothing beyond herself and her wagon. She couldn't jump from the wagon now—it was traveling too fast.

She hung on for dear life, trying to control the panic that threatened to overcome her with each ragged breath. The wind had tugged the pins from her hair and it whipped wildly about her head. She clenched her jaw to keep her teeth from rattling. The wagon sounded as if it were about to fly apart. Dear God, what was she going to do? What *could* she do?

She had to do something. She couldn't simply sit there until she was flung to the rocky ground. She grabbed the edge of the seat with one hand and leaned out as far as she could reach, but her fingers touched nothing.

"Whoa! Stop!" she shouted. "Damn you stupid beasts, *stop*!"

Over the shriek of the wind she heard a man's voice. Then she faintly saw the swift movement of a horse and rider. They came even with the lead ox, and the rider lunged out of his saddle, caught the animal around the neck and swung himself astride. He was shouting, but Megan couldn't make out what he was saying. It didn't matter, for the oxen were slowing. Her rescuer was getting them under control.

Minutes later, the team came to a halt and the man slid to the ground.

"Megan, are you all right?"

Jed! Megan threw herself from the seat and into his arms. "Jed...oh, Jed!" Fiercely she clung to him, burrowing her face into his neck. Oh, God, he felt so solid and safe.

Jed clasped her tightly to him, lifting her feet off the ground. With the dust stinging his face and neck and the wind sounding like a den of wolves, he held her, his chin resting in the soft tangle of her hair. He felt sick with the thought of what could have happened if he hadn't noticed that her team was out of control and come after her.

"Shh, Megan," he murmured, pressing his mouth against her hair. "You're safe now." She whimpered and burrowed deeper into his neck, still unable to believe that she was safe. His heart twisted. "Ah, Megan, love...."

The words hung between them like ripe fruit ready to fall. She grew suddenly still in his arms. After a moment she lifted her head and looked at him, her blue eyes inches from his. Her expression was one of shock and confusion. Slowly he let her slide down his body, lowering her to the ground. He caught her face in shaking hands.

"You saved me," she whispered. "Jed..."

Her eyes seemed to swallow him up. With a groan of surrender, he lowered his head. His mouth was a hairbreadth from hers, when a horse carrying Mason Glenhill thundered through the flying dust toward them. Mason was leading Jed's stallion by the reins.

"Jed!" Mason shouted. "The herd's stampeding!"

Jed released Megan and stepped back guiltily. Shielding her eyes with her hand, she gazed at him, knowing that her heart must be in her eyes. She couldn't seem to help it. Had he really called her "Megan, love"?

"Can you get your wagon back to camp?" he asked, his voice unsteady.

She turned her head until she saw some of the wagons in the distance, realizing for the first time that the storm was passing. She turned back to Jed. "Yes," she whispered, aware that Mason had stopped behind her and was watching them. "And...thank you, Jed."

Jed reached for his saddle and swung himself up into it. He looked down at her for an instant and something flickered in his eyes. Then he turned his horse and he and Mason galloped away. Shakily Megan walked up to the team. The oxen stood where they had halted, heads down, sides heaving, lathered with sweat. She gripped the halter of the lead ox and urged him forward. "Come on, boy. It's over now. We're all in one piece."

Walking beside the team, she led the animals toward the other wagons. She continued to talk to them quietly and calmly. "We had a narrow escape, didn't we? I thought you'd shake me to pieces, for sure. But Jed saved us."

Jed. He had saved her life, but whatever hope she'd had previously that she could reclaim her heart was gone. Her heart belonged to Jed, and may God forgive her.

Before she reached the other wagons, Rose was running toward her, her fright etched on her face. "Megan, I just heard the oxen bolted with you in the wagon! What happened?"

"I'm not sure," Megan told her. "I think the dust storm frightened them."

"It panicked the rest of the livestock, too. Abner's gone with the other men to bring them back, Lord willing. He'll be worried sick when he finds out what happened to you."

"No need to worry now, Rose. Everything turned out all right. Jed stopped the team. You should've seen him, Rose. He could have been killed...."

Rose gave her an odd look, and Megan closed her mouth on more praise of Jed. Oh, dear, she couldn't run on about Jed like some silly pubescent girl. She'd better watch what she said, especially to Rose, who seemed always to understand more than you told her.

"Well," said Megan brightly. "Let's see if we can find anything to make a cook fire."

Chapter Nine

The men returned at dark, herding the livestock they had found. Six horses were missing, along with twenty head of cattle. "We have to go on," Jed told the group who gathered around him after supper. "We can't afford to wait and look for the missing livestock again tomorrow."

He appeared dead on his feet, Megan thought. He looked tired most of the time now, as did nearly everyone. From her wagon she had watched Jed return with the other men, covered in dirt, as they all were. As soon as they'd corralled the livestock, the men went to their separate wagons to clean up as best they could before supper. In clean clothes, with his face washed, the lines of strain were even clearer than before.

"That's easy fer you to say, Jed," grumbled a hardy farmer named Bert Olmstead, "but my best saddle horse's gone."

Jed removed his dusty black hat and raked his fingers through his hair. "I'm sorry about that, Bert, but if we don't get over those mountains before winter catches us, we'll be stuck up there without food or shelter."

Olmstead continued to chafe over the loss of his horse. "I got a mind to go look for him myself come morning."

Standing beside Megan, Abner spoke up. "The Injuns'll have him by then, Bert." His voice brought Jed's eyes to him, then to Megan. She smiled at Jed and his gaze rested on her for an instant before he looked away.

Olmstead muttered under his breath, unconvinced.

"You do what you have to, Bert," Jed said tiredly, "but we're leaving in the morning with or without you."

Megan remembered that day—which seemed so long ago now—when she'd awakened to hear Thayer Goddard protesting to Jed about the party planned for a Sunday evening. "Let these people enjoy themselves while they can," Jed had said. Megan understood his words now much better than she had then. It wasn't easy to find enjoyment in the journey anymore. It had become a grueling test of strength and determination, and a race against the onset of winter.

The train pulled out early the next morning. Bert Olmstead had indeed gone in search of his horse before dawn; he caught up with the rest of the party after they'd been on the road for two hours. His face sagged with discouragement; he'd not found his animal.

Dead cattle lay all along the road that day, and the stench was nearly unbearable. Johnny Goddard fell from a wagon that afternoon and, by some miracle, escaped being run over by a wagon wheel. Almost beside herself, Carolyn dragged him from beneath the moving wagon and hugged him until he screamed that she was hurting him. Carolyn kept him with her in the wagon for the rest of the afternoon, afraid to let him out of her sight.

They pulled a good way off the road to camp that evening, where the stench of the cattle wasn't so strong. Megan and Abner ate their supper with the Schillers. Megan, Rose and the Schiller children had gathered enough buffalo chips for a good fire.

One of the Schillers' cows had broken a leg late that afternoon. Reuben and Daniel had acted quickly, shooting the injured animal, then butchering and dressing the carcass. Everybody in the party had fresh beef for supper that evening. The Schillers and the Claunches enjoyed thick steaks—a bit tough, but of a good flavor. With the steaks they had gravy made from the pan drippings, and cornbread. It was the best meal they'd had in weeks.

Rose saved a steak for Jed, and he joined the two families as they were finishing their meal. "Jed," Laura asked, "are we really in danger of having to spend the winter in the mountains like you told Mr. Olmstead?"

"It's happened to others," Jed told her.

"I thought we'd be closer to our destination by now," Megan said. "One of the guidebooks I read in Independence said the trip didn't take more than four months, but we've traveled over two months and we're not halfway there."

"The guidebooks are written by people who've never made the trip," Jed said, his eyes resting on Megan. "Either that, or they're deliberate liars. We'll be mighty lucky to see Oregon by the end of October."

They sat talking for another hour. For once Jed seemed at ease in Megan's presence and was in no hurry to leave. Megan listened to the conversation around her, enjoying the deep sound of Jed's voice whenever he spoke. Several times he met her gaze and didn't immediately avert his eyes. She didn't know how his saving her could have made so much difference, but ever since, Jed had seemed more willing to tolerate her presence—he'd even talked to her pleasantly for a few minutes earlier that day.

She went to bed with a full stomach and feeling that some invisible barrier that had existed between the two of them was now gone.

As they prepared to leave the next morning, a band of Sioux Indians appeared on the horizon and rode toward the wagons. Jed barked sharp, quick commands to the men to pull the wagons into a circle and get their guns loaded and ready. Megan had stopped on the way to her wagon to say hello to David Glenhill.

David clearly disapproved of Jed's orders. "We make the Indians hostile by meeting them with loaded guns," he said to Megan.

"Jed knows what he's doing," Megan said, defending his actions.

By the time the Indians were upon them, the wagons were circled and everyone was inside the protective barrier. The Indians, about a dozen of them, sat on their horses a few yards away, their faces inscrutable and still as stone.

"I'll go talk to them," Jed told the group.

"Let me go with you," David said eagerly.

Jed shook his head without hesitation. "Let me see what they want first. Reuben, Mason, Abner, cover me. If there's trouble, start shooting." His words sent a shiver of fear up Megan's spine. Carrying a rifle, Jed left the circle and walked toward the Indians.

"This is all so unnecessary—" David began.

"How do you know?" Megan snapped at him impatiently.

He looked offended, but she hardly noticed. Her eyes were on Jed. Jed talked to one of the Indians for a moment, mostly by means of sign language. Then he came back to the others.

"They want something to eat," he said.

"You see," David said to Megan. "I told you they were harmless."

The women went to their wagons and returned with whatever bits of food they could spare. Jed gathered the contributions into a bundle and took them to the Indians. The food was parceled out among them by the one who seemed to be their leader, and they rode off.

The wagon train traveled that day without seeing any more Indians, but Megan noticed that Jed was unnaturally alert. When they made camp that night Jed warned, "Watch your horses. We may not have seen the last of those Sioux." He assigned extra men to guard the livestock through the night.

As Megan and Rose were preparing their families' evening meal together, Carolyn Goddard rushed up to them. "Have you seen Johnny?" Carolyn's eyes darted frantically around the camp.

Rose exchanged a look with Megan. "I haven't seen him since we stopped, have you, Megan?"

"No." Megan turned to gaze slowly around them. "He has to be here somewhere, Carolyn."

Carolyn began to wring her hands. "Oh, my God . . . my God. . . ."

Rose took her skillet off the fire. "Calm down, Carolyn. We'll find him."

"I'll spread the word," Megan offered. "We'll search the wagons." She hurried off as Rose attempted to calm Carolyn, and made her way through the camp, asking if anyone had seen Johnny Goddard since they'd stopped for the day.

Jed and Thayer Goddard were leading their horses back from the river and noticed Megan running from wagon to wagon. They corralled their horses and intercepted her.

"What's wrong?" Jed asked.

Megan's eyes darted to Thayer. "We—we can't find Johnny, Thayer. Carolyn is frantic."

"Where is she?" Thayer demanded.

"With Rose Schiller." Megan pointed in the direction of the Schiller wagon and Thayer hurried off.

Megan and Jed followed him. "We've searched all the wagons," Megan said. "No one's seen him for at least two hours."

When they reached the Schiller cook fire, Carolyn was sobbing uncontrollably. Thayer grabbed his wife's shoulders and shook her roughly. "Think, woman!" he shouted. "When did you see him last?"

"That won't help," said Rose angrily. She put her arm around Carolyn's waist. Thayer's dark eyes flashed resentfully, but he dropped his hands.

"There now," Rose said soothingly to Carolyn. "You have to tell us when you saw him last, dear. So we'll know where to start looking for him."

With great effort Carolyn controlled her sobbing. She avoided looking at her husband. "I—I don't think I've seen him since about two o'clock. He—he was walking with—

with the Olmstead children. I thought Fanny was keeping an eye on them.''

Thayer grabbed her arm. ''It's your job to keep an eye on our son!''

Jed stepped forward and brushed Thayer's hand off Carolyn's arm. ''Rose, why don't you take Carolyn to her wagon and stay there with her.''

As the two women walked away, Megan told the others what she had learned. ''I talked to Fanny Olmstead. She said Johnny and her youngest boy got into a fuss and Johnny said he was going to find his mother and tell her the Olmstead boy took a pretty rock away from him. Fanny wasn't paying much attention and just assumed Johnny went to his mother. No one can remember seeing Johnny since then.''

''Carolyn has only one child to look after,'' Thayer muttered, ''and she can't even do that—stupid woman—''

''She's already blaming herself, Thayer,'' Megan said. ''What good will it do to talk like that?''

Thayer whirled on Megan furiously, but before he could speak Jed interjected, ''We have about an hour to search before dark, Thayer. Lets get the men organized.''

Megan cooked supper for the Schiller children and herself, putting enough aside for Rose, Reuben and Abner to eat later. All the men and older boys in the camp, except for those who were left to guard the train, had spread out to search the surrounding terrain.

The searchers began straggling back to camp at dark, grim faced and discouraged. They had found no sign of Johnny Goddard. Jed and Abner were among the last to return.

''We'll go out again at dawn,'' Jed said as Megan filled their plates, but his eyes were filled with resignation when he looked at Megan.

Megan imagined all sorts of horrible things that could have happened to Johnny, and she wondered what Abner and Jed were thinking. She didn't ask—she wasn't sure she really wanted to hear. Leaving the men to finish their supper, she went to the Goddard wagon.

From the look Rose gave her, Megan realized that the two women knew that all the searchers had returned and Johnny had not been found. Carolyn sat in a corner, swaying and moaning softly.

"Go and eat your supper, Rose," Megan urged. "I'll stay with her." Rose had no sooner left than Thayer Goddard climbed into the wagon. Megan was sitting beside Carolyn, holding her and making futile efforts to comfort her.

"He's out there—somewhere," Carolyn sobbed, "lost—and cold—and hungry . . . crying for his mother. . . ."

"Maybe he's found a warm place," Megan soothed. "Shhh, Carolyn dear . . ."

Thayer stalked to them and pushed Megan away from his wife. "I'll take charge of her," he said rudely. "You aren't needed here any longer."

Megan wanted to tell him how thoroughly mean and despicable he was behaving, but she realized that Thayer must be as worried as Carolyn, so she left the wagon without a word.

Through most of the night, Carolyn's wails could be heard in the camp. Megan slept little and doubted that anyone else did, either. The night seemed interminable. Megan rose before dawn and heard Abner snoring beneath the wagon. She dressed quietly so as not to wake him, knowing that he needed the rest. She left the wagon and walked restlessly around the camp. As the first hint of dawn began to lighten the dark sky, she ventured outside the perimeter of the camp, peering closely at every shadow for signs of life.

If Johnny could have made it this far, she kept telling herself, he'd have made it to the Goddards' wagon. But she continued to look, anyway, around every shadowed hillock and rock. It was something to do as she tried to drive from her mind images of little Johnny Goddard lying in some desolate landscape, his legs broken or his body torn and bleeding, perhaps dying this very minute, or already dead.

Megan was so intent on her search that she strayed farther from the camp than she'd intended. When she looked
up and saw the outlines of the wagons against the lavender
sky, she realized how far she'd gone and felt a faint stab of
alarm. She shook it off, realizing she could see well enough
now to determine that no danger was in sight.

As she was about to turn and go back, she noticed another gentle mound ahead of her and decided to walk far
enough to see beyond this one last hillock. She lifted her
skirt and hurried forward. As she reached the hillock, she
heard a low sound. She whirled to peer anxiously around
her. She saw nothing unusual, yet it had sounded like a
moan.

Megan frowned, wondering if she'd really heard anything, after all, when the sound came again. It seemed close
by. She took a few cautious steps around the hillock until
she could see the other side. There was an opening in the
mound. Someone had made a dugout. But there was no sign
of human habitation—no remains of a cook fire, no animal dung, nothing. Whoever had lived in the dugout must
have abandoned it long ago.

Megan ducked her head and peered inside. Dimly she saw
something huddled on the floor. She rushed forward into the
semidarkness as another moan came from the mound on
the floor.

"Johnny!" Megan bent down and touched hot, bare
flesh. She gasped and jerked her hand away.

The nearly naked Indian, who lay facing the back of the
dugout, stirred at her touch and turned his head. His black
eyes stared at her from a savage bronze face. Stripes of black
paint slashed his cheeks and forehead. He wore nothing but
a breechclout.

He blinked as though trying to clear his vision and mumbled some guttural words that Megan didn't understand.

Megan straightened from her crouch, intending to make
a run for it before this evil-looking heathen scalped her.
Then she realized that the Indian was too sick to hurt any-

one. He appeared to be young, not much older than Daniel Schiller.

She took a cautious step closer to him. He continued to stare at her, his black eyes glittering with fever.

Compassion welled up in her. He was lying here sick and alone. "You're very ill," she said as she reached out to touch the bronze hand that was spread on his bare chest just below the right shoulder.

He mumbled more guttural words, but the only one she understood was "no." Yet his meaning was clear. He didn't want her to touch him. "I won't hurt you," she said. He lifted his hand and Megan sucked in a quick breath. He had an angry red, festering wound—from a bullet or an arrow, she couldn't tell which. No wonder he had a fever.

"That's a bad wound," she said. "It's infected." He no longer looked savage or dangerous to her, merely sick and in pain. She couldn't turn her back on any living creature in that condition. "I'll go get my medical supplies. I'll bring some of our men back with me and—"

"No!" The Indian struggled to sit up, nearly fainting from the effort. Groaning, he stopped struggling and gasped for breath.

"Evidently you understand some of what I say. Believe me, I won't let anyone harm you. If that wound isn't treated, you will die here."

He stared at her intently as she spoke, then shook his head. "Bring no one," he said, the words so heavily accented she could barely understand them. "You come."

He must be terrified that he'd be killed if she told her party he was here, Megan thought. "All right," she said quickly. She wasn't afraid of him. In his condition he was harmless. She didn't know where his people were, but he would at least be sheltered here until he was strong enough to leave—or died. There was really no reason to tell anyone of his presence. "I'll come back as soon as I can."

She left the dugout and hurried back to camp. Everyone was up now, and she smelled food cooking. Abner was standing near their wagon.

"I've been looking for you, Meggie. I put your coffeepot on the fire. Where have you been?"

"Just walking," Megan said. "I—I thought Johnny Goddard might have come back during the night."

"He ain't back," Abner said gently. "We're going out to search for him again right after breakfast."

"I'll mix batter for pancakes," Megan said. She'd have to wait until after breakfast to return to the dugout, if she was to keep the wounded Indian's presence a secret.

Twitching with anxiety, Megan cooked their breakfast and waited for the men to leave. As soon as they rode out, she ducked into her wagon. Since she couldn't walk away from the camp carrying her carpetbag, she wore Abner's poncho. She stuffed Abner's bottle of whiskey, clean rags, a knife and a jar of salve in one deep pocket. In the other she hid pancakes left from breakfast, dried peaches and a tin cup. She grabbed the more battered of their two buckets and left the camp carrying it. If anyone noticed her, they'd assume she was going after fresh water.

When she was away from the camp, she filled the bucket at the nearby stream and lugged it to the dugout.

The Indian jerked awake when she set the bucket down beside him, his eyes wild for a moment until he recognized her. He looked at the bucket longingly. Megan emptied her pockets and dipped the cup in the water. She supported his head as he gulped the water down. Then she handed him a pancake. He wolfed it down and indicated he wanted more water.

"How long have you been here?" she asked as she supported his head again.

He drank, then his head sank to the ground. He was exhausted from the slight exertion of eating. "Two suns," he said.

He'd been without food and water for two days. Little wonder the poor thing was ravenous. Megan poured two inches of whiskey into the cup. "You'd better drink this," she said. "I have to examine that wound."

He drank the whiskey slowly, his black eyes watching her. When she touched the wound, he trembled but remained rigidly still. She probed as gently as she could. He ground his teeth and grunted. Sweat popped out on his forehead, and he closed his eyes. Megan thought he might have passed out, and she hoped he had.

"There's something in there," she said, and his eyes flew open. He hadn't passed out, after all. "A shell?" He looked at her blankly. "Gun," she said, pantomiming the action of lifting and shooting a rifle.

He understood and nodded. "I thought so," Megan said regretfully. "It has to come out." She lifted the knife so that he could see it. "Do you understand?"

He stared at her for a moment, then nodded. Pouring some of the whiskey over the knife, she shook it dry before continuing with her task. "I'll be as gentle as I can," she said as she brought the knife to the wound. He jumped and groaned once, when the tip of the knife broke the swollen flesh around the wound, then stiffened, clamped his teeth together and lay still.

As Megan probed, she talked, hoping to divert his attention. "We saw Sioux yesterday," she said. "We gave them food. Are you Sioux? Were you with them?"

He stared at her as though he didn't understand, but she felt sure he did, and went on talking. "Yesterday afternoon we discovered that a child in our party is missing. His name is Johnny Goddard and he's only four years old. Our men are searching for him right now." Occasionally Megan glanced at him as she probed and talked. He watched her carefully, his jaw and hands clenched.

"His mother is insane—loco—with worry over him. She cried all night long. Johnny is her only child. I don't know what will become of her if we don't find him. I'm afraid she'll lose her mind completely—or harm herself...." She felt the bullet with the tip of her knife. With a quick, deft movement she dug it out. She held it up so he could see it, and realized he'd fainted.

Quickly she dropped the bullet and poured whiskey over the bleeding wound. He groaned and opened his eyes. "It's out," Megan said. "That's all I can do. I'll leave the cup and water bucket with you. There are two more pancakes and some dried peaches. I'll leave them beside the bucket."

She wiped the blade of her knife on the earth floor of the dugout, capped the whiskey bottle and returned it and the knife to the poncho pocket. She spread salve from the jar gently over the wound and placed a clean rag on it, binding it in place with another long strip of cloth, which she tied above his shoulder. Through all of this, the Indian watched her intently, without speaking.

"There," Megan said, screwing the lid back on the jar of salve and dropping it into a pocket. She stood. "You'll feel better in a day or two," she said reassuringly. "You'll be able to return to your people." Or you'll be dead, she added to herself. "I have to get back to camp now before I'm missed."

"Good woman—you," he said. He touched his bare chest with his left hand. "Medicine woman. You save life."

I hope so, Megan thought. "I'm glad I could help. I won't see you again. Goodbye."

He nodded solemnly, and Megan left him.

Megan and Rose took turns sitting with Carolyn Goddard until the search parties returned about noon. Carolyn sat huddled in her wagon, staring at nothing and sobbing intermittently. The men did not find Johnny. Thayer Goddard's face was set in stone when he returned to his wagon. He stared at Carolyn with hatred in his eyes and seemed not even to notice that Megan was there. She slipped away and left them alone. Before Megan reached her wagon, she heard Carolyn scream and knew that Thayer must have told her that the searchers had returned without Johnny.

Megan halted, shocked, as she noticed that the men were hitching their teams. She saw Abner and ran to meet him. "Abner, what are you doing?"

"We're leaving," Abner said.

"But we can't leave without Johnny!"

"Jed gave the order. He's right, Meggie. We can't afford to lose any more time."

She stared after Abner as he led the oxen to the wagon. She couldn't believe it! They could not mean to leave without knowing what had become of Johnny! She caught sight of Jed near his wagon and ran toward him.

"You can't do this," Megan gasped when she reached him. "You can't be that cruel! For all we know, Johnny is still alive, injured or lost!"

Jed stared at her calmly for a long moment. "Listen to me, Megan," he said deliberately, "the chances of Johnny being alive are virtually nonexistent. We've already spent more time searching for him than we can afford to lose. If we don't keep going, winter will catch us unprepared and we will all die." He turned away from her shocked face and walked to the back of his wagon for a bucket of oats for his horse.

Megan's outrage exploded. She ran after Jed. He was reaching into the wagon, his back to her. "Jed!"

He turned around. "You're wasting your time, Megan. We're leaving."

She flew at him, pounding her balled fists on his chest. "You—you heartless beast," she sobbed. "I hate you. I—hate—you—"

Jed subdued her by wrapping his arms around her so tightly she could not move. Crying, she tried to struggle, but his arms only held her more tightly and his chest was a solid, unmovable wall. Megan cried out in fury.

"Be still," he said quietly. "I won't let you go until you stop fighting me."

She sobbed and dropped her head against his chest in surrender. He held her while she cried herself out. After a while, she became aware that he was murmuring comforts against her hair. She grew still.

"I'm sorry, Megan," he said quietly. "But there is no hope for Johnny. You ought to pray that he's dead."

She jerked her head up and stared at him, her eyes still glazed from crying. "How can you say such a thing?"

"He's better off dead, believe me," Jed went on relentlessly. "Because if he isn't dead, the Sioux have him."

Her eyes widened in stunned comprehension. "Oh, dear Lord, Jed." Every story of Indian cruelty she'd ever heard came back to her. "What will they do to him?"

"Don't think about it," he warned sternly. He looked down at her intently for another moment before releasing her. "It's time to pull out. You'd better go help your husband."

Chapter Ten

After Johnny Goddard's disappearance, Carolyn rarely left her wagon, except to make a few pathetic, abortive attempts to search for her son. She simply sat there, day after day, in heat or cold, staring at nothing. Thayer slept in their tent or in a bedroll on the ground and ate his meals alone. Megan wondered how much Carolyn ate of the food the other women prepared for her, and how much sleep she was getting. Very little of either, she suspected.

The night after they had given up searching for Johnny and traveled on, Carolyn made her first attempt to leave the train and look for her son. One of the men saw her stumbling away from camp before she had gotten very far. Jed and Thayer overtook her and brought her back, kicking and sobbing hysterically.

About the time everybody had gotten back to sleep, Carolyn had started screaming, "Thayer Goddard, you are a murderer! Jed Dossman, you are a murderer! Both of you, murderers! Murderers!" Over and over Carolyn screamed the accusations, until she woke the whole camp. Thayer made no attempt to calm her. He merely picked up his bedroll and moved farther away from the wagon. Rose Schiller left her bed and went to Carolyn and within a few minutes the distraught woman was quiet.

But after Rose left Carolyn that night, thinking she was asleep, Carolyn had tried to leave the train again. Fortunately one of the guards saw her. The next morning, Jed gave Rose the responsibility of assigning the women to watch Carolyn whenever Thayer was away from the wagon, and told Thayer it was his responsibility to care for Carolyn at night.

"I don't think Thayer Goddard would care if Carolyn wandered off and he never saw her again," Rose confided to Megan later in the day. "He's the most unfeeling man I've ever known. He acts like Carolyn is just being stubborn, when the poor woman is beside herself with grief. All Thayer seems to care about is that he has to cook his own meals and wash his own clothes."

"Do you think she'll pull out of it?" Megan asked.

Rose shook her head sadly. "I don't know. Johnny being her only child, it's like she died with him—or wished she had. Listen to me, will you? I've already accepted Johnny's death."

"There's little chance he's still alive, Rose. We all know that."

"You know, I believe somewhere deep inside Carolyn she knows that, too."

"Poor woman," Megan murmured.

"She's right pitiful," Rose agreed. "She's lost weight. And you should've heard her rambling on last night while I was trying to get her to be quiet and go to sleep. Between you and me, Megan, from what Carolyn said, Thayer forced himself on her the night after Johnny disappeared."

Megan stared at Rose in disbelief.

Rose nodded glumly. "Apparently he thinks a husband has his rights, even when his wife is grieving herself to death. That's according to Carolyn, of course. She's in such a state, you have to take anything she says with a grain of salt."

"Personally, I can believe Thayer capable of such a thing. There's something about that man that has always given me the creeps," Megan said. "Sometimes he makes me think of an animal. I've caught him staring at me like a wolf watches a rabbit he intends to kill and eat. Once he did it with an open Bible on his knees."

Rose frowned. "You be careful around him," she said. "I won't ask you to stay with Carolyn. I wouldn't trust Thayer any farther than I can throw him."

"Nor would I," Megan agreed, "but I don't feel right not doing my part in watching over Carolyn."

Rose shook her head adamantly. "You're doing more than your part taking care of the sick."

Secretly Megan was relieved. She had begun to feel more and more uneasy whenever she found herself alone with Thayer. And Rose was right. Being the party's nurse and dispenser of medicines occupied most of her waking hours.

Two small children had sickened and died that very week after drinking polluted water from a stagnant pool. Megan and the mother had cared for them for thirty-six hours without a break, but they could not save them. The mother had cried for hours on the day the children died, but the next day she had risen and gone about her duties as usual. She had three other children and a husband to care for.

That woman was much better off than Carolyn Goddard, who couldn't seem to let go of her grief. Perhaps, Megan thought sadly, Carolyn would have taken her loss better if they'd at least found Johnny's body. As it was, Carolyn continued to maintain stubbornly that her child was still alive somewhere. Whether Carolyn truly believed it, Megan didn't know.

June 17 found the party traveling over extremely rough, rocky terrain. The trail no longer rose gradually over foothills, but now moved steeply up the sides of mountains toward peaks covered with snow and through gullies with names like Emigrant's Gap and Devil's Gate. Their progress was considerably slowed by the change, and even the few miles a day they traveled were grueling.

That afternoon Abner brought Megan a bucket full of snow in one hand and a bunch of yellow wildflowers in the other. "I found them growing out of a crevice next to six feet of snow," Abner said as Megan lifted the flowers to inhale their scent.

"They're so pretty. Thank you, Abner." Megan set the flowers in a cracked cup. "Give me the bucket. We'll have good water to drink when this melts." Studying Abner, she thought that he looked terribly weary. Sometimes she worried that he would be physically broken by the time they reached Oregon. After all, Abner wasn't getting any younger.

"I would've brought you two buckets full," he said, "but I couldn't find the other bucket. Have you seen it?"

She had expected him to notice that the bucket was missing long before now. "Not lately," she said, wondering if the bucket was still in the dugout where she'd left it and if the young brave had died or recovered.

Abner started to say something else, but broke into a fit of coughing, instead. Unable to stop the sudden attack he slumped down on the trunk. Megan poured a small amount of salt into the palm of her hand. "Here, put some of this on your tongue, she instructed."

Listening to his struggle for breath, her concern deepened. She hovered over him as he managed to swallow the salt. The cough sounded tight, and she knew it should be loosened so he could bring up phlegm. "I heard you coughing several times during the night," she said. "How long have you had this cough?"

The salt seemed to control the cough, and Abner shrugged as he gasped for air. "Not long."

"I'll see what I have to make a cough syrup from." She watched him wipe his watering eyes with his shirt sleeve. "And you'll not sleep on the ground tonight. You'll sleep in the wagon where I can take care of you."

Abner didn't protest, and that worried Megan as much as the cough. Previously when she'd suggested it was too cold to sleep on the ground he'd laughed at her concern. Had he been feeling poorly for days without telling her?

Later that day they stopped at a small trading post run by a filthy-smelling Frenchman and an Indian squaw. Megan was never sure whether the squaw was the man's wife or merely the only woman around to work in the trading post and warm his bed.

The log building was small and dark, with an earth floor. They stopped there only long enough to buy a few supplies from the Frenchman's meager store. Grass for the animals had been scarce for three days, and the train's livestock feed had been depleted the previous day. But the Frenchman had no feed for sale.

The day was cold, cloudy and very windy—more like November than June. They left the trading post disheartened, deciding to travel another mile or two before darkness overtook them.

They made camp in gloomy gray dusk, amid the bawling of hungry cattle. Megan and Abner's supper consisted of hot, thick gruel made from cornmeal and sweetened with honey.

"This is good, Meggie," Abner said as he wolfed it down. "The heat soothes my sore throat."

"This is the first I've heard of a sore throat." She was exasperated with his refusal to take care of himself. "How long has it been sore?"

"Awhile," he said vaguely. "All that dust we been through scraped it raw, I reckon."

At least his appetite hadn't been affected, Megan told herself. After supper she arranged his bedding in the wagon and insisted that he get ready for bed. She gave him a dose of the cough syrup. She had concocted it earlier that day from a combination of honey and vinegar heated with elm bark and rosemary and then strained and mixed with a small portion of whiskey.

"You need a good night's sleep," she said. "I'll check the animals before I go to bed."

"I won't argue with you, Meggie," Abner replied. "I feel like I been rode hard and put up wet."

Abner was sleeping by the time Megan retired, but she awoke later to hear him thrashing in his sleep. She pulled on her warm flannel robe and went to him. Kneeling, she murmured, "Abner," and smoothed his brow, then felt his long johns just below his chin. They were drenched with sweat.

"Abner." She shook his shoulder gently.

"Wh-what?" He struggled to a sitting position. "What's wrong, Meggie?"

"You're wringing wet." She rose. "I'll get your dry underwear." She found the long johns by touch in the trunk and handed them to him. "Put these on."

He complied, modestly undressing and dressing again beneath his covers, even though it was too dark for Megan to see anything. He threw the wet long johns aside and she spread them on top of the trunk to dry.

Then he started coughing, and she gave him another dose of cough syrup. He settled back amid his covers. "How long have you had night sweats?" she asked.

"It ain't nothing to worry about, Meggie." From the sound of his voice, she knew he had turned his back on her. Megan took off her robe and crawled into her bedroll. He hadn't answered her question, she realized. She must watch him more closely—she'd insist that he sleep in the wagon every night until he was himself again, she vowed as she stared anxiously into the darkness. It was some time before she slept again.

When Megan awoke, Abner was gone. She dressed and started to roll up his bedding. But upon discovering that the quilt on which Abner had slept was damp, she spread it near his underwear to dry.

As they ate their breakfast she studied Abner more closely than usual. He had always been thin, but she thought he'd grown even thinner lately. Of course, the hard physical work and sometimes spare rations had ensured that most of the party were thinner than when they'd started. Megan had noticed that her own dresses were loose at the waist.

Abner ate heartily and left to feed the oxen a portion of their cornmeal before hitching them to the wagon. Encouraged by his continuing good appetite, Megan told herself that perhaps he wasn't seriously sick, as she'd feared, but merely exhausted.

She managed to shrug off her worry and pack their belongings back in the wagon. Then she climbed up onto the seat and guided the team into their place in line. Once the train was moving forward, she jumped down with the whip Abner had bought at a roadside trading post to replace the one she'd lost in the dust storm.

A few minutes later, she saw Aaron Schiller and asked him to walk beside her team for a while so she could check on Ben, who'd been sick the past two days.

Rose and Mary were in the wagon with Ben when Megan joined them. "How is he?"

"A little better," Rose said. "He's sleeping. That elixir you mixed up helps him rest. This journey is hard on the little ones."

"It's hard on everybody," Megan said. "Abner has a terrible cough. He broke out in such a sweat last night his underwear and bedding were wet. He insists he's all right, but I can't help being worried about him."

"Reuben hacked all night long the other night, too," Rose said. "But he was all right the next day. It's these cold nights."

"I saw Mrs. Glenhill lose her breakfast this morning," Mary put in. "She was as white as a ghost."

"Lacey's ain't a permanent condition," Rose observed. "Being in the family way takes some women like that at the first. Now me, I felt as healthy as a horse when I was carrying you children." She chuckled. "Ate like one, too."

"I think I'll find some of the girls to walk with," Mary said, getting up. "Do you want me to stay with Ben later, Mama?"

"Come back about noon," Rose said, "and help Daniel and Laura keep an eye on Jude and Aaron, will you?"

"Yes'm."

Mary left and Megan said, "Aaron's with our wagon."

"Good," said Rose. "It'll keep him out of trouble." Her gaze swept Megan's narrow waist and flat stomach. "Be glad you're not with child like poor Lacey. You'll be lucky if you can manage to wait till we're settled in Oregon.''

Megan lowered her eyes, feeling her cheeks heating. What would Rose think if she knew that Megan could not possibly be pregnant because, though she'd been married for ten weeks, she had never had intimate relations with her husband?

"Yes, I am glad," she murmured.

Rose grinned. "I'm sorry if I embarrassed you, Megan. I keep forgetting you're still a bride and nearly as young as my Mary."

Avoiding Rose's gaze, Megan glanced out the opening at the end of the wagon toward a mountain that loomed to the north. "You didn't embarrass me. I..." Her voice trailed off as she noticed several riders in the distance. "Come here, Rose. Look at that."

Rose crawled over beside Megan. "Injuns," she muttered.

They watched in silence as the Indians came nearer. Suddenly Megan drew in a quick breath. "It looks like that band of Sioux we fed before."

"If they want more food, they're out of luck," Rose said. "We can't spare any more."

Megan felt a frisson of alarm. "They've been following us." She could think of no other reason for the band to have traveled so far from where they had first intercepted the wagon train.

"Maybe they're following the road, not us," Rose said. She was silent for a moment, then added, "All the same, I think I'll go talk to Jedediah—if you don't mind sitting with Benny for a few minutes, Megan."

"Of course I don't mind, you go on."

Rose returned shortly. "The men saw the Indians before we did," she said. "Jedediah has already posted extra armed guards to ride at the rear of the train to keep an eye on them."

The Sioux were visible in the distance all day, keeping pace with the wagon train. Their silent stalking wore on everybody's nerves. Megan was actually relieved when Jed called a halt and gave the order to circle the wagons. She felt more protected with the wagons forming a barrier between the party and the Indians.

As she was carrying a pot of beans to the Schiller wagon to combine her and Abner's supper with the Schillers', she saw Carolyn Goddard leave her wagon to talk to Jed and several other men. Carolyn seemed highly agitated.

"Rose, have you noticed Carolyn?" Megan asked. "I wonder what's wrong with her?"

"No telling," Rose said. Just then Thayer appeared leading a protesting Carolyn back to their wagon. "We'll soon find out," she continued. "Here come the menfolk."

Jed joined the Schillers and the Claunches for supper that evening. "What was Carolyn saying?" Rose inquired as she served the men.

"She saw the Sioux," Reuben replied.

"Wanted us to talk to them about Johnny," Abner said. "Ask 'em if they'd seem him."

Megan noticed the three men exchange shuttered glances. She knew what they were thinking. The Sioux may well have seen Johnny. They might be responsible for his disappearance. They might even have killed him. But it would do no good to question them about it—it might even precipitate an attack.

"What do the Injuns want, Jedediah?" Rose asked.

"Food, maybe," Jed replied. "More likely, our horses. They count their wealth by the number of horses they own. When we saw them the first time and they asked for food, they were probably trying to find out how many men and firearms we have."

Laura spoke up. "I wish they'd quit following us. They make me feel uneasy."

"Maybe that's their intention," Jed said. "They could be trying to wear us down so we'll agree to any demands they might make."

Just as they finished the meal, Thayer Goddard ran up to them and announced, "I can't find Carolyn."

Jed shot to his feet. "Damn it, Thayer, I told you not to leave her alone."

"I had to get water," Thayer said defensively. "She hasn't drunk a swallow all day. I thought if I got fresh water...anyway, when I got back to the wagon she was gone."

"Where could she be?" Megan asked.

"Gone after them Injuns, I imagine," Thayer said disgustedly. "That's all she's talked about ever since she caught sight of 'em. Won't open her mouth for days, then she won't shut up about them Injuns. The woman's deranged. I swear, I don't know what I'm going to do with her."

"You'll not have to worry about that," Jed said angrily, "if we can't find her." He turned to Reuben. "Come with us, Thayer. She can't have gone far on foot. We may be able to locate her before dark."

"I'll come, too," Abner offered.

Jed's gaze raked Abner's gaunt frame. "I'd feel better if you'd stay here and take charge of the train while we're gone," he said, and Megan shot him a grateful look.

The rest watched as the three men saddled their horses and rode off. "I stand sentry tonight," Abner said. "I better go and get ready."

"I'm sure you could get somebody to relieve you," Megan protested. "You shouldn't be in the cold night air with that cough."

He patted her shoulder fondly. "I been in the night air most every night of my life, Meggie. You just get yourself some rest and don't worry about me."

"Men," said Rose when Abner was out of earshot. "You can't tell them a thing."

Laura and Mary washed the dirty dishes while Megan and Rose had another cup of coffee. "I think I'll stay here with you until the men get back," Megan said.

"None of us will rest easy until they do, anyway," Rose said. "I hope they aren't gone long."

"Do you think they'll find her, Mama?" Laura asked.

"Yes, I think they will. Like Jed said, she couldn't have gone far on foot."

Laura hung her dish towel on the corner of the wagon bed. "Maybe the Indians got her." She sounded tense.

"Hush that kind of talk, Laura," Rose warned. "You'll scare the other younguns so bad they won't sleep a wink tonight."

"I ain't afraid of Injuns," Jude announced grandly.

"No need to be, with our men on guard," Rose said, not very convincingly. "Now, Jude, you go help Benny get ready for bed. We'll be sleeping in the wagon tonight."

"It's too early to go to bed," Ben protested, even though he had been nodding over his plate moments before.

"Not when you been sick for two days," Rose said. "Now go with Jude."

"Mary, will you tell us a story?" Jude begged.

"I'll go with you, Mary," Laura offered.

A few minutes later, Daniel left for his stint at guard duty. Megan and Rose sat and waited alone as it grew dark. They heard the horses before they saw them. They jumped up and hurried to the opening in the circle of wagons through which the men would pass. They could make out three horses and riders silhouetted against the night sky.

"Thank God," Rose said, "they're all right."

A moment later, Megan made out another figure mounted in front of one of the men. "They found Carolyn!"

The men rode into the circle of wagons and dismounted. Jed reached up to lift Carolyn off his horse. "There you go, Carolyn," he said as he set her on her feet. "You get to bed now and try to rest." He spoke as though he were talking to a frightened child.

Carolyn just stood there rigidly, and Megan and Rose went to her. "We were all so worried about you, Carolyn," Megan said. "Are you all right?"

Carolyn didn't answer. She gave no indication of having heard.

"She'll be fine in the morning," Thayer said.

"I'll take care of your horse for you, Thayer," Reuben said.

Carolyn showed no sign of moving from the spot where Jed had set her. After a moment, Thayer lifted her in his arms and carried her to their wagon.

"That poor, poor woman," Rose murmured.

Reuben put his arm around his wife's waist. "Come on to bed, Rosie," he said wearily. "I'm dead on my feet." They walked away, leaving Megan and Jed alone.

"What's wrong with Carolyn?" Megan asked.

Instead of answering, Jed began unsaddling his horse. Megan wished she could see him better in the darkness so that she could judge his thoughts from his face. Was the answer to her question so terrible that Jed didn't want to tell her? He patted the stallion and the horse whinnied and trotted toward the other corralled horses at the opposite side of the circle wagons.

Still ignoring her, Jed hefted the saddle and walked toward his wagon. His attitude irritated her. Determined to have an answer to her question, she followed him. He threw the saddle into his wagon bed before turning around.

"Where's Abner?"

"On guard duty," Megan retorted. "What's wrong with Carolyn, Jed?"

Heaving a sigh, he took off his hat and tossed it into the wagon. "I don't want to talk about it here," he said quietly. He reached back in the wagon and brought out a coat. "Put this around you. It's getting chilly. Let's walk away from the wagons a little way." He draped the coat over her shoulders and Megan shivered, though she couldn't have said if it was from the night's chill or the fact that Jed had touched her. She pulled the coat together in front and followed him wordlessly.

An alert sentry approached them. Jed identified himself and the man lowered his rifle and returned to his post. Nothing was said until they'd walked several hundred yards from the camp. The night was dark, a quarter moon hazily visible through cloud cover. Megan thought about the Sioux who'd been following them all day and shivered. She was glad that Jed carried a handgun in his holster.

Jed stopped, but kept his back to her for a moment. "Jed?" she said anxiously. "What's wrong? Why was Carolyn so strange when you brought her back?"

Reluctantly he turned to face her. Her features were dim, but he knew that she was frowning with concern for her friend. He took a deep breath. His chest felt heavy, laden with the sadness of a woman who had lost her only child. "I think Carolyn's decided to die, Megan."

When they had found Carolyn, her rigid face and glazed eyes had reminded him of Penelope's. His wife had had that same look when he found her and took her away from the trapper, a vile savage, more animal than man. Jed had killed him as he would have killed an attacking grizzly, without a qualm of conscience, but that had changed nothing as far as Penelope was concerned.

"What do you mean . . . how do you know?"

"She's gone inside herself. She can't even hear you when you talk to her."

"She's just weak," Megan insisted. "Half the time she doesn't eat, and she hasn't been getting any exercise. Walking a long distance exhausted her, that's all. She'll improve once she's rested and—" She stopped talking when he placed a hand on her shoulder and squeezed gently.

"It's more than exhaustion," he said softly. "When we found Carolyn she'd stumbled on the Sioux camp. Thank God, she stopped before they heard her. They were sitting around a campfire, eating. Carolyn was sprawled on her stomach behind a hill, watching them. By the time we got there, I don't think she was seeing them or anything else anymore."

"But—"

His hand moved on her shoulder. "Let me finish, Megan. One of the Indians had a scrap of cotton cloth tied around his neck. It was a piece of the shirt Johnny was wearing when he disappeared."

Megan gasped. "Oh, dear God . . . poor Carolyn . . . oh, Jed—"

His fingers clenched, gripping her shoulder convulsively. "This is no place for any but the strongest women," he said roughly. "And Oregon isn't much better. It's still a wilderness, Megan. I've seen what it can do to a delicate woman."

He sounded so odd, almost angry, his voice thick with feeling. "You don't think I'm strong enough, is that it? You still believe I shouldn't have come."

After a moment, his hand on her shoulder relaxed. His thumb stroked the side of her neck. "You're stronger than I believed at first," he said musingly, "stronger than most of the women in our party. But, Megan, strong women can still die."

She puzzled over his words, the obvious depth of emotion behind them. "Jed, what did you mean, you've seen what Oregon can do to a delicate woman? Was your wife delicate? Did—"

"Shhh—" he said sharply, and his hand slipped below the collar of the coat she wore to curl around the back of her neck. "No more questions, Megan. Some things are best forgotten."

She didn't think he had forgotten, though. There had been too much pain in his voice. She lifted a hand to his face and felt the hard angle of his jaw. "Jed, I'm sorry."

His fingers captured her hand and brought it to his lips. He planted a warm, moist kiss in her palm. "Megan..." he said tenderly, "it's not at all wise for you to touch me. You shouldn't ..."

"I know," she murmured, but she didn't draw her hand away.

Suddenly, with an anguished sound of surrender, he pulled her into his arms. Holding her tightly, he crushed her to him, burying his face in her hair. Her throat closed achingly. She couldn't speak. She could only cling to him, filling her senses with the warmth and strength of him. He smelled of horse and the elements. The muscles of his arms, his midsection and legs were taut and straining toward her. His heartbeat was like the thunder of galloping horses, and his breath was warm and heavy in her hair. She wished she could stay like that forever, protected and sheltered in Jed's arms.

"I shouldn't be doing this," he said, his voice husky and shaken. He lifted his head. "I promised myself I wouldn't touch you again." His breath against the skin of her forehead was as intimate as a kiss.

She, too, had made promises to herself. But when Jed held her...

Jed, so strong and vital....

How could she keep promises made in the cold light of reason when she was in his arms and reason had fled? She could only tighten her arms around him and lift her face in invitation as his mouth sought blindly and desperately for hers.

Their need for each other overwhelmed them, surging through them with a power that ripped through their self-imposed restraints. Megan's blood sang with joy and relief and love, and she reveled in the taste and feel and scent of him.

His mouth tasted deeply of her; his arms tightened around her. She grew dizzy with the wonder of it, and her mouth clung to his hungrily, unable to get enough of him. Her hands crept to the back of his head to stroke his hair, her fingers burying themselves among the thick strands. The coat fell from her shoulders, but she felt no chill. Jed's heat surrounded her.

He groaned and his hands dived into her hair, scattering pins. His hot, restless mouth moved over her face, feathering feverish kisses over her forehead and the bridge of her nose, following the curve of her cheek, kissing her eyes closed. His fingers tangled in the heavy fall of her hair, stroking through its silken length.

"Jed," she whispered, "Jed..."

His hands clutched the back of her head. "Megan, I want you... I need... oh, God, I can't—"

Again his mouth claimed hers, hard and demanding. With a faint cry of mingled surrender and despair, she wound her arms around him and pressed against him, her body aching to get closer.

She trembled with weakness as his mouth moved to her throat and his hand traced the curve of her hip, the dip of her waist, and molded to the side of her breast. She drew a ragged breath as his fingers closed over the swell of her breast and his palm pressed against the hardness of the nipple. His breath heated her throat and his tongue dipped into the hollow at its base, and she felt drunk and dizzy. Glorious spirals of pleasure spread through her as his hand stroked her. Fire rushed through her blood, causing a tight, tingling sensation in the pit of her stomach.

Jed was drowning in the warm flesh of her throat and the ripe curve of her breast. Every little gasp, every soft moan drove him closer to the edge. Soon he knew he would be out of control, beyond caring about right and wrong, beyond anything but his desperate, searing need for her. If only she would stop him . . . but she was all fire and willing weakness in his arms. He felt a new wave of weakness pour through him and he was helpless beneath the onslaught of desire. God help me . . . don't let me do this. . . .

From the opposite side of the camp, the dim cry of one of the guards penetrated Jed's whirling consciousness. "Abner," the guard called, "oh, there you are . . . thought you'd gone to sleep."

Abner, still weak from his fever, stood sentry while he led Abner's wife out of the camp and made love to her. Jed's gut knotted in self-loathing, and he tore his mouth from Megan's. With hands that shook, he disengaged her hands from his neck and lowered them to her sides. It was the hardest thing he'd ever done in his life.

"We can't, Megan," he said hoarsely.

Megan stood without moving, waiting for her head to stop spinning and the throbbing of her body to ebb. As the clamoring sensations eased and her mind cleared, the unfairness of what she had been willing to let happen—had wanted desperately to happen—rushed in on her, filling her with regret and shame.

She had never imagined that love could hurt so much. "You're right, Jed," she whispered brokenly. "Thank God you were strong enough to stop us, for I wasn't. I never thought I could be so weak, until I met you." Before the tears that were gathering could spill over, she turned and ran back toward camp.

Jed moaned her name softly, but she didn't hear him and he knew it was best that she hadn't. He must get hold of himself, for he could not avoid Megan altogether. To do so would cause too much talk among the members of their party. Besides, he couldn't treat her with unkindness. His opinion of her had changed in the days since Independence. He was no longer convinced she'd tricked Abner into marrying her just to get to Oregon, where she could ply her former trade. He was beginning to believe she had always meant to leave her old life behind for good.

Chapter Eleven

Gunshots ripped through the fabric of the night. The sounds jerked Megan from sleep. She sat up, clutching the covers around her. "Abner?"

In the silence that followed, she remembered that Abner wasn't there—he was on guard duty. Abner! She scrambled from her bedroll and groped frantically around her in the darkness for her clothes.

She heard people calling excitedly to one another from their tents or wagons. Her fingers felt the rough fabric of her gray dress. She pulled off her gown and dropped the homespun over her head, too anxious to concern herself with underclothing. Her fingers fumbled with buttons as she shoved her feet into a pair of boots.

Twisting her hair with one hand to keep it out of her face, she picked her way through the jumble of boxes and cartons to the end of the wagon and climbed out.

She saw a man hurrying past and called, "Wait! What's happened?"

The man stopped. "Megan?"

She recognized David Glenhill's voice. "Oh, it's you, David. I didn't know you in the darkness." She hugged herself against the night chill. "Have you seen Abner? He's on guard duty tonight."

David Glenhill hurried over to her and took her arm. "I haven't seen anyone. I heard shots and was going to investigate. Come with me."

A few people had congregated near the opening in the circle of wagons. David and Megan ran toward them. "I never heard a thing until it was too late, Jed," Abner was saying. "Injuns can move as quick as lightning and as silent as shadows."

Megan went to Abner and grabbed his arm. "I heard gunshots and thought . . . oh, Abner thank goodness you aren't hurt."

He patted her hand. "Nobody's hurt, Meggie, but those heathen stole some of our horses. Cut the rope and came right in here, and me none the wiser."

Megan shivered at the thought of Indians slipping silently through the camp while they all slept. They must have been only a few feet from where she had lain, unaware.

"What about you, Bert?" Jed asked. "Did you hear anything?" Until he spoke, Megan hadn't recognized any of the other men in the group. Now that her eyes were growing accustomed to the darkness, she could pick out Bert Olmstead's stocky form.

"Just the horses running after the Indians got away from the camp," Bert replied. "That's when I started shooting. I think I winged one of 'em. I heard him yelp like he'd been hit. Hope I killed the thieving dog."

"Do you know how many horses are missing?" Jed asked.

"Five, for sure," Abner said. "Maybe more. We can't get a good head count till daylight."

"They'll be miles away by then," Jed muttered with obvious discouragement.

"I fired three times myself," Abner put in. "Maybe I got one of 'em, too. Their wounded could slow 'em down."

"They won't let that hamper their getaway," Jed told him. "Anybody who can't keep up gets left behind."

Megan remembered the wounded Indian in the dugout and knew Jed was right. By morning the stolen horses would be far away.

"Damned no account bas—" Olmstead muttered, then caught himself as he remembered a woman was present and added, "Excuse me, ma'am."

"You're shivering, Meggie," Abner said. "Go on back to bed. We ain't gonna see them Indians again tonight."

"I'll walk you back," David offered quickly. Megan had almost forgotten his presence. He hadn't said a word since they'd joined the other men.

She took David's arm and they walked away from the men. "I guess we should feel lucky they stole horses instead of children," Megan said.

"This whole thing makes me so angry and sad," David told her. "It merely proves the harmful influence whites have had on the Indians."

Megan darted a surprised look at David's shadowed face. "I don't understand you. The Indians stole from us, not the other way around."

"Where do you think the Indians learned to steal?"

"That's assuming a lot, David."

"You don't know their culture," he said impatiently. "They don't understand that stealing is wrong. They're like children who ape the behavior of the adults around them, Megan."

Megan felt a sudden flash of fear for David Glenhill, who was going, blithely and blindly, into a wilderness with some romantic vision of taming childlike natives. He knew no more about the culture of the Indians than she. He'd merely created a culture in his imagination that appealed to his romantic nature.

"You're being naive, David," she said flatly. "There must be good Indians and bad Indians, even by their own standards. And their standards aren't even civilized ones."

"Because they are different from us, you fail to appreciate the natural nobility of the red man, the—"

"Nobility!" Megan's patience with David's stubborn blindness where the Indians were concerned came to an abrupt end. She halted and faced him. "Let me tell you how noble the Sioux are, David. They stole a four-year-old child from his family, carried him off—probably to be tortured and killed. Don't talk to me about the red man's nobility!''

"You don't know that, Megan," David said, sounding stunned by her accusation. "Nobody knows what happened to Johnny Goddard."

"Apparently you haven't heard. The last time Carolyn ran off she found the Sioux camp. The men caught up with her before the Sioux spotted her, but not before she saw a piece of Johnny's shirt tied around the neck of one of them. Is it any wonder Carolyn's in the state she's in? Can't you just imagine the visions she's conjured up since she saw that scrap of fabric?''

He had taken a step back as Megan talked, as though to protect himself from her barrage of words. "I—well—people can't be held accountable for what—''

Exasperated, Megan cut him off. "Oh, never mind. I'm going to bed." She turned on her heels and left him standing there, still trying to come up with a more palatable explanation for the fact that a Sioux warrior was sporting a piece of Johnny Goddard's shirt.

By the time Megan reached her wagon, her irritation with David was already turning to pity. The poor innocent had no idea what he would have to deal with if he stuck to his resolve to work among the Indians to convert them to what he was convinced was their "lost heritage." David was heading for sad disillusionment.

Sighing, she climbed up into the pitch-black interior of her wagon. She yawned and started to unbutton her dress. Then her hand stilled as she sensed a furtive movement in the darkness.

Her heart jerked in alarm. A shiver of fear ran up her spine and pricked the base of her skull. "Abner?" she whispered.

She heard a grunt and another movement, as swift as the dive of a hawk, and a hand covered her mouth. The intruder had moved behind her, and his arm imprisoned her against him. The unpleasant smell of him was overpowering. Megan swayed and almost fainted in terror.

He brought his mouth close to her ear. "No move. No talk." The guttural voice shot terror through Megan. An Indian had entered her wagon . . . waited for her! What did he mean to do?

Pure panic swept over her and she began to struggle, clawing at his arm, screaming silently into the dirty hand clamped over her mouth.

"No!" he commanded. "Be still. I bring boy to Medicine Woman."

Megan continued her futile struggling until his words slowly penetrated the hysteria clouding her brain. Boy, he had said. What boy? She grew still, her chest heaving. If only he would move his hand—she couldn't get enough air.

They stood there in tense, unmoving silence for a few moments, like children in a game of Statues. "Let me go," she tried to say. "I can't breathe." But her words were muffled noises behind his hand.

After another moment, he lifted his hand fractionally. "No talk," he said sternly. "Be still."

She nodded, hoping her acquiescence was communicated to him in the darkness. He waited for what seemed an eternity before he dropped his arm and stepped back. She whirled around, but could see only a faint, black outline of a man's head and shoulders. Growing in Megan was the feeling that his voice was familiar. What had he called her?

"You save life, Medicine Woman," he said in a low voice. "I bring boy. He sleep." He stood there for another moment, then slipped quietly from the wagon. With a little cry, Megan stumbled to the end of the wagon and peered out. She could see nothing, and she didn't hear the sounds of his retreat. How could he move so quietly?

She remembered the strength of his arm clamped around her and trembled. What if he hadn't felt grateful to her? But he had called her "Medicine Woman." Obviously he had recovered completely from his wound. She had saved his life, he'd said. And he . . . Suddenly she crouched down and felt her way over cartons and around boxes. She found her bedroll and ran her hand over it. She touched something solid, a small foot.

"Johnny?" she cried.

The boy stirred and mumbled something in his sleep. Oh, thank God, it was Johnny, and he was alive! They hadn't killed him. She had heard of white children being abducted by Indians and raised as members of the tribe. Perhaps that was to have been Johnny's fate, but the Indian whose life she had saved had brought him back to her in payment. Odd, she didn't even know the Indian's name.

She touched Johnny's face, felt his tangled hair. "Oh, Johnny, are you all right?"

He mumbled again and then, with a cry of alarm, sat up. She put her arms around him and held him tight. "Shh, it's all right, Johnny. You're back with the wagon train now. Shh, don't cry."

Johnny threw his arms around her and clung to her. "Mama," he whimpered. "I want my mama."

"I'll take you to her, honey." Megan rose and lifted him to his feet. "Let's get out of the wagon, and I'll carry you."

Clutching the dirty, exhausted child, Megan hurried as fast as she dared through the darkness to where she remembered seeing the Goddard wagon earlier that evening. She didn't know where Thayer Goddard was sleeping tonight. He had ignored Jed's order to always sleep close to the wagon. But Carolyn would be there, her determination to find her son finally broken.

Hugging Johnny's warm little body against her, Megan thrust her head through the canvas opening. "Carolyn," she called. "Wake up, Carolyn. I have Johnny. He's come home."

"Who's there? Who is it?" Carolyn's voice was sharp and alert, as though she hadn't been asleep at all.

"It's Megan, Carolyn. I've brought Johnny."

Johnny struggled out of Megan's arms and crawled into the wagon. "Mama?"

Recognizing her child's voice, even in the state of living death in which she had existed for weeks, Carolyn choked out, "Johnny!" Megan heard Carolyn stumbling through the wagon. When she reached Johnny and felt his solid little body in her arms, she burst into tears. Megan waited outside, not wanting to intrude, until Carolyn stopped crying and began talking excitedly to the child.

Carolyn was oblivious to anyone else's presence. Dashing a tear from her cheek, Megan turned away and returned to her wagon. If she had known where Thayer was sleeping, she would have told him that Johnny was back. Since she had no idea, she went to bed. Thayer would learn the good news from Carolyn in the morning.

By the time Megan awoke the next morning, the news of Johnny's return was already spreading through the camp. Several people approached her, as she was cooking breakfast, wanting to know how she had found Johnny. Somehow she didn't think they'd understand about her nursing and feeding the wounded Indian. And she wasn't sure she could explain. She knew only that she would do the same thing again.

She said the same thing to everyone who asked. "I was disturbed by the gunshots last night and went to find Abner. When I returned to my wagon, I found Johnny in my bed. I have no idea how he got there. You'll have to ask him."

Jed, hearing her say this to one of the women, eyed her thoughtfully and might have questioned her with more persistence than the others, but at that moment Rose Schiller ran up to him, wringing her hands.

"Jedediah, come quick! Benny's been bit by a rattler and I can't find Reuben."

Jed ran to the Schiller wagon. Megan left Abner eating breakfast to see if she could be of any help. Jed had opened the snakebite wound with his knife and sucked out the poison. Ben was sitting in his mother's lap, crying.

"Is there anything I can do?" Megan asked.

Rose hugged her son and shook her head. "I think he'll be all right," Jed said, "but he might be sick for a day or two."

"Have you fixed breakfast, Rose?" Megan asked.

"No—when I heard Benny screaming, I clean forgot about it. Mary and Laura can do it. I sent them after water. They should be back any minute." She gave Jed a wan smile. "Thank you, Jedediah. I couldn't think what to do. I was in a panic."

Jed laid a hand on the child's head for a moment. "You'll be fine, Ben. I got the nasty old poison out of your leg."

"I'll get your breakfast started, Rose," Megan offered after Jed left. "The girls can take over when they get back."

Rose put Ben to bed in the wagon and came back out to help her. "Poor Benny. Everything happens to him." She started mixing flapjack batter. "I heard about you finding Johnny Goddard in your wagon last night, Megan," Rose went on. "Strangest thing I ever heard. Do you reckon he's been wandering around, lost, all this time and just happened to stumble on our camp?"

"No, I think he was with the Sioux—don't forget that scrap of his shirt Carolyn saw on the Indian. How he got away from them and back to us, I couldn't say. I'm just grateful that he did. Now Carolyn will be herself again."

"I hope so," Rose said with no great conviction. "She's been through more than a lot of women could take and keep their right minds."

Megan remembered Jed's saying that this was no place for any but the strongest women and wondered if Carolyn's store of strength had been used up in grieving.

During the next several days, Carolyn resumed the activities she'd abandoned when Johnny had disappeared. Megan watched her go about her duties and made a special effort to engage her in conversation. Carolyn seemed to be slowly returning to normal, but she remained obsessed with her son. She was unwilling to let Johnny out of her sight. Megan also noticed a change in Carolyn's attitude toward Thayer. She ignored him most of the time, and on the rare occasions when Megan saw Carolyn look at her husband there was hatred in her eyes.

A week after Johnny's return, Megan confided to Rose her concern about Carolyn's attitude toward her husband. "I know he wasn't very sympathetic with Carolyn's prolonged grieving," Megan said, "but she has to forget that and look ahead, or her marriage will never be right again."

"I'm afraid there's too much for Carolyn to forget," Rose responded.

"Well, I know Thayer went all over the camp complaining about Carolyn and saying she was deranged to anybody who would listen."

"It's not only that," Rose said. "It's his brutish behavior." She sighed, then added, "Don't breathe a word of this to anyone else, but the night after Carolyn got Johnny back, I had a backache and couldn't sleep. I got dressed and went for a walk to keep from disturbing Reuben. I heard Thayer and Carolyn in their wagon...mostly it was Thayer I heard, berating Carolyn and calling her dimwitted and a poor excuse for a wife. He was so loud he woke Johnny, and Carolyn trying to shush him the whole time. Then—well, then he forced himself on her, pure and simple. I'd convinced myself I'd misjudged Thayer that other time—the one I told you about. But this time there was no mistake. He claimed his husbandly right, as he called it, with Johnny and Carolyn both crying and begging him to stop."

"Oh, no—"

"I don't think little Johnny knew what was happening— he just knew Thayer was hurting his mother."

"He must have been frightened out of his wits."

"Remember," Rose cautioned, "don't speak of this to anyone else. It won't help Carolyn if Thayer hears talk critical of him going around."

Megan agreed. Though she would have liked to go to Carolyn and offer to take her and Johnny into her and Abner's wagon, she realized that would probably make things worse for Carolyn in the long run, since Carolyn and

Johnny would have to go with Thayer when they reached Oregon.

As the last days of June passed, Megan was too busy to keep an eye on Carolyn or even to think about her very often. A fever spread through the train like a prairie fire, and Abner was one of the first to come down with it. His cough had hung on, weakening his resistance, and with the fever he developed chest congestion and his night sweats returned.

For days they had been passing travelers heading back East with tales of cholera sweeping through wagon trains. When the first members of their party fell ill with the fever, Megan feared it was the beginning of a cholera epidemic. But when the severe stomach cramps and diarrhea of the dread disease didn't develop, that particular fear abated, and Megan spent her days and much of her nights caring first for Abner and, when he was resting quietly, for the other sick members of the party.

She brewed the strong boneset tea every day and carried it to all the wagons where the fever had struck. At each wagon she left instructions that the patient be given plenty of water and that his feet be kept as warm as possible, even when he was sweating and didn't want the lightest cover touching him. Mrs. Valentine had impressed upon Megan the importance of keeping the feet of fever patients warm. When she tended a patient who was delirious or huddled in blankets, shaking with a violent chill, she wished she had a few drops of laudanum to administer so they could have a few hours' rest.

Abner's condition improved somewhat as long as he stayed in bed, but as soon as he felt a little better, he was up and about, despite Megan's pleading.

Before the fever left the stricken, four more of the party had been buried beside the trail. By that time Megan was worn out and disheartened.

One evening Jed saw her going to the river for fresh water and followed her. Catching up with her, he took the bucket from her hand and walked beside her.

"Are you going to keep on taking care of other people until you drop?" he asked accusingly.

She looked up at him with a tired smile. "Don't worry about me, Jed. I must have extraordinarily good health or I'd have caught something by now."

"It's extraordinarily good luck, I think. But no one has good luck all the time. Yours could run out any day." They reached the river and walked along the bank until they found a place where it sloped gently to the water.

As Jed went down to fill the bucket, Megan sat on a smooth, flat rock in a lopsided circle of scrubby willow trees. The sun had set, and she pulled her wool shawl close around her to protect against the cool air that settled over the mountains when the sun dropped from sight.

She leaned back against a tree trunk and closed her eyes. She didn't open them again until she heard Jed coming up the bank with the water. He set the bucket beside the rock and, stuffing his hands in his pockets, gazed down at her. She looked up at him, her head cocked.

"Were you sleeping?" he asked gently.

"No, just relaxing for a minute." She stirred and started to get up, but he placed his hands on her shoulders and pressed her down again.

"You can relax for a few more minutes. God knows you need it."

She studied him gravely. "Do you know what you are? The pot calling the kettle black. You work harder than I do, Jed. I watched you yesterday when we had to pull the wagons up that steep cliff. All the other men rested every little while and let somebody else take their place. But you stayed on that rope for hours without a break. Let me see your hands." She reached out and caught his wrists, turning them palms up. They were ridged with calluses that had formed since they'd left Independence, and an angry red from the rope burns he'd suffered the previous day.

Megan drew in a sharp breath at the sight and smoothed her thumb over the reddest welt. "Oh, Jed, you'll get an infection if you don't take better care of your hands."

He watched her with an odd expression, but didn't pull his hands away. "I rubbed some grease on them last night."

"I have a salve that will help. I'll give you some, and you should bandage these for a few days." Suddenly she became aware of the heat of his skin and let go of him. Looking away, she tightened the shawl around her shoulders.

After a moment he asked, "What really happened the night Johnny Goddard came back, Megan?"

She darted a quick look at his face. "I told you, I found Johnny asleep in my wagon."

"I know that's the story you've been telling, but I think there's a lot more to it than that. You don't have to confide in me, but if you do, it'll stay between the two of us."

She gave him a hesitant smile. He was the only one who hadn't accepted her story with no questions asked.

"Jed Dossman, you're too clever."

He grinned. "So what really happened?"

"Not long after Johnny disappeared, I found an abandoned dugout. There was a wounded Indian inside and I—well, I couldn't just leave him there to die, could I?"

He gaped at her. "You damn well could have."

"Well, I didn't. I dug the bullet out of his shoulder and gave him food and water. That's the last I saw of him until he brought Johnny to my wagon that night. I think he felt he had a debt to pay me for saving his life."

"You dug the bullet out? He could have killed you!"

She shook her head. "He was too weak to hurt anyone, Jed. I was in no danger."

He had known for a long time that she had strength. Now he realized just how much courage she possessed. He was learning new things about her all the time. "You are the most amazing woman," he said.

The caressing edge to his voice made her fearful of meeting his eyes. Gazing at the river, she groped for another topic of conversation. "Tomorrow's the first day of July," she pointed out. "It seems we've been traveling forever. I suppose I should feel encouraged because we've come halfway...."

"The worst part of the trip comes after we reach South Pass." Jed's tone had hardened and it caused her to look around at him. He was eyeing her intensely. "That's why I keep after you to get more rest. You're going to need your strength."

"I'll try," she promised, her gaze caught by his. "Most of our sick are recovering, except . . . oh, Jed, I'm so worried about Abner." Without any warning, her voice broke, and she bowed her head to hide the tears that sprang to her eyes. She cleared her throat. "He can't seem to shake that cough, and his chest stays congested all the time. He hasn't felt really well in ages. He thinks he hides it from me, but I can see him getting weaker every day."

Unable to resist touching her, Jed brushed a coiling black curl back off her forehead. She sounded so forlorn. His gentleness surprised her and she looked up at him warily. "You really care for Abner, don't you?" he asked.

She felt a little hurt that he seemed startled by her concern. "Of course I do. I'll never be able to repay him for—for all he's done for me."

"Yeah," he muttered. "I think I understand. He made you respectable when he married you."

She stared at him. This wasn't the first time he'd implied that marrying Abner had somehow saved her reputation. On the day they'd left Independence he'd said something about marriage making her "an honest woman." Was he referring to her attempt at posing as Abner's daughter? It was true she had lied about that, and somehow Jed had found her out. But she and Abner had been desperate to get away from Independence, and it had seemed a necessary lie. They hadn't hurt anyone by it.

A worrisome thought struck her. Was it possible that Jed knew about her background, knew about her mother's trade? No, she told herself, there was no way Jed could know that. Still, she didn't like how he'd said that her marriage had made her respectable. She didn't know quite why, but it made her angry.

She stood abruptly, the sudden movement startling him. "Please excuse me," she said coolly. "I have to get back and cook supper."

As she brushed past him, he snagged her waist and forced her to stand there, facing him. "What's wrong, Megan?"

To her mortification, her bottom lip began to tremble. She lowered her lashes, trying to get control of herself. The truth was, she didn't know what was wrong with her. Why did the tiniest hint of ridicule from Jed hurt her so deeply? Maybe he hadn't even meant to mock her. She caught her bottom lip between her teeth to stop the trembling.

He took her chin in his fingers and lifted it gently. His eyes were dark and brooding. "I'm just tired," she said weakly.

Still he held her chin in his fingers and his eyes probed hers. "If it's what I said—I didn't mean to hurt your feelings, Megan. I never want to hurt you."

For a moment she looked at him and it felt as though the entire world had stopped. Somehow she and Jed had been sealed in a private little world of their own. In that moment, nobody else existed but the two of them. He gazed at her with yearning in his eyes and she gazed back, knowing what he was feeling because she was feeling it, too. It was a golden moment, brilliant and filled with emotion. She knew the second before it happened that he was going to kiss her, and she could do nothing to stop it.

"Oh, Jed . . ." she breathed helplessly in the instant before his mouth claimed hers.

Overpowering need rose up in both of them. Megan didn't know how it could have happened, but he drew her to the ground and she let him. The earth was hard and cold beneath her, but he wrapped her in his arms and his mouth tasted hers with a desperate hunger.

She moved her lips beneath his, parting them in invitation, as she clung tightly to him. Again and again her mouth drew his closer. She was unable to get enough of him.

Jed's heat covered her and his lips roamed the skin of her face and throat. Closing her eyes with a sigh of pleasure, she stroked his hair. If only they didn't have to go back to the wagon train. If only there were really just the two of them in all the world. If only...

Her thoughts spun away into sensation. Inside her there was a trembling, dizzying wonder, a mindlessness as his fingers loosed the buttons of her dress and his hand moved urgently beneath her underclothes to touch her naked breast. Groaning, he moved his mouth lower and, cupping her breast in his hand, kissed the warm rosy flesh.

His breath heated her skin and kindled a flame that traveled all the way to the center of her being. Megan gasped as he took her nipple into his mouth. The thrill of the hot, moist sensation made her senses reel with mounting pleasure as heat surged through her blood.

He reveled in the warm flesh of her breast, her taste, the sweet sensation of her taut nipple between his lips. His hand moved restlessly downward, finding her smooth, flat abdomen and the gentle curve of a hipbone. With every tightening of her arms around him, with every movement and every soft sound she made, he felt closer to losing his grip on his straining self-control.

Through an intoxicating daze, Megan felt his hand burrow beneath her skirts and push them up. The shock of cool air washing over her heated skin made her tremble. She opened her eyes and stared up at the dusky sky between the branches of a willow tree, and was assaulted by a flood of sensations. As his fingers brushed against her thigh, the terrible aching deep inside her intensified.

Dimly she was aware of the cold ground beneath her and Jed's unsteady breathing and her own wild, erratic heartbeat. And slowly she became aware of the recklessness of what was happening, of their compromising situation should anyone see them, of Abner back at camp, Abner, growing weaker every day.

With a shuddering effort of will, Megan gasped, "Please...oh, Jed, stop...you must." Pushing at his hands, she rolled away from him. She stood up, her knees trembling and threatening to collapse under her. After a few moments to get her breathing under control, she straightened her clothing and buttoned the front of her dress, never looking at him.

Jed got to his feet and watched her furtive, embarrassed movements. Desire for her was like a hot branding iron in his gut. "We wouldn't be hurting anyone," he said hoarsely. "Nobody would know." He heard the pleading sound of the words and hated himself.

Her face white, Megan clutched her shawl around her in an effort to still her shaking. "We would know, Jed," she whispered. "It's wrong. I'm a married woman." She couldn't stand the look of accusation and betrayal in his eyes and turned to stare unseeing at the river. "Please, just leave me. Please."

Jed stared at her for an endless moment. Then he uttered a hollow, angry sound and did as she had asked.

Chapter Twelve

July-August, 1850

Megan was awake most of the night, tending to Abner. When she'd returned from the river, she had found him huddled beneath every blanket and quilt they owned, shaking with a violent chill. Immediately guilt had overwhelmed her as she remembered how she had lingered by the river with Jed when Abner needed her.

She made a poultice of ground, dried horseradish leaves, applied it to the soles of his feet and wrapped them in clean rags. But he still shook, and she lay down with only the top blanket covering her and wrapped her arms around him, curling her body to the shape of his backside, adding her body heat to the blankets.

She held him until the chill left him and he fell into an exhausted sleep. Then, she lay awake, tortured by guilt. While she was forgetting her wedding vows with Jed, Abner had taken a turn for the worse. He'd needed her more than ever before, and she had been indulging herself with the forbidden kisses of another man.

Was Abner's illness a judgment from God against Megan for betraying her husband? The Reverend Donovan's sermons had been full of thundered warnings about God's anger and judgment against the wicked, and as Megan lay curled around Abner, every warning she had ever heard from Donovan's pulpit echoed in her head.

After a while, she managed to push such thoughts away from her and remember the Reverend Valentine's loving, merciful and forgiving God. Over and over she prayed, Please forgive me, Lord. Help me be a better wife to Abner.

The next day Jed ordered Abner to stay in his wagon until Megan decided he was well enough to resume his duties. Megan thanked him stiffly and promised herself she would avoid being alone with Jed again.

On July 4, Independence Day, they traveled through dust from morning until night. That evening as they set up camp on the bank of Raft River, they were beset by swarms of gnats and mosquitoes. They hurried to gather the wild sagebrush that grew all around them, building big fires to ward off the insects.

Megan brewed a strong, medicinal tea and made hot broth from a rabbit Daniel Schiller had given her. She coaxed the tea and a cup of the broth down Abner and straightened his bedding. He'd burned with fever all day, but his temperature dropped with the coming of evening. Megan herself didn't eat until Abner was resting comfortably.

Abner's illness hung on, and Megan's days took on a weary sameness. She stayed with the wagon, tending Abner and driving the ox team forward. Rose Schiller offered to take over for a few hours so Megan could rest, but Megan refused. She had a duty to care for her husband and she wouldn't shift it to someone else. Perhaps she could atone a little for betraying Abner by falling in love with Jed.

She didn't see much of Jed and hardly spoke to him when she did. Several times she caught him watching her with an anxious expression on his face, and wished he wouldn't worry about her. She told herself that she didn't want Jed thinking about her at all. She told herself that she wanted him to forget her and the stolen kisses they had exchanged.

They traveled through country that Reuben Schiller called Digger Indian Country, but they saw no Indians. They crossed Swamp Creek and later Goose Creek, its high banks almost straight up and down.

At South Pass they traveled through snow, which excited the children. They had a snowball fight, while the adults watched with somber eyes, knowing that the worst of the trip still lay ahead of them.

One night in the middle of July, they camped on Rock Creek. For miles, tales of Indian scalpings at that place had traveled through the train. The men guarded the stock all night. Megan, along with most of the women, was so tense and frightened that she lay awake all night, waiting for the Indians to attack. They broke camp the next morning, greatly relieved that they had, by God's mercy, escaped an Indian raid.

The fever and chills finally left Abner, but they had wracked his body for so long that he teetered around the wagon, clutching at boxes to steady himself. He was so pale and weak that Megan worried about him constantly. When she was called upon to visit other sick people, she made her visits in haste and returned to Abner as soon as she could. Other men in the party took charge of the Claunches' wagon and livestock at every river and creek crossing.

Two more of Abner's longhorns died. They appeared to have been poisoned, and Abner said the animals had drunk bad water or eaten poisonous weeds. One or two head of livestock died almost daily now, and their party wasn't alone in their misfortune. They passed dead cattle every day along the trail.

The crossing at Bridge Creek was the worst since they'd started. The creek took its name from the natural rock bridge that spanned it. The bridge was just wide enough for one person to walk over it, and the crossing, with water roaring and tumbling fifteen feet below, was terrifying. The wagons had to be dismantled and ferried across farther up the river, where more livestock was lost to the swift, roaring water. They camped that night on solid rock, with camps of other emigrant parties all around them.

The one bright spot in their tortuous journey was that the Indians they came in contact with after leaving Rock Creek were peaceful and friendly. Better still, the red men had plenty of fish to trade cheaply. Megan and Abner feasted on fresh trout, bass and salmon for days.

When they crossed the Snake River in early August, they bargained with a band of Indians to swim the stock across and didn't lose a single head. Perhaps their luck was turning for the better, Megan thought. She was convinced of it when their tired, dirty bedraggled party reached Fort Hall south of the Snake River, and Jed announced they would rest there for two days to replenish supplies and repair wagons before going on.

To the weary travelers Fort Hall seemed like a palace. Its walls were constructed of thick, oak logs caulked with clay and the floors were made of wide wood slabs. There were stone fireplaces in the trading post, dining hall and barracks.

Megan had left her wagon and stock for Daniel Schiller to take care of while she walked with Rose Schiller, the five younger Schiller children, Carolyn and Johnny Goddard and a still weak Abner to the trading post attached to the fort.

The store seemed to be filled with hairy men clad in rough animal skin pants and tunics. They all stopped what they were doing to stare at the bedraggled settlers.

A Scotsman and his wife ran the trading post. While the man waited on Carolyn and Rose, the woman assisted Megan.

"We need everything," Megan said, trying not to dwell on their shrinking store of cash. "Cornmeal, oats, grain for the livestock, flour, molasses... well, you'd better add that up before I order anything else."

"We have a few fresh hen eggs," the woman said. She was small and swarthy skinned, and her eyes were a surprising bright green. "There won't be any more for a while, either. Our hens have about quit laying."

Megan hadn't seen fresh eggs in so long she'd forgotten
what they tasted like. "Just the thought of fresh eggs makes
my mouth water," she said, adding wistfully, "how much
do you want for them?"

The price the woman named was exorbitant. Fresh pro-
duce of any kind was as precious as gold on the wagon trail.
Any that was for sale was usually taken by trains traveling
ahead of theirs.

"I can let you have six," the woman said.

Megan swallowed. "I'll take three," she decided finally.
She'd fix two of them for Abner and have one herself.

"How about some fresh bacon to go with 'em?"

Megan could smell the bacon frying and couldn't resist
purchasing a small slab. In another corner of the store she
heard Ben and Jude Schiller clamoring for licorice sticks.

The strange men had gone back to talking in low, rough-
sounding voices. Occasionally one of them laughed loudly.
As the woman was sacking up Megan's grain and flour,
Megan noticed a big, burly, bearded man standing in a dim
corner apart from the others. He was staring at her.

She turned away quickly. "Who are these men?" she
asked the Scotswoman.

"Trappers. Ain't seen women and children in so long they
don't know how to act. Trappers are a breed unto themselves. This is a rough crew, but they're harmless, except
when they're drunk. But they ain't gonna cause no trouble
around here. We got more than seventy soldiers at the fort.
Major Southern don't hesitate to throw any man, soldier,
trapper or Indian into the stockade if he even looks like he
wants to start something."

"That one in the corner keeps staring at me."

The woman glanced up and shrugged. "He's a strange
one—quiet. I don't think he's with the others. Keeps to
himself. Pay him no mind."

Nevertheless Megan was glad to leave the trading post.
The way the big man kept staring at her made her skin crawl.
When she and Abner got back to camp with their supplies,
somebody had set up their tent for them.

Seeing it, Abner grumbled, "I hope I ain't gonna have to depend on somebody else to do my work for the rest of the trip."

"You're getting a little stronger each day," Megan told him, though in truth she was worried at how long it was taking for him to regain his strength. "Why don't you sit down and rest while I fix supper. I have a special treat for you."

"What is it?"

"Be patient. You'll see in a little while."

He grinned, "Oh, Meggie, you're a fine young woman, you are. Don't know what I'd have done these past few weeks without you to take care of me."

"Well, I don't know what I'd have done if you hadn't agreed to take me to Oregon. So it evens out. Now sit down before you fall down, Abner. That was a pretty strenuous walk to the trading post and back."

He grunted. "I wouldn't even be breathing hard if I had my normal strength." He sat in the opening of the tent and watched her build a fire from wood she'd bought from an Indian who hung around the fort. She mixed biscuit dough, forming fat, smooth rounds with her hands and arranging them in a pan. Setting a lid on the pan, she placed it at the edge of the fire to bake. The first few times she had baked biscuits over a wood fire, they'd been burned on the bottom and doughy in the middle. But by now her biscuits consistently came out golden brown and cooked clear through.

While the biscuits baked, she measured ground coffee into the big tin pot, then cut the bacon into thick slices, enjoying the delicious smell of the meat sizzling in the skillet.

"I know what the treat is," Abner called to her from the tent. "We ain't tasted bacon in a spell, but I still remember what it smells like. Hurry up, Megan. I'm hungry."

She smiled. "I can't hurry. I want this to be perfect. And, anyway, the biscuits aren't done yet."

When the bacon was fried just right, she poured some of the bacon grease into another pan, in which she scrambled the eggs. From the drippings left in the first pan she made gravy. Abner's eyes lit up when she carried him his plate.

"Is that eggs? Lord, I can't even remember when I last had an egg."

"They're very fresh," Megan said, sitting down beside him. Her tin coffee cup was balanced on the edge of her plate. "But so expensive I could only buy three. You know, we could get rich if we wanted to build a trading post somewhere along the western trail."

"Being a storekeeper ain't my idea of life, Meggie. I have to be outdoors, working with my hands."

"I know. I wasn't really serious. I want to see Oregon as much as you do. Sometimes I . . . oh, never mind."

"No, tell me."

She sipped the steaming coffee cautiously. "It's just, sometimes I wonder if we'll ever get to Oregon."

"We'll get there, Meggie—at least, some of us."

She looked at him sharply. "I wonder what you're thinking when you say things like that."

"I'm just being realistic, sugar. How many of our party have we lost already, ten—twelve? Stands to reason we'll lose more before we get there."

"Well, you and I are going to make it," Megan said staunchly.

He chuckled. "If it's up to you, we will for sure. I never seen a woman work as hard as you do and never have a sick day."

"I'm too stubborn to get sick," she said, and he laughed.

They heard footsteps approaching and looked up to see a tall, dark-haired man in a military uniform walking toward them. Abner set his plate down and got to his feet.

"Good afternoon, folks," the man said. "I'm Major Southern, commander at the fort."

"Abner Claunch, Major." The men shook hands. "This is my wife, Megan."

"How do you do, ma'am. Don't let me disturb your supper. Sit down, Claunch. Finish that fine-looking meal before it gets cold." Abner readily complied and Major

Southern went on, "Just came to invite you folks to a party in the dining hall tonight. We'll have eats and dancing—" he smiled at Megan "—if some of you ladies will favor us with your presence."

Abner looked at Megan. "What do you say, Meggie? Would you like to go?"

She hesitated. "Are you sure you feel up to it?"

"Shucks, I can sit in the dining hall as well as here." He looked up at the captain. "We'll be there, Major. Thanks for inviting us."

"Good. Now, if you'll excuse me, I have more invitations to deliver."

They watched Major Southern stride away. "I reckon we better enjoy this party while we can, Meggie. Ain't had one since April, and ain't likely to have another till we reach Oregon."

Whenever Megan looked back to that April evening when their party had celebrated the end of their first week on the trail, she could hardly believe how young and naive she'd been. She wondered if she would have wanted to turn back if she had known then what hardships they would face. Reflecting on it, she didn't think so, but it was just as well that she hadn't known. One of Mrs. Valentine's favorite Scriptures had been "Sufficient unto the day is the evil thereof." Megan hadn't really appreciated the Scripture then, but now she could see the blessing in not being able to look into the future.

"When we finish supper," she said, "I'll take the bucket and get fresh water. We can't go to a party without a bath."

"Heck, I was afraid you'd say that," Abner drawled.

She cocked her head. "Yes, and a good head washing, too, Mr. Claunch."

He made a sound of mock pain. "Why is it that women have to always be trying to clean up their menfolk?"

"Because we have to smell you, that's why," Megan retorted with a grin.

"One thing about being on a cattle drive, the cows don't care how you smell."

"That may be true," Megan agreed, "but has a cow ever cooked a nice hot supper for you?"

"No, no," he said, shaking his head, "that's a good point, Meggie girl. Sure as thunder."

Lively music flowed from the dining hall, signaling the start of the party. People left the camp by twos and threes, drawn by the sound. Megan wore the blue dress she'd made over for the party in April. It had to be taken in another two inches in the waist for tonight. She'd washed her hair, and by brushing it for over an hour had managed to dry it. Then she put it up in a braid coiled at the back of her head. Curling wisps of hair were already escaping to frame her face.

The music came from several fiddles, a harmonica and a French horn, played by members of the fort's company. Mary Schiller, pretty and smiling in a pink dress, was already dancing with a handsome, young soldier when Megan and Abner entered the room. Laura Schiller was standing against the wall with another young soldier, giggling and tossing her head. A born flirt, Megan thought, smiling at Laura's easy friendliness and comparing it with her own painful shyness at Laura's age. That was about the time she had learned the truth about her mother. It was unlikely that Laura, surrounded by her loving family, would ever have to experience such humiliation and disappointment. Laura would never be the brunt of cruel taunts from her peers or spend a moment wondering who her father was.

A refreshment table in the corner of the big room offered punch and cookies. Megan and Abner were headed that way, when Jed intercepted them. He, too, had found time to bathe and wash his hair, which was still damp. He looked so tall and strong and tan in his clean brown trousers and cotton broadcloth shirt with a string tie. He hadn't gone out of his way to speak to Megan for a month and she was unprepared when he approached her directly. "May I have this dance, Megan?" he asked, looking questioningly at Abner. "If it's all right with your husband."

He appeared as at ease as if nothing more than a friendly exchange of conversation had ever passed between them, but Megan felt flustered. "Oh, no—we just got here. We were about to visit the refreshment table."

"Go on and dance, Meggie," Abner urged her. "I'll grab a handful of those cookies and find a place to sit and watch. If you don't enjoy yourself, I'll feel like it's my fault."

"Don't be silly, Abner. I'll enjoy sitting with you." She was finding it difficult to meet Jed's gaze.

"I want you to dance, Meggie," Abner insisted. "You can sit when you're an old lady with rheumatism in your joints."

"Megan?" Jed prompted, forcing her to look at him.

She realized it would be simpler to dance with him than to explain why she couldn't. "All right. I'll come and sit with you after a while, Abner."

She walked stiffly in front of Jed toward the other end of the room, and held herself carefully when he took her hand, placing his other at her waist.

They danced in silence for a few minutes. Megan searched desperately for something casual, but not overly friendly to say.

Suddenly Jed asked, "Are you still mad at me?"

Her eyes flew to his face. "I was never mad at you, Jed."

"Oh?" His dark brows rose in disbelief. He gave her a lopsided smile, and her heart caught in her throat. "You sure acted mad that day on the riverbank when you told me to get away from you."

She gazed up at him in astonishment. How could his memory of that event be so different from her own? She hadn't been angry. She'd been heartsick and hopeless because she could not stop wanting him to hold her and kiss her—and more. Because she couldn't stop loving him. "I asked you to leave me alone because I was embarrassed and ashamed," she said softly.

He studied her for a long moment. "Then I should apologize. I'm sorry, Megan. I—I seem to be always making a fool of myself around you."

"I'm the fool," she said. "I—I don't know how you can stand to look at me after..." Her voice trailed off. She couldn't put into words what had happened between them.

"I'll never stop wanting to look at you," he said huskily.

She didn't know how to respond. No doubt she would have found much to say if she were free, but she wasn't. His dark eyes appeared as deep as pools and full of secret longings. She couldn't look into them without wanting to lose herself in them.

Hastily she averted her gaze and fixed it on Mary Schiller and the soldier dancing with her. She watched them for a moment before she noticed the man beyond them, standing against the wall alone. It was the big, bearded man who had stared at her in the trading post. He was staring at her now as he had then—his expression somehow calculating.

She shivered and focused on Jed's string tie. "That man," she murmured, "the one with the beard, standing against the south wall. He watched me the whole time I was in the trading post this afternoon, just as he's doing now."

Jed grinned. "He probably hasn't seen anything as pretty as you in years."

"No." She lifted her chin and shook her head emphatically. "He doesn't look at me like that. It's strange...it makes me want to run and hide."

Jed frowned and swung her around so he could see the man. "Oh," he said after a moment. "He's a trapper. That's just a half step above an animal. Stay away from him."

There was contempt in his tone. "Are all trappers dangerous men?" she asked curiously.

"The ones I've had dealings with are. They treat women worse than animals."

His expression was grim, his eyes narrowed, and she could actually see the muscles in his face grow taut. He wasn't looking at her now. "What dealings have you had with trappers?"

"Violent ones."

"When? Where?"

He looked down at her, and the anger in eyes that had been so warm a few moments before shocked her. "In Oregon, a couple of years ago."

She knew that his memories of Oregon were sad. "It had something to do with your wife, didn't it?"

He hadn't expected her to realize that. She saw it in his eyes. For a moment he seemed to be arguing with himself. Then he said, "Yes. A man—no, not a man, he wasn't worthy of the name—a trapper took her from our house. I'd gone after supplies, and when I got back, she had vanished. I found her three weeks later and took her home, but she'd already been destroyed—inside."

Megan expelled a deep breath. "Oh . . ." she said reflectively. "The trapper was responsible for her death."

"Yes."

She wanted to say she was glad he felt he could tell her. She wanted to say she was sorry. She wanted to say, "Don't grieve for her, Jed. Let me comfort you." But of course she couldn't say any of those things. "Did they catch him?" she finally asked.

"*I* caught him." The way he spit the words out made her remember the rumor Carolyn Goddard had repeated to her and Rose months ago that Jed had killed a man in Oregon. She looked into Jed's eyes, which were now as hard as stones, and knew that he'd killed the trapper who'd taken his wife.

The realization saddened her. How terrible it must have been for Jed to come home and find the woman he loved gone, carried off by a barbarian. How he must have suffered during the three weeks he'd searched for them. What had he seen when he'd found them? Whatever it was, it had made him kill. He must have loved his wife very much. He'd probably never love another woman that way.

She forced herself to stop thinking such thoughts. It couldn't make any difference to her how much Jed had loved his wife or whether he could ever feel that deeply for another woman. Even if he could, she would never be that woman. She wasn't free to love Jed, and that made her wish she hadn't come to the party. It was torment to have Jed's arms around her and know she could never have him.

"This wasn't a good idea," she said.

"What?"

"Dancing with you."

He didn't reply, and as soon as she could, she excused herself and went to find Abner. She stayed by Abner's side the rest of the evening, turning down all invitations to dance. The pleasure had gone out of the party for her.

Chapter Thirteen

During the night after the party at Fort Hall, Abner's fever returned. His thrashing and mumbling in his sleep woke Megan. Before falling asleep, she assured herself that the fever was gone for good. But, hearing Abner, she knew even before she touched him that it was back, and she was filled with a feeling of complete helplessness.

She left her bed to bathe his face with a cloth dipped in cool water. She'd already given him every concoction she knew of to combat fever, and there seemed nothing else to do.

"Oh, Abner, you overdid it yourself today," she said fretfully. "Walking to the trading post and then attending the party... we shouldn't have gone."

"Meggie, I didn't do a thing at that party but sit on my behind," Abner muttered. "That didn't hurt me. Whatever is making me sick stays in my body, even when the fever leaves—sort of goes into hiding, I reckon. When it comes out, the fever comes with it."

Megan was thinking along the same lines herself. She feared that Abner had malaria or some similar sickness. But she said stubbornly, "You'll be completely well soon." She dipped the cloth in cool water again, wrung it out, folded it and laid it on his forehead.

"Sugar," Abner said after a while, "on the off chance I don't make it, there are a few things we ought to talk about—"

"Nonsense," Megan cut him off sharply. His words caused a flutter of panic in her stomach. She couldn't let him give up. "You need your rest, Abner, you *will* make it."

Ignoring Abner's repeated requests that she go to bed, she sat with him until dawn. Her wool shawl pulled around her, she dozed intermittently, her head resting against a wagon bow. When the fever made him restless, she woke to bathe him with cool water.

Fever racked Abner's gaunt body all the next day, and Megan stayed with him in the tent, leaving him only for brief periods to prepare their meals and take care of other necessary duties.

Several bands of Indians were camped near the fort and, hearing Jed say some of them were Sioux, Megan found herself looking for the young Sioux warrior who had returned Johnny to her. She had been too frightened to thank him at the time, and would have liked to do so now. But she didn't see him. Perhaps his band didn't roam this far west.

They broke camp early the next morning. Reuben Schiller sent Daniel to help Megan with her wagon and team. It was cold enough for winter coats, but they passed through several patches where there was grass for the livestock to eat. The animals' grazing slowed them down, but no one complained. Grain was hard to come by now, and too expensive when it could be found. Grass was a blessing.

Abner seemed better that morning and as soon as they were under way, Megan left him resting and Daniel in charge of the wagon. She wanted to find Reuben and thank him for sending Daniel to her rescue.

"I wish I could repay you and Rose for all the help you've been to me while Abner's been sick," she told Reuben.

"You've already repaid us, Megan," Reuben said, "by helping care for our children when they were poorly."

"Somehow that doesn't seem enough."

He laughed. "It sure seems more then enough to Rose and me."

She walked with Rose, Carolyn Goddard and Lacey Glenhill for a short while. "I hated leaving the fort," Lacey said wistfully. "Even with all those Indians and trappers around, I felt I'd found civilization again." Lacey had entered her fifth month of pregnancy and was no longer plagued with morning sickness.

"I know what you mean," Rose said. "Major Southern and his soldiers were right hospitable to us. My Mary and that young soldier took a shine to each other, I think. She seemed unhappy when we broke camp. I hope my girls can find suitable young men to marry in Oregon."

"There will be plenty of young men, Rose," Lacey said. "Think of the number we've seen just on the road." She heaved another sigh. "But we have to get to Oregon first, don't we? In the meantime, we've Fort Boise to look forward to. Do you think Jed will let us stop there for a rest?"

"I don't think Jed wants to stop any longer than we have to from now on," Megan told her. "Summer will be over before you know it, and I've heard the snows start in early autumn in these mountains."

"Mason says we're making pretty good time." Lacey looked around at the other women for confirmation. Megan knew Lacey wanted desperately to reach Oregon before her child was born. If Lacey carried full term, the baby would come in early December, and they should be in Oregon, barring trouble. But the rigors of traveling could cause a premature birth. And who knew when terrible calamity might strike?

"If I had it to do over," Carolyn said, her gaze constantly moving to keep Johnny in her sight, "I wouldn't leave Illinois."

"I imagine there are many who would say that," Rose put in. "Lately I've heard several of our women pining for the homes they left in the East. You'd think they'd lived in Paradise before they started west. They seem to have forgotten all the reasons why they wanted to come."

"Complaining only makes you and everybody around you miserable," Megan said. She couldn't help comparing the attitudes of the complainers with Rose Schiller's, who most of the time had a sick child to care for along with her other duties, yet remained cheerful and optimistic. "It's better to think about the rich farmland in Oregon."

"Mmm," Rose agreed, "and the houses our men will build. I want a grand place with at least five rooms. Reuben says we'll have to start with two, but I mean to have more before two years have passed."

"I'd rather live in a town," Carolyn announced.

Megan looked at her in surprise. Thayer was a farmer. "I'm not sure there's a settlement in Oregon worthy of the word 'town' yet."

Carolyn shrugged. "A settlement then. I want to start a business of my own so I can support myself and Johnny...if I have to."

The other women exchanged thoughtful glances, wondering if Carolyn planned to leave Thayer once they reached Oregon. Nobody dared to ask, however. There was something distant, almost secretive, about Carolyn now. It was as if she had erected a protective wall between herself and everyone else, except Johnny.

Megan wondered if Thayer was still forcing himself on his unwilling wife and felt a deep compassion for Carolyn. Thayer was such a strange man. On three occasions lately, she had become aware that she was being watched, and when she'd looked up it was Thayer she'd found studying her. How terrible to have to live with and share the bed of such a man.

Even though she was not in love with her husband, Megan felt so much more fortunate than Carolyn Goddard.

She remembered Abner's words of the day before: "On the off chance I don't make it, there are a few things we ought to talk about." No, she told herself, she wouldn't even consider the possibility of Abner's not making it.

Megan forced her mind back to her companions. "I've thought I might open a dressmaking shop sometime in the future," she said. "What kind of business would you like to have, Carolyn?"

"A boarding house," Carolyn replied without hesitation. Evidently she had given it considerable thought.

"There must be many single men in Oregon already and more will be coming each year. I should think a woman could do well for herself supplying them with clean beds and hearty meals."

"Well, I shudder at the thought of having more than two men to cook and clean for," Lacey said. "Mason and David are good to help me now, but they'll be too busy to help in the house once we get settled."

"Maybe your baby will be a girl," Rose told her. "Before you know it she'll be helping you. I know I'll miss Mary's and Laura's hands when they marry."

"I wouldn't wish that on anyone," Carolyn said, causing the other three to stare at her.

"What?" Rose asked. "Having a girl child?"

"Being a girl child," Carolyn corrected. "Girls grow up to be women, and most women spend their lives being men's chattel."

"I have to disagree with you there, Carolyn," Rose said gently. "I certainly don't feel like chattel, and if Reuben ever treated me as such, I'd hit him."

Megan and Lacey laughed, picturing Rose taking after her husband with a clenched fist. But Carolyn wasn't amused. "Johnny, come back here," she called, clasping his hand when he ran to her. "I'm taking you to the wagon, young man. You'll run until you make yourself sick." She murmured goodbye to the other women and left them.

"She just wants him in the wagon so he won't be out of her sight," Megan commented.

"I'm worried about her," Lacey said. "She's so bitter lately."

"Do you really think Thayer will let her open a boarding house?" Megan asked the other two.

"I don't reckon she'll ask Thayer's permission if she decides to do it," Rose said, frowning. "I suspect she's thinking of leaving him."

"I can't imagine him letting her leave," Megan remarked.

Lacey nodded. "Nor can I, and that's something else that worries me."

Jed left Mason Glenhill leading the wagon train and spurred his stallion to the rear. He saw Megan, Rose and Lacey walking together and, tipping his hat, called hello to them. He was glad to see Megan with her friends. She had been confined to her wagon so much lately because of Abner's ill health. He must be feeling better today, Jed thought, or Megan would not have left him alone.

Rarely had he seen a more dutiful wife. During the party at Fort Hall she had danced only once, with him, and then only because he'd pressed her. She had turned down all the other invitations in order to sit with Abner.

Megan had surprised him on this journey—more than that, she had amazed him. He had long ago come to regret confronting Abner with his knowledge that Megan was not his daughter, thereby forcing Abner to marry her. If he'd only left well enough alone, she would not now be another man's wife and . . .

He muttered an oath and hauled his mind back from insane fantasies. She *was* another man's wife, and that was the end of it. Or should be . . . had to be.

He reached the end of the train and pulled up on the reins to stop the stallion. He peered back along the trail, scanning the horizon, then turned his head to study the surrounding mountains.

He'd felt a sharp wariness ever since they left Fort Hall, like an itch that he couldn't scratch. He was reminded of the feeling he'd had weeks back as he'd waited for the first Indians to show themselves. But this was even stronger. Once the hairs on the back of his neck had stood on end, and he'd been certain he was being spied on. But when he'd whirled around, no one in his party had been paying any particular attention to him, and he'd detected no one following them or watching from the surrounding mountainous countryside.

Nevertheless the feeling stayed with him. He couldn't shake the sensation of being watched. He had a strong suspicion that the party was being tracked. There had been nearly two hundred Indians camped near Fort Hall, mostly Sioux and Cheyenne. Maybe a band had followed them. If so, they would be waiting for the opportunity to steal the horses—or attack the party and ransack their goods.

Jed turned his mount and caught up with the last wagon. He rode at the back of the train all day, watchful and alert, continually scanning the country around them. If an attack was imminent, he wanted some warning.

After supper, Jed began patrolling the perimeter of the camp and kept it up all night, stopping for only a few moments now and then to lean back against a wagon and doze, his hand resting on the stock of his rifle.

On one of his trips around the camp he ran into Reuben Schiller, who was standing guard. "What's eating you tonight, Jed?" Reuben asked.

"Don't know," Jed replied. "I've had an uneasy feeling all day, as though there's somebody—" he gestured vaguely with one hand "—out there, watching. Keep alert, will you, Reuben?"

"I always do when I'm on sentry duty," Reuben said, watching Jed stride away in the darkness and wondering if Jed's uneasiness wasn't caused by someone within the camp, rather than outside. Several times he had seen Jed look at Megan Claunch in a way that a man ought not to look at another man's wife. Reuben didn't know if Megan was aware of it or not, but in any case, Megan was a woman of high morals. If Jed was feeling the way Reuben suspected he felt about Megan, he couldn't expect anything but heartache.

Reuben hadn't mentioned his suspicion to anyone but Rose, and she'd said Jed missed being married and that he'd find a suitable woman once they reached Oregon. Reuben wasn't so sure. Jed didn't strike him as a man whose affections could be so easily shifted.

* * *

In midafternoon of a day in late August, they camped on the southern bank of the Snake River in preparation for crossing on the morrow. Daniel Schiller handled the Claunch wagon and team every day now. As Megan helped Daniel unhitch the team that afternoon, she glanced apprehensively at the swift, rapids-filled river. There was no telling how many head of cattle they would lose in the next day's crossing. She wondered if they would reach Oregon with a single one of Abner's longhorns.

She lifted her gaze to the slate-colored sky. As Daniel loosed the fourth ox, thunder rumbled ominously. The men drove the livestock to water, and the women hurried to build their cook fires before rain made cooking impossible.

While the men were gone with the livestock, three Cayuse Indians approached the camp. Several women went after their shotguns and two of the men left to guard the camp met the Indians. Very shortly the men were escorting the Indians, who had salmon and potatoes to sell, into the camp. The Indians were unarmed and friendly, and the tension that had gripped the camp with their appearance relaxed.

Megan relinquished another of her and Abner's dwindling store of coins in exchange for a salmon and two potatoes. The supper would surely tempt Abner's appetite, which had flagged in recent days.

Although Abner was usually fever free when he awoke each morning, he was too weak to leave the wagon for more than a few minutes at a time. The fever returned every evening now with the regularity of the sun setting and he was forced to take to his bed while Megan prepared their supper.

It was Jed who brought the Claunches' livestock back from the watering hole. Daniel had stayed to help Reuben with the Schillers' mules, who were stubbornly refusing to take a step away from the water.

Jed drove the livestock into the pen that had been roped off inside the circle of wagons, then came to the fire where

Megan was keeping an eye on the salmon sizzling in a frying pan.

He watched the graceful movement of her wrist as she turned the salmon before she realized he was there.

She looked around with a little start, smiling when she saw who it was. "Hello, Jed. Thank you for corralling our livestock."

"It was no trouble," he murmured. "Daniel asked me to bring you this bucket of water. He had to stay and help Reuben with the mules."

"Oh, good. Now I can make coffee. I didn't know he'd taken the water bucket with him. Daniel has become my right arm." She poured water from the bucket into the tin pot and added coffee grounds. Jed stood, watching her but not speaking. "The salmon smells wonderful, doesn't it?" she asked. "There's enough for three here, if you'd like to join Abner and me for supper."

"I already told Reuben I'd eat with his family." His gaze raked her slender form in the worn, cotton dress. He lifted his eyes to her face. Although he knew she, like the other women, tried to protect her skin from the sun as much as possible, her face and hands were lightly tanned. The angles of her delicate features had become a little sharper with loss of weight, giving her face an elfin quality. At the moment her cheeks glowed with hectic color from the fire.

To Jed, she was lovelier every time he looked at her. She continued to care for Abner and other ill members of their party, and he was convinced she would wear herself out before they reached their destination. But no matter what he said, she refused to make things any easier for herself. "Are you getting along all right?"

"I'm just fine," she told him. Her gaze stayed on his face a little longer this time before she turned back to the fire. "How about you?"

"I'm surviving." Barely, he could have added. Wanting her had become a permanent gnawing in his innards. It disturbed his sleep and filled his days with awareness of her—he could have said where she was and what she was doing at almost any hour of the day or night. "Is Abner feeling any better?"

She shook her head sadly without looking at him. "The fever comes up in the evening," she said quietly. "It's sapping the strength from him." She had almost said "life," but caught herself before the word was formed. "And lately, he has so little appetite...he takes a few bites and pushes his plate away. He says nothing tastes right."

"I'm sorry, Megan."

His earnest tone made her glance up at him gratefully. For one brief instant, his eyes held yearning and a touch of bitter agony before he managed to hide his feelings from her. She wanted to put her arms around him and say everything would be all right, but she wondered if things would indeed be all right. What did the remainder of their journey hold for any of them, she wondered.

"I know you are, Jed," she said simply, ladling the salmon from the pan into a tin plate.

"If there's anything I can do..."

She took the pan off the fire and turned to face him. "There's nothing right now, but if there ever is, I'll ask."

"Promise?"

She smiled. "I swear it." She watched him walk away from her, biting her lip to keep from calling him back. After all, what was there to say? She certainly couldn't confess her true feelings—that she simply wanted to be near him for a few minutes longer.

Jed.

For her, it would always be Jed, and she had known it for some time. If she'd had any idea how powerful and consuming love was, she would not have married Abner, even if Jed had stuck to his decision not to take them with his party. Of course, if she hadn't come with Jed's party, she wouldn't have fallen in love with him. But it was futile to think of what might have been. She knew only that love was nothing like the gentle fondness she felt for Abner. How could she ever have believed that the affection and gratitude she had for her husband would in time develop naturally into love?

A raindrop plopped on her nose, bringing her thoughts back to supper. Hastily she fished the potatoes from the ashes with a fork and divided the food on two plates. She carried the plates to the wagon and came back for the coffeepot. As she ducked beneath the canvas a second time, the rain began to fall steadily.

Abner was leaning back against the trunk in his long johns, a quilt covering him from the waist down. He had already wolfed down a good portion of the salmon, Megan noted, pleased.

"Thank the Lord for fish, eh, Meggie?" he said, forking another bite. "If not for the fish you've bought from the Indians these past weeks, we'd be having beans, rice or cornmeal mush and molasses three times a day."

"I hate spending our money on it," Megan said, "but you need the nourishment."

"We both need it, sugar. If we get to Oregon without a dime to our name, we'll get along somehow."

She placed the back of her hand against his hot cheek and coaxed, "Eat your potato, too."

Under her watchful gaze, he managed to eat most of his meal. But the effort exhausted him, and he lay back down with a weary little groan. Megan tucked the quilt around him and finished eating. She pulled Abner's wool poncho over her head before taking the dirty dishes outside to wash them hurriedly, using water from the bucket Jed had brought her.

As she put the clean dishes back in the wagon, someone called her name. She turned and saw Fanny Olmstead running through the rain toward her.

"Where's your coat, Fanny?" Megan asked when Fanny reached her, gasping for breath. "You're soaked through."

"Never mind that," Fanny gulped, and her fingers clutched Megan's arm. "Ginny's having some kind of fit! Come and see what you can do for her, Megan."

Megan stuck her head through the opening in the canvas. "Abner, I'm needed at the Olmstead wagon. I'll be back in a little while."

He was sleeping and didn't answer. She pulled her medicine bag from the wagon, then took off the poncho and held it over her head with her free hand. "Get under here with me, Fanny, and help me hold this up." Fanny was wringing her hands and only half heard Megan's words. Megan moved close to Fanny and draped the poncho over the two of them. "Don't you dare go into hysterics, Fanny Olmstead. Ginny's probably just had a convulsion." They hurried through the rain to the Olmstead wagon. "Has she had a fever?"

"All day," Fanny said. "I heated that tea you gave me the last time she was sick and got some of it down her. It seemed to help for a little while, but later her face got red and her skin was hot enough to scorch you."

They climbed up into the Olmstead wagon. Bert and the three Olmstead boys were sitting around six-year-old Ginny's pallet, watching her helplessly. Megan went forward and knelt beside the child. Bert and the boys moved away from the pallet and sat down on a box at the other end of the wagon.

Ginny was no longer convulsing, but she was twisting and turning and muttering in delirium. Megan ran her hand over the little girls' face and upper body. "She's still burning up. Fanny, get a clean cloth and a bucket of cool water." She squinted into the dim depths of her bag. "Bert, would you please light a candle? I can't see what I'm doing."

Bert fumbled through boxes until he found a half-burned candle. He set it on a tin plate, placed it near Megan and lit it. Megan mixed bittersweet root and scullcap herb in a cup. When Fanny came back with the bucket and cloth, Megan said, "You should boil a teaspoon of this in about a pint of water—if you can find enough dry wood to build a fire in the morning. When it cools, strain it through a clean cloth."

Fanny set the bucket down. "Maybe I could boil a small amount of water by holding the pan over that candle."

"It's certainly worth a try," Megan agreed. "She should have about half a cupful of the brew three times a day until she's taken all of it. In the meantime, we have to get her fever down." Megan dipped the cloth in the water and began bathing Ginny's face, neck, arms and chest. The cloth had to be dipped repeatedly because Ginny's feverish skin quickly heated it.

Fanny assigned Bert to hold the pan over the candle flame and relieved Megan. In about five minutes, Ginny's skin felt a little cooler and she was sleeping quietly. "Good," Megan said. "If she can rest, she should be better by morning. Fanny, you or Bert should sit with her tonight and bathe her with cool water every time her fever comes up. If her temperature gets too high, she could have another convulsion."

Watching her daughter apprehensively, Fanny nodded and took a deep breath. "Thank you, Megan. Me and Bert didn't know what to do when she started drawing up and shaking like that."

"Children go into convulsions more easily than adults," Megan said. "I don't think it will happen again if you can keep her fever down."

"We'll keep it down," Bert said.

"I think you two have this under control now," Megan said, "so I'd better get back to Abner. If you need me again, don't hesitate to send for me."

It was raining harder than ever when Megan left the Olmstead wagon. The water poured down in sheets so fast and hard she could barely see a foot in front of her. She ran to the perimeter of the circle of wagons and found her way by touching wagon beds as she moved along.

She hadn't gone far, when suddenly hailstones as big as fists started pounding down around her with a sound like a hundred continuous drumrolls. When a hailstone landed on Megan's head, she yelped and ducked down beneath the nearest wagon to wait out the storm.

Water ran from the poncho in streams. She took it off. The rain had penetrated the poncho and soaked the bodice of her dress. Shivering, she sat down on the damp ground, wrapped her arms around her knees and huddled for warmth.

If the hail didn't stop soon, she told herself, she'd go on, anyway. Abner's bedding would be damp, and she would need to change it and figure out some way to keep his bed dry until the rain stopped.

She heard the scrape of shoes in the wagon bed above her head, and somebody stepped out of it and ducked beneath the wagon with her. It was Thayer Goddard. Apparently she had chosen the Goddard wagon for shelter.

At first she was too surprised to do anything but stare at him. Crouching, he half walked, half crawled to her and peered into her face. "Well, look who's here."

Megan instinctively scooted away from him, too confused by his odd expression to explain her presence beneath his wagon. His cold eyes roamed over her and a slow grin twisted his mouth.

"The prim-and-proper Mrs. Claunch," he said. "I thought it was a bitch dog slinking under my wagon to whelp her pups."

Megan's heart raced in sudden alarm, and she edged away a bit farther. "Thayer..." she managed, intending to explain that she'd ducked beneath his wagon to escape the hail. But immediately she realized he would have already reached that conclusion. As she scooted backward he advanced on her. Now that he was close enough, she could see the gleam in his eyes.

"Hail makes a powerful noise, doesn't it?" he asked, and with rising fear Megan realized he wanted her to know that neither Carolyn nor anybody else would hear her if she called for help.

She raised up, banging her head on the bottom of the wagon bed. Rubbing the throbbing spot above her ear, she moved back. His gaze was fixed on her bosom, and looking down, she saw with horror that her wet dress clung to her, outlining both hardened nipples plainly. Gasping, she folded her arms over her chest, covering herself. "I—I have to get back to Abner."

His hand snaked out, his fingers closing on his arm. "Those hailstones are big enough to knock you cold. You'd better stay right here till it stops."

Megan's teeth chattered. "Take your—h-hand off m-me," she stuttered.

He looked at his fingers curled around her arm, then back at her, and grinned, a sickening grin. "Now, Megan, I'm just being neighborly. Why don't you come back over here and sit down. I'll put my coat around you and warm you up."

She stared at him. "No, thank you, Thayer. Now p-please let go of me."

His eyes narrowed. "You don't really mean that, do you, Megan? With that sick husband of yours, you must have been a long time without a man."

She opened her mouth to scream, but before she could make a sound, Thayer's heavy hand clamped across her mouth. Her breath left her lungs in a rush.

"I ain't gonna hurt you, Megan," he said in a wheedling tone that made her skin crawl. "It ain't as if you ain't accommodated men before." She stood rigidly still; her eyes above his hand fixed on his flushed face. "You understand what I'm saying?" he asked.

She was very much afraid she did, but she knew that her only hope lay in making him think he'd allayed her fears. She nodded quickly. "Good," he said. "I'll take my hand off your mouth if you promise to keep still."

She looked at him, trying to mask her hatred, and finally nodded. He removed his hand from her face, but his other hand still gripped her arm.

Megan forced her voice to remain steady. "I'll take you up on the offer of your coat, Thayer."

He stared at her suspiciously for a moment. He would have to release her to remove his coat. She could see him debating with himself. Finally greed won out and he grinned, his fingers on her arm relaxed and he dropped his hand as he began shrugging quickly out of his coat.

Megan didn't wait for a better opportunity. There would be none. Without taking time to grab the poncho, which still lay on the ground in a sopping heap, she ducked and ran all in one movement. When she sensed she was clear of the wagon bed, she straightened. But she'd misjudged by a few inches and banged her head in the same spot she'd hit before. Pain exploded above her ear, and for an instant everything went black. She swayed, stunned and dizzy.

Behind her, Thayer shouted something. She didn't catch all of what he said, but she heard the contemptuous name he called her and that galvanized her. As she ran precariously over ground strewn with hailstones, the hail stopped as suddenly as it had started.

The heel of her boot came down on a hailstone, and she slowed, barely managing to remain upright. "Somebody help me," she wailed, and Thayer grabbed her from behind.

Chapter Fourteen

Sobbing, Megan tried to wrench free. She twisted back and forth, attempting frantically to escape. But it was no use. Thayer's hand crushed her lips against her teeth, and she could taste her own blood. His other arm was clamped about her waist, holding her back against him so tightly she could hardly breathe. His sharp fingers dug into her wet clothing as he tried to pull her skirts up without letting go of her. His breath came in grunts of effort as he struggled with the heavy, wet fabric of her dress.

"Confounded dress—worse than a spider web," he hissed furiously. "You can fight me all you want to, harlot. It ain't gonna stop me." His fingers had found the hem of her dress at last and now tore at her petticoat.

"I'm not your wife, Thayer," Megan panted. "I won't stand still for this!" She lifted her foot and brought her boot heel down on his instep as hard as she could. In the same instant she bit down hard on the finger that was wedged against her mouth. When he jerked away, she screamed and struggled free of his grasp. But before she had run three steps he snatched a handful of her wet hair and hauled her back.

The pain was excruciating. She cried out. He jerked her around to face him and grabbed her shoulders. Megan's head bobbed back and forth as he shook her.

"I reckon you want to be paid first," he sneered. She screamed and he shook her harder. "Save your breath, you filthy little harlot! Nobody can hear you." His breath was hot against her cheek. His hands were bruising on her arms, and the sound of the rain was drowning out her screams. It was no use. No one would hear. No one would come to help her.

One hand held her in a viselike grip, while the other started tearing at her clothes again. With a cry of rage and terror she jerked her hand up, her fingers rigid and curled like claws. With a lunge she raked her nails down his face and felt the skin rip. Good, she thought hysterically, I wish I'd torn his evil face off.

He yelled in agony and shoved her back against a wagon with his body. "You'll pay for that, whore!"

The middle of her back hit the wagon bed and drove the breath from her lungs. She gasped and felt the earth tilting. She grabbed at the wagon bed and her breath came back with a whistling sound.

Megan blinked and stared at her attacker. Dark blood trickled down one side of his face where she had scratched him. He'll kill me now, she thought. But she would not let him kill her or rape her without a fight. She gathered her strength and lifted her balled fists to pound his shoulders and chest.

All at once Thayer staggered back away from her. Megan had a moment to think, I didn't hit him that hard. Before she realized what was happening, Thayer was sprawled in the mud at her feet, and suddenly none of it seemed real. All she could think was that she had to get back to her wagon, back to Abner.

Jed had been patrolling the camp, worried that the rain would provide cover for an Indian attack. He was almost upon Thayer Goddard before he saw him, struggling with a woman, heard him say, "You'll pay for that, whore." It was another second before he recognized Megan, and in one blinding flash of understanding took it all in.

His vision blurred with rage, Jed had grabbed Thayer's shoulders, almost lifting him off the ground, and dragged him off her, flinging him aside so suddenly that Thayer lost his balance and fell to his hands and knees in the mud.

Megan cowered against the wagon, in shock, as she gulped air. Thayer Goddard was trying to rape her, Jed thought, attempting to assimilate the knowledge without losing control of himself completely. Before Jed could go to Megan, Thayer managed to get to his feet. He spoke so close to Jed's ear it made Jed jump and whirl around.

"What in tarnation's wrong with you, Dossman? There's enough for both of us."

Jed's already fragile control snapped. His fist shot out and cracked against Thayer's jaw so hard he thought he might have broken a bone. Thayer rocked back on his heels, teetered there for an instant, then sprawled in the mud again.

Jed stood over him, holding himself back with all his strength. He wanted nothing more than to go after Thayer Goddard again. He wanted to beat him with his fists until his face was a bloody pulp. He wanted to kill him.

"If you ever touch her again," Jed said, his voice shaking but deadly, "I'll kill you."

Thayer sat up, groaning and cradling his jaw. "I think you broke it, Dossman," he whined.

"Get on your feet, damn it! Get away from me before I change my mind and kill you here and now."

Thayer scrambled to his feet and glared furiously at Jed before he staggered toward his wagon. Jed turned to Megan. She was shaking uncontrollably. "Megan, honey, are you all right?"

Jed's face wouldn't quite come into focus for her, and she couldn't stop shaking. She couldn't think. The one thing she did take in was that Jed was there, Jed had rescued her.

"He—he was going to—to attack me."

Jed's gaze swept down her, and his mouth set in a grim, disapproving line. "What were you doing with him, looking like that?"

Her dress was soaked through everywhere now, the material clinging to every curve and line. But she couldn't help that. Jed's accusing tone bewildered her, and tears sprang to her eyes. No doubt it was a delayed reaction to what had happened with Thayer, but once the tears started, she couldn't stop them.

Jed was immediately repentant. "Oh, hell..." He pulled her into his arms, one hand cradling her wet head on his shoulder. "Megan, don't..." he said miserably. "We got enough water here without adding more." It was a poor effort to make a joke, and it fell flat.

She didn't laugh. She had gone very still in his arms. "I ducked under his wagon to escape the hail." Her voice was muffled against his coat. "I didn't know it was the Goddard wagon until he came out and found me. I was wearing a poncho, but I took it off because it was soaked... it's still under the wagon. I couldn't take time to get it. I tried to run for it, but when I did he—he stopped me."

"I'm sorry."

A shiver ran through her. "Thank goodness you saw us before he..."

"It's over now," he murmured quietly. "Just—please, Megan, stay away from him."

He still sounded angry with her. What had she done? Didn't he know she'd been trying to stay away from Thayer for weeks? Did he think she'd gone out of her way to seek shelter beneath the Goddard wagon?

She took a bracing breath and lifted her head. "I went to the Olmstead wagon. Ginny's terribly sick. On the way back the hail started, and the Goddard wagon was the closest and..." She'd already said that. She was babbling. "I...I'd better get back. My husband needs me. I've been gone too long, he'll be worried." She stepped away from him. "Thank you, Jed." The words came out sounding stiff, and she hadn't intended that.

"I'll get the poncho for you," he said. "I'll dry it and return it later."

She nodded and, turning, hurried toward her wagon. Jed watched her go, still struggling with his anger—at Thayer for what he'd tried to do, at himself for practically accusing

Megan of asking for it, and even at Megan, though he couldn't have said why.

When Megan reached the wagon, Abner was standing on one foot and trying to stuff the other into his trousers. He was so weak he was trembling all over. When Megan climbed in the wagon, he stopped and stared at her, forgetting for the moment that he stood in nothing but his long johns.

"You're too weak to get up, Abner," she said tremulously. She was still shaken from her encounter with Thayer, and she continued to feel as though she could cry at the drop of a hat. "Get back in bed. And turn your back so I can take off these wet clothes."

"I ain't doing anything till you tell me what's wrong."

"Please, Abner," she said wearily. Turning her back, she started unbuttoning her dress.

"Meggie, you're nearly drowned—and you look like you've seen a ghost. What happened to the poncho?"

"I left it..." She trailed off, hoping he'd assume she'd left it at the Olmstead wagon.

"Megan, do you think I'm blind as well as sick? Something's wrong."

"Nothing's wrong—not now." Her shoulders sagged. "Let me change my clothes, and I'll tell you what happened." After a moment she heard him arranging his bedclothes. Quickly she stripped off her wet things and pulled on dry underclothes and a dress from the trunk. Then she bent down beside Abner. "Is your bed wet?"

He lay on his back, studying her with concern. "Not much. I scooted over here where the canvas wasn't leaking so bad. I'm dry enough."

"Good. I've been trying to think of a way to use the tent to protect our bedding when it rains. There isn't room to set it up in here, but maybe I could drape it over boxes and the trunk and make a dry little cave."

"Meggie," he said sharply, "quit trying to change the subject. You're gonna tell me what's wrong with you, besides being as wet as a drowned rat. Did you get caught in the hail and get the wits scared out of you?''

He had offered her a convenient way out, but she couldn't bring herself to lie to Abner. Sighing, she sat down between two cartons and pulled the edge of Abner's quilt over her legs. "I got caught in the hail, yes. So I ducked under the nearest wagon to wait it out. It turned out to be the Goddard wagon, and Thayer came out and found me. He was—very unpleasant."

"What?" He struggled half-upright. "What did he do?"

"He scared me. He looked strange, and when I started to leave, he—well, he grabbed me."

"Damn his hide!"

He obviously meant to get up again and get dressed. Megan pushed him back down. He was too weak to oppose her, and apparently, he realized it, for he didn't try to get up again.

"I'm all right," she assured him. "Really. He didn't hurt me." Abner's skin felt much too hot. "Jed came along and told Thayer to leave me alone. Now lie still and I'll get a cool cloth to put on your forehead." She found a clean rag and dipped it in the water bucket. After bathing Abner's face slowly and gently, she folded the cloth and pressed it against his brow.

"I never trusted that coyote, Goddard," Abner muttered angrily.

"I never did, either, and you know, I believe Carolyn actually hates him."

"Can't say I blame her." He took her hand and folded it between both of his, enveloping it in feverish heat. "Good thing Jed saw what was going on."

"Thayer was so angry, he—he called me a—a whore. And him always pretending to be so religious."

"He's got about as much religion as a dog," Abner spit. "He's a hypocrite. When he was in Independence I saw him at the Gilded Lily more than once. He went upstairs with Dolly."

Megan's mouth dropped open. "He did? He left his wife and child to go to a prostitute? Why, that no-good piece of dirt!" It occurred to her that if Thayer had frequented the Gilded Lily while in Independence, he might have known Kate. "Abner, he could've met Kate. He might even know I'm her daughter."

"Don't worry about it, sugar," Abner said. "I mean to have a talk with Mr. High-and-mighty Goddard."

"It can wait until you're feeling better," Megan said. She pulled her hand from his and went to dip the cloth in the water bucket again. Coming back, she ran the cloth over his face and neck. "I thought I could get away from my background by going west," she mused, "but if Thayer knows..."

"Meggie, I've watched you grow up while we been on the trail—you were just an untried girl when we started, but now you're a strong woman. Strong enough not to worry any longer about your background. Kate was Kate, and you're you. You didn't have nothing to do with how she lived her life."

Megan folded the cloth and placed it once more on his forehead. "When I found out the truth I begged her to stop." She said with a sad little smile. "I was silly enough to think she loved me enough to do it just because I asked."

"She did love you, Meggie. If I don't know another thing in this life, I do know that."

She looked down at him thoughtfully. "How long did you know her, Abner?"

"Since she was twelve or thirteen." He gazed at her for an instant before he went on. "I always meant to tell you when you was old enough, and now I reckon you are. Kate's ma died when she was a little tyke, and her pa drank too much. One day they came to Independence. He went into a saloon and told her to wait for him outside. Only he left by the back door. She never laid eyes on him again."

Megan sucked in a breath. "I never knew any of that," she said softly. "She never talked to me about her parents or her childhood."

"I think all she remembered of her childhood was painful, so she tried to forget it."

"What did she do when her father ran off and left her alone in a strange town?"

"She wandered around Independence for a few days, sleeping in barns and abandoned buildings and begging food from housewives. Then Royce Waddell noticed her. He took her to the Gilded Lily, cleaned her up and put her to work helping in the kitchen."

"I see," Megan said reflectively. "She must have been very grateful to him."

"Honey, she thought he was God. You can understand that. She was just a kid, and he saved her life and gave her a place to sleep and let her eat her meals in the kitchen with the cook. Why, for a long, long time, Kate thought Royce Waddell hung the moon every night."

"But what happened? How did she end up working upstairs?"

"She didn't do it all in one step, sugar. When she was fifteen, Waddell moved her things into his room. Poor little gal thought she was in love with him, Megan. He was the only man in her whole life who had ever been kind to her. She became Waddell's woman, but she was still just a kid. She was *proud* to be Royce Waddell's woman. She couldn't see nothing but that he'd saved her, and when he wanted her in his bed, she went. She told me once that he promised to marry her. Maybe he did and maybe she just wanted to believe he would. I don't know. Women will do crazy things for love, Meggie. Maybe you don't believe that now, but you'll understand someday."

Abner had no way of knowing that she already understood all too well. It still appalled her when she thought about how close she had come with Jed to breaking her wedding vows and betraying Abner. Thinking over what Abner had told her, she could even understand how fifteen-year-old Kate could have become Waddell's mistress. Kate had been in love with Waddell. It was as simple as that.

As simple as her being in love with Jed. Oh, Jed... if he hadn't come along and stopped Thayer...if she hadn't been able to fight Thayer off...

It was the second time Jed had saved her from a terrible fate. The first time he'd stopped her ox team from carrying her off in the middle of a dust storm. Somehow he always seemed to be near when she desperately needed him. It was as though there were some mysterious link between them, something that made him sense when she was in trouble. She felt warm inside at the thought, then guiltily pushed it away. She had to stop thinking about Jed like this. Abner was her husband.

She wondered if she would've been so vulnerable to Jed if she and Abner had had a real marriage from the start. Perhaps she *could* learn to love him as a husband, if only... She glanced down at him and her eyes widened in sudden horror.

"Abner, you can't mean Waddell is my father!"

"No," he said hastily. "Kate told me herself he wasn't. He got tired of her months before she got in the family way. One night he got Kate drunk and sent a customer to her bed. Kate wasn't used to strong drink, and she didn't realize what had happened until the next morning. That's when she finally admitted to herself that Waddell never had any intention of marrying her."

"She—she should have left right then."

"Maybe she should have, Meggie, but she was still just fifteen and scared of starving to death. Waddell told her she could work upstairs after that or get out. To her it seemed like she had no choice. It must have been five or six months later when she got pregnant."

"Abner, do you know who my father is?"

He shook his head. "She never told me, Meggie—if she knew. And I never asked. She did say that when Waddell found out, he told her she'd have to give the baby away— give you away, Meggie—as soon as you were born. He said he'd find a family to adopt the baby, and they'd all be better off. But Kate just couldn't give you up completely—to her it would've been abandoning you, the same thing as her pa did to her. So when you came she took you to the Valentines. She said she picked them because they had no children and they'd always seemed like kind, loving people to her. But she wouldn't let them adopt you. It was always understood that she could visit you whenever she wanted.'' He searched her face. ''She did the best she could by you, Meggie. You gotta believe that.''

''I suppose she did,'' Megan agreed reluctantly. ''Abner, I'm glad you told me all this. Naturally, I've wondered—I couldn't help it.'' She managed a smile. ''Now you'd better stop talking and rest a bit.''

''In a minute. First I got something else to tell you. I reckon I owe you an apology, Meggie girl. That money we been spending ain't all the money I got for the forty acres I sold before we left Missouri. I left half of it in the bank in Independence. I wasn't trying to deceive you exactly, Meggie. I just wanted something for a rainy day.''

Megan couldn't help laughing. ''Do you think we'll ever have a rainier day than this?''

He grinned sheepishly. ''What I'm trying to say is I wasn't trying to sneak around and hold some back just for myself.''

''Will you hush about that money? Goodness, Abner, it was your land, and it's your money. You can do what you want with it.''

''I'm glad you see it that way, sugar.'' His voice was sounding strained, as though merely talking was becoming too much of an effort. ''I wrote out a will, leaving the money and everything else I got to you—though, the Lord knows, I ain't got much else except my horse and saddle. Anyway, I wanted you to know I put the will in the bottom of the trunk. If anything happens to me, you'll have a little something to get you started in Oregon.''

"I don't want to hear you talking like that," she said, exasperated. "Now hush and—" She stopped talking when she realized that his eyes were already closed and he was breathing deeply and evenly. He's fallen asleep talking.

She got up and unrolled their tent. Working as quietly as she could, she pushed the trunk and several boxes near to where Abner slept, arranging half on either side of him, with a space between them wide enough to accommodate her bedroll as well as Abner's. After spreading the tent over the boxes, she arranged her bedroll in the narrow strip beside Abner's.

She crawled into the darkness beneath the tent and pulled a quilt over her. Curling up, she listened to the rain and tried not to think about Jed—about how he magically appeared when she needed him the most, about how sheltered and safe she felt in his arms, about how easy it was simply to close her eyes and see every detail of his face.

How strange life was. She was married, yet not married. She didn't think Abner was any more able to think of her as his wife than she was able to think of him as her husband. Yet legally that is what they were to each other. That is what they would be as long as they both were alive.

Thinking about life and death made her uncomfortable. Sometimes Abner said things that worried her. It was almost as though he'd settled it in his own mind that he wasn't going to live until they reached Oregon. It wasn't that he wanted to die, but simply that he believed it. Could people really *know* when they were going to die and simply give in to it without a fight?

Mrs. Valentine had told her some odd stories about people she had known or heard of who had been near death and lived to tell about it. They'd described it as being in a tunnel, walking toward a glorious light and having a feeling of profound peace. All of them had said they hadn't wanted to come back. They had *wanted* to die, so that they could live where that glorious light was and have that peace, which they'd said was like nothing they'd ever known in this life.

It was comforting to think that, if Abner had to die—but, no, she couldn't start thinking like that. If Abner died, he might be in a better world, but how could she go on without him?

Chapter Fifteen

When the rain stopped, Jed slogged through ankle-deep mud to saddle his horse. The stallion seemed as restless as Jed himself, and clearly glad to get out of the muck created by the hooves of the milling livestock inside the circle of wagons. Jed rode away from camp to scout the surrounding country.

Once he'd had some time alone to calm down after his confrontation with Thayer Goddard, his recollection of what Goddard had said made him uneasy.

"You'll pay for that, whore!"

"What in tarnation's wrong with you, Dossman? There's enough for both of us."

Goddard had sneered the words, as if Megan were mere merchandise to be divided between reasonable men, and he'd called her a whore. It was almost as though Goddard knew about Megan's activities in Independence. But how could he know?

Jed held the stallion to an easy trot, his eyes searching the wet terrain, as his thoughts ran along their own course. Goddard had gone into town alone several times while they were camped outside Independence. Once Jed had seem him walking away from the Gilded Lily. At the time it hadn't occurred to him that Goddard might have actually been inside the gambling hall, because he'd assumed Goddard disapproved of gambling. But now he thought about the possibility.

According to Royce Waddell, Megan's mother had been a prostitute, plying her trade in a room above the gambling hall. Maybe Goddard knew that. Maybe Goddard had been coming from one of the Gilded Lily's second-floor rooms when Jed saw him. After the unsympathetic way Goddard had treated his wife when their son disappeared, Jed had begun to suspect the man's straitlaced religion was barely skin-deep. Goddard's attempt to rape Megan confirmed it. Jed no longer found it difficult to believe that Goddard could have visited one of Waddell's prostitutes while in Independence.

It was conceivable that the woman had told Goddard about Megan and her "private house." Perhaps she'd been complaining about the competition, or perhaps they'd seen Megan walking along the street from the woman's window. The subject could have come up in any number of ways.

At any rate, Thayer Goddard had acted and talked as though he knew of Megan's past. Had he told anyone else? Upon reflection, Jed thought Goddard was the kind of man who would hold on to such a tidbit of information, waiting for a time when he could use it to his own advantage. But use it he would when the time was right, with no regard for the fact that Megan had turned over a new leaf.

If Megan's past became common knowledge, it couldn't help but alter the attitude of Megan's friends and neighbors in Oregon. People who were carving homes out of wilderness were generally more tolerant of past mistakes because they needed one another. But if Megan's past became common knowledge, their acceptance would be altered, if only subtly. Jed didn't want that to happen.

As he urged his horse up a steep incline, his mouth twisted into an ironic grin. Not long ago he wouldn't have cared what Goddard said about Megan or to whom. Now he wanted to protect her. He couldn't have her, but by God, maybe he could keep her past from following her to Oregon. To do that, he'd have to find a way to guarantee Goddard's silence.

The stallion scrambled up the last few feet of the incline to stand on a small plateau, and Jed found what he'd been looking for—the remains of a campfire. He dismounted and examined the pile of partially burned logs. The rain had scattered and obliterated the ashes, making it impossible to tell how long the logs had lain there like that. But Jed's instincts told him it hadn't been long. Whoever it was must have wanted to avoid detection. Nobody would make camp in such an inaccessible place otherwise.

Upon closer inspection, Jed could see the outlines of a horse's hooves in the mud and a single human boot print. A lone rider had camped here, hidden from the sight of anyone on the wagon trail below by a rock cliff. Jed's party's camp could be observed through a narrow slit between two rocks.

Jed swung back into the saddle and gently urged the stallion down the rocky incline, thinking that whoever had been tracking them might have called off the chase—for some reason, which he couldn't begin to know since he didn't know who was tracking them in the first place, or why. It was just as likely, though, that the tracker had gone on ahead and even now was waiting for them somewhere on the route.

The stallion reached level ground and Jed spurred him toward camp. It was time, he reflected, to talk to someone about his conviction that the train was being tracked. He needed another pair of eyes to help him watch for signs of the culprit.

His confidante would have to be someone he could trust to keep his suspicions quiet. Too many in their party had been worn down by sickness and exhaustion, until they were on the verge of cracking, and Jed didn't know if they could handle the news that the train had been relentlessly stalked since leaving Fort Hall, perhaps even before that.

He decided to confide in Reuben Schiller.

Chapter Sixteen

September-October, 1850

Two weeks after Jed found the tracker's abandoned campsite, Abner stopped taking any food or water. He was so weak that the effort of chewing and swallowing was too much for him, and most of the time he drifted in and out of consciousness.

Megan had spent forty-eight hours straight at his bedside as the wagon jolted over rocky ground and through the long, cold nights. So exhausted that she hung on the edge of delirium herself, Megan looked out the canvas opening in the deep darkness of the second night and saw the light of a lantern bobbing toward her. Or perhaps she was only dreaming it, she thought fuzzily as she raked a weary hand through her falling, tangled hair.

Never had she known such total fatigue. She was too tired to move, so she sat holding Abner's hot, bony hand and gazed at his wasted face in the last flickering light from a burned-down candle. His cheekbones appeared to have been sharpened on stone, and they looked like they were about to slice through the waxy skin that covered them. His cheeks were sunken like craters in his face.

Abner's breathing was so shallow, Megan couldn't detect his chest moving. She stared at the fever-ravaged face, realizing that he looked truly at rest for the first time in weeks, and dread swelled in her throat. It spread down into her chest and stomach and formed cold drops of sweat on her forehead.

She stared at the man she had known and loved longer than any person alive. And as she did so, she heard the distinct sound of footsteps approaching, yet was loath to look away, fearing that Abner would shrink to nothing while her attention was fixed elsewhere and she would turn back to find an empty bedroll.

Someone was coming. Who could be walking around the camp in the middle of the night? Oh, dear God...Abner didn't appear to be breathing. She jerked forward and laid her hand over his nostrils—and felt his breath, faint but warm and even. Despair racked Megan. "Don't leave me, Abner," she begged. "Oh, God—please, please don't die.

The footsteps stopped at her wagon. "Megan?" The whispered voice was low and gentle.

Was it her own voice that finally spoke, so calm and steady, when inside it felt as though her heart had turned to stone? "Come in, Jed, if you want to."

He was standing beside her when she finally looked away from Abner. An enveloping numbness pressed in on Megan. She could even look at Jed and feel nothing... nothing.

"You can't hold up to this any longer without some rest," Jed said softly, his voice full of concern.

Megan sat forward and rubbed her hands over her face. It felt like someone else's hands and face.

Jed touched her hair. "Megan?"

Her whole body seemed to sag and collapse in on itself. "Oh, Jed...he can't eat or drink...he doesn't even know me." A sob lodged in her throat and she covered her mouth with her hand. Tears rolled down her face.

Jed set the lantern down and lifted her in his arms. Her head fell against his shoulder as if her neck wasn't strong enough to support it. She weighed almost nothing. He kicked back a quilt that was spread over a second bedroll on the opposite side of the wagon bed from Abner's and laid her down. He pulled the quilt up to her chin and dried her tears with its corner, smoothing back her rumpled hair with gentle fingers.

"Go to sleep. I'll sit with Abner."

"Wake me," she whispered, her lashes already drooping closed, "if he needs anything . . . promise me."

"I will," he assured her. "Now rest."

Sighing, she curled up on her side and was instantly asleep. He watched her for a moment, his eyes softening with love. Then he turned away and moved back to Abner.

The sky in the canvas opening was gray with dawn when Megan jerked awake and sat bolt upright in bed. Disoriented, she looked around the dim interior of the wagon. Jed was sitting beside Abner's bed, his head tipped back and propped against a wagon bow, his black slouch hat tilted down over his eyes.

She had slept for hours. Megan threw back the covers and rose from her bed. She grabbed up the hairpins that had fallen among the covers during the night and pinned up her hair by feel as she knelt beside Abner's bed. He opened his eyes when she touched his face. He didn't feel feverish; but, then, the fever usually didn't come up until later in the day.

"Feeling better?" she whispered.

He just looked at her for a moment, his eyes bright with the glitter of the illness that had ravaged his body for so long. "Meggie?"

He knew her! As she smiled, Jed stirred and sat up. "I just dropped off for a minute," he mumbled, pushing his hat back on his head.

Still smiling, Megan looked at Jed. "Thank you for coming last night. I was at the end of my tether. But I feel quite rested now." She turned back to Abner. "He's better, I think."

Jed got to his feet and picked up the lantern, averting his eyes from Megan. He knew that Abner wasn't better—Abner was dying. At some level he thought that Megan knew it, too. "I'll bring you some fresh water before we break camp."

"I'd appreciate that, Jed. Thank you." As Jed left the wagon she straightened Abner's bedclothes. "You feel well enough to eat something this morning, don't you?" she asked, but didn't wait for an answer. "I'll make biscuits and gravy."

Abner reached out and took her hand. His fingers were so bony they looked like claws. "You can fix my breakfast in a minute, sugar. Right now I want you to listen to me."

"Abner, there isn't time—"

"Meggie," he said almost sternly. "I have to say this now. I—oh, Lord, I don't know where to start—" His glittering eyes, fixed on her face, were so bright she thought they might burn right through her skin. "Meggie, didn't you ever wonder why I was always around, always came to see you when I was in Independence and brought you presents, even when you were a little tyke?"

Megan sat very still, her fingers clutching his. "I often wondered about that through the years. Why, Abner, I can't even remember the first time you came to see me, I was that young. I don't know why I never asked you about it. I guess I knew you'd tell me if you wanted to."

"I meant to tell you many times," he said, "but then I'd change my mind at the last minute—because—" He moved restlessly on the bed. "What I mean is, I can't prove...I mean I don't *know* anything for sure." He struggled as though to sit up.

She drew her hand from his and laid both hands on his chest to press him gently down. "Shh, lie still." She could feel his heart beat, much too rapidly, beneath her palm. She smoothed the quilt over his shoulders. "This is upsetting you, Abner. Why don't you wait until you're stronger to talk to me about it?"

"No," he said adamantly, and managed a weary smile. "I want to do it now. You see, Meggie, I always thought—hoped—that you were my daughter."

For an instant she thought he had slipped back into delirium. But in the next instant she realized that his eyes, though too bright with the sickness, were clear. Through the opening in the canvas, she could see the sun peeking over the horizon, coloring the mountains with pale yellow light and the sky with streaks of vivid pink. To Megan it seemed that the whole world had shifted, that she was looking at it with fresh eyes. A part of her wasn't even surprised by Abner's confession. "Abner... you mean, you and Kate..."

"Only the once, Meggie, and then I left on a cattle drive, and when I got back to Independence, you'd been born and she'd put you with the Valentines. I went to see you right away, you were such a tiny little thing, still kind of red and nearly bald." He smiled, remembering. "You took one look at me and started squalling. But the next time I came, about six months later, we hit it off fine."

He sounded so proud. "Oh, Abner..." she said tremulously.

"Aw, I know the odds are against me being your pa, sugar, but I always wanted it to be true. I couldn't love you any more if I had an iron-clad, gold-plated guarantee. You're the spittin' image of Kate, but sometimes you do have a way of tilting your head that reminds me of my ma."

She smiled. "Do I really?"

"Yep."

"Abner," she said seriously, "I'd be proud to be your daughter. I never told anyone this, but I used to pretend that I was."

"Aw, you're just trying to make me feel good."

"I swear it."

She could tell she'd pleased him. His expression turned suddenly grave. "Now maybe you can understand why I was plumb sick with shock when you wanted to get married— why I didn't want to do it."

Oddly, Megan hadn't thought about being married to Abner for days, but his words brought the memory of their wedding day flooding back. "Oh, Abner... and I literally begged you to marry me. In front of all those people, where you couldn't very well say no. I'm so sorry..." All at once her throat thickened. "It—everything that's happened—it's all my fault. If we'd stayed in Missouri, you wouldn't have gotten sick.''

"Meggie, listen to me." He paused to gather his strength for more words. "I couldn't let you stay there. Royce Waddell would never have left you alone. He wanted you in one of those upstairs rooms, and he'd have made your life unbearable, trying to get you there."

"I know, but—'' Her voice broke and she couldn't go on.

"No buts, Meggie." He sounded so tired. He closed his eyes. After a moment, he went on, "Nobody hog-tied me and made me come. I wanted to come, sugar, just not as your husband... Well, that ain't gonna be a problem now." His words trailed off weakly. At length he muttered, "My only regret is I can't finish the trip and see you settled in Oregon."

"Don't talk like that," Megan insisted, bending over to kiss his sunken cheek. "I think I heard Jed come back with the water. You take a little nap while I make your breakfast. I'll wake you when it's ready."

"You do that, Meggie," he murmured, his lips barely moving.

Megan sat still for a moment, her hands clutched in her lap and tears burning her eyelids. Then she collected herself and went in search of fuel for a cook fire.

Never had her coffee smelled so rich as it brewed. Never had her baking powder biscuits risen so high or baked to such a perfect golden brown. Never had her sowbelly gravy turned out so smooth and creamy. As Megan arranged the food on his plate, she thought, not even Abner's delicate appetite could resist this breakfast.

She poured a mug of coffee and carried the meal to him. She set it down on the nearest box and, kneeling, placed her hand on his shoulder to give him a gentle shake. "Abner, wake—'' But the words died in her throat. He was too still. He wasn't breathing.

Megan sank down beside him as her throat closed. Her heart wrenched with sorrow. She squeezed her eyes shut and tears squirted out at the corners. Love welled up in her, mixed with grief and despair. "I'm so sorry," she whispered brokenly, "Abner—oh, Abner, you were my father in all the ways that mattered."

' She sat there until Daniel Schiller came to hitch up the ox team and found her. He took one look at Abner and tried to get Megan to stand and let him lead her out of the wagon.

She resisted, saying nothing, just shaking her head.

Daniel knew when he was in over his head. He left her sitting there and ran for the Schiller wagon. "Ma!" he croaked, "Ma, come quick! Megan needs you!"

Chapter Seventeen

The mountains seemed endless. Summer had passed and autumn, which came early to the mountains, was well under way; and always there were more mountains to cross, rising through the white mists of frosty mornings. They had thrown away everything that could conceivably be parted with to lighten the loads, even the deck boards of some of the wagons. Fort Boise was somewhere not far ahead, and they longed for sight of it as for their first look at Paradise.

Although the members of the party had said it before, they now knew that *this* was the worst road ever made—up and down steep, rocky hills, through mud holes and forests so dense that they traveled in twilight at high noon, continually turning and winding around tree roots and fallen trees.

Everybody agreed they had "seen the elephant," an expression passed along by earlier emigrants, which meant that they had surely faced the worst that could be faced.

Some days they traveled only two miles before falling into their bedrolls; the very best days ended with thirteen or fourteen additional miles behind them. Mouths had a grim set to them now, and eyes held resignation or defeat or just plain bone tiredness.

Megan's eyes, Jed noticed, revealed little of her thoughts or feelings. Something had gone out of her when Abner died. She held her grief inside and shuttered her eyes. She ate and walked alone, even when she was in the company of others. She still tended the sick, but stayed only long enough to see the patients and instruct their families how best to care for them. People watched her walk through the camp, self-absorbed, often not hearing when someone called to her, and they looked at one another and shook their heads.

Jed tried to talk to her—he wanted to help her, to comfort her—but she had withdrawn from him and from everyone except perhaps Daniel Schiller, who managed her team and wagon and slept nearby at night. Her withdrawal made Jed feel frustrated and helpless. She had changed. She was so unlike the woman he had come to know and love since they'd left Independence.

On a day in mid-September, they had to cross a twisting creek four times and progressed less than two miles. When they stopped to make camp, Jed sought out Rose Schiller, who was mixing cornbread batter for her family's supper.

Rose smiled as Jed approached her makeshift table. "There's enough cornbread and beans here for you, too, Jedediah."

"Nobody ever said you had to take me to raise, Rosie," he chided.

She laughed. "Throwing an extra portion in the pot makes no more work for me, and we have the pleasure of your company. Get one of those cups and pour yourself some coffee, and tell me what's weighing so heavy on your mind."

Jed got the coffee, then propped one boot on an upright log and blew on the steaming brew. He watched her drop a spoonful of lard into an iron skillet and set the skillet on the fire next to a big pot of beans. "How do you know I have something heavy on my mind?"

"You have that crease between your eyebrows. I know all your moods by now, Jedediah." She stirred the beans, then wrapped a dish towel around her hand and lifted the skillet off the fire before pouring the cornbread batter into the melted grease. Between them, orange flames licked at the cedar logs. "We're not likely to be interrupted for a few minutes. Reuben and Daniel are seeing to the livestock, and I sent Mary with the other children down to the creek to wash a few clothes. It'll give me a head start on the laundry I have to wash tomorrow."

Jed measured her a moment before he spoke. "It's Megan."

"Can't say that surprises me none." She glanced at the sliver of moon in a patch of darkening sky between two towering pines. The air was brittle and the fire felt good. Sounds of women's voices, talking in desultory tones as they prepared the evening meal, drifted around them. "You noticed it smells like rain?"

"Yeah."

"So it's Megan on your mind, is it?" she observed at length. "I saw you talking to her this morning, and I saw her walk off like she didn't hear you."

"I'm worried about her..." He trailed off then started again. "She keeps to herself too much."

"It's only been two weeks since Abner died, Jedediah. You have to give her time.

Testing the coffee, he found it cool enough to drink. He sipped it slowly. "Guess I don't fully agree with that, Rosie. It seems to me she needs some help getting over Abner's death so she can go back to being her old self again. She'll not get over it holding her feelings in and avoiding contact with other people, as she's doing."

Rose picked up a stick and poked at a log. "It appears to me she's let you know she doesn't want *your* help."

"She has. It'll take another woman to get around her defenses right now. She'll try to brush you off, so you'll have to be persistent. Will you talk to her, Rosie?"

"I always meant to when I thought she'd had enough time to feel like talking. We're going to ask her to throw in with us for the rest of the trip. We could combine all our goods in one wagon, and with two teams the animals could have every second or third day off from pulling that heavy load."

"That's good of you and Reuben. It sounds like the best solution to me."

"It's not only Megan we're thinking of. Reuben needs more of Daniel's help than he's getting now. When will we reach Fort Boise?"

"Tomorrow, if we're lucky."

She chuckled humorlessly. "Well, I won't count on getting there tomorrow then. But when we do get there, I'll make her talk about what she's feeling—if I can. And I'll put our proposition to her."

"Good."

She stirred the beans again and checked the cornbread. "Tell me to stick my nose somewhere else if you like, but you love her, don't you, Jedediah?"

Jed didn't reply for a long moment. "Where'd you come up with that notion?"

"I told you, I know your moods."

He looked unhappy. "Rosie, I didn't set out to fall in love with her." Knowing of her past, he had meant to keep a watchful eye on her while maintaining his distance. It was keeping his distance that he'd not been able to manage, because Megan had turned out to be so different from the scheming little piece of goods he'd imagined. "I sure didn't have any right to—I mean, she was a married woman—and after my wife died, I didn't think I'd ever want another woman in my life. I had a lot of regard for Abner, too, and that made it worse. I've felt guilty as hell for weeks now."

"Jedediah, don't torture yourself. We don't really have much choice about who we fall in love with. We don't get to pick the time, either."

He nodded glumly and took a swallow of coffee.

It was dark enough now to see a single faraway star, and Rose peered at it before shifting her gaze back to him over the flickering orange flames of the cook fire. "How does Megan feel about you?"

Jed's head came up. Rose had put into words the very question that nagged him in the long, sleepless night hours. "I don't know." He knew that when he kissed Megan, she kissed him back. When he held her, she responded, she wanted him. But that wasn't the same thing as love. He knew also that Megan felt as guilty as he about those clandestine kisses. Abner's death had probably only increased her guilt.

"Maybe she doesn't know yet herself."

Jed hoped that was the case. If Megan was avoiding him because she was confused about her feelings, he could deal with that. But what would he do if she had made up her mind she could never love him?

"You and me buried Abner two weeks ago," Rose went on, "but it's not that easy to leave a husband behind. Give her time to forget, Jedediah."

He knew that Rose's counsel was wise, but it was hard to stand aside and wait, when he wanted desperately to be with Megan, to touch her, talk to her, find out what was going on in her mind. He heard the voices of the Schiller children, coming back from the creek, and said quietly, "I don't have any other choice, do I? I'll rest easier, though, if she agrees to throw in with you and Reuben."

Fort Boise was a collection of log buildings enclosed within a high stockade. There was a small trading post and fields for the livestock. The grass had already been killed by frost, but it was still palatable to the hungry animals. Jed found a level place to set up camp near the fort, where the wagon train party could rest and repair the wagons.

At least three hundred Indians—Nez Pierce and Cheyenne—were encamped nearby and most of them seemed to stay drunk. Jed assigned camp guards around the clock to keep the Indians from stealing everything that wasn't nailed down.

Daniel staked Megan's oxen in the grass near a mountain stream fed by the Snake River and returned to help her gather wood for a fire. "Your lead ox is sick," he told her. "I don't think he'll be strong enough to pull the wagon for a while—if he lives, that is."

Megan looked at him with eyes like a startled fawn's. She'd been so self-absorbed she hadn't even noticed the ox was ailing. This was dire news indeed, because she had no replacement. The mules had died weeks ago. "Can three oxen pull the wagon?"

Daniel shrugged. "Dunno. It's hard enough with four in this country."

She nodded. "We'll not borrow trouble. We'll figure out what to do when and if the ox dies. Now you go on and have supper with your family."

Daniel told his parents about Megan's sick ox at supper. It gave Rose the opening she'd been waiting for. As soon as they finished eating, she assigned Mary and Laura to tidy up and put things away, and paid a call on Megan.

She found her sitting in her wagon, a shawl pulled around her shoulders, nursing a mug of hot coffee. Rose tapped on the side of the wagon and poked her head through the opening in the canvas. "Can I come in and sit a spell?"

"Of course. Would you like a cup of coffee?"

Rose climbed into the wagon. "No, thanks. I've had plenty." She tested the sturdiness of the metal trunk, then sat on it, facing Megan. "Daniel says you've got a sick ox."

Megan nodded. "I was just thinking about what I'll do if the ox dies." She lifted a brow. "Maybe I'll end up like that Dutchman we met going to California with everything he owned in a wheelbarrow. Except I don't own a wheelbarrow."

"I have a suggestion that'll beat that one all to pieces. Reuben and I have discussed it, and we want you to join forces with us."

Megan paused with her cup halfway to her mouth. "Join forces? What do you have in mind?"

"We could make one good wagon out of the best parts of our two and combine our teams. Four of the animals can pull the wagon while the other two get a day off. They'll all last longer that way."

"But can we store all our provisions in one wagon?"

"Shouldn't be any trouble with what we have left."

Megan was hesitant. "The sleeping arrangements—"

"You, Mary and Laura can have the wagon. The rest of us can sleep in the tent."

Rose seemed to have thought of everything. She sounded so earnest and determined that Megan was amused.

Rose grinned. "It's good to see you smile again, Megan."

"I haven't had much to smile about lately."

"I know," Rose sympathized. "I could tell you wanted to be left alone. That's why I haven't come around to pester you. But, Megan, your friends can help you get through this bad time if you'll let us."

Rose held Megan's gaze and Megan felt the tears gathering behind her eyes. She seemed to tear up over the silliest things lately. Rose's reference to "friends" had reminded her that she'd never had any friends before, unless you counted Abner and the Valentines. She looked down into her coffee.

"I have felt a need to be alone," she murmured.

"I know how that feels. I lost twins in a flu epidemic back in Illinois."

When Megan had conquered her tears, she glanced up. "I'm sorry, Rose. How old were they?"

"Six months. Like to tore my heart out."

"But you're so strong. I should think you could weather almost any heartbreak."

Rose shrugged. "I kept going because I had a family to care for. Keeping busy helps, Megan."

Megan nodded, accepting the truth of Rose's statement. "I'm grateful to you and Reuben for your offer. I'll think about it—I really will."

Rose knew it wouldn't help to press Megan for an answer just then. From what Daniel had said, the sick ox would be dead by morning and Megan's choice would be made for her. "Good." She hesitated. "Reuben says we won't be leaving here till day after tomorrow. It'll be nice to have a day to get the washing done. My children rinsed out a few things today, but I need to wash all our bedding."

"I'm looking forward to giving myself a good wash, as well as my bedding and clothes," Megan said. "I'm sick of taking spit baths with a few inches of water in the bottom of the bucket.''

"I reckon we all could use a vigorous scrub.'' Rose pushed herself off the trunk with her hands. "I better get back and see that the younguns put the tent up before dark.''

"We'll talk tomorrow,'' Megan said. After Rose left, Megan sat in the wagon, blanketed by the cold night, and pondered the Schillers' offer. If she had to join up with anyone, she would rather it be the Schillers. She knew they wouldn't make her feel as though she were imposing. She was imposing now, anyway, by depending on Daniel so much. There must be times when Rose and Reuben needed him.

It was just that she'd gotten used to being alone with her thoughts. Maybe that wasn't all to the good, she reflected as she finished her coffee. Rose was undoubtedly right; she had spent too much time alone with her memories and regrets. Too much time worrying and feeling sorry for herself. Abner would want her to look ahead. She was here by her own choice and now she had to make a decent life for herself in Oregon—to honor Abner's memory.

She wouldn't decide anything tonight, she told herself. But if the ox died before they left this camp, the only sensible thing to do would be to join the Schillers.

A brief rain shower blew in during the night, but passed on before morning. Megan woke to find her bedding wet. She thrust her head out of the wagon to examine the sky. It was clear. The eastern mountains were shrouded in pink and lavender mists, and shimmered with golden fire from the rising sun.

For the first time in weeks, she felt a lightness in her body and was eager to be doing something. Enough wood remained, from the supply she and Daniel had gathered yesterday, for a fire. She cooked rice and brewed coffee and, after eating, began pulling the bedding out of the wagon. She tied it in a bundle for transporting to the stream.

While she was thus engaged, Daniel appeared. "Megan, I've got some bad news. The lead ox is dead, and another one's head's drooping, like he's feeling poorly."

She tied the last knot firmly on the laundry bundle, then straightened and placed her hands on her hips. "That's that then, isn't it?"

He seemed to have expected some female outburst, and was clearly relieved that she was taking the news so calmly. "Yep. Too bad so many beasts have to die to get us to Oregon. All the teams are worn down to a frazzle. It's a good thing they're getting a day of rest."

"Tell your folks I'll have to take them up on their offer, will you? I'll sort through my goods after I've finished my laundry, and if you'll help me, we'll take my things to your wagon this afternoon."

"All right. Megan, we're all gonna be real glad to have you with us."

She smiled. "Thank you, Daniel. I'll try not to be a burden." She lifted her skirts to step up into the wagon. "I'd better get started on my laundry."

"You want me to carry it for you?"

"No, thanks," she called from inside, "I can manage."

She tied the dirty clothes in a second bundle. With the two bundles of laundry thrown over one shoulder, she tucked a comb and a bar of lye soap in her pocket and folded a clean change of clothing over her arm. She walked along the bank of the stream, returning greetings as she passed other women from the train who were already scrubbing their clothes and offspring. The children were complaining at the top of their lungs about the cold water, but their mothers' determination to leave Fort Boise with clean clothes and equally clean children prevailed.

Megan followed the stream until she found a big rock that would serve as a washboard. Apparently nobody else had ventured this far upstream from the others, so she had the rock to herself. Pine and cedar trees edged a semicircular clearing with the rock at its center. She dropped her bundle, rolled up her sleeves and set to work.

After scrubbing and wringing each piece, she spread it on a rock or bush to dry. By the time she'd finished, she'd discarded her shawl and her heavy gray dress felt too warm. Walking even farther up the stream in search of a secluded place to bathe, she found the perfect spot where the water had eaten into the bank forming a U-shaped pool surrounded on three sides by trees and brush. The water was so clear she could see the rocks on the bottom, and it appeared to be no more than knee-deep.

With a little murmur of pleasure, Megan scanned the opposite bank and the surrounding vegetation. Confident that she was alone, she hastily stripped off her clothes. Gritting her teeth, she stepped into the water and instantly submerged herself in the pool to her shoulders.

The shock of the cold water nearly paralyzed her. "Oh, mercy... brr-rrr," she groaned, her teeth chattering. Standing again, she locked her muscles to keep from shaking and scrubbed everywhere with the lye soap, assuring herself she'd feel warm by comparison when she was dressed again.

Last of all she washed her hair, then waded out of the water to grab the towel and dry herself quickly. She wound the towel around her head and dressed in clean underclothes and cotton dress. By the time she was fully clothed, she no longer felt cold.

She looked around for a sunny rock smooth enough to sit on while her hair dried. Choosing the flattest-looking one, she had started toward it, when, right in front of her, Jed stepped out of the trees.

Megan froze. She did not know how long she stood there, muscles paralyzed, breath suspended. Visions of herself standing in the pool stark naked whirled through her mind and plunged her from fiery embarrassment to frigid disbelief so fast she felt dizzy. If only I could faint, she thought, or die—anything, so I wouldn't have to face this.

Jed couldn't think of anything to say to smooth over the situation. Before she'd arrived he'd bathed in the pool. He'd been drying himself, when he heard someone coming.

Hardly thinking, he'd grabbed his clothes and run into the cover of the trees.

By the time he'd dressed and was ready to leave the woods, she'd gone into the pool. He hadn't known what else to do but keep quiet and wait until she'd dressed and returned to camp. There was no other way back except along the bank of the stream.

But instead of leaving when she was dressed, she'd looked around and headed for that rock, and he'd realized she meant to stay there and dry her hair. That might take an hour, and he didn't fancy hiding in the trees that long. There was nothing for it, he'd decided, but to brazen it out.

Now that he was alone with her, as he'd dreamed of being through so many restless nights, he felt anything but brazen. He felt a tingling excitement and a wary caution all at once, and he still didn't know what to say. He wasn't used to feeling unsure of himself, and he didn't like the feeling. "Megan, I—"

Warmth suffused her throat. "What are you doing here?"

He raised his hand, which clutched his dirty shirt and trousers, then let it drop. "Same as you. I needed a bath. I thought I'd be alone this far from camp."

She stared at him. Her cheeks felt as if they were on fire. "You were there—all the time—you—"

"I heard you coming," he hastened to explain. "I didn't know who it was—and I didn't have any clothes on. I ran into the trees to dress. When I came back, you were already—uh, in the water. I couldn't come out then."

She didn't know which she felt more, angry or embarrassed. "So you stood there and watched me?"

Her eyes were wide and a little stunned as she stared at him. He took one step and her chin jerked up, dislodging the towel she had wrapped around her wet hair. As though she were glad to have something to snatch, she ripped off the towel and threw it to the ground. She drew a comb from her pocket and began to pull impatiently at the snarls.

Jed lifted his hat from his still damp hair and crushed it in his hand with his dirty clothes. He watched her attacking her tangled hair for a moment, yanking the comb through a strand and tossing it over her shoulder to do battle with another.

When he spoke, his voice was husky, as though he'd caught a cold between one second and the next. "Do you want me to lie and say I turned my back? Or that I didn't enjoy watching you?"

Her hand stilled and her head tilted up, her eyes lifting to his from beneath dark lashes. They stood less than a foot apart, rapt. She could hear him breathing and see the rise and fall of his chest beneath the homespun shirt. "I wouldn't believe you, anyway."

His mischievous grin further unsettled her. "I could say I'm sorry, but that would be a lie, too."

She tossed back her hair and gazed at him, her blue eyes issuing what might have been a challenge. "I hope you don't expect to receive a commendation for honesty."

He chuckled and, just for an instant, thought he saw the corner of her mouth twitch. He regarded her silently, not wanting to anger her again. She'd already tolerated his company longer than at any time since Abner's death. She seemed different today. He didn't want to do anything to spoil it.

Lifting her shoulders, she drew a deep breath and let it out slowly, as though to say, what's done is done. Looking away from him, she walked to the rock she'd been headed for when he stepped out of the trees. She settled in the sun with her back to him, arranged her skirts around her, leaned back on her hands and closed her eyes.

Jed watched her, fascinated. In the sunlight, her hair glistened like black patent leather. Hat, shirt and trousers dropped from his hand. He walked up behind her. She didn't open her eyes, but she knew he was there. He saw the tensing of her arms and shoulders. He lifted his hands and placed them on her shoulders and waited. Slowly she relaxed and opened her eyes, looking at him upside down.

His eyes were as dark as the deepest part of the forest, Megan thought as she listened to the racing of her own pulse, as loud as thunder in her ears. His hand lifted the heavy weight of her hair off her shoulders, his fingers playing through the strands. She couldn't move.

He saw the erratic pulse beat leaping in the hollow of her throat and swallowed convulsively. Gathering her hair in one hand, he brought it forward over her shoulder as he lowered himself to sit beside her, his feet on one side of the rock and hers on the other.

"I watched you bathing because I couldn't look away," he said with honesty. "You're so beautiful." Her dress fit closely over her breasts, the fabric lifting and falling with her rapid breathing. He lifted his eyes to her lips. They were parted, the pink, moist tip of her tongue caught between her teeth.

He bent to touch her mouth with his. The kiss was light, gentle, but when he lifted his head, his breathing was ragged, fanning the top of her hair. His arms came around her, and his breath caught in his throat.

Megan wanted to sob aloud. The numbness that had enveloped her for days was melting, and she was awash with feeling. So many feelings, and all so intense. The only thing she could do was tighten her arms around him and lift her face to his and welcome his greedy, hungry mouth.

A desperate, releasing emotion washed through her. It was more than need, more than pleasure. It was gratitude and joy for being young and alive, for being there with Jed, for whatever he saw in her that made him want her. She did not question the sensation that overpowered her; she merely received it.

Jed's hands drove themselves into her hair. "Megan, I need..." And then his mouth covered hers again, hard and possessive, and a sob rose in her throat as she pressed against him, unable to get close enough, wanting something else, something more, something mysterious that she barely understood.

She made no protest when he lifted her and drew her with him to the ground, fashioning a pillow for her head from her discarded towel. She knew only that his arms were wrapped around her once more and his mouth was tasting hers again.

Dazzled by wonder, her lips moved beneath his, opening for him, drawing his mouth back to hers again and again. The ground was cool and damp beneath her, but Jed's heat covered her. Her hands played over his back, feeling the breadth of hard muscle beneath his shirt, tracing the ridge of his spine, marveling in the wonderful maleness of him.

A few, fleeting cautions drifted through her hazy mind. Abner had died only weeks ago—what would people think? But the question was quickly lost under the onslaught of love and need.

She was seized by an inner trembling and overcome by mindless pleasure as his lips tasted her throat. His fingers fumbled clumsily with the tiny buttons of her dress, abandoning them to trace the swell of her breasts and then return to take up where they'd left off.

He's undressing me and I'm letting him, Megan thought as his hand slipped inside the opening of her dress to close firmly, warmly over her breast. She gasped as he lowered his head and pressed his mouth there.

Megan closed her eyes and gave herself up to the drowning, tingling sensations that sent ripples of pleasure racing through her and set her blood on fire. She moaned, helpless with need. Jed. This was Jed, whom she loved, would always love.

Oh, Jed, touch me there...

Jed exposed the ivory curve of her breast. Seeing the rosy tip engorged, he groaned. His shaking fingers somehow finished opening her dress and drew it down and away from her.

Each sweet, soft sound of pleasure, each dazed smile, each taste of her mouth, each scent of her clean flesh buried him deeper in need. She was so beautiful. She tasted so good, smelled so sweet. She was so soft and yielding beneath him. Her glazed eyes held awakening and wonder, as though all of this were new, as though he were the first.

He let himself believe in her innocence for a little while because he would give anything to have been the first. He forgot her past, forgot that her husband and been dead less than a month. It was too late to think of any of that—it didn't matter. He knew only that he had needed her for what seemed all his life, that he had to have her.

Megan felt his hand beneath her thin petticoat, warm on her thigh. There was a tense, heavy feeling in the pit of her stomach. She trembled and the blue sky above her was moving, spinning. She closed her eyes as his hand moved upward, and the tenseness in her stomach tightened into a clenched, aching knot.

He spread his palm on her stomach, and for the space of a few heartbeats, she stopped breathing. Then he was fumbling with her undergarments, and Jed's unsteady breathing was the only sound in all the world.

She lay still, weak and waiting, feeling his fingers brush her naked skin. She knew vaguely what was going to happen, but she had never imagined the power of the feelings that would accompany it. Had never realized that she would never, ever be the same person again.

She was grateful it was Jed who was teaching her about love. She wasn't afraid. She wanted this. She knew now that she had wanted it for a long time. And maybe, when he'd stepped out of the woods and she realized he'd seen her bathing, she had known this would happen and she had been glad the inevitable moment had finally come.

He slipped her undergarments down her legs and off her feet. His fevered gaze raked over her, and without ever taking his eyes from her, he stripped off his clothes.

Why, Jed, you're beautiful!

His body covered her, pressing hard and hot against her naked thighs and stomach and aching breasts. She could never even have imagined the pleasure of his bare flesh against hers.

Then he was kissing her hair, her brow, her nose, her cheeks, her throat. She could feel the part of him that would enter her, hard and hot against her stomach, strange and frightening and exciting.

"Jed," she whispered, and buried her face in the hollow of his neck. "Jed, help me. I don't know what—how—"

He dimly heard her words, but he didn't comprehend them, and he didn't let her finish. He couldn't wait any longer to have her. He had waited so long now that he was all driving need and power without gentleness or care.

The pain she felt was sharp and searing. Megan would have cried out if she hadn't bitten down on her bottom lip. She had wanted this, she told herself. This was Jed, and he would make it all right.

Jed was lost in a paroxysm of need so intense he almost didn't realize what had happened. But at the last second, as he pushed against the barrier of her maidenhood and at last it gave, the impossible, inconceivable truth rushed in on him. He felt as though he'd been flung on the shore of a foreign country, where there were no guideposts to tell him where he was or in which direction he was going.

She was a virgin!

For a blinding instant, he froze, trying to make some sense out of it. Then his need drove everything else from his mind. But this time the need was tempered with a great tenderness, an impulse to cherish her. Lifting himself up with his hands, he looked into her lovely face. Her eyes were closed and tears dampened her cheeks. In that moment, he hated himself for judging her and hurting her with his blundering male hunger.

Tenderly he kissed her tear-stained cheeks and her closed eyes. "I'm sorry...it'll be all right..." She opened her eyes, and looking deeply into them, he began to move slowly within her.

She could feel him holding himself back as he gazed at her with a mixture of tenderness and hunger in his eyes. The pain had faded and a warm, languid feeling filled her. Instinctively she matched his rhythm. This was the mystery she had wondered about for so long. Megan's heart overflowed with love.

There was release, more rending and powerful than any Jed had ever known. And there was more. Even in the moment when his world exploded, he felt the wonder and the glory.

Chapter Eighteen

Afterward Jed held her, poignantly aware of how small and fragile she felt in his arms. He wanted to hold her like that forever and feel her light, warm breath on his neck and the slow, steady beat of his own heart.

While his body rested and his weakness receded, his mind whirled with sensations and emotions and confused thoughts. Deep inside of him a single truth was repeated again and again. She had never known a man before. He could not conceive how that could be possible, but it was true.

Megan. She filled his mind, his very soul. She had given her innocence to him freely; she had given him herself; and he had never known such joy in making love to a woman before. He had never felt so many things so intensely. What had happened was indescribably wonderful, and it had left him stunned and shaken and horrified at the disreputable things he'd been sure he knew about her. All that he thought he knew had been destroyed. Now he blindly groped his way toward a new understanding of the one woman in all the world who had made him feel the shattering, uttermost depths of love.

Megan.

He wanted to drown out the confusion by kissing her and burying himself in her warm, yielding sweetness again. He wanted to wipe out the past few months since that day he first saw her in Independence, and love her and keep her safe always.

But the questions wouldn't stop. Why hadn't Abner ever bedded her? Why had Royce Waddell lied to him about her? Why? Why?

Jed listened to the sound of his own heartbeat and watched the lazy drifting of a cloud across the blue sky. What had happened between them was touched with splendor. He felt reborn. Everything was different now. He had been totally wrong about her from the beginning, so self-righteous and condemning. He had taken her without comprehending the magnitude of what he was doing. It made him feel deeply ashamed.

She lay so still and soft against him that he wondered if she'd fallen asleep. Tenderness made his throat ache painfully and his eyes burn. How could he have been so pigheadedly wrong about her?

"Megan." His voice was husky. He rubbed his thumb lightly over her cheek. She murmured and snuggled against him. His arms went around her to keep her close. He couldn't look at her until he'd said what he must say. "Honey, I'm so sorry. I didn't know...please forgive me."

She eased out of his arms and sat up, her hair falling in a tangled black glory over her shoulders. Her eyes were gentle and still a little dazed. Her smile was sweet and soft; it turned his insides to jelly.

"There's nothing to forgive. I wanted this as much as you." She toyed with the lock of hair on his forehead. "It's all right, Jed. I love you." She looked at him for a long moment, disturbed by the confusion in his eyes. "Surely that doesn't surprise you. I thought—that is, I assumed you felt...I mean...oh, dear..."

It had not entered her mind before that Jed didn't love her as much as she loved him. How could he be so hungry for her and give her such pleasure without loving her? It occurred to her that she knew very little about men. Why had she assumed she knew what Jed felt?

She was suddenly aware of the tangled mass of hair falling down her back and about her face and of her nakedness. Removing his hand from her hip, she reached for her dirt-smudged petticoat and slipped it over her head. She rose and found her dress, also smudged. Turning her back to Jed, she stepped into it, staring fixedly at the nearest pine tree as she fastened the buttons. Why didn't Jed say something? Had she embarrassed him by declaring her love? Dear God, what had she done?

She heard him dressing, but she didn't turn around. She couldn't look at him. He didn't love her, or he'd have said so by now. If only he would leave her alone with her humiliation. She wasn't expecting the touch of his hand on her shoulder, and jerked violently. He wrapped his arms around her, pulling her back against him and resting his chin on top of her head.

"Don't turn away from me, Megan," he muttered. "I'm just trying to sort things out. I've been thrown for a hell of a loop. I never dreamed you were innocent."

"Does that change things? Are you sorry you made love to me? Do you think less of me now?"

His arms tightened around her. "Oh, no—never. Don't you think that for a second." He placed a gentle kiss on top of her head. "But you were Abner's wife, Megan. How—why didn't he ever...?"

She sighed. "You never understood about Abner and me. We were—friends. Getting married was the the last thing either of us wanted. When we came to your camp that morning in Independence and you told us we couldn't travel with your party because we weren't related...well, it seemed at the time that getting married was the only thing left for us to do. We wanted to go to Oregon, and we'd spent all our money on our rig. We knew it wouldn't be safe to travel alone. We did what we had to get you to take us."

He had virtually forced her to marry Abner. He saw that now. "Why couldn't you have explained the situation to me? Why did you have to fabricate that story about being Abner's daughter in the first place?"

She let her head fall back to rest on his shoulder. "Abner said no wagon master would take a young, single woman without a family. So I decided to say I was his daughter. It was my idea completely. Abner wasn't crazy about it, and he was even less crazy about getting married." She trailed her fingers over the arm wound around her just below her breasts and felt the springy, dark hairs. "But you could tell that, couldn't you? He only did it because I begged him to and...oh, there were a number of reasons that neither of us wanted to stay in Independence."

He thought of Royce Waddell and wondered what the gambler had hoped to gain by lying to him about Megan. She made a soft sound. "I fully expected to be a real wife to Abner. I thought it was my duty and that he'd expect it, but he wouldn't touch me. To be honest, I was relieved, but I didn't understand why until—until he was dying." She lifted her head from his shoulder and stepped out of his arms. She turned to face him, knowing that she had to tell him everything now. She didn't want any more secrets between them. If he couldn't love a prostitute's daughter, she might as well learn it now.

"My mother, Kate, worked at the Gilded Lily, in one of the rooms over the gambling hall," she said. "When I was born, she left me in the care of a Baptist minister and his wife. I never knew who—who my father was. If my mother knew, she never talked about it. But...before Abner died, he told me that he could be my father. There's no way of knowing for sure, of course, but it was a possibility. He said he had always wanted to be my father. I'd known him all my life, and he was good to me. He was the nearest thing to a father I ever had. I guess that's why the marriage never seemed completely real to Abner, or to me."

Jed reached out for her, pulling her against him to kiss her tenderly. What a blind fool he had been. When he discovered that Abner was sleeping beneath the wagon, he'd felt sorry for the man, assuming that Megan had kicked him out of her bed. As usual, he'd leaped to the wrong conclusion. His entire attitude toward Megan since the party had left

Independence had been based on the lying words of a devious gambler.

Megan drew away a little to look up into his face. "What I still don't understand is why you disliked and distrusted me on sight."

Looking pained, he brushed his knuckles beneath her chin, then, resting his hand on her shoulder, wound an ebony lock of hair around his finger. "Because of something I heard about you in Independence."

Her face went very still. "What my mother did for a living, you mean?"

"I knew that, but I didn't blame you for what your mother was. There was something else."

"Please tell me, Jed. Let's not hide things from each other anymore."

He drew a deep breath and studied her face. Her cheeks were faintly flushed, and her eyes were questioning. "Royce Waddell told me that you—well, that you had followed in your mother's footsteps."

"That I—" For a moment Megan didn't understand what he meant.

"He said you kept a private house at the edge of town. So when you and Abner showed up, I thought—well, I figured you'd cause no end of trouble before we saw Oregon."

She felt the blood leave her face, and something inside her shrank to a diamond-hard core of disillusionment. And then it shattered, like a treasured crystal vase flying into a thousand tiny slivers. Every piece cut her heart.

"You thought I—all this time, you've thought I was a—a whore? You believed what that evil man said? How could you, Jed?" She shook her head as though to negate the horrible truth. All at once, everything fell into place—Jed's sneering contempt for her that first day, his attitude toward her marriage to Abner, the things he'd said to her that hadn't made sense before. Every time he'd sought her out, he'd merely been seeking the services of a prostitute. He had never meant for their lovemaking today to be anything but a business transaction. Had he meant to offer her money before he found out how wrong he'd been about her?

"Megan, don't look at me like that . . . please."

He reached for her and she spun away. "Don't touch me, Jed." Her voice was cold, and she hated the sound of it. She hated herself for being so stupid and naive. But most of all she hated Jed for taking her love and twisting it into something ugly. "Don't ever touch me again."

"Megan, you can't mean . . . I'm sorry. How was I to know Waddell lied? Honey, forgive me."

"You ask too much, Jed—too much." Deliberately she turned her back on him and walked to the edge of the trees. "When my mother died, Waddell wanted me to work for him," she said tonelessly, knowing explanations could change nothing. "I refused." Why was she bothering to tell him all this? she wondered. None of it mattered now. "If you knew me at all, you'd know I'd have done anything to survive before I'd have agreed to his offer."

"Megan, give me a chance to make it up to you."

She uttered a short, bitter laugh. "Now that you have proof that Waddell lied? I'm afraid that's the very reason you can't make it up to me, Jed. It's too late. You had to have the evidence, didn't you?"

"I won't let you do this, Megan . . . after what we just shared—"

"What we shared! You were merely availing yourself of the services of a whore, Jed. Don't pretend you meant it as anything more."

"No, you couldn't be more wrong!"

She covered her ears with her hands and waited for him to leave. After a long silence, she dropped her hands and heard his soft, frustrated oath as he picked up his dirty clothes and felt hat. She stood still, letting the awful, rending pain rack her. She squeezed her eyes shut and clenched her fists to keep from sobbing.

"Megan . . ."

She didn't move, didn't look at him. In barely more than a whisper she said, "You make me feel dirty. Just go away and leave me alone."

Everything in him railed against doing what she asked. Desperately he wondered what he could do, what he could say to make it better. But there was nothing. Later she might listen to him, but not now.

He jammed his hat down on his head and walked away from her. It was as hard as anything he'd ever done.

He'd gone only a few steps, when he heard a movement in the trees to his left. Halting, he peered into the dense, green forest. The sound came again, a soft rustling, like the sound of furtive footsteps. Jed stood listening for another few moments, but heard nothing more.

"Megan," he called, "you'd better go back to camp. It's not safe for you to be alone this far from the others."

Jed's voice was like a thunderclap in the tense silence. It made Megan feel, on top of everything else, suddenly exposed and frightened. The idea of remaining for another minute at the scene of her shame was painful. She never wanted to see the place again. Running to where she'd left her laundry, Megan bundled the wet things into her arms and hurried back to camp.

Wordlessly Jed waited until she'd brushed past him, then he veered into the trees in the direction of the rustling sound he'd heard moments earlier. He was remembering the numerous occasions recently when his sixth sense had warned him that the train was being watched. If Indians were tracking them, why the hell didn't they make their move? What were they waiting for?

But was it Indians? The abandoned camp he'd found on a high plateau above his party's camp had been used by a single man. For a moment he thought about the Indian who had returned Johnny Goddard to Megan's wagon. Was he in the woods nearby? But why would he still be tracking them?

Turning the thoughts over and over in his mind, Jed scouted the forested area next to the creek bank, walking deeper into the trees at several points. Once he thought he caught a movement from the corner of his eye, but when he whirled to stare at the spot, he saw nothing unusual. On closer inspection, he found several places where the under-brush was crushed, as though it had been walked on re-cently. But he found nothing else to indicate that anybody had been there. Eventually he became convinced that look-ing any farther would be a waste of time. If somebody had been hiding in the trees, he'd gotten away by now.

Jed's mind returned to Megan as he walked back to camp. Was the Indian who returned Johnny Goddard after Me-gan now? A shiver of alarm shot through him at the thought. But immediately he realized that if the Indian had wanted to take Megan, he could have done so when he'd brought Johnny to her wagon.

Just the same, Jed decided to try to keep a closer eye on Megan. He didn't want her wandering away from camp alone as she had done today. He hoped she'd agree to join the Schillers for the remainder of the journey. He'd worry about her less if she wasn't traveling alone. But his feelings on that score weren't entirely settled. If Megan joined up with the Schillers, it would be more difficult to see her alone.

Nevertheless he had to get her alone and make her listen to him. Somehow he had to make things right between them again.

Megan and Daniel moved her things out of the wagon that afternoon. After Reuben finished repairing the Schil-lers' wagon, salvaging a wheel and other spare parts from Megan's wagon, he and Daniel helped Rose and Megan pack Megan's goods with the Schillers' in their wagon.

Though Megan did more than her share of the work that afternoon, Rose noticed that she seemed distracted. Sev-eral times she took no notice when Rose spoke to her.

That evening, as soon as Jed joined them for supper, Megan excused herself, saying she was tired and wanted to retire early. Rose raised a questioning brow at Jed, but he merely shrugged and looked away. Rose wasn't fooled, however. Clearly something had happened between Jed and Megan earlier that day. Whatever it was, it had made Jed miserable and Megan angry. Rose sighed inwardly, wishing that Jed had taken her advice and given Megan more time.

Rose observed the situation between Jed and Megan for several days. She saw him try to talk to her numerous times, and watched her turn her back and walk away. After the night when Megan excused herself from supper because Jed was there, Jed cooked his own meals and ate alone. The Schillers missed him and they rarely sat down to a meal without one of the children asking why Jed didn't eat with them anymore.

It was Laura who finally looked at Megan at supper late one afternoon and said a bit accusingly, "Megan's mad at him. Jed knows she won't eat with us if he's here."

All the Schillers turned to look at Megan, and she felt herself blushing. She hadn't realized that her feelings had become so obvious to everyone.

"That's enough, Laura," Reuben said sharply. "It's Megan's business and none of yours."

"Well, *I* think she's being awful hard on Jed," Laura retorted.

"Laura!" This time Reuben's voice brooked no opposition, and Laura bowed her head and finished her supper in stony silence.

The family dispersed after supper, leaving Rose and Megan alone. "Laura had no business saying what she did," Rose said, "but I have to tell you I think she was right. Don't you think you ought to ease up on Jedediah, Megan. Every time he comes near you, you snap at him like a dog with a new litter of pups."

"You don't understand."

Rose studied her. "Maybe I understand more than you think."

Megan shook her head. Nobody but she and Jed knew what had happened that day beside the pool. If she wasn't sure of that, she wouldn't be able to face kindhearted Rose Schiller. "No, you don't."

After a moment Rose shrugged. "All right, Megan, but I know Jedediah. He's a good man, and he cares about you." Megan didn't respond, and Rose added, "Have you decided what you'll do once we get to Oregon?"

"Not yet."

"You know you're welcome to stay with us for as long as you want to."

Megan managed a smile. "Thank you, Rose, but I'm not sure Laura would like that."

Rose waved a hand. "Pshaw, don't pay Laura any mind. She thinks Jed's right near perfect, which makes her rush to his defense without knowing what she's talking about. She's fond of you, too, Megan. She'll be fine tomorrow."

Megan knew that Rose was right. Laura was impulsive and quick-tempered, but her anger never lasted. "You and Reuben will have a tough enough time without another mouth to feed."

Rose chuckled. "You'll earn your keep, never fear."

"I really haven't given much thought to what I'll do in Oregon," Megan admitted. "Until a few weeks ago I'd planned to help my husband build a house and farm. Now . . . well, I may try to go into business as a seamstress." She wasn't sure the money Abner had left in the bank in Independence would be enough to establish her in a shop, but it would be a start.

"You'll still need a place to stay until you're making enough to support yourself," Rose said. "Think about staying with us."

"All right," Megan agreed. "Thank you, Rose." Impulsively she hugged Rose, then said, "I believe I'll go for a walk before dark. Do you mind?"

"Don't mind at all," Rose said. "I know a big family can be kind of overwhelming when you're used to being alone."

Megan wrapped her wool shawl around her shoulders before setting off. Feeling the need to be alone, she made her way out of the circle of wagons, where she wouldn't be stumbling over someone who wanted to chat every few minutes.

Seeing Megan leave the encampment, Jed followed. He caught up with her quickly. "I want to talk to you, Megan."

She stiffened. "There's nothing you can say that I want to hear." She whirled and started back to the wagons.

Jed grasped her shoulder and stopped her. "Damn it, you're going to listen to me. I've waited a week for a chance to talk to you alone."

"Let go of me," she demanded.

"I will if you promise to stay and hear what I have to say."

She stared at him furiously for a moment before finally nodding. He dropped his hand. "Last week," he said, "when I saw you bathing, I wasn't thinking about what Waddell told me or about anything except how beautiful you were and how much I wanted you. That's the truth, I swear it, Megan."

"That doesn't alter the fact that for months you thought I was a whore who was taking advantage of Abner to get to Oregon. I remember what you said to Abner back in Independence. I remember every word. 'Give her some money,' you said, 'but don't marry her.' *You* didn't even offer me money, Jed. You thought I was free for the taking, didn't you? When I think of the times I let you touch me— Tell me, Jed, what did you think I'd do when we got to Oregon? Desert Abner and open a house for entertaining gentlemen?" She spit the word "gentlemen" as though it were dirty.

Her words hit too close to home, and Jed winced. "I was a blind fool. I admit it. I don't deserve your forgiveness, but I'm asking for it."

"Why?" she shot back. "So you can stop feeling guilty? Well, I won't make it that easy for you, Jed. I am not a whore, but I am damaged goods. You saw to that. You don't really want me, Jed, except in your bed when the need strikes you. I'm not a perfect lady like your wife, and I never will be."

"You don't know what you're talking about." He tore off his hat and dragged his fingers through his hair in frustration. "Penelope was far from perfect. She was spoiled and selfish. She whined every mile of the way to Oregon, and she didn't stop when we got there. Our marriage was the biggest mistake of my life. I'd decided to take her back to her family in Illinois the next spring—but that damned barbarian kidnapped her and beat her and raped her before I tracked them down." He balled his fingers into a fist, crushing his hat. "She blamed me for all of it, just as she blamed me for everything else that was wrong in her life."

For an instant the anguish in his voice penetrated Megan's anger and wounded pride. She had an impulse to reach out to him in comfort, but she stopped herself. "I don't know what to say, Jed. I don't think I'm the one you should be telling all this to."

"You're the only one I want to know anything about it! I'm trying to tell you you're more woman than Penelope could ever have been if she'd lived to be a hundred. Megan, honey, listen to me—"

Megan stepped back abruptly. "No, don't touch me." She pulled her shawl more tightly around her, gripping it with both hands. "I can't deal with this right now, Jed. I came out here for a peaceful stroll. Please let me get on with it."

He uttered a curse and jammed his crushed hat back on his head. "I'll go, Megan, but I'm not giving up." She looked at him stonily. "And I'm going to keep an eye on you, so don't walk far from camp."

He left her, his long strides eating up the ground, and Megan resumed her walk, keeping the wagons in sight. She was disconcerted by what Jed had said about Penelope and his marriage. All this time she'd been imagining that Jed's had been an ideal marriage and thinking that he'd never love another woman as much as the wife he'd lost. It appeared that Jed wasn't such a shrewd judge of women, after all. He'd misjudged his wife, and he'd certainly misjudged Megan.

That didn't make it easier to forgive him, however. Blast
the man. How could he have swallowed anything that snake
Royce Waddell told him? The least he could have done, in
all fairness, was give Megan an opportunity to deny Waddell's charges.

Sighing, she told herself she'd been awfully dumb to fall
in love with a man who held such a low opinion of her. But
love Jed she did, and she had no idea what she was going to
do about that.

Some fifteen minutes later, Megan was pulled from her
deep thoughts by the sound of a male voice calling her
name. She turned to see David Glenhill loping toward her.

"I saw you from my wagon," David greeted her, "and
decided to come and walk with you, if you don't mind."

Physically David had matured in the course of their
journey. His shoulders in his deerskin jacket looked
broader, his wrists extended from the now too short sleeves
and his once soft hands were rough and calloused from
manual labor.

Since his uncle's death, David had taken charge of Hollis's wagon and livestock, working as hard as any man in the
party at hauling wagons over mountains and fording the
dangerous, frigid streams. It had been weeks since he'd had
time to discuss literature and life with Megan, and she'd
missed their conversations. She had always found David's
presence calming, perhaps because he aroused no strong
emotions in her.

"I'd welcome your company," Megan assured him as he
fell into step beside her.

"You've moved in with the Schillers," he observed. "I'm
glad. You shouldn't be alone."

"I realized that when my lead ox died," Megan told him
with a smile. "How's Lacey? I haven't talked to her in a
while."

"She feels as well as any woman could, under the circumstances," David said, avoiding her gaze, as though it
embarrassed him to be discussing his sister-in-law's delicate

condition with a woman. "Mason and I take as much of the work off her as we can."

"She's strong and healthy. She'll be all right," Megan assured him. "We'll reach Oregon before her baby comes. Fort Boise was our last planned stopover." She became aware that David wasn't listening. He was staring straight ahead with an intent expression. "What is it, David?"

"Indians. Up there."

Megan looked where he was pointing. Dusk was falling, and it was difficult to make out how many of them rode astride the horses that snaked down the side of a nearby mountain. "We'd better alert the others," Megan said.

"Wait." As she started to reverse her steps, David grabbed her arm with surprising strength and said urgently, "Bert Olmstead is just itching for an excuse to shoot an Indian, and he's not the only one. Look. They're not trying to sneak up on us. They're probably Cheyenne—from the fort. They don't mean any harm."

Megan glanced at David in alarm. His altered physical appearance had lulled her into believing he'd matured in other ways, as well. But apparently his naive view of Indians hadn't changed. "You have no way of knowing that," she said sharply. "I'm going back to camp and sound the warning."

"Megan, please," he pleaded. "I talked to many Cheyenne at Fort Boise. They're peaceful, I tell you."

"Those were fort Indians. They gave up their old ways to move to the fort so they could receive food from the government."

"And be turned into thieves and drunkards," David added contemptuously.

"Be that as it may," Megan said in exasperation, "these are no fort Indians."

"They're Cheyenne," he said stubbornly. "I'll just talk to them first. Then if I judge there's any cause for concern, you can tell the others." He released her and started forward.

He actually meant to intercept them! "David, don't be foolhardy—David, come back!" He strode purposely toward the Cheyenne, who were gathering at the base of the mountain, looking toward the wagons. They were close enough now for Megan to see that they numbered at least twenty. They carried bows and a few rifles. One of the Indians spoke rapidly and gestured toward David.

Alarmed, Megan threw a glance over her shoulder, realizing for the first time how far from the wagons they had walked. David would reach the Indians before she could find anyone to stop him. There wasn't time to go back. She'd have to stop him herself. "David!" She broke into a run.

When David was within a few dozen yards of the mounted Indians, he started waving his arms and talking in an excited manner. Megan caught the words "come as a friend" and "tell you of God's love." The Indians reacted with sullen stares that sent fear shooting through Megan.

"Come back, David . . . something's wrong . . . !"

Her voice dwindled off when she caught a movement from the corner of her eye. She jerked her head to the left and stopped in her tracks. Her hand flew to her mouth as she realized that what she'd seen was a bow being raised and an arrow fit to it.

There was a swishing sound, followed by a thump. The arrow had traveled through the dusk too fast for sight. Megan stared at David as the arrow struck him at the base of the throat. His head jerked back and he crumpled to the ground without a sound.

This isn't happening, Megan told herself. But she knew it was. Terrified, she spun and ran blindly in the direction of the wagons, smacking into a solid wall before she'd taken ten steps. Strong hands steadied her and she looked into Jed's face with wide, panic-stricken eyes.

"I saw," Jed answered, grabbing her hand and running for the wagons, dragging her so fast her feet barely touched the ground. Together they stumbled over a wagon tongue and tumbled over and over on the ground. Jed's arms encircled her as he shielded her with his body. They lay on the hard ground, gasping for breath, with shouts of "Indian attack! Take cover! Arm yourselves!" all around them.

Then Jed was on his feet again, hauling her up. "Come on," he yelled. In the confusion and darkness, she didn't know where he was taking her until he stopped and she realized they'd reached his wagon. Turning, he lifted her in his arms and dropped her unceremoniously inside. "Get down between those barrels and don't get up until it's over." He grabbed a rifle and shells and was gone before she had caught her breath enough to answer.

She crawled through the darkness of the wagon bed and stumbled over Jed's bedroll, hugging it to her breast. Jed's scent was still in the bedding, and it was oddly comforting. She clutched the bedroll in one arm and felt around until she found the barrels, then crouched between them. Over and over, she saw the arrow strike David's neck and the dark spurt of blood.

"Oh, David, you poor, sweet child," Megan moaned to herself. The words were wrenched from her aching throat as tears streamed down her face.

Chapter Nineteen

Megan had no idea how long she huddled in the darkness of Jed's wagon, listening to gunshots and the shouts of the men and wondering what was happening. The battle seemed to go on forever, but it probably lasted only a few minutes.

Finally there was a break in the gunfire and a male voice shouted, "We've got 'em on the run! Keep firing!" There was a final rapid burst of gunfire and then silence.

Cautiously Megan straightened, groaning at the soreness of her muscles, cramped too long in an uncomfortable position. She waited another few moments before edging toward the end of the wagon, where the night sky was now only faintly less dark than the black interior of the wagon.

Jed returned as she was climbing to the ground. Shivering, she hunched her shoulders and pulled her shawl tight beneath her chin. For a wordless instant he clasped the curve of her shoulder as though to reassure her.

"Will they be back?" she asked.

"I don't think so. We hit at least four of them."

"Oh, God." All at once she felt the strength go out of her, and leaned against the wagon bed. "Were any of our people hurt?"

"Two men took arrows," he said grimly, "and Bert Olmstead's got a bullet in his shoulder."

Gathering her wits, she said, "I'll get my nursing bag."

He held her against him for a moment and buried his face in her hair, breathing in her sweet scent. At length, he let her go without a word.

Megan tended the three wounded men all night, going from wagon to wagon throughout the cold, dark hours until dawn. One of the wounded was Thayer Goddard, who'd been hit by an arrow in the back just below his neck. Carolyn sat up with him, giving him periodic sips of strong medicinal tea brewed according to Megan's instructions and making him as comfortable as possible. It was the closest Carolyn and Thayer had been in weeks, Megan realized, and wondered if Thayer's brush with death would bring them back together permanently.

Carolyn answered Megan's silent question when she followed her from the Goddard wagon just before dawn. "You're very kind to come here to tend Thayer," Carolyn whispered when they were a few feet from the wagon, "after what he tried to do to you. I don't think I could be so generous."

Megan hardly knew how to respond. It was the first indication she'd had that Carolyn knew what had happened beneath her wagon during the hailstorm. "I'm not really doing it for Thayer," she said at length. "I'm doing it for the rest of us. We need every able-bodied man we can get."

Carolyn's thin fingers closed over Megan's hand for an instant. "You would see it that way," she said with a touch of irony, "because you're a realist, like Rose Schiller. You're able to put your personal feelings aside when you see something that needs doing. I think I've become more like the two of you lately. I hope so. I admire you very much, Megan."

Megan returned the pressure of Carolyn's fingers. "Thank you. Carolyn, I do hope distance doesn't prevent our seeing each other once we're both settled."

"We'll see each other," Carolyn said with conviction. "I've definitely made up my mind to open a rooming house, and you'll be coming to town occasionally."

"How does Thayer feel about your plan?"

"I haven't asked him, since he'll have no part in it. I'm leaving him as soon as our journey ends."

"Oh, Carolyn..."

"I know what I'm doing," she said reassuringly. "I've thought it through and worked out my plan. All I feel now is relief at finally having made up my mind and eagerness to be rid of Thayer."

"A divorce may be difficult."

"I don't care. He can't force me to live with him, even if we're not legally divorced. I never want to marry again, anyway. Johnny and I will be fine."

Megan gave her an impulsive hug. "Yes, you will be. You can always turn to your friends for help."

Carolyn returned Megan's hug and went back to the wifely duties she wanted so desperately to be free of.

The next morning, digging in the hard, rocky ground proved impossible. After a few words from Mason Glenhill and one of the other men in memory of the preacher killed by those he'd wanted to save, they laid David in a shallow depression in the rocks and piled stones on top of him to protect his body from scavenging wild beasts. The entire undertaking required less than half an hour, and without further pause they journeyed on, the actions of breaking camp and hitching teams to wagons now performed by rote.

That evening, Megan did not excuse herself when Jed joined the Schillers for supper. As she had visited the wounded men and gone about the other activities of the day, she'd spent a great deal of time in reflection.

They could all have been killed by Indians yesterday. They'd survived that attack with the loss of only one life, but the next attack might have a much worse outcome. Even if they encountered no more Indians, they could fall victim to cholera or another deadly disease, or die of drowning or exposure and starvation. Everyone of us, Megan mused, holds on to life by a thread that could be snapped at any moment of the day or night.

When considered against such odds, holding a grudge seemed like an enormous waste of time and energy. Though that didn't mean she was over the hurt Jed had inflicted on her, or that she would ever be able to put it completely behind her.

A few evenings later Jed lingered after supper, drinking coffee with Reuben, his eyes straying again and again to Megan as she washed dishes in a dishpan resting on an up-ended carton. Rose supervised the setting up of the tent and, as soon as it was fully dark, sent the children to bed, even Mary and Laura, who protested loudly that it was too early to go to bed.

Megan dried the last dish and stored it with its fellows in the carton, then carried the carton to the wagon. "Do you want the last of the coffee before I rinse the pot, Rose?" Megan asked.

"No, thanks." Rose yawned behind her hand. "I'm going to turn in. I'm plumb tuckered out."

Megan poured the coffee into her own mug and rinsed the pot, turning it upside down to drain on top of the emptied dishpan. When she looked around, Reuben was disappearing into the shadows surrounding the tent and she could just make out Jed's form still lazing on a log beside the dying fire.

She carried her mug to the fire and sat down beside him. She felt his eyes on her and was thankful for the darkness to cover her awkwardness. Although she and Jed had supped with the Schillers for three evenings now, they had not been alone or engaged in any but the most guarded conversations. Realizing that Rose and Reuben had disappeared to give them some privacy, Megan decided it was as good a time as any to break the wary reserve that remained between them.

She held the cup close to her face to savor the smell and feel its warmth on her skin. "How much longer will it be before we see Oregon?" she asked. It was the first week of October, and yesterday they'd traveled through snow flurries that had left a thin white blanket on the ground over which they passed.

He leaned forward and gazed into the glowing red embers, his elbows resting on his knees. "In two weeks, three at most, we ought to reach the Columbia. From there we'll go by raft downriver to the Williamette Valley."

"Barring calamity, like a heavy snowfall." She bent her head to sip her coffee.

He made a sound of assent, turning his head to study the line of her cheek and chin in the dim illumination provided by the embers of the fire. In the silence a horse whinnied. "Have you forgiven me, Megan?" he asked softly.

She didn't look at him, but he thought he saw a softening at the corner of her mouth. After hesitating for a moment, she replied, "I'm working on it." She held her coffee toward him. "Would you like a sip?"

He took the cup, drank and returned it to her, his fingers brushing hers in the process. She lifted the cup and took a swallow, imagining she could taste Jed's mouth on the rim. "Sometimes, Jed, I wonder if any of us will be alive when we get to Oregon."

"Those who've made it this far are strong," he assured her, "even stronger than when we started. They're worn out and discouraged, but underneath it all is strength."

She peered at him in the darkness. "You told me once before that I was strong. Funny, but I never thought of myself that way. Before I joined the Schillers, I hated having to depend on Daniel to break down the wagon and put it back together and swim the livestock across every body of water we had to ford. I wanted to do everything myself, but it was a physical impossibility."

"There are many kinds of strength, Megan. The kind that makes you keep on in the face of severe hardship is inside. Most of us don't know if we have it or not until it's tested. My grandmother stood less than five feet tall and weighed about ninety pounds, but she was one of the strongest women I've ever known. You're like her in many ways."

She smiled pensively. "I think you've just paid me a compliment."

He chuckled. "Honey, saying you're like my grandmother is the highest form of praise. She raised me after my mother died. Losing her was one of the worst things I've ever had to endure."

She finished her coffee and set the mug beside her on the log. "I understand." Megan twined her fingers and cupped them around her knees. "When someone you love dies, a little part of you dies with them."

His warm hand covered both of hers. "You're thinking about Abner now."

"All my life I always knew he'd come if I needed him. It may sound selfish, but the worst thing about losing Abner was the feeling of abandonment. Before I moved in with the Schillers, I'd wake up at night in a panic, and then I'd remember that Abner was dead and I was alone. I'd stay awake the rest of the night worrying about whether I could make it alone."

His hand tightened convulsively over hers. "You can do anything you have to do, Megan. Women like you wrest civilization out of the wilderness. But, sweetheart, you don't have to be alone. Let me be there for you when you need someone, Megan."

All he had to do was touch her and say something kind to her, and she felt her resistance melting. With all her heart, she wanted to throw herself into his arms and feel safe in his strong embrace. But her mind wasn't so ready to trample over caution again. She needed to find out if she was as strong as Jed said. To see if she had the courage and confidence to get by on her own. It was the only way to be sure she wouldn't be disillusioned and hurt again. She drew her trembling hands from his and stood. "I—I'd better go to bed now."

He followed her around the fading embers and ashes of the fire, both hands reaching out in desperation to stop her. "Megan..."

She stiffened herself against the need to step into his arms in sweet, yielding surrender. To wrap her arms around his neck and let him comfort and reassure her. What he must think was her coldness, perhaps even strength, was really a terrible fear that she couldn't hold Jed, that he would leave her eventually. If that happened, the pain would surely kill her.

"Don't tear my heart out . . ." His voice cracked and she could hear the pain in it. He took a step toward her. "I love you. I've never loved anyone the way I love you, and I never will again."

The words hung suspended between them in the cold, dark night. A few days ago, Megan would have given her soul to hear those words. But now even they did not melt the last frozen barrier that encased her heart. Perhaps too much had happened for them ever to go back. Perhaps he'd hurt her so deeply that the wound would never heal and she could never trust him again.

"I can't forget everything that's happened so quickly," she said. "I need time to work it out, Jed. I'm sorry. I hope you're right about my strength, because I will need it."

He knew he had no choice but to give her time, but, dear God, what would he do if she hadn't worked things out by the time they reached Oregon. What if she went away without telling him where she was going? What if she met somebody else, married somebody else?

He could not think about that now. One day at a time, he told himself, one obstacle at a time. If he had killed her love and he couldn't restore it, then he would have to go on without her. There his mind rebelled. He could not make himself imagine a life without her. She was the only good and precious thing that had been in his life for a long time, and he hadn't even known how good or precious she was until he'd hurt her, perhaps beyond healing. Just as he hadn't understood Penelope until it was too late to do anything. Why did he destroy everything he touched?

Megan wrapped her arms around herself to stop her trembling. Although she could not see him clearly, she sensed his anguish and his need as sharply as if they were her own. She was filled with yearning for him, this man who a few days ago had lain with her and taught her what it really meant to love a man. But then he had smashed her trust. If only he hadn't told her...but, no, without honesty there could be nothing worth having between them.

Despair overcame her. Her voice shook as she said, "Oh, Jed, I'm not trying to hurt you. I'm really not." She closed her eyes, feeling tears burning them, and held herself more tightly. "I don't want you to suffer because of me." Her voice broke, everything within her reaching out to him, but she couldn't make herself take a step toward him. "I'm—so terribly confused."

"You said you loved me," he said unsteadily. "Has that changed?"

Inside Megan her whole being cried out that she would never, ever stop loving him, but she couldn't get the words past her throat. The words that finally did come were "I don't know. I don't know anything right now. I wish you could understand how much you hurt me, how much—"

He stepped toward her and when he spoke there was torment in his voice. "Don't," he pleaded. Even though his tone was harsh, the anguish beneath the surface went through her like a knife. "What happened the other day..." Words failed him for a moment, and he felt helpless to make her understand, hating his own inadequacy.

He clenched his hands, digging his fingernails into his calloused palms to keep from touching her. "I know that most people would say it was wrong. But I can't make myself believe that something that beautiful could be wrong. I never knew I could feel anything so deeply. Megan, it felt like you opened up my chest and crawled inside. And you're still there. You'll always be there."

How many times had she wished, since that day, that it had never happened? But Jed's words moved her, and a calm sureness settled upon her. Jed was right. Perhaps they had sinned in the eyes of the world, but she could not feel ashamed for it. The only shame she felt was for what came after. Nor could she wish that it had been some other man who had shown her the true meaning of being a woman.

She spoke in a low voice, but clearly enough for Jed to hear every word. "I can't regret what happened, and Lord knows I've tried. I can't even say that it wouldn't happen again if we could live that day over. And maybe, with time, what you told me afterward will become so unimportant that the other won't be tarnished anymore. I hope so, Jed. You don't know how much I hope so."

His hands slowly unclenched. One hand reached out to touch her hair so lightly it might have been a whisper. "Thank you for that much, at least." He sighed and pulled his hand away. "Just remember that I love you. Will you do that for me, honey?"

"I'll remember," she murmured. "Good night, Jed."

She made her way through the silent night to the wagon. Even though Mary and Laura had protested indignantly about being sent to bed so early, she could tell from their deep even breathing that they were asleep. Megan was thankful that she wouldn't have to answer any questions about what she and Jed had talked about.

She undressed as quietly as she could and felt around in the inky darkness for her gown and bedroll. Shivering, she crawled between the covers and drew herself into a ball until her body warmth had heated the bedding. Then she relaxed slowly, stretching out on her back, with the covers tucked under her chin.

She knew she would not sleep for a while; her emotions had been thoroughly shredded. Jed loved her. She said the words over and over to herself as she stared into the blackness. Jed loved her. The words sank in, like jewels floating gently down to earth from the hand of God.

Why couldn't that be enough for her? Life wasn't a fairy tale where nothing bad ever happened. She'd told Jed she didn't want to hurt him, but was that really true? If she hadn't wanted to hurt him, why had she said she didn't know if she still loved him? Of course she loved him. If she didn't love him desperately, she wouldn't be putting herself through such agony right now. Couldn't she at least have told him so?

She thought about Jed lying awake in his own wagon, worried and hurting. If she'd had a little more courage she would have dressed again and gone there to tell him that she had never stopped loving him, that there could never be another man in all the world for her. She would explain that it wasn't her love that she doubted, but whether that love was enough to cancel out the bad things between them.

But she didn't move. It could wait a few more hours until they were both calmer.

It might take a while for her to be able to trust him again, but she could tell him she loved him, and she would. Very soon.

Chapter Twenty

Megan was awake the next morning before the first hint of daylight. She had spent a fitful night, wishing she'd confessed her true feelings to Jed. The more she thought about it, the more urgency she felt. "Let's not hide things from each other any more," she'd once said to him. Yet she'd gone back on that last night and she had to rectify it.

Although it was still gray dark, she dressed by feel and left the wagon without waking Mary and Laura. She'd work off her restlessness gathering deadwood, which was plentiful in the forested area near their campsite. The Schillers would be stirring by the time she returned with an armload. Perhaps after breakfast she would have an opportunity to speak to Jed alone for a few minutes.

Shivering a little in the early morning chill, she made her way toward the trees, glad she'd had the foresight to wear her coat. She walked briskly, seeing no one else, and was soon swallowed up by forest. Dead and disintegrating trees were so thick on the ground that she hardly had to use the hatchet she'd brought with her. She quickly gathered enough wood for a breakfast fire.

With the hatchet resting on top of the stack of wood, she started back to camp. Before she was clear of the trees, she realized she'd gathered up more of a load than she could carry all the way to the wagons.

She stopped and lowered the wood to the ground, discarding several pieces. Then she picked up the remaining lengths and arranged them in the crook of her left arm, leaving the hatchet until last.

As she reached down for it, she heard a sound behind her. Instantly a big, hairy hand clamped over her mouth. She dropped the wood and it tumbled around her, one log striking her shin with a stab of pain.

Megan hardly noticed her throbbing shin. In that first second she was too shocked to react, but then she tried frantically to fight off the man behind her. She couldn't see him, but she was certain he meant to rape her.

She threw her hands over her head, pummeling something solid, which she hoped was his face—and was quickly restrained. One arm was wrenched behind her back and held there firmly in one hand, while the other remained glued to her mouth.

"Keep quiet, and I won't hurt you." The voice was low and gravelly. Megan couldn't identify the man by his voice, but she was so overcome with fright that she might not have recognized the voice of her closest friend. All she could tell for sure was that he was as strong as a mule—and he stank!

It's Thayer Goddard, she thought, remembering the horror of being trapped beneath his wagon with him during the hailstorm. He had not come near her since Jed threatened him, but ever since that day Thayer's sullen gaze followed her whenever she came in his line of sight. It's Thayer, and this time there's no one to stop him doing whatever he wants with me!

She tried to bite the hand clamped over her mouth, but he anticipated her and ground his fingers hard against her lips. Panic and lack of air brought her close to fainting. She went suddenly limp, fighting the black unconsciousness that threatened to overcome her.

Mistaking her limpness for compliance, the man relaxed his grip on her wrists. Megan swam out of the blackness and seized the chance to renew her struggle. As she tried to wrench free, her hands flailing, one hand landed on his face, briefly clutching hair. He had a full beard! Thayer Goddard was clean-shaven. It wasn't Thayer!

The swift realization gave her no comfort, for her captor quickly subdued her again and she still hadn't gotten a look at him. She had no idea who grappled with her, grunting and growling like an angry grizzly.

Dear God, he stank like a grizzly, too.

Without warning, he stuffed a dirty rag in her mouth and knotted it at the back of her head. "That'll keep you quiet," he said with a note of satisfaction as he bound her hands behind her back. Then he lifted her and threw her over his shoulder like a sack of corn. As her head flew through the air, she caught one brief glimpse of her captor and her heart froze. She didn't know him, yet he seemed vaguely familiar.

Then her head was hanging down his back, the pins flying out of her hair. He grabbed her behind the knees and she jostled and bounced on his shoulder as he carried her through the trees. Oh, dear Lord, if he was going to rape her, why didn't he do it and get it over with? Where was he taking her? If he took her far from the camp, she would never find her way back when he was finished with her.

Maybe he didn't intend to let her go back. The thought turned her blood to ice water.

The man halted abruptly. Through her falling hair, she saw a horse. He threw her across the animal in front of the saddle and mounted, grasping the reins in one hand and planting the other on her buttocks to keep her from sliding off.

The horse took a tortuous route through the forest, as if he knew the way. Megan's bound arms felt as though they were about to break, and her head bobbed with the horse's gait, her hair nearly dragging the ground.

Pain soon enveloped her whole body and filled her mind, driving out any thought of what would happen as soon as they stopped. All she could think about was that the pain was going to kill her any minute. Since death seemed inevitable, she hoped it came sooner rather than later.

Megan had no idea how long they rode like that. Before they stopped she was drifting in and out of consciousness.

When the horse stopped and the man dismounted, she was barely aware of what was happening. She longed to close her eyes and drift away from the pain.

She was brought to instant, agonizing alertness when he dumped her on the ground. She thought her arms had lost all feeling, but the pain that shot up them when she hit the earth made beads of cold sweat pop out all over her skin.

He bent down, removed the gag and untied her wrists, which made the pain worse, though she wouldn't have believed it possible. She clutched her arms to her breasts and screamed in agony.

"Yell all you want to," he said matter-of-factly. "Ain't nobody to hear you now."

She huddled on the ground, lying on her side, her knees drawn up. As the feeling came back to her arms she moaned and cried. He stood over her, watching curiously, as though she were some strange and exotic animal he'd never seen before.

Slowly the pain ebbed, and she stopped writhing and lay still, staring up at him. She realized for the first time that the patches of sky she could see between the trees were a clear blue. They had ridden long enough for the sun to rise—an hour, two? The Schillers would have missed her by now, and a search party would be combing the woods for her. She had no hope that they would find her. Her captor had had too great a head start, and they'd traveled far.

He spit on the ground and grinned. "I knew I'd find a good chance to take you," he said, "if I jest bided my time."

She peered up at him, trying to think where she'd seen him before. He was a big man, tall and barrel chested. His dark hair and beard looked dirty and matted. Whoever he was, he obviously didn't put much stock in bathing.

One of his front teeth had been broken off close to the gum and his eyes were an unusual shade of greenish gray. He was watching her with an odd detachment, considering what he must be planning to do to her. He was patient in a perverse sort of way—perhaps the anticipation excited him as much as the act itself.

"Who are you?" she questioned.

He seemed to find that amusing. At least, Megan thought the guttural sound he made in his throat was a laugh. "Name's Orson Gurwell. Oh, you don't know me, but I know you. I've come to know you real good since Fort Hall."

Fort Hall? That had been weeks ago, in another lifetime. She had still been frivolous enough to spend hours making herself attractive for Major Southern's party. But by then Abner had been sick for weeks, though he'd felt well enough to escort her to the party and insist that she dance with Jed, and—

In a flash of recognition, she knew who the smelly giant was—the trapper who had watched her so intently in the trading post and during the party in the dining hall. Merciful heaven, he must have been following the train all that time. Waiting for the chance to abduct her. But why her? And when in heaven's name did he mean to rape her? Any minute now, she was sure. Oh, God . . .

She struggled to a sitting position, pushing her tangled hair out of her face to look around wildly for a place to run to—provided her legs would support her. She ached in every muscle. While he watched alertly, she braced one hand gingerly on the nearest tree trunk and slowly, painfully, got to her feet.

When she straightened and looked at him again, a gun had materialized in his hand. "Don't get no bright ideas about going somewhere without me."

"I—I have to—to relieve myself."

He jerked the gun, indicating a nearby bush. "Go behind there." He followed her, staring down at her as she squatted, holding her skirts off the ground but keeping herself covered.

She was beyond embarrassment over anything so unremarkable as a simple bodily function, and it didn't seem to embarrass him, either. He seemed totally disinterested, in fact, except to make sure he didn't let her out of his sight. Now that he had her at his mercy, he was in no hurry to use her. An odd sort of rapist. Yet there was a sick kind of torture in the mere waiting, not knowing when he would fall upon her.

Megan only hoped his seeming disinterest in her as a woman would continue until she could escape from him. And she would escape, she told herself, for the simple reason that she would not allow herself to consider any other alternative.

When she stood, he motioned with the gun, indicating where she was to sit on the ground. Then, never taking his eyes off her, he reached into his saddlebag with his free hand and took out a canteen and jerked meat. He gnawed off a bite of the jerky, chewed vigorously and drank from the canteen. When he walked toward her, she cringed, in spite of her effort not to reveal how afraid she was.

He squatted in front of her. "Jest aiming to give you a bite of this here venison." She shook her head, knowing she wouldn't be able to keep it down. Riding flung across his horse had jarred her insides until she wondered if they would ever sort themselves out again. When he came so close, his smell made her feel sick to her stomach. He shrugged and offered her the canteen. She took it in both hands and drank greedily.

After he had eaten, he sat down with his back against a tree, the gun resting on his thigh. He sat like that for about an hour, barely blinking, his mouth hanging half open. He said nothing to her; she might have been just another tree, except that he watched her all the time. Perhaps he had trained himself to sleep with his eyes open, but she was afraid to act on the theory.

At the same time that Megan was sitting on the ground a few feet from her abductor, Rose and Reuben Schiller were reporting to Jed that she was missing. He was saddling his horse when they found him. It had looked as though they'd get started that morning a little earlier than usual, but when he heard what Rose and Reuben had to say, the early start was forgotten.

"She has to be around here somewhere," he insisted, a dreadful chill enveloping his heart. "Someone must have seen her this morning."

"We've been through the camp," Rose said with agitation. "No one's seen her. She left the wagon before Laura and Mary woke up."

"We couldn't find our hatchet—" Reuben began.

Relief washed through Jed. "Well, there you are. She's gone to cut wood. Wait till I see her. She knows better than to leave camp alone."

"We found the hatchet, Jed," Reuben said. "In the woods back there—" he pointed "—beside a pile of wood she'd gathered. But Megan was nowhere around."

Jed stared at Reuben for an instant, then grabbed his shoulders and shook him roughly. "You didn't look hard enough! She must have fallen. She's hurt—"

Rose grasped Jed's arm. "We took the children and combed that whole part of the woods, Jed," she said gently. "Megan is gone."

"We have to get a search party together," Reuben said.

Jed dropped his hands. "Oh, God . . ." His fists clenched helplessly at his sides. Megan . . . what had happened to her? He closed his eyes to steady himself. They would find her. "I'm sorry, Reuben. You're right. Get eight or ten men. We ride out of here in three minutes with whomever is ready."

The hastily assembled party consisted of eight men. They were mounting, when Bert Olmstead noticed a contingent of men on horseback, galloping hard toward them.

"Hold up, men!" Bert yelled. "Riders coming."

"Looks like soldiers," Mason Glenhill said.

The company drew closer, and Jed saw that Mason was correct. As the soldiers rode up to them, Jed recognized one or two of them from their stopover at Fort Hall.

The leader, a ruddy-skinned man of medium height, swung to the ground. "Lieutenant Taggert, sir." He extended his hand to Jed. "Mr. Dossman, the wagon master,

I believe. Your party stopped with us at Fort Hall some weeks back.''

"You're a long way from home, Lieutenant," Jed said, impatient to mount and start the search. "We were just about to go in search of a young woman from our party who is missing this morning. We can't delay. I'm sure some of our women will be glad to offer you something to eat.''

As Jed started to mount, Taggert said, "One question before you go, Mr. Dossman. We've been tracking a man who stole the payroll money from Major Southern's office at the fort. By coincidence, the robbery occurred while your party was staying with us there.''

Jed frowned. "If you're hinting that somebody in our party robbed you—''

"Oh, no, sir," Taggert said hastily. "We know who the thief is. A trapper named Gurwell—Orson Gurwell. A big man—tall, broad, dark hair and beard. You may have seen him while you were at Fort Hall. As far as we know he's traveling alone. Have you run across anyone fitting that description?''

Jed stared at Taggert. "Did you say his name was Gurwell?''

"That's right. Orson Gurwell. Do you know him?''

Jed shook his head, his fingers gripping the saddle horn so tightly the knuckles were white.

Reuben watched Jed's jaw clench and his face harden. "Jed, are you all right?''

Jed looked up, his mouth set grimly. "Reuben, I want you to take over the wagon train. Break camp and get on the road.''

"What?" The men in the search party exchanged confused glances. "Jed, what's wrong with you? Have you lost your mind? We can't go without Megan.''

"Megan's with Orson Gurwell. I'm going to stay with Lieutenant Taggert and his men until we find them.''

"Lord Almighty," Bert Olmstead declared. "What's he talking about?''

"Jed—" Reuben began.

"Two years ago I killed a man named Aaron Gurwell," Jed said as he swung into his saddle. "Orson Gurwell must be some relation of his. He's after me, and Megan's in the middle. I can't take time to explain it all to you now. Just get the train on the trail. When I find Megan, we'll catch up with you." Jed looked at the lieutenant, who had been listening openmouthed. "Let's go, Lieutenant. I can show you where Megan was when he took her."

"Yes, sir!" Taggert said. He mounted and they rode toward the woods, leaving Reuben and the other men in the dust stirred up by the horses.

After an hour's rest, Megan's abductor ordered her to get to her feet. "If you behave yourself, I won't tie you up."

"I'll behave myself," she said without hesitation. Bound, she could not possibly escape.

He laughed. "I know you're thinking you can get away when I'm not looking. But you can't, so don't try. If you do, you'll be sorry."

The seeming mildness of the threat was in itself chilling, and she had no doubt he would make her very sorry indeed if she tried to get away and failed. He lifted her into the saddle and mounted behind her, reaching around her to flip the reins. At least he was going to let her ride upright this time. She was pathetically grateful for this concession.

They'd been together for at least two hours. Megan could hardly believe he hadn't raped her yet. He'd hardly touched her, and when he had it was out of necessity, to untie her or put her on the horse.

Now, her back pressed against his chest, but she could sense no lust in him. She concentrated on breathing through her mouth to keep from smelling him and thanked God that her captor was evidently a single-minded man. Right now he was occupied with putting distance between them and the wagon train. When they stopped...

Megan quickly put the thought out of her mind. When they stopped, she would get away from him somehow. Jed, where are you? Will I ever see you again? Oh, Jed, I love you and I didn't tell you.

She had no idea where they were or in which direction they were now traveling. Every beat of the horse's hooves on the ground was a reminder that she was one step farther from Jed and the wagon train. How long would they look for her before they traveled on?

She knew that Jed had to think about the safety of the entire party. He couldn't delay the train for days, looking for her. At noon they would have to travel on without her. She didn't blame Jed for that. She didn't blame anyone. But if she could escape soon, perhaps she could find her way back to the trail and catch up with them. To entertain any other outcome was unthinkable.

They didn't stop again until dusk. Megan had been astride the horse so long she felt as though her back had grown into her captor's chest. When Gurwell pushed her rudely to the ground, her legs folded beneath her. Besides being sore all over, she hadn't eaten all day. She was so weak that she saw bright splashes of color before her eyes and for a few seconds she couldn't hear anything. She shook her head, and the sound came back and her vision cleared.

While she was conquering her lightheadedness, Gurwell staked the horse. She didn't see or hear him coming toward her, and when he touched her, she shot to her feet and pummeled him with her fists. All she could think was, now he's going to do it, right now!

He grabbed both wrists in one hand and slapped her once so hard he knocked her head halfway around. "Damn little wildcat," he growled, and dragged her to a tree. "All I aim to do is tie you up so I can get some rest."

He used the rope that had been secured to his saddle to tie her, forcing her to sit with her back against the trunk. Pulling her arms back on either side of the tree, he tied her wrists together, knotting the rope on the back side of the trunk. Then he left her and unsaddled the horse.

He sat on the ground close to her and ate more jerked venison, washing it down with water from the canteen, gazing at her gloomily as he ate.

Slowly Megan became aware that her coat was open in front and that her dress was ripped. Half the bodice hung down to her waist, exposing one breast covered only by her thin petticoat. It was growing dark, but he was close enough to see the darkness of her nipple through her petticoat.

"Please," she said, "won't you untie me long enough for me to cover myself?"

His upper lip curled in contempt. "If I wanted a woman, it wouldn't be a ragged, dirty bag of bones like you." His gaze raked her tangled hair and her face, which she knew must be grimy. "Leastways not till you'd had a bath."

He sounded as though he were the soul of cleanliness. He sat there gnawing on jerky and smelling worse than a goat in heat and had the nerve to tell her she was dirty! She was hungry and weak and sore and half-naked and scared, and he squatted on the ground, chomping and wiping his mouth with his filthy jacket sleeve. It was too much to bear without complaint.

"I may be dirty, but I couldn't possibly smell as rank as you!"

He chortled as though it were a great joke. "Reckon I insulted you, calling you a bag o'bones." He took another bite of jerky and spoke around it. "Don't get your bowels in an uproar. There ain't nothing too bad wrong with you, except you're a woman."

"I don't *care* how you feel about me or what you call me!" Megan burst out.

He gazed at her calmly for an instant. "Don't cotton to females, I don't. Never knowed 'em to be anything but trouble to a man. 'Twas my brother, Aaron Gurwell, who hankered after women. When he stayed in the woods too long without having one, he turned downright mean and there weren't no pleasing him."

When he spoke of his brother, his voice became tense and determined, showing more feeling than Megan had thought him capable of. She watched him wash down the jerky with a drink from the canteen and her mouth watered. She felt utterly hopeless. "I don't see what that has to do with me."

Instead of answering her question, he fished another piece of jerky out of his saddle bag. "Eat this. Can't have you dying on me. You ain't much good to me dead."

He poked the jerky into her mouth with a dirty finger. In spite of the jerky's nauseating smell, not to mention Gurwell's, she chewed off a bite ravenously. She had to keep up her strength to she could act when a chance of escape presented itself. She swallowed water from the canteen when he offered it and ate more of the salty, rancid-smelling jerky.

After she had eaten, he ignored her while he arranged his saddle blanket on the ground, placing the saddle at one end of it. The temperature was dropping quickly and Megan longed for the warmth of a fire. Evidently he wasn't going to build one, probably for fear of giving away their location in case searchers were still looking. He stretched out on the blanket, pushed his hat down over his face and propped his head on the saddle. He seemed to be settling in for the night.

Megan squirmed against the tree, trying to find a comfortable position, but it was impossible. She glared at his sprawled form resentfully. "Just tell me one thing. Why did you abduct me if you dislike women so much?"

"You're nothing to me but bait." He spoke from beneath his hat. "I took you for my brother."

Megan went rigid as fresh fear shot through her. She was just about to convince herself that he really didn't intend to rape her, but it appeared he wasn't the one she had to worry about; it was his brother. She darted a look at the darkening woods to her right and then to her left. "Where is he?"

"You don't know nothing, do you? Stupid female," he grumbled. He turned on his side and pulled the saddle blanket over him.

Megan wanted to scream. *"Where is he?"*

"Aaron's dead, killed for lusting after a yellow-haired woman—a bag o'bones, like you. I told him to get him a squaw. At least they know their place. And they know how to be quiet and leave a man be. But Aaron had a hunger for a white woman. So he took her out of her house. She weren't feisty like you, but she got him shot in the back."

Megan's abduction was somehow a balancing of accounts or an act of revenge, it seemed, but she still couldn't comprehend how she was connected to that other woman or Gurwell's brother. Nor could she fathom what he meant to do with her now. "Did the woman shoot your brother?"

He grunted contemptuously. "That one? She couldn't do nothing but cry and carry on. It was her man. He came after her. Ain't he bragged to you about it?"

Was it possible he had mistaken her for some other woman? "I don't know what you're talking about. I don't even know this man you say killed your brother."

"You know him all right. He's your man."

"*My man?* You've made a terrible mistake, Mr. Gurwell. My man died on the trail."

"The old geezer you married—I know *he* died. But you got you a new one now—Dossman."

"Jed?" The name came out with a gasp of understanding. It was finally beginning to make a crazy, chilling kind of sense.

Aaron Gurwell must be the man who'd abducted Penelope, who'd beaten and raped her—the man Jed had killed in Oregon. Orson Gurwell must have been following Jed even before they reached Fort Hall, and he'd been following him ever since. "But surely Jed only did what any man would have done. Your brother kidnapped his wife and abused her. What would you have done if she'd been your wife?"

"Ain't got no wife. I told you, I got no use for women. I had my brother and my traps and my shack in the woods. Didn't need nothing else except fer a bottle of whiskey now and then. Dossman came into my territory and killed my brother. I aim to make him pay for it."

"Well, you have a strange way of going about it," Megan said bewilderedly. "Jed's fifty miles away by now. The wagon train is traveling in the opposite direction."

"He won't go without you."

"You're wrong. He's responsible for our entire party. He'll be forced to go on. You've gone to a lot of trouble for nothing, Mr. Gurwell."

He shifted to his other side. "You don't believe that, no more'n I do. Dossman's got a bad itch for you, and it's gonna be his downfall. I seen the hankering way he looks at you. I seen the two of you out there by the river, wallering in the dirt."

His words filled Megan with horror. He had been watching her, as well as Jed. He'd seen her remove her clothes and bathe, watched as Jed made love to her.

"Why haven't you shot him before now? You must've had plenty of opportunity."

"That'd be too easy," he said with a chilling cackle. "I want him separated from the pack, and I want him to sweat a while before I kill him. Right now he's being eaten up with pictures in his mind of what he thinks I'm doing to you. He's seeing another man wallering with his woman, maybe a pack of men. By now he's in a hell of his own making and he's crazy mad. He'll be here, sure as thunder, and I'll be ready for him."

Clearly he had planned this for months, and Megan's greatest fear was that he was right about Jed. "What good will it do to kill Jed? It won't bring your brother back."

"It'd take a woman to say that," he snorted contemptuously. "A life for a life. I heard tell that's what the Bible says, and it's what I live by. Killing Dossman won't bring my brother back, but it will settle the score. You behave yourself and I'll let you go after I kill him."

"But—"

"Quit your yapping," he commanded, his tolerance at an end, "and let me get some sleep." He turned on his back and heaved a heavy sigh. "Damned females, worse than a swarm of gnats, all the time nipping and nagging at a man. If it wasn't a matter of honor, I'd send you back to Dossman. Serve him right.''

"Honor! You don't know the meaning of the word!"

"I ain't gonna tell you again to shut your mouth!"

She bit back her anger, knowing that he'd hit her again if she didn't keep quiet. Elaborating on her opinion of his low character might release some of her outrage, but it wouldn't help Jed. Her anger would be much better used in trying to free herself from her bonds while he slept.

Sometime later, Megan slumped against the tree in exhaustion, her wrists raw and bleeding. She had not succeeded in getting free; in fact, her struggling seemed to have tightened the rope.

Shivering, she closed her eyes and tried to think of another way to free herself and save Jed. Reasoning or appealing to Gurwell's better nature wouldn't move him. He had no better nature, and she suspected he was pretty dim in the reasoning department, as well. She couldn't even pretend to be attracted to him to make him let down his guard. He had no interest in the opposite sex. Besides, she didn't think she was that good an actress. She could not physically overpower him. She couldn't escape. What else was left to try?

Unable to arrive at any plausible answer, she fell into a fitful sleep.

Chapter Twenty-One

Jed lay, belly down, peering up through a tangle of vines to a shelter of scrubby trees on a high bluff. Gurwell and Megan were up there. Jed had seen movement through the trees a while ago but nothing since. Gurwell had chosen the rendezvous site well. Between where Jed and the soldiers were hidden and the base of the bluff was a stretch of bare ground. Gurwell could see anybody crossing that stretch and pick him off before he could reach the bluff.

Jed and the soldiers—all except two men who waited some distance away with the horses—had been secreted near the bluff for more than an hour, and the waiting was getting to him. It was all he could do not to risk rushing Gurwell's stronghold, regardless of the odds against his reaching it. When he thought of what Megan must be going through up there, it filled him with a hot, reckless frenzy to *do* something.

Lieutenant Taggert crawled over to him. "My men and I are going to withdraw to a safe distance," Taggert whispered, "while we discuss strategy."

"We take no chances with Megan's life," Jed said with a hard edge to his voice.

"Of course."

"Gurwell has all the advantages. We could take him by sheer force of numbers, but not without the loss of some lives, and he might decide to start with Megan's. He knows that would hurt me more than killing me."

Taggert gave Jed's shoulder a brief, sympathetic grip. During the ride through the forest, Jed had told Taggert the full story of Penelope's abduction and its aftermath. "I'm sorry he had to involve the woman, Dossman."

Jed studied the shelter of trees, but he couldn't see any sign of life now. "Darkness will make the odds a little more even. We have to wait until night to make our move."

"That's what I've been thinking," Taggert agreed.

"When it gets dark, have your men fan out," Jed said. "I'll work my way around to the other side of the bluff and climb up it as soon as there's enough daylight to see where I'm going. If I can get to the top without Gurwell seeing me, I'll have a chance to take him."

Taggert frowned. "A slim one. There's not enough scrub high up on the side of the bluff to hide behind. If you make it that far, you'll have to hit him with the first shot, or he'll bring you down."

"I don't care what the odds are. It's Megan I'm concerned about. It's the only way, Taggert."

After hesitating a moment, Taggert grudgingly agreed. "I guess you're right. I'll tell my men. You might as well draw back a ways until dark."

"I'll stay here," Jed said. "Maybe we'll get lucky and Gurwell will decide it's safe to venture out into the open."

"I wouldn't count on it," Taggert said. "It looks to me like he's planned this thing down to the last detail." After a few seconds, he again clapped his hand on Jed's shoulder, then crawled away back to his waiting men.

Megan and Gurwell had been on the bluff since early the previous afternoon. In the center of the scrubby patch of trees a camp of sorts awaited them—drinking water in lidded containers and a stack of cut wood. Gurwell had obviously chosen this spot carefully before he'd abducted her. After looking around, Megan understood why. On the bluff they were higher than the surrounding terrain and could see anyone approaching long before he reached them.

At dawn Gurwell untied Megan and ordered her to build a fire and make coffee. She was glad to be allowed to move about, and gladder still to taste fresh-brewed coffee. She was also allowed to mix cornmeal batter and fry it over the fire using meal and a frying pan from Gurwell's saddle bag. He sprawled nearby while she made their breakfast, giving no indication of having anything else to do. Evidently Gurwell meant to wait patiently for Jed to appear, then kill him.

Don't walk into this trap, Jed . . . please, don't.

Megan gave Gurwell three of the hot cornmeal cakes with his coffee, reserving two for herself. She sat down beneath a tree to eat her breakfast, praying that he wouldn't decide to tie her up again as soon as she finished eating. Perhaps if she stayed still and said nothing, he'd leave her be for a while. She ate her cakes slowly, savoring every bite.

Gurwell kept an eye on her, while appearing not to, his gun always only a few inches from his hand. Megan was fully aware of the alertness beneath his deceptively relaxed manner, and stayed where she was.

After eating the last bite of her second cornmeal cake, Megan leaned her head back against the tree to sip her coffee from the battered tin cup Gurwell had fished out of his saddle bag.

From the corner of her eye, she caught a movement higher up on the side of the cliff above them. Instinctively she flicked her glance that way, and almost gasped aloud. Jed was crawling down the side of the bluff from above. In a flash she looked away. Hardly knowing what she was doing, she brought the cup to her lips again, gripping it in both hands and staring hard at her feet, which were stretched out in front of her.

Her heart beat loudly in her ears, and her mind raced. If Gurwell turned around and saw Jed, he'd shoot him before Jed could draw his gun. Why didn't Jed shoot Gurwell now? He must not be close enough yet, or not in a position to be accurate. She didn't dare look at the bluff again to see what Jed was doing.

Hurry, Jed, hurry . . .

Gurwell got up slowly and Megan's heart jumped to her throat. The trapper stretched and walked to the fire to refill his cup. He brought the coffee to his mouth and tipped his head back to drink. He'd notice Jed any second!

Jed, why don't you shoot?

She had to distract Gurwell. She said the first thing that came into her head. "What do you trap, Gurwell?" The question surprised Megan almost as much as Gurwell, who was staring at her with a puzzled look. "You said you have traps," Megan went on in desperate haste. "I was just wondering what you catch in them."

"Beaver, fox, muskrat." His eyes narrowed as he studied her. "Why are you talking to me all of a sudden? You ain't said two words since I made you shut up the other night. Been poutin', I reckon. That's what females do, ain't it?"

"I suppose—some females."

"Humph."

Megan struggled not to glance at the bluff again. "I thought—since it appears we'll be here a spell—well, it might make the time go faster if we talk to each other, like civilized people."

His lips curled. "That ain't what you think a'tall. You already made it clear you don't consider me civilized. You're trying to put something over on me, woman. Are you scheming to sweet-talk me into letting you go?" He laughed cruelly. "Save your breath."

At that moment, Jed, in his agonizingly slow descent down the cliff, dislodged a stone, and it clattered down the bluff. To Megan, the noise was loud as a round of gunfire. Gurwell dived for his gun and Megan screamed.

"Jed, look out!"

In one swift movement Gurwell grasped his gun, whirled and brought the firearm up. The explosion shook the bluff.

Jed threw himself to one side and jerked his gun from its holster, cocking it as he brought it around. Before he could pull the trigger, Gurwell got off another shot. Jed felt a stinging stab of pain in the fleshy part of his left arm. Wincing, he fell on his stomach, rolled and brought his hand up to shoot. Gurwell threw himself behind a boulder. Jed's shot pinged off the boulder, whizzing through the air where Gurwell's head had been the instant before.

Megan hadn't moved from beneath the tree. She was paralyzed. She thought dimly that Gurwell had shot Jed, and suddenly she was on her feet, screaming, "No, no, no!" and running.

From somewhere behind her a man shouted, "Get down, miss! Get down!"

Confused, Megan whirled and saw soldiers swarming up over the side of the bluff. One of them ran toward her, knocking her to the ground and covering her with his body. He aimed his gun at the boulder behind which Gurwell had taken cover.

"You're surrounded, Gurwell. Throw out your gun and come out."

The man's weight wa' heavy on Megan, and she couldn't breathe. Hysterically she concluded that she was dying, that Jed was already dead, and she didn't want to live, anyway. Suddenly the heavy weight rolled off her and the soldier was on his feet.

"Kick the gun over here, Gurwell. That's it. Now come out with your hands up."

Megan sat up shakily, only half hearing the soldier ask solicitously, "Are you all right, miss?

"Jed," she whispered. "Gurwell shot him."

The soldier grinned. "He'll be all right, miss. Two of my men are helping him down off that cliff now. Can't you hear him cussing?"

Megan whirled around to see Jed shaking off the hands of the two soldiers. "Let go of me, damn it! He just grazed me. Oh, hell, I wish I'd killed the bastard."

Megan flew to him, grabbing him around the waist and hugging him to her. "Jed...I thought he'd killed you...oh, Jed, I love you! I love you!" She burst into tears.

Jed's good arm came around her to press her close. He buried his face in her tangled hair, unable to speak for a moment. Then he said brokenly, "Honey, everything's going to be all right. Whatever he did to you, it doesn't matter. We'll make it good again. Megan...Megan, do you understand what I'm saying?''

She couldn't seem to stop shaking. When she lifted her head, his face was a dark blur before her. She tried to say something, but couldn't speak for crying. All she knew was that Jed was there; Jed was alive; Jed would hold her and make it all right.

The next few minutes were a confusion of images and voices to Megan. Some of the soldiers ransacked the campsite, looking for the money Gurwell had stolen from Fort Hall, but they didn't find it. Megan heard one of them say, "Before we're through with him, he'll tell us where it is."

Then the soldiers tied Gurwell's wrists together, put him on his horse and bound his ankles, passing the rope beneath the horse, behind its front legs. Confident at leaving Jed in Megan's care, the commanding officer, Lieutenant Taggert, ordered his men to mount up and ride. They were taking Gurwell back to the fort to stand trial.

As soon as the soldiers were gone, Jed kissed Megan hungrily. "Sweetheart," he said fiercely, "I nearly lost my mind when I realized who'd taken you. Thank God, you're alive. That's all that matters."

When she wound her arms around his neck, he winced. She jumped back and saw blood seeping through the sleeve of his shirt. "Jed, you're bleeding! Why didn't you tell me? Let me see."

He grimaced, and as she watched, the blood left his face. Abruptly he sat down on the ground, lowering his head to his knees. Megan knelt beside him, her pulse pounding as she stared at the blood on his sleeve.

Swiftly she unbuttoned his shirt sleeve and ripped it open until the bloody wound was exposed. Gently she pressed her fingers against the mouth of the wound. He grunted with the pain.

"Grazed you, did he? Jed, the bullet's still in there. It has to come out now."

"There's a knife and whisky in my saddle bag. I left my horse tied to the tallest pine at the edge of the trees down below." He sounded strange, his voice too slow and dreamlike.

"Don't try to get up," Megan said. "I'll be right back."

Megan rushed down the bluff. She found the stallion easily. Along with the knife and bottle of whiskey she grabbed Jed's bedroll and carried everything back up. After undoing his bedroll, she spread it in the shelter of trees and helped Jed to the pallet. His eyes remained closed as she cleansed the wound with whiskey.

"I'll do this as quickly as I can," she told him. She poured whiskey over the blade of the knife and probed the wound until she'd maneuvered the tip beneath the bullet and worked it out.

Jed moaned only once. After pouring more whiskey on the wound, Megan ripped the cleanest-looking strip from the skirt of her petticoat and used it to bandage his arm.

"There. It's over, sweetheart. I'm sorry I had to hurt you."

He didn't respond. He'd passed out. With a little cry, Megan cupped his face in her hands. "Jed, talk to me." But he was dead to the world. "You will not die, Jed Dossman," she said fiercely. "I won't let you die, do you hear me?"

She pulled a blanket over him and stood, watching him anxiously until she was convinced he was breathing deeply and evenly. She added wood to the embers of the campfire, wishing she could have something nourishing for Jed to eat when he woke up.

Jed smelled something wonderful. He opened his eyes and tried to move. Immediately soft, gentle hands were there, helping him sit up. "Megan...sweetheart...what happened?"

He knew her! And his brow felt cool. She didn't think he had any fever. Megan thought her heart would burst with joy just looking at him. "Nothing much. You passed out when I dug the bullet out of your arm."

He gazed at her with love in his eyes, and she was thankful she'd had time to wash her face and hands and get the worst tangles out of her hair. She was on her knees before him, and he gently touched her face. She bent forward and pressed her lips to his. The kiss was slow and deep and tender.

"I love you, Megan," he whispered hoarsely.

Her heart soared. "And I love you," she returned, blinking and sitting back on her heels. "Now I'm going to feed you."

"What smells so good?"

"Rabbit. I shot him with your gun."

He laughed. "I didn't know you could hit the broad side of a barn."

"There are many things you don't know about me yet, Jed Dossman," she said pertly as she set the pot in which she'd cooked the rabbit beside him. The pot had been left behind by Gurwell, along with a skillet and two cups. Megan dipped one of the cups into the pot and held it for Jed to drink from. "The broth will be very nourishing," she said, smiling as their eyes met. "It'll make you feel stronger."

He took the cup from her hands and drank hungrily, his eyes continuing to smile at her over the rim. "I'm feeling stronger by the second, love. Umm, that's good."

"Help yourself to the meat," she said. "We'll have to use our fingers."

In short order, they had emptied the pot of meat and broth, and Megan set it aside. Brushing the hair off Jed's forehead, she felt his brow. "Feeling better?"

"Much." His hand covered hers, turning it over, palm up. Watching her intently, he brought her palm to his mouth. "Have you forgiven me, Megan?"

She gazed at him through hot, springing tears. "Completely. I can't stay mad at you because I love you. I have loved you for a very long time, and I will love you forever."

A flare of hope lit his eyes. "I don't deserve your love," he muttered unsteadily, "but I thank God for it. Will you marry me, Megan?"

Blinking away her tears, she wrapped her arms around his shoulders. "Oh, Jed...yes!" Then, remembering his wound, she drew back quickly. "Did I hurt you, darling?"

He grinned and with one arm pulled her hard against him. "Come here," he growled, and lay back, pulling her down on top of him. His arm tightened around her, holding on tight. Her breaths were muffled in his shirt, and his face was pressed into her neck. "Megan, Megan, I adore you."

She lifted her head. With a new instinct of confidence and welcome, she brought her mouth down to his. The kiss was filled with joy and need and tenderness. Without breaking the kiss, she opened her coat so that her body could absorb the feel of him.

His right hand moved to her hair, cupping the long, loose waves, caressing them. Then he tangled his fingers in the silky strands as he tilted her head to gain deeper access to her mouth. His mouth opened on hers greedily, drawing from her more nuances of need and love.

Megan felt the flow of hot, heady weakness through her blood, and her fingers slid beneath the open collar of his shirt, absorbing the damp, warm texture of his skin. And then, restlessly, her hand moved down over his chest, feeling the tensing of his muscles.

She lifted her head and looked down at him, her eyes glazed and dreamy. "Jed, if we don't stop, we won't be able to...and you'll hurt yourself," she said breathlessly.

His eyes were dark with intensity and hunger. "I don't care. I don't want to stop."

Searching his face with adoring eyes, she whispered, "Neither do I." Then she relaxed against him and her lips moved lightly across his face. He groaned and his lashes drifted closed and she kissed the lids. With utmost care, she opened his shirt and removed his boots and trousers. With a shy smile and the boldness of a woman who loves and knows she is loved in return, she reached for him. His eyes went as dark as the night with desire.

"I know this isn't easy for you, sweetheart," he said softly, earnestly. "After Gurwell—if you're not ready to do this yet, I'll understand."

"Oh, Jed, he didn't touch me. He said he didn't like women. Sweetheart, there's been no one but you. There never will be."

She felt the tension go out of him as her fingers stroked his cheek, scratchy with the night's growth of beard. His eyes were moist. "My sweet love..."

They touched each other gently, discovering the beauty and mystery of each other's body. Their eyes spoke of things they could not put into words. There was no time, no urgency, nothing and no one but the two of them and the love they shared.

He lifted her breasts from her petticoat to kiss and caress them. Megan sighed with happiness, her shyness vanishing when she saw the awe and pleasure in Jed's eyes. When he looked at her, she no longer felt tattered and disheveled, but beautiful.

She let her hands slide over the smooth muscled contours of his shoulders, down over his stomach, over the jut of his hipbone, discovering him. It was more wonderful than anything she had ever known.

Jed's movements were hampered by his injury, but he was content to lie beneath her and feel the pleasure of her touch. He wanted her to take all the time she needed, wanted the moment to last forever. But as her fingers explored and caressed him, he needed her so badly that his stomach ached.

His hot gaze raked her face and naked breasts above him, making her blush, and when he slipped his hand beneath her skirts to run it over the silken texture of her skin, she trembled. "It won't hurt this time, sweetheart," he whispered.

She drew in a quick breath and felt her stomach quiver. She lifted her hips and guided him into her. The entry was moist and easy, filling her with heat and hardness, filling her with Jed.

She felt his muscles quiver as his hand cupped her hip and he pushed himself deeper inside her. With a moan of pleasure, Megan felt herself opening to him. They lay still for a moment, gazing at each other with adoration. Then she reached a trembling hand to smooth the hair off his forehead, watching the fire fill his eyes.

"Megan . . . I can't wait . . ."

She dropped her face to his chest and felt his hand tighten on her thigh. He lifted his hips in a series of long, slow thrusts, and she could feel herself moving with him, withdrawing a little and being filled anew, until Jed and that moment were all that existed.

Soon his strokes quickened, and her body instinctively matched his pace, rising and lowering to meet him. The fire in her belly spread, and a fierce need grew in her, swelling and aching deep inside. Her hands gripped his shoulders as she clung to him helplessly, and she heard the moan of her own breath and Jed's groans.

Then Jed shifted subtly, and without warning, the release came, a flicker at first that began deep inside her and rippled out in warm, ever more powerful waves of pleasure that enveloped her and left her breathless and quivering and spent.

She felt Jed's body tense, then shudder again and again with release.

Afterward Jed held her in the tight, protective circle of his right arm, her head on his chest. In a little while, they would have to leave, but for now, they were both reluctant to move.

"We have to go, honey," Jed urged gently, a few minutes later. "I sent the wagon train on ahead and I want to catch up with them before they reach the Columbia."

"Jed, are you sure you're up to riding just yet?"

He grinned. "Absolutely." She slid off him and he got to his feet, swaying a little.

Megan jumped up. "You're not up to it!"

"I was a little dizzy for a minute, but I'm all right now."

Unconvinced, she planted her hands on her hips and cocked her head. "You've got a stubborn streak, Jed Dossman."

Suddenly he scooped her up with his good arm and hauled her against him. His eyes danced. "You see how strong I am?"

She tightened her arms around his neck. "I'd like to stay here with you forever," she said with a sigh.

"Nope, we have to get to Oregon and get a house built before the first baby comes."

She laughed. "Aren't you forgetting something?"

"What?"

"The wedding ceremony."

"That's number one on my list, sweetheart," he said in a husky voice. "I'm getting your promise before witnesses to stay with me till death do us part, before you change your mind."

"I'll never change my mind," she said, and pulled his head down for her kiss.

Epilogue

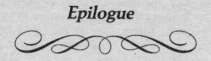

Spring 1851

Megan took a pan of golden-brown rolls from the oven and set it on top of the new stove. She covered the rolls with a clean dish towel and cast a critical glance around the large kitchen. The long table Jed had improvised, of wide wood planks resting on sturdy sawhorses, was covered with a red-checked cloth. It easily accommodated the fourteen place settings arranged six to a side and one on each end.

The big black cook stove and the fire roaring on the hearth in the adjoining parlor filled the two rooms with cozy warmth. Although it was the last day of April, a late snowstorm had blown in two days earlier, depositing nearly a foot of snow. Today the temperature had climbed above freezing for the first time in a week and the sun reflected off the snow beyond the kitchen window with a blinding whiteness.

Going to the table, Megan straightened a fork beside one of the plates.

"Everything ready?" Jed asked from the doorway. Megan turned and smiled as he sniffed the air. "Something smells wonderful—and I'm starving."

"They should be arriving any minute," Megan said as he crossed the room. He slipped his arm around her and she rested her head lightly on his shoulder. "I'm so eager to see everyone again."

The Glenhills and the Goddards had settled in Salem, twenty miles west of them. Jed had started the new house immediately after their wedding last November. Even with delays caused by cold weather, he'd now finished four large rooms. The Schillers lived only two miles to the north, but traveling over the rough country road had been difficult during the harsh winter months, and Megan hadn't seen Rose and the children for weeks. Since Jed and Reuben were partners in a lumbering operation, they saw each other much more frequently. But neither Megan nor Jed had seen the Glenhills or Goddards in three months.

"Have you heard anything more about Thayer?" Megan murmured as Jed nuzzled her neck, finding the sensitive spot beneath her ear.

"Nothing since he went to California to mine for gold."

"That was before Christmas last year, when Carolyn opened her boardinghouse."

"Mmmm." He kissed her gently, then drew away to look at her. Her cheeks were rosy from standing over the cook stove. Or was it pregnancy that gave her skin that special glow? "Maybe Thayer will return a rich man. Do you think Carolyn will have him back?"

"No." She brushed a lock of hair off his forehead. "He killed whatever love she once felt for him long before we reached Oregon. It's so sad. It makes me realize how lucky I am to have you." Smiling, she cupped his face in her hands. "I love you, Jed."

"I don't deserve you, sweetheart. But, Lord, I'm glad I have you. I adore you." He drew her close until their mouths met.

She relaxed against him with a sigh. The kiss was slow and sweet, and Jed's arms tightened around her. Megan was enjoying the mingling of soft pleasure with heating passion, when suddenly she felt a flutter in her stomach. She uttered a surprised "Oh" and stepped back.

"What?"

A look of wonder filled her shining eyes. "I felt the baby move. It's the first time." She took his hand and pressed it against the gentle mound of her stomach. "There, he did it again. Did you feel it?"

He grinned. "Yes, I think so."

"Leave your hand there. Maybe he'll do it again."

He bent over to plant a gentle kiss on her lips. "'He,' eh? Have you decided it's a boy?"

She savored the kiss briefly before she broke it to reply, "Not really. It doesn't matter to me whether it's a girl or a boy. Does it to you?"

"All I care about is that both of you come through all right." He caught her head in his hands and resumed kissing her. "Ah," he murmured after a while. "Are you sure we don't have time to—"

Reluctantly she stepped out of his arms. "I'm sure. Listen, I hear a wagon outside."

"Wagons," Jed corrected.

Minutes later, Jed threw open the front door and the Schiller family crowded into the house, all trying to get through the door at once. Jed kissed Rose's cold-reddened cheek and pumped Reuben's hand. "Welcome," he shouted over the din of six youngsters all talking at once and the delighted squeals of Rose and Megan as they embraced each other.

"The Glenhills are right behind us," Reuben said. "They have Carolyn and Johnny with them."

"Oh, give me the baby," Megan exclaimed as Lacey Glenhill stepped inside.

Lacey handed the blanket-wrapped bundle to Megan and hugged Rose, then Mary and Laura. With Megan's free arm, she patted Johnny Goddard's cold cheek before squeezing Carolyn's gloved hand. "I'm so happy to see all of you," Megan said. "Now let's have a look at this little man." Relinquishing Carolyn's hand, she folded back the baby's blanket to expose the round, sleeping face of Mason and Lacey's four-month-old son. Carolyn, Rose, Mary and

Laura all crowded around Megan for a closer look. "Isn't he precious?" Megan murmured.

"What's his name, Lacey?" Laura asked as she unwound the scarf from her head and shook out her auburn hair.

"David Mason Glenhill," Lacey said softly. The women exchanged thoughtful looks tinged with sadness as they remembered Mason's brother, David, and his death from a swift, sure Cheyenne arrow.

Mary shrugged off her coat. "May I hold little David?" she asked, and Megan shifted the baby to the young girl's arms.

"When do we eat?" Ben Schiller inquired loudly, and there was a flurry of laughter and movement as coats were removed and carried to Jed and Megan's bedroom, where they were piled on the big bed. Megan led the women on a quick tour of the house, ending in the kitchen.

"It's real nice, Megan," Rose said.

"How's your house coming along?" Megan asked.

"We have four rooms and a loft over the kitchen, where the boys sleep. It's enough to do us until Reuben has time to build on more."

"I expect we'll both wait awhile for more room. From what Jed says, orders are pouring in at the lumber mill."

"Mercy, yes," Rose agreed. "The way this country is booming, there's no end in sight to their need for lumber."

As the women dished up the food Megan had prepared, Megan had a chance to ask Carolyn, "How are you and Johnny getting along?"

"Just fine," Carolyn assured her. "We have four men living with us now, and rooms for three more, which I expect to fill soon. Keeps me busy, but I enjoy it."

"That's good to hear, Carolyn. Have you had any word from Thayer since he left?"

Carolyn shook her head. "I don't expect to. When I asked him to move out, he said that if he went he wouldn't be back. I guess he thought I'd back down and ask him to stay."

"How is Johnny adjusting to his father's absence?"

"He hasn't asked about Thayer in months, and he seems quite happy."

"Laura," Rose said, "tell those men to come to the table before Jed and Reuben start talking about the lumbering business and you can't get a word in edgewise."

Everyone took a seat. Jed sat at the head of the table, with Megan on his right. "Megan and I have an announcement to make," Jed said proudly as the guests quieted. "We're expecting an addition to our family in about four and a half months."

When the exclamations of surprise and congratulations had died down, Reuben raised his glass. "A toast to Jed and Megan. May their baby be healthy and happy and a joy to his parents all their lives."

"Hear, hear."

"For all gathered at this table," Mason said, "here's to good health and prosperity."

"And good friends," Jed added, sending a smile around the table.

When they had drunk, Megan said, "Reuben, will you say grace before we eat?"

They reached to join hands around the table and bowed their heads. As Reuben asked God's blessings on the gathering, Jed's warm, calloused hand enveloped Megan's and squeezed.

Megan closed her eyes. As she listened to Reuben's prayer, her heart filled with the warmth of friendship, gratitude for the safe journey to Oregon and boundless adoration for her husband and unborn child. When Reuben's prayer came to an end, she joined the others in a heartfelt "Amen."

As she lifted her head, her eyes met Jed's, and they exchanged a wordless message of love that grew deeper with each passing day.

* * * * *

COMING NEXT MONTH

#19 RIDES A HERO—Heather Graham Pozzessere

Shannon McCahy despised the cruel Civil War that had robbed her of all but her precious land. Though the conflict was over, a new breed of ruthless men had descended upon the Missouri border to threaten her loved ones. But only the fugitive Rebel Malachi Slater would shatter her defenses and claim the beautiful Yankee's heart as they joined forces in a desperate rescue mission.

#20 SAMARA—Patricia Potter

As war threatened the uneasy peace between England and America in 1812, fiery Samara O'Neill would not sit idle. But when she rashly hid herself aboard her brother's schooner, she hadn't counted on being taken prisoner by dangerous British privateer Reese Hampton. Within her reckless heart Samara had never imagined her greatest adventure would be loving Reese.

AVAILABLE NOW:

#17 A GENTLE PASSION
Cassie Edwards

#18 WILD HORIZONS
Jeanne Stephens

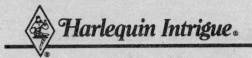 **Harlequin Intrigue**®

They went in through the terrace door. The house was dark, most of the servants were down at the circus, and only Nelbert's hired security guards were in sight. It was child's play for Blackheart to move past them, the work of two seconds to go through the solid lock on the terrace door. And then they were creeping through the darkened house, up the long curving stairs, Ferris fully as noiseless as the more experienced Blackheart.

They stopped on the second floor landing. "What if they have guns?" Ferris mouthed silently.

Blackheart shrugged. "Then duck."

"How reassuring," she responded. Footsteps directly above them signaled that the thieves were on the move, and so should they be.

For more romance, suspense and adventure, read Harlequin Intrigue. Two exciting titles each month, available wherever Harlequin Books are sold.

INTA-1

COMING IN MARCH FROM

Harlequin Superromance

Book Two of the Merriman County Trilogy AFTER ALL THESE YEARS the sizzle of Eve Gladstone's *One Hot Summer* continues!

Sarah Crewes is at it again, throwing Merriman County into a tailspin with her archival diggings. In *One Hot Summer* (September 1988) she discovered that the town of Ramsey Falls was celebrating its tricentennial one year too early.

Now she's found that Riveredge, the Creweses' ancestral home and property, does not rightfully belong to her family. Worse, the legitimate heir to Riveredge may be none other than the disquieting Australian, Tyler Lassiter.

Sarah's not sure why Tyler's in town, but she suspects he is out to right some old wrongs—and some new ones!

The unforgettable characters of *One Hot Summer* and *After All These Years* will continue to delight you in book three of the trilogy. Watch for *Wouldn't It Be Lovely* in November 1989.

SR349-1

Give in to Temptation! Harlequin Temptation

The story of a woman who knows her own mind, her own heart...and of the man who touches her, body and soul.

Intimate, sexy stories of today's woman—her troubles, her triumphs, her tears, her laughter.

And her ultimate commitment to love.

Four new titles each month—get 'em while they're hot. Available wherever paperbacks are sold. Temp-1